LAND OF NO PITY II
The Lost Generation

By:
Toni T-Shakir

PUBLISHING

Cover by Kleshaam Shakir

ISBN: 9780998609256
Library of Congress Control Number: 2017904550
Shakir Publishing, Los Angeles, California

DEDICATION

TO THERON "BIG MICRON" SHAKIR

The founder of the tribe. 90th and Budlong's Finest. . .
Long live the Shakir Mob!

AUTHOR'S NOTE

I grew up as part of America's lower class. The characters I have created in this story are the people I can write about with the most honesty and knowledge. The profanity, the terminology, and the modes of expression contained in this novel are purely for the realism of this world.

For the gang members who may happen upon this book: If a disrespectful term is used about your hood, please do not take it personally. It is not intended as an attack on you or your tribe. It is only a testament to the book's authenticity.

All events and characters in this book are fictional. Any resemblance to persons living or dead is purely coincidental.

In a different day and age, they would have been the demigods that legends were made from.

A blended cocktail of Malcolm X, Huey Newton, and Priest from *The Mack*. Strong, intelligent, dangerous young Black men in their prime. At the height of the pharaonic reign of Egypt, they would have been the elite of the Royal Guard. During the conquests of Alexander the Great, they would have been the warriors chosen for single combat. When the Roman Empire ruled most of the known world, they would have been the Barbarians crossing the Alps on the backs of elephants with Hannibal the Conqueror. But this was no longer the age of legends. This was 1970s America, and by then, the gods of Mount Olympus had fallen to the hardened pavements of South Central Los Angeles, where not even their super-human traits could save them from the drugs, decay, and violence that was to come.

These were the individuals who taught us how to fight, how to be cool, how to be hustlers, how to be violent, and how to not take shit from nothing or nobody. But they were in a fallen state, so they also taught us to be ignorant, irrational, and destructive to ourselves. By their lessons we die in droves. We fill the prisons with our young and beautiful, and we endure tears of pain and grief from the cradle to the grave. Yet, to them we still salute, knowing that they gave what they had. To the masses, they are considered savage predators, unworthy of anything but a cage or a cold slab in the morgue. Yet to us, they are still our fallen princes who gave us both good and evil, beauty and ugliness, and regardless of what others may say, they did it with a style unmatched.

So, to who is this homage due?

THE BIG HOMIES!

PROLOGUE

Lil Teflon-Black struggled to place one foot in front of the other on the slow-moving treadmill, his dark features and eyes strained in a mask of anger, pain, and determination. The minimal movement took a monumental effort. He turned the machine off and paused to catch his breath. He looked around the private rehabilitation room and grew angrier. The deep metal tub, the restraint bands scattered loosely across the floor, and the assorted exercise equipment in the otherwise empty room were a stark reminder of what happened to him.

He scratched his matted afro as he caught a glimpse of his reflection in the walled mirror in the far corner of the room. The hot slug that Lil Wizard pumped through his face at close range had ripped through his upper cheek and cracked the right side of his skull, then traveled out the lower backside of his head. He was lucky the bullet didn't lodge in his brain. The gunpowder left a ghastly burn and severe disfigurement on the left side of his face, adding slivers of pink to his midnight-dark skin. The bags under his deeply sunken eyes appeared even darker than his skin tone. The fifteen-pound weight gain, after the wires that sealed his mouth were removed, added nothing to his already thin five-foot, six-inch frame. He appeared almost anorexic.

Son of a bitch, he thought, as he gritted his teeth at his reflection. The flip phone sitting on the metal stand next to the treadmill vibrated.

"Yep," he answered. He already knew who was calling without having to hear the voice on the other end.

"What's crackin', loco?" Baby Devil chimed from the other end.

"Aw, you know . . . just tryin' to speed up the process of fully gettin' back on my feet. This rehab facility shit is like bein' in prison, but the good part is I have plenty of time alone to plot and plan out here in Palm Desert."

"That's right, Cuzzo." Baby Devil coughed. "On the plottin' and plannin' note, I did what you asked. I'm sittin' on the prize right now."

Lil Teflon smiled. "Good . . . good. Was it smooth?"

"As butter." Baby Devil laughed. "Once you get the final results, you'll be proud of the kid."

"I'm already proud-a you. You the only mothafucka I trust."

"That's what's up. Just take your time and get back on your feet. *Everything'll b*e in place when you make your appearance again. Don't trip, I'm on the job," Baby Devil reassured.

"For sure, lil homie. When you unwrap the gift, make sure you send my blessings."

"Alright, big homie. Nine minutes, no seconds."

"Rollin'." Lil Teflon ended the call and placed the phone back on the stand. He made his way over to the chair and sat down heavily. He grabbed the folder that was lying next to his feet, then he leaned back in the chair and studied the contents of the folder. He examined the photos and neatly typed writing that accompanied each one. He removed the pen clamped to the folder cover and carefully marked an *X* over one of the faces of the photos.

"Nobody get a pass," he mumbled. "Everybody's a piece on the chessboard in this game of war."

His mind went back to the day of the shooting. The recurring nightmare of seeing Lil Wizard's face and demonic smile behind the blazing pistol was not just a dream. Big Wizard, Hitter, and Lil 9 had laid a carefully made trap that he had walked right into. Lil Wizard was just the one to carry it out. They'd figured out that he was behind the hit on Lil 9-Lives.

"My sorry-ass team let them niggas get up on me and almost snuffed me out. But that's another issue for another day. I got bigger fish to fry." He shook his head at the thought, put the folder down, and stood up. The pain gnawed as he grabbed his side and made his way over to the treadmill. He got back on it and began his slow trek once again.

"They thought they silenced me," he uttered as his resilience grew stronger. "But the Loc is back."

*   *   *   *

Baby Devil stood over the figure in front of him. The man's cornrowed hair was disheveled, and blood and sweat rolled from his head down the right side of his face. His eyes were blackened and almost swollen shut. Duct tape covered his mouth and held his arms and legs secured to the plush leather office chair serving as a torture device.

Baby Devil took his gaze from the man and looked around the room. *This is a nice hideaway*, he thought. The basement was converted into the ultimate man cave: arcade-size games lined one of the walls; a large movie screen covered the opposite side; a custom-made oak pool table sat in the middle of the room with a matching oak bookshelf and desk placed in a corner area of the room.

He had never been in a basement before. Houses in South Central Los Angeles did not have basements, but he had heard they had them in Texas for the tornados or something. Still, he envisioned them as shelter-like bunkers, not a damn sports bar.

He turned his attention back to his victim. "I know you haven't figured out why this happenin', huh?"

The barely conscious man simply stared at him.

"Why, after inviting us here, would we turn around and take your life?" Baby Devil asked rhetorically. "Well, to tell you the truth, I don't even know the whole reasoning. I just follow orders. All I know is you went from ally to enemy fast. So something you did or said really rubbed Lil Teflon the wrong way."

The man let out a loud moan.

"The super-soldier from Underground," Baby Devil mocked. "I hate to see you go out like this, but an order is an order." He turned to Murder-Min, his Laotian partner in crime, who was watching with emotionless eyes. He nodded to her. She produced a small .380 pistol with a silencer attached from her waist and walked over to their victim.

"Hold up." He suddenly raised his hand.

Murder-Min looked at him with confusion.

"Let's not make this too messy." He gently lowered her hand. He looked around the room, then walked over to a trashcan in the corner. He removed the plastic liner, emptied the contents, and handed Murder-Min the empty plastic bag.

Her eyes sparkled.

"This'll be a lot cleaner. Less mess to clean up."

Murder-Min slowly draped the plastic bag over the man's head and wrapped the bottom of it to seal off any air circulation. The man's shallow, rapid breaths caused the plastic to patter with the sick sound of panic as he struggled for air. His bladder and bowels emptied as he faded into nothingness.

Baby Devil moved to the front of the chair with a disposable camera in his hand. Murder-Min carefully held the man's head back, his swollen eyes staring at the ceiling in vacant horror. Baby Devil snapped pictures. After five good shots from different angles, he was satisfied. He lowered the camera and stared silently at the dead man.

"Now ends the reign of Lil Crip," Baby Devil said. "May he find shade on the other side."

They gathered all that they brought with them, wiped away any trace of their presence, and made their quiet getaway from the house and the state of Texas.

* * * *

Soft rain fell from the gray sky as Elijah nervously peered from behind the wheel of his V-12 600 Series Benz. Traffic moved slowly up Central Avenue. Rainy weather was uncommon in Southern California and it was apparent by the reactions of the reckless drivers.

His eyes constantly darted from the rearview mirror to traffic ahead and to the side. With his black beanie pulled low to his eyebrows, his puffy Avirex jacket, and thick wool gloves, he appeared to be dressed for the snow than for a light rain and slightly below average temperature. His light brown eyes were intense with anticipation and stress. The fine lines at the corners of his eyes and tautness of his high cheekbones were a contrast to his usually youthful features.

"This lil nigga need to come on," he whispered.

The door to the small storefront abruptly swung open and his young homie stepped out, looking both ways up and down Central Avenue before heading toward Elijah's car in a carefree stroll.

Elijah watched him as he approached. *This lil nigga got balls the size of Texas,* he thought as Baby E.C. got closer. He immediately felt uneasy from the negative unseen energy that surrounded Baby E.C. as he opened the car door and got in the passenger seat.

"Roll out, Cuzz," Baby E.C. directed, looking straight ahead. His dark eyes, long eyelashes, and thick eyebrows contrasted his small chestnut-brown face.

Elijah dropped the gear in drive and smashed off. "How did it go?" He maneuvered the Benz through traffic.

"It went how it was supposed to go. I told you when you send a Eastside nigga to take care of something, it's always gonna get handled . . . on Eight-Nine Crip." Baby E.C. unzipped his windbreaker, threw it on the back seat, pulled a large envelope from his waistband, and tossed it in Elijah's lap.

Elijah chuckled. "Stop it with that Eastside shit. You know the West is the best."

Baby E.C. glanced at him sideways. "You know the real. That's why you fuckin' with the young Eastsider."

Elijah smiled and nodded. He could see the loyalty in the youngster. At times, he marveled at how a person could influence those he encountered without knowing it. Baby E.C. had been a snotty nose, abandoned, dusty kid running around the Eastside with his friends, pumping gas and helping old ladies carry their groceries to their cars for pocket change. Elijah saw him from time to time when he visited the older Eight-Nine East Coast homies. He always gave Baby E.C. and his friends money and weed. As Baby E.C. got older and earned his own street notoriety, he gravitated to Elijah. His separation from most of his homies and the dope game made Baby E.C. the perfect soldier and ally. They had a bond based on mutual respect and honor as men, not on flimsy notions like being from the same hood. Their allegiance surpassed all of that, and Baby E.C. would smash one of his own homies if they crossed Elijah.

Elijah peeped inside the envelope as they stopped at the red light. "Did it take much persuading?"

"Nah, I told him he had his opportunity to just pay us the monthly tax and he chose not to. So he could either accept the money and sign over the deed, or he could accept a bullet in his forehead. I think he realized the money was a better option," Baby E.C. explained.

"That's what's up." Elijah turned on Grand Avenue and got on the 110 freeway heading north. "Fuck that. Motherfuckas think they can just come into our communities and look down on us and treat us like shit. This the new move . . . we gonna take back the dollars they get from our hoods.

"I feel you." Baby E.C. nodded and reached for the blunt in the ashtray. He lit it up, took a deep toke, and stared at the big white Hollywood sign in the distance.

The phone in the center console vibrated. Elijah picked it up and sent it straight to voicemail without looking to see who was calling. Before he could put it down, it vibrated again. This time he looked and saw it was his uncle, Big 9-Lives. "Hold up, Cuzz, this Unc."

He answered the phone. "What?" He listened intently. "Any word on who caught up with him?" A hint of a smile creased his lips. "Alright, Unc. I'm gonna finish takin' care of this lil business, then I'll hit Big Wiz up and we'll all get together to see what this all mean for us." A pause, then, "Yep, ninety minutes." He hung up and put the phone back in the center console.

"Everything straight?" Baby E.C. asked with concern.

"Yeah, just some unexpected news." He merged across lanes and hit the Vernon Avenue exit. "I'm gonna drop you at your car. We'll get to the rest of the business later. I gotta go get up with the homies."

"You sure everything good, Cuzz? You need me on something?" Baby E.C. pushed.

"Take my word, lil bro, I'm straight. You know I'll keep you in the loop if it was something detrimental. We just got word that Lil Crip was found gutted in a spot in Texas. So it's just some lil internal politics. Once I rap with the homies and learn more, I'll let you know what's up."

Baby E.C. nodded and sat silently for the rest of the ride.

Elijah turned off Vernon on to Fourth Avenue and came to a stop in front of a well-kept, green one-story house. "I'll holla at you in a bit."

He gave Elijah daps, hopped out the car, and walked over to his smoked-gray Buick Regal.

Elijah waited for him to get in the car and pulled off.

Just when shit was cooling down, these niggas throw a monkey wrench in the game, he thought, as he drove back toward the freeway. *This seems like some of Lil Wizard's work.* He shook his head with a smirk.

One thing's for sure, karma's a bitch. He turned the volume up on the radio. Snoop Dogg's "Lay Low" boomed as he merged onto the freeway and got deep into traffic.

CHAPTER 1

2003

Elijah and Big 9-Lives stood in the middle of a clearing surrounded by large bright green Georgia pines. The brisk chill bit through their puffy windbreakers, gloves, and beanies. Frost formed on the leaves, giving them the appearance of large Christmas trees. Both men cradled twelve-gauge shotguns. Elijah lodged the rifle under his armpit, then blew into his palms and rubbed them together.

"Damn, my fuckin' hands 'bout to freeze off," Elijah said, his warm breath visible in the cold air. "And when the fuck you start hunting?"

Big 9-Lives looked at him with dark piercing eyes and frost forming on his goatee. "It helps to ease my nerves. I can clear my mind out here." He chuckled. "You been enjoying that year-round California sun for too long . . . done made you tender to the real elements. Out here shaking like Don Knots, looking like an Indian lost in the snowy hills of Montana." He laughed.

"Now all of a sudden you know about the hills of Montana. Nigga, if you don't stop it with this Daniel Boone shit. You been out the city for a few years, now you a mountain man?"

Big 9-Lives laughed harder. "Don't hate 'cause I'm versatile." He paused. "Hold up, be quiet." He crouched low and scanned the trees and the sky. "You hear that?"

"Nah. What you . . .?"

"Shhhh," Big 9-Lives waved at him.

Elijah scanned in the same direction.

Big 9-Lives leveled the rifle on his shoulder and stared down the path as he eased forward one soft step at a time. Twigs and debris crunched under his rubber-soled boots. Elijah mimicked his movement, clueless to what they were stalking.

Suddenly, a patch of bushes ahead erupted into vigorous activity as a flock of geese flew into the air.

Big 9-Lives instantly rose from his crouching position and calmly trailed one with the barrel of his rifle. Then he pulled the trigger, and the intended bird plummeted to the ground simultaneously with the loud bang of the rifle. He racked the used shell casing out of the chamber with the twelve-gauge's pump action, trailed the birds for another millisecond, and squeezed the trigger. Another bird fell from the sky.

Elijah let off shot after shot, working the pump action, in the same instant. With each shot the resounding boom grew louder in his ears. The torque from the rifle nearly threw him off balance, altering his aim. He didn't hit anything. "Fuck." He let off a few more shots in frustration.

Big 9-Lives watched him and burst into laughter as soon as the eighth and final shot was spent from the rifle. "You ain't hit shit but the sky."

"Bullshit, nigga. I dropped one, you saw it," Elijah argued.

"I ain't see you do shit but waste my bullets," Big 9-Lives teased.

"Yeah right, I'm tellin' you, you shot the first one, then I hit the second one. Watch, let's go find them, you gon' see two dead." Elijah walked to where the birds fell from the sky.

"I know it's two because that's how many I dropped." Big 9-Lives trailed him.

"See, you still a bullshit nigga. Don't try to take my kill." Elijah looked back at him.

Big 9-Lives laughed as they walked into the brush among the trees. It was refreshing for them to be together again. After the war with Lil Teflon ended, Elijah and the crew had all faded into their separate corners of the world to let the smoke settle. Elijah had been laying low at his home in Malibu. All his assets were hidden in shelf corporations unattached to him, so he was totally off the grid. He stayed out of the Hood and encountering the police. Big 9-Lives made his home in Atlanta. He occasionally dipped in and out of LA for business and to check on the family property. He never stayed long or let too many people know he was there. So their visits with each other were sporadic and infrequent.

Elijah had been keeping his nose to the ground and constantly on the grind with his new passion: purchasing real estate and running his record and investment companies. But with the new developments with Lil Teflon, he set everything aside to get his uncle's counseling.

They stalked through a wooded trail where they found the first dead bird. Big 9-Lives grabbed the bird callously by the neck and carried it as they searched for the second bird. "So, what's the word? How y'all plan to deal with the rumor that Lil Teflon is still alive if that proves to be true?" The dead bird dangled by his side. He breathed heavily as they continued their trek up a small hill toward more trees.

A sudden surge of anxiety welled up in the pit of Elijah's stomach; his mind a mixture of frustration, worries, and anger. It had been years since he had to concern himself with his childhood friend and now adversary, Lil Teflon. It still baffled him how someone he flipped with on dirty mattresses and played with in the sandbox could turn on him for no valid or understandable reason. Friends had arguments and fights, but he could not wrap his head around Lil Teflon wanting him dead. Finally, it all came to a head when Lil Wizard shot Lil Teflon in the face at a funeral, and the feds had swarmed the Hood.

"I'm not considering it a rumor no more. I got it from some reliable sources that Cuzz is still on deck. And with me knowin' how Cuzz roll, it's only a matter of time before he starts makin' some noise."

"So you should know that he's a loose end that y'all can't leave dangling." Big 9-Lives reached the crest of the hill and used the binoculars hanging from his neck to view further into the distance.

"I'm already knowin'." Elijah reached his side. "Big Wiz already doin' some homework to try and get a location. I really just been lettin' him run point on the issue."

"Why's that? It's your problem as much as it is his, probably even more so because Lil Teflon blames you more than he do Hitt and Wiz for what happened. In his head, he think you jumped sides on your childhood road dogs, that's how he justifies his hate. This way . . ." He led them through more trees.

Elijah thought about it momentarily. He knew Lil Teflon probably blamed him for half his face nearly being blown off more than he blamed Lil Wizard.

"Honestly, Unc, I just been tryna stay low and enjoy my sons, my family. All the politics of the Hood gets tiresome. It's like we constantly wrestling with some cutthroat, lowlife niggas over some shit that don't even matter in the grand scheme of things. I mean, majority of the homies don't have no worthwhile goals or dreams. They whole life is that bullshit five-mile square from the Forties to the Hundreds. Life is way bigger, Unc. I never got to know my pops. I wanna be there for my kids. I wanna do like you taught me long ago, to give the next generation the things we never had."

They walked up to the second dead bird. Big 9-Lives stooped down and inspected it, then laid the first carcass next to it. "I can dig that. But remember, at the same time don't leave a serious threat to chance or in the hands of the next man. Don't underestimate strong enemies. Whenever there's a threat and you can eliminate it, you make sure it gets done." He stood and gazed at the two dead birds.

"Yeah, you right for the most part," Elijah said.

"For the most part? What does that mean?" He side-eyed Elijah.

"I mean . . . we good financially. We out of the Hood, for the dmost part, except when we wanna be over there. I just feel like tryin' to figure out how to continue to grow our legal businesses and makin' our families stronger should be the top priority right now. I'm not even in the game no more, so it ain't like I got to war with niggas over territory or dope money. So, at this point we just going to war and hunting niggas down out of ego. An ego that can lead us into destruction. I'm tryin' to live in peace and prosperity now. Lil Tef don't seem as important to me as he once would have."

Big 9-Lives regarded him briefly. "I get all that. But don't forget who we are. We pursue peace but don't shun war when it confronts us. Don't become one of them niggas that money makes soft."

"Never." Elijah was offended.

Big 9-Lives stared at him, then averted his gaze back to the birds at his feet. "Neph, I want you to always remember something. We're lions." He laid his rifle on the ground and unsheathed the Swiss army knife from its holster. "A lion is born a lion; he don't wake up one morning and decide to become one." He bent down and flipped the birds on their backs. He looked up at Elijah with a serious expression, the knife clenched in his fist. "In that spirit, a lion can't wake up one morning and say he's a cat." He jammed the tip of the knife into the soft belly of the bird and ripped upward, exposing its innards.

Elijah flinched.

Big 9-Lives did the same to the second bird. Then he grabbed the birds by the neck and stood, holding the bloody birds in one hand and his bloody knife in the other. "No matter how much peace life grants, don't never lose your lion instinct, nigga."

Elijah locked eyes with him and nodded a silent affirmation.

Big 9-Lives wiped his bloodied knife on his pants leg and sheathed it. He picked up his rifle and walked back toward the way they came.

After they entered the thick part of the brush, he spoke without looking back at Elijah, "And for the record, these are both my kills. You gotta get your own tomorrow."

He pushed through a rough patch before Elijah could protest. The noise of moving leaves and cracking twigs were the only sounds left as they made their way back to Big 9-Lives's truck.

CHAPTER 2

Elise gazed out of the back passenger window of the rugged Range Rover. Her dark shades covered the excitement in her eyes. Crossing the border from San Diego into Tijuana, Mexico, always fascinated her. It was like stepping through a time portal into another world. A blend of the modern with Stone Age desperation. Seeing those people struggle for their survival sparked something in Elise. In Mexico, violence and the energy of death seemed to hang over the cities. It was the spirit of cocaine, Elise always thought. The devil's dust, with the power to allure the desperate and brave into a deadly game. It promised the possibility of wealth and power, but for most, it was a fleeting illusion that ended with the player in a cage for the rest of their lives, or more likely, with their severed head being delivered in a box to their family. Yet many signed up daily to play. The thought always brought a slight smile to her face. Something within her loved the game.

Living on the edge of life and disaster was what made life worth living. She loved her young son, Amaru, and Elijah. She understood why Elijah did not want her in the streets anymore, but she was not ready to give up the game. Her time away giving birth and getting her home life together was wonderful. She and Lauren, who she sometimes jokingly referred to as her "sister wife," shared a home and children by Elijah. She considered Lauren and Elijah's son, Toussaint, her second son and loved him as such. Never in a million years would she had ever thought she would have agreed to such an arrangement. Naturally, it was difficult at times, but she would not trade her family for anything, no matter how much others frowned on it. They were a young, successful, beautiful family, and together they were a working machine. They each played their part well, and that was what made the whole thing flow. But despite all of that, she still longed to be in the trenches. She missed the power of running a multi-million-dollar drug network and being a boss in the underworld. The game was calling, and she finally made the decision to answer that call. The landscape of the noisy hustle and bustle gave way to a more rural area. The truck turned on to a long stretch of dirt road. Vendors with carts and produce stalls lined the roadside. Some of the buildings were dilapidated and run down, while others were occupied by the locals. Animals wandered the road lazily as the SUV swerved slightly to avoid a horse-driven carriage. She rested her head against the headrest and closed her eyes. Her mind drifted back to the brief conversation she had had with Elijah earlier that morning before leaving the hotel. The anguish of having to lie to him when he asked about her whereabouts pained her deeply. He had completely caught her off guard and she had to cover her tracks. She never kept anything from him before. *It's too late to worry about that now,* she thought. *It is what it is.*

The blaring honk from a cargo truck and a bumpy dip from a pothole in the road jarred her back to reality.

"Are ju okay?" the Mexican driver in a cowboy hat and dark shades asked.

"Si, si . . . *Bueno, gracias.*" Elise reached in her multicolor Louis Vuitton purse for her satellite phone. She dialed a number, and after a few rings, someone picked up.

"Hey," Elise said. "Everything is good here. How's my baby?" She listened, gazing out the window at the moving scenery. "Okay good. Hug and kiss him for me. Tell him Mommy will be home soon." She hung up the phone and put it back in her purse.

She caught the driver looking at her through the rearview mirror. He quickly returned his attention to the road. She looked in the mirror, smoothed her center-parted ponytail, and applied another coat of lip gloss, smiling as she caught the driver stealing another glance at her.

The SUV turned down another half-dirt half gravel road. A modest single-story brick house with an adjoining farm nestled in the distance appeared through the clearing of the dust. They reached a gate checkpoint where two Mexican men dressed in black military uniforms with AR-15s strapped to their shoulders promptly waved them through. As the truck drew closer to the house, Elise saw Guzman waiting on the front porch surrounded by his customary multiple-armed guards. His carefully cropped curly hair and broad shoulders on his six-foot-three frame instantly separated him from his crowd of short, stoic bodyguards. He wore a light gray suit jacket with a white button-up shirt, and gray slacks with black loafers.

He approached the truck as it came to a stop in front of the house. Elise noticed that he had aged slightly around the eyes, but he still carried the look of a rugged Antonio Banderas.

He opened the door for her with a warm greeting. "*Buenos dias, hermosa.*" He held her hand to help her climb from the truck and kissed both cheeks in a familial fashion. "What a refreshing surprise," he charmed in his heavy accent.

"*Buenos dias, gracias por invitarme.*" She smiled. Her white silk Donna Karan blouse, black wool Armani slacks, paired with block-heeled ankle boots gave her a casual-sexy but chic style.

"Any time, any time. How is the young lion?" He led her toward the house.

"He's good. Just trying to stay true to his transition," she replied.

"That's good to hear," Guzman said.

He opened the front door and allowed her to step in first. Elise scanned the surroundings with familiarity. The modestly furnished house contrasted with a man of his stature. Plain linoleum covered the floor throughout the house. An inexpensive maroon couch and loveseat faced a fifty-inch television sitting on a sturdy oak chest. The simple and tidy adjoining dining room displayed a durable cast aluminum table and matching chairs; a vase of artificial flowers sat in the middle of the table. The immaculately clean house smelled of wax and Pine-Sol, giving it a rustic yet homey feel.

Guzman gestured to a spot on the couch and waited for her to sit before joining her. "I'm proud of what he's trying to do. Most of us, myself included, stay in too long. The more we get, the more we want. But I guess it's the nature of the beast; we're greedy. What else can I say?" He looked in her eyes.

"For some of us, it's just for the sport of it." She set her shades on the coffee table and smirked.

"True, true. For me, it's a little of both. The sport of it and a lot of greed." He chuckled. "But anyway, how is my godson? Is he getting big and strong?"

"Yes. He's growing like a weed and keeps me on my toes, just like his father."

"I can imagine. He's going to be smart like his papa as well. I have a few gifts for you to take back to him." He looked over his shoulder and called, "Maria, Maria?"

A short, stout, middle-aged woman in an apron over a traditional Mexican dress stepped from the kitchen drying her hands with a small towel. "*¿Si, señor?*"

"Maria, *trae a nuestra invitada un vaso de limonada.*"

"*Si, si, de inmediato.*" Maria disappeared back into the kitchen.

"So I guess we get to the matters at hand." Guzman reached into his side jacket pocket and removed a letter-sized envelope. "It's all there . . . every telephone number and address he's had within the last five years."

Elise's hands trembled slightly as she played with the thought of unsealing the envelope. She had dreamt about this many nights and was still uncertain if she wanted the information. Her sense of wanting to know was outweighing her bitterness. It was time to get the answers she deserved so she could close this chapter in her life.

"I know this is a big situation for you." He patted her gently on the arm. "It may be better if you open it when you're alone."

Maria returned holding a tray with two crystal glasses with a lemon slice perched on each glass, and a glass pitcher filled with lemonade and ice. She sat the glasses down and poured each of them lemonade.

"*Gracias.*" Elise smiled graciously and picked up the glass, taking a sip.

Guzman did the same.

"*¿Algo más, señor?*"

"*No, eso será todo, Maria.*"

Maria nodded, then went back to the kitchen.

"From the looks of it, he's in Jamaica now. I have people there if you need any assistance on that end." Guzman reclined back and crossed his leg.

"I'll take it from here. Are you sure all of this information is accurate?" Elise stared at the unopened envelope in her hand with uncertainty.

"Trust me, it's one hundred percent on point. I have people who work in the government here. This you ask of me is a small thing. Unless someone is an international spy with multiple identities, my guys can find them."

"Thank you so much. I will repay you for this one day." She placed the envelope into her purse.

"Don't worry. It is my pleasure to be able to help, and you renewing our work together now is payment enough." He smiled cunningly.

"Speaking of, how do you want to proceed on that front?" She readied herself for the negotiations. This was her first solo dealings with Guzman. Their past interactions were based on Elijah.

"We don't have to make this too complicated. Now that 9-Lives is not your foundation, it's a matter of how many you can handle."

"I want to start off with fifty kilos just to get my feet wet again." She intentionally ignored his veiled inquiry into Elijah's role in their arrangement.

"If you can handle fifty, why not start with the whole hundred?" he countered.

"Because I'm paying up front and don't want to tie up too much money until I know my machine is rolling right. It's been a while since I been in the field you know?" She sipped her lemonade.

"I understand." He paused for a moment. "I don't want you under any undue pressure, so don't worry about how long it will take you to sell them. I got your back. I'll give you a hundred and you take whatever time you need to make them fly on this first go around."

"At what price are you talking?"

"Uh . . . fifteen per," he quickly responded.

"Alright now give me your real number."

He laughed. "You have learned well, *soldado*. But you know prices have changed since our last business . . . inflation."

"I know. I'm a smart businesswoman, and I did my homework before coming here. Let's not waste each other's time. I'll do twelve per on the ones I pay for up front, and thirteen on the ones fronted."

"Add five hundred dollars on each of those numbers—"

"Done," she quickly answered.

He clapped his hands. "A woman who is decisive, that is a great trait. My man will contact you with the details. For the first one, we drop in San Diego and you take it from there. Once you see how things are going to work for you, we can figure out if you need me to get them down to the South or the Midwest, and we discuss the price for me getting them there then."

She nodded. "Sounds good. I know how the bull rides in this rodeo. We'll make whatever adjustments we need to and make it work."

"Okay good. And I'll assume that you will make sure 9-Lives is not going to have a problem with our new arrangement." He studied Elise intensely.

"That's not your worry. I'm a big girl, I got it."

"It's a deal then." He reached over and squeezed her hand.

"Now get your men to take us to the roughest part of town that serves the best Mexican food because I'm going to buy you lunch."

"Are you sure you want to go to that area? Shootouts take place in the roughest parts of Mexico," he cautioned with a raised brow.

"I wouldn't have suggested if I wasn't game. You're supposed to be the king lion in these parts. I know a little excitement doesn't make you uneasy," she jeered.

He stood and extended a hand to help her from her seat. He turned to the bodyguard who was standing off to the side. "Chuco, *prepara los autos y las armas, iremos a la ciudad.*"

Guzman's head security barked out orders in Spanish to the other guards, and the compound became abuzz with their activities preparing the caravan.

"After you, Mia." He gestured toward the front door.

Elise smiled at him, put on her oversized Chanel shades, and strutted confidently out into the dust and bright sunrays.

CHAPTER 3

JuJu stepped onto his front porch dressed in a wife beater, blue cut-off khakis, and corduroy house shoes nursing a forty-ounce bottle of Old English 800. His cornrows were intact on one side of his head, and the other side was a spry of wild, crinkly hair. He was waiting for the homegirl to come back and finish braiding. He took a swig from his beer and watched the tiny chipping sparrows fly from one tree to another, chirping their constant morning music. *LA mornings are beautiful*, he thought. That was a drastic contrast to the reality of living there. For him, the recent past had been a series of betrayals, wars, and deaths that sent many of his peers to the graveyard or prison. Those who were able to escape those fates had faded back from the Hood for their own strategic reasons.

With all the shifts and changes, Ju-Ju became one of the de facto leaders in the day-to-day operations of the Nine-Os. He had managed to maintain neutrality in the war between Lil 9-Lives and Lil Teflon, which kept him off the FBI's radar and in good standing with most of the homies in the Set. Meanwhile, he was the driving force in the ongoing wars with the Hoovers, the Eight-Tray Gangsters, and the Bloods. There was even a short spell where he was warring with former allies from the Rollin' Forties and the One-Hundreds. Most of the young up-and-comers in the Hood loved and respected him. Although he was only a few years older than them, he had survived a ten-year period in South Central's killing field with his sanity and honor intact, which made him a veteran in the streets. A lot of headaches and stress came with all the responsibilities, so the calmness of these early mornings was his favorite time of day.

An even breeze coursed through the trees, swaying the leaves, washing over his face as kids were already outside riding bikes and playing. Ju-Ju closed his eyes and took in a deep breath. His once soft and pudgy face was now hard and chiseled, with dark areas underneath his eyes that contrasted the rest of his light skin. He stretched out his muscular six-foot-three-inch frame to work out the morning kinks and took a seat on the stone stoop.

A young kid with a dusty afro, tight and ragged clothes, stopped his bike in front of Ju-Ju's front gate. "What's up, Ju-Ju?"

"What up, killa? What you up to?"

"Nothin'. We gon' ride our bikes all the way to the beach today."

"Lil Dude, y'all gon' have Fred Flintstone feet doin' all that ridin.'" He chuckled. "Don't you supposed to be in school? How the hell you ridin' to the beach?"

"It's Saturday, ain't no school on Saturday." The boy perched on the opposite side of the bike and rested his foot on the pedal.

"Oh yeah, I'm trippin'. I don't know where time be goin'," Ju-Ju mumbled more to himself than the little boy.

"Yep, I'm gon' ride Tyrone on my handlebars. He won't have no bike, so we gon' try and jack for one on the way to the beach," the boy babbled excitedly.

"I see the cycle don't stop. We used to do the same shit as kids. How old are you now?"

"I'm twelve."

"Lil nigga, you ain't no damn twelve."

"Uh-huh . . . yes I am." The boy frowned.

Ju-Ju took a sip of his drink, the lukewarm alcohol fizzing in his mouth. "It don't matter either way. You old enough to go to the halls if you keep bullshittin'."

"What's the halls?"

"Juvenile hall . . . jail, lil motherfucka." Ju-Ju glared at the boy. "You know what they do to lil dudes like you when you go to the halls? They beat yo motherfuckin' ass. Niggas in there gon' have you washin' they clothes."

"I ain't washin' no motherfucka's clothes."

"Watch yo mouth, boy." Ju-Ju hopped from the stone stoop as a midnight-blue Lexus pulled up blasting Tupac's "Shed So Many Tears". "Go on, get up the block. And stop tryna steal your way through life. It's other ways to get money."

"Alright. Can I get five dollars?" The boy smiled innocently, showing yellow stained teeth.

Ju-Ju stared at him for a moment, then dug in his pocket, mumbling, "Lil slick ass always tryna hustle somebody . . . here." He gave the boy a twenty-dollar bill. "You better make it last."

"I will. Later, big homie!" The boy excitedly gave the bike's pedal a swift, hard pump to get on his way. Ju-Ju chuckled as the boy sped down the block.

The music from the car went off and a short, plump, brown-skinned youngster with a close-crop haircut bounced from the driver's seat wearing a blue Dickies suit and blue Chuck Taylors.

"What's up with it, Loc?" Lil Bar-Dog held out his fist and Ju-Ju bumped it.

"What's crackin', Cuzz?" Ju-Ju noticed the sexy light-skinned young woman sitting in the passenger seat. "Is that Stella niece?"

"Yeah, big bro, kill game, she don't want it all out there like that."

"Fuck you mean she don't want it out there but ridin' through the Hood with you?" Ju-Ju walked over and sat on the stoop. He lit a blunt. "The whole Hood gon' be talkin' about her ridin' in the Lexus with Lil Bar-Dog, so I guess her secret is shot." He laughed.

"It don't matter to me one way or another. I just gotta act like I care about her reputation." Little Bar-Dog rolled his eyes and smirked. "But fuck that bitch, I wanna holler at you about the politics in the Hood. It's like the Hood splittin' up. A lot of the young homies fuck with Baby Devil, and he's team Teflon, so it's a lot of bullshit talk about Lil 9, Hitt, Wiz, and them."

"Niggas don't even know what all goin' on. How they gon' take sides? Even with Lil Teflon, I heard all the rumors about he supposed to still be alive, but I ain't seen him."

"Nah, it's official, Cuzz, you ain't heard?"

Ju-Ju took a long drag from his blunt. "Heard what?"

"He slid through the park last night on some wicked shit."

Ju-Ju perked up at the news. "Who was he with?"

"He bumped through solo, with the lil Asian bitch Murder-Min driving. They say Cuzz got out with the MAC-11 strapped around his shoulder."

"What he say? Who was he lookin' for?" Ju-Ju asked.

"They say he ain't say shit. Pulled up in front of the gym, got out with the strap, and just stood there mean-muggin' the crowd with Murder-Min standing next to him with a pistol. He got back in the car and they skirted off after a few minutes."

"Is that right?" Ju-Ju chuckled and shook his head. "So Baby Devil is ridin' with Lil Teflon against the empire?"

"He ain't just came out and said it recently, but you know he fuck with Lil Teflon. And it's a group of young homies that's talkin' about Lil 9 and them not bein' in the Hood as much, and how they not feeding the Set the way they suppose to—just all the hater shit they pickin' up from other niggas."

"First off, what Lil Teflon got goin' on with Lil 9 ain't even niggas business. It don't have nothin' to do with Nine-O. That's some next level shit that them youngsters better keep out of. Believe me, they don't wanna see the homies."

Lil Bar-Dog sat on the steps next to Ju-Ju. "I'm with you, Loc. Just let me know how we rollin'."

"For now, you and your circle don't speak on the issue either way. I'm callin' a meeting for next Sunday. Get the word out that every Nine-O better be at Jesse Owens Park on that day or they will be disciplined." He stood up.

"Easy call, Cuzz. I'm on it now." Lil Bar-Dog stood, gave Ju-Ju daps, and walked back to his car. "Ninety minutes, Loc."

"Yep, Long Gang." Ju-Ju threw up the Nine-O fingers and walked back into the house.

Lil Bar-Dog's music cranked back up, then gradually faded down the block. Ju-Ju picked up the phone, started to dial, then paused. He slowly sat the phone down, picked up the remote control, and kicked his feet up on the coffee table. He turned on the

TV, settled in, and rested his head on the couch pillow.

*　　*　　*　　*

A hard knock on the front door startled Ju-Ju out of his slumber. He looked around, confused for a moment. The TV screen was black. He'd dozed off again. He scratched hard at the undone side of his hair.

Another hard knock. "What the fuck?" He got up and peeped through the curtains. "Don't be knockin' on my door like the fuckin' police." He dropped the curtain and opened the door.

"You should have your ass up then," Big Teflon-Black said in a deep voice. A wide grin was plastered on his face.

"My nigga." Ju-Ju greeted enthusiastically, grabbing Big Teflon-Black in a strong bear hug. "Fuck you doin' down here? You shoulda let me know you was coming."

"Just some spur-of-the-moment shit." Big Teflon stepped inside. His teal-green eyes did not seem to fit with his jet-black skin and strong African features. "What you got goin' on?"

"You already know, same shit different toilet. What's up with you? I see you been tryna keep that thang tight with yo new lil haircut." He playfully squeezed Big Teflon's muscles.

Big Teflon pulled back. "Watch out, nigga. Don't be tryna size up the guns. You know I keep 'em loaded!" He looked in the mantle mirror and rubbed his bald-fade haircut from all angles. "Yeah, and you see it too. You see them thangs dippin' on you. You can get your surfboard and go surfing on them waves right there."

"Ol' bougie-ass dude. You ain't doin' nothing but cheatin' with that Murray's grease to get them lil kiddie waves in your hair," Ju-Ju teased. "That Murray's gonna have your shit fallin' out in a couple years. Nigga gon' be looking like George Jefferson."

Ju-Ju walked to the kitchen and grabbed a forty-ounce bottle of beer from the refrigerator. "You want one a these?" He held up the bottle.

"Nah, I'm straight." Big Teflon sat heavily on the couch.

Ju-Ju twisted the cap off the beer and took a long, deep chug.

"Damn, Cuzz, you drinkin' this early? You turned into a real alchy, ain't you?"

"Fuck you." He sat down in the La-Z-Boy recliner. "I got problems, nigga. I ain't up in San Diego enjoying the sun and family life like you. I'm still here wrestlin' with the bear. Dealin' with the Set is stressful."

Big Teflon took the blunt that was tucked behind his ear and lit it. "Don't get it twisted. Family life ain't all what it's cracked up to be. I find myself just wantin' to move back to the Hood and thug it out at times."

"Don't do it. It's almost like suicide, and it's gettin' even more hectic by the day." He grabbed the remote and flipped to the news.

"If it's suicide, why you still in the thick of it?"

"Because I don't have nothin' else. I love the Set, but I wouldn't recommend the life to no one else who ain't in it or got the means to get out. Right now, with the wars flaring back up with the enemies, the Set need me. All y'all not around much, so it's on me to keep our side goin'."

"On that note, that's what I really came for. I heard my brother was through here. What you heard about it?"

"Nothin'." Ju-Ju lied and took another drink. He wanted to

gauge if Big Teflon was going to continue bullshitting him about Lil Teflon. Big Teflon had been one of his closest friends in the Hood, but he had flat-out lied about his brother being dead. Ju-Ju was curious how Big Teflon planned on recovering from feeding him a fake story for all these years. He assessed that Big Teflon was there to figure out whose side he was going to be on if the war kicked back up. He measured his words and tried to sound casual. "You told me Lil Teflon passed, so I've been dismissing any rumors that say different. Are you now sayin' the rumors are true? He still alive?"

Big Teflon averted his eyes to the TV. There was silence. Ju-Ju held his breath, anticipating what Big Teflon's response would be.

Finally, Big Teflon said, "Look, I didn't wanna lie to you, but the family decided it was best to let those who thought he was dead continue to think that."

Ju-Ju kept a straight face. He decided to continue playing dumb. He had known that Lil Teflon was alive for months. News like that didn't stay hidden in the Hood. Someone was bound to slip and let the cat out the bag.

"And you felt it was alright to have niggas grievin' and goin' through changes for nothing?" Ju-Ju said.

"War is deception, Cuzz, you know that. Sometimes what's best for the greater good may hurt others, that's just how it goes. And you mean to tell me you haven't confirmed till now that he been around here?"

"I just told you I hadn't." His mood shifted. He was getting agitated with all the suspicious questioning.

"Well, now you know. And now that he's made himself known, you know what's to follow. I need to know where you stand when the storm comes." Big Teflon grew serious now. His eyes studied Ju-Ju.

Ju-Ju considered him with leveled eyes. "Where I stand? I stand for Nine-O. The question is, where do you stand?"

"He's my brother. I've thought about it long and hard, and at the end of the day, I can't just stand by and watch them hurt him again. Is there a way we can get this squashed?"

"I don't know. Lil Tef did the unspeakable. I can try to reach out to Lil 9, but you already know there're other factors involved."

"I wanna try and get it squashed if there's a chance. If we can't, I'd like to know where you stand. Lil Tef did the unspeakable plottin' with the dude to smoke Lil 9, but so did Lil Wiz when he damn near blew my brother's face off," Big Teflon said.

"I told you I stand with Nine-O."

"What do that mean?" Big Teflon snapped.

"It means I'm not on no one man's side. Whatever's best to keep the Set from imploding, that's what I'm gon' do. No one is bigger than the program. I'm loyal to the soil. We already at war with damn near every hood in the vicinity. The police tryna bag everybody, and now we got to contend among ourselves. So again, whatever's best for the Set, that's where I'll stand."

Big Teflon smashed the end of his blunt in the ashtray. "I got you." He stood. "All I can do is ask you to reach out to Lil 9 or Big 9-Lives. Tell 'em I wanna end this."

Ju-Ju stood and walked Big Teflon to the door. "Is Lil Tef ready to squash it? I mean because if he ain't with it, then tryin' to negotiate is worthless."

"Leave that part to me, I'll talk to him."

They walked out onto the porch. The warm California sun washed over them.

"I'll do my part," Ju-Ju promised. "I'll find a way to get at Big 9-Lives, that's who our best chance is with."

"I appreciate it." Big Teflon stared at him. "But you know if this don't work what it spells." He let the question linger. "And if it comes to that, it ain't gonna be about who's right and who's wrong for me. I'm gonna pick my side and ride until the wheels fall off."

Ju-Ju extended his hand and he gripped it firmly. "I hear you, killa. As long as you can stand under the heat, I respect it."

"Me and my brother was born in the heat, so it ain't shit." Big Teflon walked toward his Yukon. "Let me know when you hear something," he said without looking back at Ju-Ju.

Ju-Ju watched Big Teflon climb into his truck. He continued watching as he sped off up the block and disappeared around the corner, Scarface's "Watch Ya Step" blaring in the wind.

CHAPTER 4

Baby Devil walked out of the liquor store on Ninety-Second and Western with a brown paper bag cuffed under one armpit, and a bag of sunflower seeds in his hand. If not for the blue-gray cascade shirt, blue painter pants, and blue croquetsacks that identified him as an active Crip, his dark brown skin, big, combed-out afro, dark Locs shades, and natural scowl resembled a Black Panther Party member of the past. He surveyed his surroundings as he walked to the nearby 1996 Chevy Impala parked in a space in front of the laundromat. He chirped the alarm, opened the passenger door, and reached for his cell phone sitting in the middle console.

He raised back out of the car just as Cisco, a local neighborhood crackhead was walking up.

"What's up, Devil, you got a bump for me this morning?" She shifted from one foot to another, her jaw rocking side to side, and body swaying back and forth as if she was grooving to a tune that only she heard.

"You got some money?" He stared at her blackened hands and dirty clothes.

"Not right now, but I got a trick around the corner." She looked suspiciously both ways. "Soon as I take care of him, I got you."

"Why don't you go take care of him first then get at me? Yo ass always tryna run game."

"Come on, Devil, you know Aunty good for it. I got you, just need a lil bump to get started."

"Go on up to the spot. I'll tell the homies to look out for you, but you better have my money later."

"Alright, alright, you know I don't play, Devil. I got you." She walked off rapidly toward the spot on Ninety-Fourth and Western.

Baby Devil made a quick phone call. "Hey, Cisco 'bout to come your way, throw her a dime till later." He hung up the phone and put it in his pocket.

He went into the laundromat and put the brown bag on one of the washing machines, then sat on top of the machine next to it. There were a few patrons moving around loading and emptying machines and folding clothes, while others waited for their washer or dryer to finish their cycles. He stared out the window and watched the activity on Western, popping the sunflower seeds into his mouth, cracking the shells, and spitting them out in rapid succession.

Many had come and gone before him who operated this strip of land, but now he knew it was his time to call the dogs. His childhood crew, the Tiny Toons, had grown to over fifty members separate from the other Nine-Os. Apart from Lil Bar-Dog and Lil Time-Bomb, they all looked up to Baby Devil as the hardest among them. If it wasn't for a group of active older homies, such as Ju-Ju, Baby Devil possibly could have the keys to the whole Hood. He had earned his stripes against the Hoovers and Eight-Tray Gangsters with three confirmed kills, multiple shootings, and rumbles with the enemies. It was also an open secret that he was Lil Teflon's main triggerman during the inhouse political wars. He knew Ju-Ju and others would probably try to kill him if they could do it secretly, but he didn't care. He stayed strapped and kept a loyal crew of Tiny

Toons around whenever he was in the Set. He was the chief Devil on this strip from Eighty-Ninth to Century, and the days of him taking orders from the elders were quickly coming to an end. He was growing more independent as he got older and was starting to realize that there was more to gain looking out for his own interest than indulging in the war between Lil Teflon and Lil 9-Lives. In all reality, it wasn't his war to fight; he had jumped in it to prove his loyalty to Lil Teflon. He was a kid when Lil Teflon snatched him off Western Avenue to rob banks and do his dirty work. He didn't know any better then. He thought the crumbs Lil Teflon was giving him off the licks was big money. Now that he was more streetwise, it was obvious that Lil Teflon was using him all along. He wasn't mad at Lil Teflon because he'd taught him the ropes of street life and hustling, and he still had love and admiration for him. But things had changed, and Baby Devil had his own army of young homies that was ready to move on his call. The older homies had shined long enough.

He retrieved a bottle of beer from the paper bag, twisted the cap off, and drank from the bottle. Just then, a black Cadillac STS with dark tint turned into the parking lot and came to a stop behind Baby Devil's Impala. Three young Crips got out of the car, laughing, and talking as they made their way into the laundromat.

Skip, Tiny Looney, and Droopy were all a part of the Tiny Toons, Baby Devil's original crew within the Nine-Os. All three wore powder-blue North Carolina Tar Heels hats with the intertwined *NC* logo for the Ninety-Crip and various styles of gang attire.

They all greeted Baby Devil with daps and hugs. "What's up with the Crips?" Baby Devil chimed.

"What's up with it, Cuzz?" Tiny Looney sat on top of one of the washing machines. He was bright skinned and handsome.

"Same ol, same ol. Y'all hollered at the other homies?" Baby Devil inquired.

"Yeah, some of 'em should be here any minute now." Tiny Looney turned to Skip. "You brought the weed?"

"Yep." Skip pulled out a sandwich bag of weed from the top pocket of his blue Pendleton jacket.

"Roll up." Tiny Looney tossed Skip a blunt cigar. Skip split the cigar down the middle. Then he emptied out the tobacco in the nearby trash can; and broke down the buds of weed to go inside the emptied cigar.

"What you been hearing?" Tiny Looney asked Baby Devil.

"The same shit y'all have." Baby Devil took another drink and passed it to Droopy. "I don't know the reason Lil Tef went up to the park the other night and showed his face. The plan was that he was supposed to lay low until the time was right."

"Nigga probably got stir-crazy playing dead for so long." Droopy laughed in a slow, goofy manner, his large lips jiggling.

"Tell me 'bout it." Baby Devil chuckled. "Seriously though, Cuzz do dumb shit sometimes that I don't get. I guess he feels like he makin' a statement or something."

"I'm sure it shocked some motherfuckas to see him live in the flesh, so I guess his statement was felt." Tiny Looney took the freshly rolled blunt from Skip and lit it.

"Yeah, but to what extent? The niggas who really count ain't around right now. Lil 9, Hitter, and Wizard is who he bangin' with, so making a statement to anybody other than them is really irrelevant." Baby Devil took another swig of beer.

"Here come the cavalry, Cuzz," Droopy drawled.

Ten young Tiny Toons were waiting to cross at the light on the opposite side of Western. Simultaneously, two old bucket cars whipped into the parking lot with four to five people in each. They parked and poured out into the laundromat. They all dapped and hugged as the Nine-Os on foot made it across the street and into the laundromat.

After all the greetings were finished, Baby Devil gave Baby Grape and Tiny Chaos two pistols and walkie-talkies. "Go post up in the auto-mechanic shops on both sides of Western. Keep an eye out for enemies and the police."

The adolescent youngsters obediently walked out of the laundromat and headed in the direction of the auto shop.

Baby Devil and the rest of the crowd moved to the back of the laundromat, as all the other patrons cleared out, leaving the area free for their group. Small talk and jokes ensued until Baby Devil commanded everyone's attention. Everyone got quiet and gathered around him.

"Listen up. This ain't gon' take long." He looked at the crowd with a menacing scowl. "I called y'all up here specifically because I feel we all represent the Tiny Toons first and foremost. I mean, Nine-O above all, but our loyalty within Nine-O is to our generation: the Tiny Toons."

A chorus of "fashos" and "you know its" sounded around the room.

"Just so we all know where we at, I wanna know if any of you is already taking one side or another with this Lil Teflon-Lil 9 shit?" Baby Devil studied the crowd carefully.

A youngster with crooked teeth said, "I mean, we know you fuck with Lil Teflon, but we don't know all the ins and outs to what all this shit is even about. Big Peso told us to stay out that shit."

"Anybody else got something they wanna add?" Baby Devil paused to give others the opportunity to speak.

Tiny Looney chimed in. "You already kinda in the mix with this shit. And the older homies feel like you ride with Lil Teflon, period. If that's the case, and niggas comin' for you, then I'm ridin' with ya. So, I'm not takin' Lil 9's side or Lil Teflon's . . . I'm ridin' with you."

A low grumble of agreements went around the room.

"But ain't that still us gettin' in a mix that we don't know who's right or wrong?" the youngster with crooked teeth said. "Not to mention this shit is just causin' chaos in the Hood like Big P said."

The crowd again stirred.

"You right, Cuzz," Baby Devil surprisingly agreed. "I'm lookin' at all this from a different standpoint than before. Really, I shouldn't have even took sides in the beginning. I was young and being loyal. It is what it is now. But I feel like we got an opportunity before us. It ain't about Lil Tef or Lil 9 and them, it's about us. We out here on the frontline against the Tramps, the Snoovas, and the Faggots, not the older homies."

A chorus of agreement echoed among the crowd.

"So why take sides to keep either of them in control?" Baby Devil continued. "I say we keep our cards close to the vest as much as possible. Like the homie said, I'm already in they lil scrimmage because of what happened in the past, but I'm gonna try and holla at Nine and them and try to pull myself from that shit. If they not tryna hear it, then I gotta do what I gotta do, and it won't have nothin' to do with y'all, so don't feel obligated to get in it. If Nine and them force me to ride with Lil Tef, then I will. But know that when the dust clear, I'm aimin' for the Tiny Toons to run the Set, not none of them. They time is over. It's time for us to call the shots around here."

"Tiny Toon Gang, on Nine-O," Skip blurted out.

They all verbalized or nodded their agreement.

"So are we all in agreement that we pushin' for our takeover of the Hood?" Baby Devil waited as the question prompted a surge of excitement in the group.

"Tiny Toons or nothin'," Tiny Looney shouted.

"Tiny Toons or nothin'!" they all consented.

"That's what's up." Baby Devil smiled. "So we keep our stance on this silent outside of us. Ju-Ju called a meeting for Sunday. I already know the question is gonna be put to y'all 'bout where your heads at on this in-house beef. Everybody stay neutral. Don't show no favoritism to Lil Tef, Lil 9, or me. Let him talk—all y'all do is listen. Everybody got it?"

The crowd expressed their consent and understanding.

"Let's fall out." Baby Devil grabbed his phone. "Tell the homies over the walkie-talkie we headin' out. Let's head to the Sixties and see what's up with that issue. Y'all ready for the Thunderdome?"

The crowd got animated as they crowded for the door in anticipation of the prospect of Thunderdoming with the Rollin 60's. Cheers and tough talk resounded among them as they stepped outside.

In a frenzy of excitement, they all piled into their respective vehicles and pulled out on to Western like over-crowded clown cars, headed northbound toward the Sixties.

* * * *

A beat-up gray Datsun B-210 waited in the Penny Pinchers' parking lot across the street from the laundromat. A stocky, brown skinned, bald-head man sat behind the steering wheel, watching through his large bifocal glasses, as the Nine-Owes drove from the parking lot on to Western.

He fidgeted and glanced out the side and rear windows as people moved around his vehicle. "A bunch of dumb motherfuckas," he mumbled. He picked up the box of Lemonheads from the passenger seat, tossed a few into his mouth, and chewed rapidly. He watched as the caravan continued their exit from the laundromat parking lot.

As the last car pulled out, he turned the ignition, pushed his glasses further up the bridge of his nose, and let out a spontaneous giggle. He backed out of the parking space and zoomed on to Western, unbeknownst to anyone.

CHAPTER 5

Big 9-Lives drove down Peach Tree Boulevard in a money-green 735i BMW on his way to Lennox Mall. The Temprees played softly through the stereo system as he tried to ease his mind from the gnawing feeling in his gut. A drive through the gleaming metropolis of Atlanta, Georgia, was just what the doctor ordered to let his mind drift. He chose this city as his sanctuary outside of South Central Los Angeles because of the Black progress here and the smooth balance of country with city life. He could go from his hideaway in the sticks in small county Georgia to a city rivaling the likes of Los Angeles and New York in twenty minutes.

Beautiful Black men and women moved throughout the busy streets dressed in casual and formal attire, going in and out of cafés and shops, heading to their various destinations as the sun fought for dominance against the slightly overcast clouds. The traffic flowed with ease, unlike the gridlock, bumper-to-bumper jams in Los Angeles. He took it all in as he contemplated the problematic situation with the Teflon Brothers. It threatened the very fabric of the gang and the financial empire that he and Elijah built. He stayed up nights questioning if he had left the Hood in the hands of Elijah, Hitter, and Big Wizard too soon.

The Teflon brothers were not his only concern. He noticed a new group of youngsters calling themselves the Tiny Toons springing up out of Jesse Owens Park during his infrequent trips to Los Angeles. They were a hybrid of Western birth being raised under the influence of the West Coast side. Only a small remnant remained active on the Orchard side. The Eighty-Seventh Street clique of Nine-Os became a ghost town due to mass incarceration and the gang and drug wars that left a trail of dead bodies. The Budlong clique was the last stronghold of the West Coast side, as most of the other homies migrated to the western side after the takeover by Wizard and Hitter of the Neighborvilles and Jesse Owens Park.

The Tiny Toons were mostly youngsters who came from good homes and grew up playing basketball at the park. Their first impression of Nine-O was seeing Big Wizard and Hitter after their transformation from hood gangbangers to rich Crip mobsters. He assessed the Tiny Toons were not joining Nine-O out of tribalism as the first- and second-generation homies once did. They were joining due to the allurement of the fast cars, money, women, and the glamour they thought Nine-O would afford them. They knew nothing of the decades of bloodshed and war in the trenches, earning stripes for defending the honor of the Hood, and going hard against those who opposed it.

Some of the new youngsters thought they had a voice in the Set before they even had an enemy under their belt. They were fly-crippin' without going through the proper rites of passage, and this new phenomenon was taking on a life of its own. He knew something had to be done to extinguish this or it was going to present major problems for them in the future, and at some point he would have to give up his comforts in Georgia and head back to the Land to get things back in order.

The sight of the expansive Lenox Square jarred him out of his thoughts. He pulled into the parking lot and drove for a few minutes unsuccessful in finding a parking space. As his frustration mounted, a red Honda Accord, slowly reversed out of a space. He stepped on his breaks and waited.

His cell phone vibrated. He grabbed it from the center console. "Hello," he said, as the Accord sped off and he inched forward into the parking space.

"What's up with the general?" Lady Rawdog asked.

"I'm straight. What's the word?"

"Same ol' politics." She lowered her voice. "Ju-Ju here . . . he in the living room. He wanna talk to you. What you want me to tell him?"

He put the car in park and turned off the engine. "Put him on the phone," he ordered.

"Alright hold on…"

He heard her walking through her house, as music and voices became more distinct. Ju-Ju was one of his most loyal soldiers in the Hood. He kept him in the know about everything. He knew that if Ju-Ju wanted to discuss something it was important. He was curious to hear what Ju-Ju had to say.

"Hello," Ju-Ju said. A door slammed and the music in the background faded.

"What's the word, solider?"

"Aw, what's up, big homie? Man . . . stressful shit around here."

"I can imagine. You holdin' it down though, right?" Big 9-Lives asked.

"You already know that Imma stay ten toes down with it."

"That's what's up. I don't expect nothin' less. You need

something?" Big 9-Lives lit a cigarette.

"Nah, I'm straight, Cuzz." Ju-Ju's tone changed. "I'm callin' about this Lil Teflon issue. Big Tef came by my house and he wanted me to reach out to you."

"What he talkin' 'bout?" Big 9-Lives blew smoke out the car window.

"You know how Big Tef is. He a good homie. He wanna try and get this thing with his lil bro squashed. He don't wanna see homies go at it. But you know at the same time that if it can't be squashed, Big Tef is not gon' stand by and watch niggas hurt his peeps."

Big 9-Lives paused in silence. He felt conflicted. He had practically raised the Teflon brothers. During the hard times when their father had abandoned their family and their mother, Virginia, was strung out on crack, Big 9-Lives was the one who made sure they had food to eat. He taught the brothers the ways of survival in the treacherous streets of LA. "It's understandable on his part," he said thoughtfully. "Where he say Lil Tef stand with gettin' shit squashed? And what you think about the whole situation?"

"He didn't give me a direct answer on Lil Tef—he just said he'll bring him around, basically. I think this is a fucked-up situation. It's already sending a lot of unexpected ripples through the Hood. It's gonna divide everything."

"I know it's a fucked-up situation, but that doesn't answer where you stand and how you feel it should be handled," Big 9-Lives snapped.

Silence.

"Cuzz," Ju-Ju spoke hesitantly. "Just to keep it one hundred with you, big homie, I wanna see the in-house fighting put to rest. I love all y'all niggas. You and Cannon raised me, and Lil 9 been havin' my back when I was green to everything. I'll never try and go against y'all. You already know, I grew up with Big and Lil Tef too, so I'll hate to see them hurt on some in-house shit. I know Lil Tef fucked up, and he really deserves what he got comin' . . . it's just hard to see it come to this."

"Yeah, I can dig it." Big 9-Lives got out of the car with the phone to his ear and walked toward the front entrance of the mall. "I'll talk to the circle and see what I can do. But if it can't be worked out, you know there'll be lines drawn in the sand."

"Yeah, I know," Ju-Ju responded.

"So, I'll let you know what's up after we get together and rap." Big 9-Lives was ready to end the call, but Ju-Ju continued to give him an earful. Ju-Ju detailed that he'd called a meeting for Sunday to try to stem the tide of division. There was all this talk of people picking sides, but most of them didn't even know what the beef was about. There were the Western niggas who were whispering in the youngsters' ears to go against Hitter and Wiz for their own hidden agendas. He assured Big 9-Lives that they were going to get things in order before finally saying their goodbyes.

As Big 9-Lives made his way into the mall, an uneasy feeling came over him. A lot was going on, and he wasn't there. He took a deep breath. He made his way down the corridor, admiring the array of attractive women, surveying the store window displays. It was a good distraction.

He entered Foot Locker and browsed the shoes in the aisle. He picked up a pair of Air Max and examined them from top to bottom. His phone vibrated and he rolled his eyes. It was Big Wizard.

"What's crackin' with you?" Big 9-Lives said as he pressed the phone to his ear.

"Sittin' here choppin' it up with bro. What you got goin'?"

"Same ol'. In the mall tryna find a lil fit." He held up the shoe to one of the referee-uniformed workers and said, "Hey, let me see these in an eleven." The employee nodded and went into the back room. "You still there, Wiz?" Big 9-Lives asked.

"Yeah, I'm here," he answered.

"What's goin' on about the situation in the Set?"

Big Wizard sighed. "I don't know why everybody talkin' about it like it's breakin' news or something. We ain't worried about that peon."

"When we all o.t. we really don't have to worry about it. But when y'all in the city, that's a threat that shouldn't be taken lightly," Big 9-Lives warned.

"We in the city right now, and we still ain't worried about him." Big Wizard laughed.

The salesperson brought him two boxes with the Air Max in black and gray. Big 9-Lives thanked him.

He turned back to his conversation with Big Wizard. "When you get back to the Land and how long you stayin'?" he asked. "I thought you was still in South Carolina layin' low?" He sat down in a chair to try on the shoes.

"Don't know yet. It was supposed to be a quick trip to check on a few things. But with this new thing with Lil Tef, I may stick around just a lil longer."

"Anything I can help out with?"

"Nah, nothing for you to worry about; just something my pops got me on."

Big 9-Lives shook his head. "Anyway, Ju-Ju callin' a meeting Sunday, y'all goin'?" he asked.

"Hell nah. Somebody over there a rat, Cuzz. CRASH officers and the detectives still got our names in they mouth after all this time. And they speakin' on shit no pig should know about. They gettin' they info from somebody in the Set. I ain't got nothin' to go talk to them niggas about. If it ain't my day-one niggas, fuck 'em."

"Ju-Ju say it's a under-current over there that's happenin', the G-Western homies tryna get the youngsters to go against us. Before that shit take root, and Lil Tef gathers more allies, we need to address it. And he say Big Tef came through his spot and he tryna get us to squash the beef."

"We gon' squash something alright. We gon' squash him."

"Don't make a decision so quick. We gotta consider all angles," Big 9-Lives cautioned.

"Look, bro, y'all taught us that we don't negotiate with terrorists. Fuck Lil Tef and all them Tiny Toon niggas, and the Western heads who're tryna stoke the fire. They ain't ready for what we bring. We can introduce all them niggas to the show."

Big 9-Lives tried on the shoes and liked them. "Just hold off on any in-house moves until I get back, Big Wiz," he said. "I see it's not an option that I gotta get back."

He waved over the salesman. "Ring both pairs of these up," he said. The salesman nodded and took the shoes away.

"When will you be this way?" Big Wizard asked.

"I'll let you know when I work my schedule out."

"Say no more, rollin'," Big Wizard concluded.

"Rollin'," Big 9-Lives said, and ended the call.

He went to the counter and paid for the shoes. The total was $463.27, so he gave the salesman five one-hundred-dollar bills.

He took his receipt and change from the salesman, grabbed his bag from the counter, and headed out of the store.

His mind raced a mile a minute. Calling off the war had to be given a chance, but the conversation with Big Wizard let him know that it might be more difficult than he anticipated. Big Wizard and Hitter were his lil homies, but his relationship with them was built on mutual respect, not a dictatorship on his part. He had to proceed with the situation with Lil Teflon using great tact. He walked to the food court and got a lemonade from Hot Dog on a Stick. He sat and stared at the passersby as he sipped the lemonade absentmindedly. Then a wave of anger swept over him. Lil Teflon had betrayed them in the worst way, and they had acted accordingly. The stress from his thoughts suddenly turned into an iron resolve. He straightened his shoulders, broadened his chest, his eyes burning fiercely with steel determination. "Shit gon' go however I want it to go. I'm OG motherfuckin' 9-Lives the Loc. I *am* Nine-O," he muttered to himself.

With his bag in hand, he stormed toward the exit.

CHAPTER 6

The sun was disappearing from the sky, leaving in its wake an artistic canvas of orange and purple hues. The last remnants of light splayed gently through the balcony glass doors and windows as Hitter unrolled a maroon-and-beige prayer rug with an image of the Kaaba in Mecca on it. His clean-shaved head, smooth brown skin, stout frame, and serious brown eyes gave him the mystique of a majestic python. The Marina Del Ray beachfront condo had sparse furniture: two white futons, a fifty-inch television, and a few pieces of inexpensive art adorned the living room. The adjoining dining room contained a simple Plexiglass and cream leather dinette set, leading to a spacious modern black and chrome kitchen with state-of-the-art appliances. The scent of Egyptian musk permeated the air as the Adhan, a Muslim call to prayer, played softly from a small stereo system somewhere in the back room.

Hitter smoothed out the rug on the living room floor and stood to remove his shoes. Big Wizard emerged from the back room with a similar rolled-up prayer rug under his armpit as he wiped the excess water from his face, arms, and feet with a towel. He'd just performed *wudu*, a ritual washing. The audio of the Adhan ended as Big Wizard placed his prayer rug to the right side of Hitter's but a little further back.

They stood on their rugs. Hitter led the prayer. Raising both hands to the side of his head, palms forward, he declared, "Allahu

Akbar."

Big Wizard mimicked the action.

They folded their arms below the navel.

Hitter began the recitation of *Al Fatihah: "Bismillaah ar-Rahman ar-Raheem, Al hamdu lillaahi rabbil 'alameen, Ar Rahman ar-Raheem Maaliki yaumid Deen, Iyyaaka na'abudu wa iyyaaka nasta'een, Ihdinas siraatal mustaqeem, Siraatal ladheena an 'amta' alaihim, Ghairil maghduubi' alaihim waladaaleen."*

"Ameen," they recited in unison.

They proceeded into a series of bows, raises, and prostrations.

They ended the ten-minute routine with turning their head, first to the right to Salaam, then to the left. Hitter cupped his hands in front of him to end with a personal supplication. "O'Allah, we pray that you watch over us and grant us victory over our enemies and adversaries in the spiritual and in the physical realm this night. Ameen."

They arose from their knees and rolled up their prayer rugs in silence. Big Wizard, an unassuming looking man of average stature, rubbed the waves in his bald-faded haircut as he gazed out at the sky momentarily.

Hitter exited to the sparsely furnished bedroom. He placed the neatly rolled-up prayer rugs on a shelf in the closet and walked back to the living room. Big Wizard was resting on the futon.

"What's on the agenda?" Hitter sat next to him, kicking up his feet.

"This moment of peace. Sometimes the agenda got to be to just sit down and be when we have that opportunity and get the feeling to do so. Because the next storm is always right around the corner waitin' to happen."

"Fasho, but I've learned that the true master of self can find that same peace, that same stillness, even while in the storm."

Big Wizard considered his brother for a moment. He did not respond; he simply smiled and went back to his thoughts.

A light knock on the door disturbed the peaceful quietness that filled the room. Hitter got up and went to open it.

Their father, Clarence X, an elderly, smooth-faced man with salt-and-pepper wavy hair, greeted Hitter with a strong embrace. "*Salaamu Alaikum.*"

"*Walaikum As Salaam,*" Hitter returned.

Big Wizard stood up eagerly. "What's up, old man?" They embraced, touched cheeks three times, alternating from one side of the face to the other.

Clarence X was the model of discipline and order. His icy gray suit, white button-up shirt, and gray bowtie was immaculately clean, pressed, and pristine. His black Bertoni hard-bottom loafers were shined. Except for his gray hair, his appearance was youthful and ageless.

"I told you, you going to wish you look this good when you my age."

"He know, Pops, he just hatin'," Hitter added. "You want something to drink?"

"Yeah, let's all have some tea together." Clarence X walked toward the window and sat down on the futon. "You guys sure got a nice view here."

Big Wizard sat down next to him. "It's our little hideaway when we come to town, a peaceful getaway." He kicked up his feet on the coffee table.

"That's good. Always have to find some semblance of peace through the madness. It's about maintaining your square. How have things been on the home front?"

"Everything stable. Can't complain about much. I bought another piece of rental property down there. Dealin' with the tenants always got its drama, but nothin' I can't handle," Big Wizard said.

"*Al hamdulilah.*" Clarence X leaned forward slightly and lowered his voice a notch. "How's he been doing mentally?" He indicated to Hitter, who was still in the kitchen.

"He straight. Stubborn as hell still, but you know that's just him being who he is."

Clarence X relaxed. "That he is. You been down there with him to check on my grandbabies?"

"Yeah. I drive up to his house at least once a month. The kids are doing excellent. I think they're what's helpin' him to mature and transition. He's homeschooling Ali right now. Kid's as sharp as a tack."

Hitter came out of the kitchen balancing a circular metal tray with three teacups and a matching teapot. He allowed his brother and father to grab their cups and fill them with tea. After they finished pouring, he filled his cup.

"So, what did you need us to come out for?" Hitter sat down on the other futon, getting straight to business.

"Always the bottom line with you, huh?" Clarence X studied Hitter briefly. "Take your foot off the gas sometimes. Life's not always a rush."

Hitter smiled at his father and remained silent.

Clarence X slowly sipped his tea, savoring the taste, admiring the cup. He set the teacup on the coffee table, settled back, and exhaled. "Well, two reasons I requested your presence. First thing is I want you to go see your grandmother first thing in the morning. She's not doing well."

"What's wrong with her?" Hitter asked in alarm.

His father held up a calming hand. "She's old, son."

"We know that. That still don't say what's wrong."

"What's wrong is she's old and she's sick and may not have much longer with us."

Big Wizard scooted to the edge of his seat and rested his forearm on his leg. "Don't have long? Why we just now knowin' it was this serious of a situation?"

"Because she and your mother didn't want to worry you guys. She's my mother, so it's me and your mother's duty to care of her, just as it will be your duty to care for us in our old age. We're not supposed to burden the young members of the family when there are elders to handle it. Your duty right now is to be stable and prosperous so that the next generation of gods in your care can be raised to be healthy, wealthy, and wise."

"Yeah, but that's Grandma. We have a right to always know what's goin' on with her," Hitter insisted with an attitude.

"I'm letting you know what's going on now, when it's proper timing for you to know."

"You seem real calm about the possibility of losin' your mother," Big Wizard added.

"It's the cycle of life, son. The Quran says, we came here weak, then grow strong, then back to weakness again, to return to our true origin. A true Muslim mourns the absence of his loved ones' presence when they go, but we don't despair.'

A pregnant silence filled the room, allowing the words to sink in.

Clarence X sipped from his teacup. "On to other matters. The brothers are hosting a convention Saturday, and I want you both to be on security detail."

"There are a thousand FOI soldiers in the city. Why we need to be on the detail?" Big Wizard chuckled.

"Because I said so."

Big Wizard held up his hands in surrender and smiled. "Hey, hey, I was just askin'. You got that. Just let us know what time to be there."

"That's what I wanted to hear in the first place. Not no extra questions."

Hitter and Big Wizard grumbled their objections jokingly.

Clarence X laughed heartily. After a brief pause, he looked at Big Wizard. "I heard about this situation with the young brotha who used to run with little Elijah growing up."

"How you knew about any of that?" Hitter asked, surprised.

"Boy, I was a staple in this community before you was even born. Just because I'm not in the streets don't mean I don't keep my ear to 'em."

"It's nothing we can't handle, Pops. Don't worry about it." Big Wizard tried to calm his concerns.

"I'm not worried at all. I know you are more than capable of taking care of yourselves. But I want you to consider things from every direction before violence becomes the solution."

"We're always gonna do that," Big Wizard assured.

Hitter listened intently and nodded but said nothing.

Clarence X sighed deeply. He rubbed his hands together, then studied his palms. The stillness in the room was neither tension-filled nor ease; there was simply an air of neutrality, each in his own pensive mood.

Clarence X searched his sons' faces. "You know, when Micron was still a baby and I was in them streets, I ran that little strip from Eighty-Eighth Street to Ninety-Second, over on Vermont. We had all the pool halls, bookie joints, and the lil club, the Rose Room, booming. I had my hand in everything: number running, heroin, pills, you name it. But one of my favorite hustles was beating what I then called 'suckas' out of their money playing pool, and with trick dice that I was a master at using. All this was before the Nation of Islam, under the Honorable Elijah Muhammad, found me and breathed life into me.

"But there was this one particular night when I laid on some brothers from out of Detroit who was at the Rose Room. They were at the pool table playing for fun. I asked if they wanted to place a small friendly wager. We started off playing twenty dollars a game. I lost five games straight on purpose. I let them see the big wad of money I was pulling the twenties from every time I lost. Their eyes got big, thinking they had a mark. They enticed me to bet bigger. We went up to a hundred a game. I'd win two, lose one. Finally, they went to five hundred a game. I blitzed them twelve games straight for an easy six grand. The main cat was furious; it didn't take a rocket scientist to realize I had hustled them. But he willingly bet the money. Hell, he was the one who was bumping up the amounts, so he should've been mad at himself, not me.

"Long story short, he pulled a switchblade on me. He and his two partners surrounded me demanding his money back. They underestimated their surroundings. Before they knew it, Big John came from behind the bar with a sawed-off shotgun pointed at their heads. All my people who was playing like they weren't with me was suddenly up on them with enough weaponry to fight off a cavalry. We disarmed them and took them into the alley behind the club. My partner at the time was egging me on to kill them. He said we needed to make an example to anyone who might think they can challenge us. I wrestled with myself. The gangster in me said to kill, but there was something in me as I looked into them brothas' eyes that just screamed, 'No, don't do it.' I finally told my partner to untie them. I slapped them up a bit and told them to get on and don't come back."

Hitter shook his head. "I don't know if I coulda been kind like that. Them dudes was tryna bring harm to you."

Clarence X held up his right index finger and continued, "But look how Allah works. Ten years later, after I joined the Nation, we were in Chicago for Savior's Day. I ran into that very brother, now working security detail, a FOI member for the nation. We both recognized each other instantly and embraced. He thanked me for sparing his life that night, and I begged his forgiveness for my role in the incident. For years I contemplated that situation. Had I killed that brother, not only would I had killed his redemption, but I would have possibly killed my own redemption. Both of our souls were at stake that night. And on the one decision to lean toward mercy, two Muslims were born."

"Pops, that's a deep story," Big Wizard marveled.

"Yeah, it is," Clarence X affirmed. "And I tell you that story to relay to you balance and mercy. Sometimes there's no recourse but violence to remedy a situation. And when that's the case, you apply it swift and effectively. But if there is any room for mercy, let it prevail. It takes wisdom and guidance to know when to apply which one." Clarence X picked up the teapot and refilled his cup.

They bonded in silent understanding, drinking their tea, watching the sun set in all its fading glory. Not a single word was necessary; what needed to be said had already been spoken.

CHAPTER 7

"We are now making our descent. Please fasten your seat belts and place all seats and trays in an upright position," the captain announced over the intercom. Elijah stared from a window seat in first class over Los Angeles County. The dense clouds gave way as the airplane lowered in altitude, revealing a calm view. He smiled as the distinct landmarks came into view, Big Randy's Donut the most noticeable. "Home," he mumbled.

The stewardess walked the aisles checking the cabin, ensuring the passengers' seat belts were fastened and trays were in the upright position. "Prepare for landing," the captain announced. The stewardesses hurried to their seats.

Takeoff and landing were Elijah's favorite aspects of flying. He could feel the plane's power and speed in those moments. The plane descended aggressively, making its distinctive wail and slightly turbulent movements. His thoughts about the problems and events that awaited consumed him and made his body tense. The plane groaned as the wheel well opened and the tires unfolded. It lowered to near rooftop level in the neighborhoods surrounding LAX. He smiled broadly seeing his favorite, Shakey's Pizza.

The landscape passed swiftly as the belly of the big iron bird glided closely to the chain-link fences that surrounded the enormous airfield. The plane leveled with the runway at tremendous speed as the tires tapped asphalt, then bounced up and down. The rubber screeched against the pavement, gradually coming to a complete stop.

The tension dissipated from Elijah's body as the plane slowly taxied toward the gate.

"Welcome to Los Angeles. Please wait until we are at the gate before you leave your seats. We hope you enjoyed your flight, and thanks for flying with Delta Airlines."

Once the plane came to a stop, Elijah unfastened his seatbelt, stood, and grabbed his rollaway bag from the overhead compartment. After a brief wait, he exited the plane. His cell phone vibrated as he walked from the gangway into the terminal. He ignored it and made his way down to the baggage claim.

He spotted Elise standing by the phone booths with their two-year-old son, Amaru, who was playing with his toy action figure. Elise turned Amaru toward him and pointed. "Look, baby. See Daddy?"

Amaru looked at his father, his greenish-blue eyes and brown face a perfect blend of Elijah and Elise. He dropped his toy and ran toward Elijah as fast as his little legs would take him, smiling and giggling. Elijah's face lit up with a huge smile and he spread his arms wide. "Heyyy," he cooed before snatching Amaru off his feet and smothering his face with kisses. "What you been doin', Son-Son? You missed Daddy?" Elijah held him on his hip.

Amaru giggled and buried his face in Elijah's neck. Elise greeted him with a peck on the lips and a warm smile.

"How was your flight?" She grabbed the handle of his trolley bag, and they walked toward the carrousel to wait for the rest of his luggage.

"It was cool. A lil long, you know how that goes."

"Yeah. You hungry?"

"I got a taste for some Shakey's Pizza." He smiled.

"Boy, you are not about to be eating no Shakey's at ten in the morning." She laughed. "You must've flown over it and saw it, and now you think you want some."

"No, I didn't." He laughed. "I just have a taste for it, and me and Son-Son can play the video games there."

"I bet." She rolled her eyes. "Tryna act like it's about him. Yo ass just saw that damn Shakey's comin' in. You can go another time."

"Who you think you is?" He turned to Amaru in his arms and playfully repeated the question, "Who Mommy think she is, huh?" He kissed his cheek again. "Say 'Mommy don't run nothin' . . . say it."

Amaru giggled and hid his face.

Elise's phone rang, and she answered on the third ring. "I can't hear you . . . I'm at the airport. Hold on." She turned to Elijah. "I'm gonna step outside real quick to try and get some reception."

He nodded.

"I'll take this." She grabbed the handle to his bag and walked toward the sliding glass doors.

Elijah and Amaru headed toward the carrousel, with the flashing red light, where bags began descending from the shoot on to the slow-moving belt.

* * * *

Taxis lined up at the outer terminal. Friends and family members bustled, putting luggage in trunks. People embraced one another, laughed, talked. Some boarded hotel shuttles, rental car, and charter buses, while others waited to cross over to the parking structure. Elise pressed the phone to her ear and moved to a less populated area toward the end of the terminal.

"What's the word?" She nervously looked over her shoulder toward the area she exited.

"I hope I'm not disturbing you, but I need to ask you a favor."

This immediately got her undivided attention. "What is it?"

"There was a mix up on my end, and an extra twenty-five keys were put in your truck's stash. Can your people just take all of it and give the twenty-five to my cousin in San Fernando Valley when it gets on your end? This will save me the hassle of having to unseal the stash to take them back out which will probably cost us an extra day."

She knew Guzman was bullshitting her. No one accidentally mixed up twenty-five kilos of cocaine. *This motherfucka tryna run game. I ain't got time to go back and forth with him right now.* She looked at the exit door; Elijah and Amaru would be coming out soon.

She sighed. "I'll do it this one time, but we're not goin' to make this a habit. I'm not into giving out free rides, as I'm sure you're not either."

"Oh no, it won't become a habit, just a small incidental bump that happens sometimes in the business."

"Okay. Remember this favor; I may need it repaid one day. And one more thing, if a mishap happens with the police while my driver is bringing the truck in, I'm not responsible for the payment of those twenty-five."

"Fair enough."

"I'll get your cousin's information once my people are safely back." She looked at the sliding door again just as Elijah exited with a suitcase in one hand and cradling Amaru in his opposite arm.

"Sounds good, talk to you then. *Que estés bien.*"

"*Tú también, mi amigo.*" She ended the call and walked to Elijah and Amaru.

They crossed the street over to the parking structure and took the elevator to the third level. Her red 2003 Range Rover was parked in a space a few feet ahead of them. She opened the back hatch, and he loaded the luggage in. Then he sat down in the passenger's seat with Amaru on his lap.

Elise squinted her eyes at him. "He has to go in his car seat." She put the key in the ignition.

"He's alright." Elijah squeezed him as he sat perched on his lap.

"Dada," Amaru blurted.

Elijah laughed. "Yeah, say 'Dada, we want Shakey's.'"

"Dada . . . Shakeyyy," Amaru drawled excitedly.

Elise shook her head and chuckled. "Won't be no Shakey's this morning. Come on, put him in the back."

Elijah reluctantly got out and fastened Amaru in his car seat. Moments later, Elise merged with the heavy flow of traffic to La Cienega Boulevard, then on to the 405 freeway, then to the 10 West freeway, which took them to the Pacific Coast Highway.

"Ah, nothin' like the air from the Pacific in Cali," Elijah said. The breeze whipped through the open window as they rode along the coastline. The hypnotic effect of the blowing wind lulled Amaru into a spell of nodding, and finally peaceful sleep.

"Look at it. It look like a big baby-blue infinity pool." He stared out the window at the expansive ocean. "I'm officially home."

A serene silence filled the vehicle as the cool, salty sea breeze caressed them, and Ashanti's "Baby" softly played from the stereo.

"So how was Unc doin'?" She glanced at him briefly, then returned her attention back to the road.

"He straight." He chuckled softly. "Thinkin' he a damn hunter now."

"A hunter?" She laughed.

"Yeah, he had me out there runnin' through the woods and shit with rifles. Guess it was cool though, takes your mind away from the usual day-to-day shit."

"I bet it does. You probably gotta take me one day." She smiled at him.

"You ain't ready for the woods, you too prissy now," he teased.

"That's what you think. Don't let the smooth taste fool you. Your girl still with all the shit."

Elijah was quiet as he stared out the window at the rolling waves.

"What's on your mind?" She noticed his melancholy mood.

"Nothin'. It ain't nothin', I'm good."

"You think I don't know you? Something's on your mind. What's up?" Her eyes darted back and forth between Elijah and the road.

"Aw, just same ol' shit. You know how the constant drama go

in the Hood." He looked at her. "It's that situation with Lil Tef. It raised its head again and Unc feel like I'm not givin' it enough attention."

Elise had already heard the whispers from her own contacts in the streets. She knew Lil Teflon's sudden appearance posed a tremendous threat to their family. "If it's true that he's alive and plottin', then it gotta be addressed," she said bluntly.

Elijah shook his head. "Ain't no more *if*. Nigga came up to the park strapped up." He stared out the window again. "It's like these dudes force your hand to get on some ignorant shit. I'm tryna live my life—tryna figure shit out the right way—but the past keeps hauntin' me." He was frustrated.

She reached over and stroked the back of his head. "Don't overthink it. And don't let no one pressure you into doin' anything that you don't feel in your heart you should do."

"I hear you. But Unc is right. There's that part of me that just wanna say fuck that neighborhood and ignore that whole situation. That shit over there have given me nothin' but pain and bad memories. But there's the part Unc talkin' about; just 'cause you bury your head in the sand don't mean what's goin' on around you go away. Lil Teflon don't care that I'm out the way, he want revenge. LA not as big as it seems. Anybody can be found or bumped into randomly, and I'm not 'bout to be runnin' from no nigga. My blood run through them streets literally. I've sacrificed too much to the Set to ever feel like I can't go sit on my family front porch when I want to." His voiced raised, causing Amaru to stir.

Elise took a moment before responding. "I'm gonna give you my truth," she finally said. "If anyone is a threat to our family even a little bit, we don't let it fester. But that doesn't mean you have to jump back out there. There's a way to do things without your hands gettin' dirty."

"Either way it go, if I'm responsible for gettin' him, then my hands is dirty."

Elise looked at him curiously. "Well, if you feel you can't stand to get your hands dirty no more, then wash 'em of it." She focused on the road. "I'll take care of it and you don't have to have no parts period."

"What the fuck are you talkin' about?" he barked aggressively. "I've already told you that you out the life. You not takin' care of shit but our son."

"I never said I was out the game or wanted out the game. This is a decision that you made for me without my consent." Her voice rose defiantly. Amaru stirred slightly.

"So fuckin' what? I said what I said, and that's it. You ain't bigger than the program," Elijah growled.

She glared at him.

"What?" he challenged, openly hostile.

She slowly averted her eyes back to the traffic with undisguised defiance. They settled back in the thick tension.

Beautiful clouds created a ceiling over the ocean. The waves continued to roll; the seagulls squawked. They rode in silence, both drifting into their own world of thoughts.

*   *   *   *

The house was tucked away in the hilly mountains of Malibu, parallel to the Pacific Coast Highway. Two eight-foot-high cast-iron gates with their family coat-of-arms parted to let them through. The driveway winded about a quarter mile and landed in front of a fifteen-thousand-square-foot Spanish colonial style mansion with Mediterranean accents. The surrounding property was immaculate. The plush green lawns, exotic plants, and flowers were expertly landscaped. A stone sculpture of Hannibal the Conqueror with a waterfall flowing behind it, into a coy pond, stood in the middle.

The Range Rover parked in front of the large wooden double doors. Elijah handed Amaru to Elise, then removed his luggage from the trunk. He followed a few paces behind Elise as she opened the enormous front door, holding Amaru on her hip.

The fresh aromatic scent of the house greeted them as they entered. Their footsteps echoed against the polished hardwood floor, the interior an impeccable mixture of elegance and modern contemporary design. A six-foot hand-painted portrait of Elijah, Elise, and Lauren dressed in formal attire hung on the living room wall along with an array of art. The furniture blended sophistication and tasteful opulence with a hint of medieval flair. A pearl white Baby Grand piano sat below the spiral staircase that led to the other three levels of the house.

Elise put Amaru down to the floor. He bolted around the corner and down the hall.

An elderly dark-skinned woman wearing a *hijab* around her head, a modest long dress with an apron over it, and plain comfortable shoes came around the corner from the kitchen.

"Hey," she greeted in a sweet motherly voice. "I thought I heard you guys pull up."

"Hey, Sistah Raheema." Elijah hugged her.

She embraced him, then gave him a once-over. "Looks like the trip did you some good. Hope you got you some good rest." She smiled.

"I did. Got to enjoy my uncle and my lil cousins. Where's Lauren and Toussaint?"

"I just put him down for his nap. Lauren left for the office early this morning, as usual."

Elijah nodded. "Gonna go peep in on him and wash the travel off me." He headed for the stairs.

"You hungry?" she called out.

"Nah, I'm good." He climbed the stairs and disappeared.

Sistah Raheema turned to Elise. "You hungry, sweetheart?"

"Uh . . . no, no, I'm alright. We just ate."

Sistah Raheema studied her with a concerned look. "Ok I guess I'll start getting the boys lunch together." She walked back towards the kitchen.

Elise stood alone staring at the empty room for a moment. She picked up her purse and keys off the console table and exited through the front door. She walked swiftly to her Range Rover, got in, and sped down the long driveway.

*　*　*　*

Elijah walked down the hallway of the second floor of the house and entered his sons' room. He walked over to a playpen in the corner of the room. His youngest son, Toussaint, peacefully slept. Elijah stood over him watching him breathe. As if sensing his presence, Toussaint stirred, slowly opening his eyes. He squinted as he tried to focus. His tiny fingers rubbed his eyelids; they fluttered a few times and opened wide. Elijah smiled down at him. A cute chubby-cheeked smile suddenly spread across Toussaint's face.

Elijah reached in and lifted him gently from the playpen. "Hey, what you doin'? He kissed Toussaint's cheek and held him back to look at him. His fair skin, hazel-brown eyes, and sandy-brown curly hair were his only features not like Elijah. He reached up and grabbed Elijah's nose.

Elijah playfully turned his head to break Toussaint's baby grip. "Don't be grabbin' Daddy's nose." He turned back and nudged him with it. "Don't be tryin' to grab Daddy."

He reached his tiny wobbly hands for Elijah's nose again but grabbed his lips instead. Elijah wiggled away and blew a flatulent sound under the baby's neck; he giggled joyfully.

"I said don't be grabbin' me." Elijah carried him over to the rocking chair in front of the window facing the ocean and sat down. He stroked his head, staring at him as he rocked back and forth.

There was rumbling in the hallway and Amaru suddenly appeared at the door. He made his way over to where they sat, climbed up, and perched on Elijah's lap, the opposite side from Toussaint. He coldly stared at Toussaint with unhidden annoyance.

Elijah laughed and kissed Amaru on his cheek. "This is what I do it for." He looked back and forth between his two sons. "This is what really matters."

He turned his eyes toward the ocean view, held his sons close, and rocked the chair slowly.

CHAPTER 8

JuJu rode in silence past the Neighborville huts that spanned from Ninety-Second to Ninety-Sixth Street on Western Avenue in his white '65 Chevy on fourteen-inch Daytons. The break from his usually loud music was much needed to gather his thoughts for the occasion. The quiet solitude steadied his mind and calmed his nerves from anticipating what was coming.

The graffiti-plagued Neighborvilles resembled a relic from another time. The tiny huts built in the 1940s stood in stark contrast to the commercial properties and new apartments that had been built around them. Crackheads moved in and out of the shortcuts that led from Western to the alley that ran behind the duplexes. Unattended children played aimlessly in the dirt patches that served as yards. While the work-hour traffic moved heavily in both directions toward jobs and schools, the Neighborvilles stood in suspended animation, a world of its own. Daily shootings and beatings were the norm around here. Domestic violence was a source of entertainment for the drug dealers and gang members who ruled this small stretch of soil, originally claimed by the Westside Crips before they broke up into subsections. The area became the territory of the Western-side Nine-Os after the split.

He observed the movements of the "Villes," as they were affectionately called, as he made it to Ninety-Sixth Street. The small white huts gave way to a space of plush green grass that led to a unit of well-kept tennis courts as it transitioned into the park. Ju-Ju came to a crawl at the streetlight and made a right into the entrance. A green sign read "Jesse Owens Park."

A group of about twenty Crips standing in front of the indoor swimming pool entrance came into view as he pulled in. He threw up the Nine-O sign with one hand, cruising slowly past them toward the gym high up the hill of the park. More Nine-Os loitered at the bottom of the steps, up to the door of the basketball gym as others sprinkled further to the back where the snack-shack to the golf course stood. Ju-Ju continued his slow trek to the back of the park, made the loop around, and parked on the other side of the island.

A black forked comb with a fist at the top protruded from his big combed-out afro. A navy-blue plaid Pendleton, blue 501 Levi jeans, and blue and white Nike Cortez made up his attire for the day. Ju-Ju was still crippin' like it was the 1980s. Many of the young homies were gravitating toward the preppy fly-guy look. He tucked his Colt 45 in his waistband, pulled his Pendleton down to conceal it and walked towards the grassy picnic play area between the basketball gym and golf course. The crowd that was standing by the swimming pool made their way to the area along with all the other loose groups of Nine-Os hanging out throughout the park. The cluster of about twenty-five Tiny Toons stayed near one another.

After all the greetings and preliminaries were done, Ju-Ju positioned himself in the center circle of the core group of elder Nine-Os and called the meeting to order. "Alright y'all listen up!" He got everyone's attention. "Before I get to the meat of why we here, we wanna know what that situation was about with the Six-Os?" He looked directly at the cluster of Tiny Toons.

"Just a lil squabble," Baby Devil said nonchalantly.

"That ain't tellin' me shit," Ju-Ju said, openly showing his dislike for Baby Devil.

"I mean, what you want me to say?" Baby Devil shrugged his shoulders, shook his head, and smiled arrogantly. "They rat-packed Tiny Punch over on Brynhurst, so we went back and lined it up."

"And you didn't feel like we shoulda known about that first?" Ju-Ju asked sarcastically.

"We didn't know we had to check in before we go to a homie's defense," Baby Devil shot back.

Before Ju-Ju could respond, a man with a goatee and serious features spoke. "It's protocol to let the homies know what's goin' on."

"Well, our bad, Mega," Baby Devil responded condescendingly, looking toward the other Tiny Toons.

"Yeah, yo bad, tough guy," Megatron snapped. "Keep that energy up 'cause I told them to come through in 'bout an hour from now for a runback in the Thunderdome." The Thunderdome was an event where hoodstas mutually came together for physical combat to settle their differences or sometimes just for the sport of it.

"Sounds good to me," Baby Devil quipped.

An animated murmur ran through the crowd.

"Let's get to our business before they get here." Ju-Ju brought the meeting back to order. "The elephant in the Hood is this situation with Lil Teflon. I'm hearin' that niggas is callin' themselves taking sides between him and Lil 9, Hitt, and Big Wiz."

No one said anything. Eyes averted and feet shifted at the topic. Ju-Ju analyzed the silent crowd, settling in on Baby Devil's expressionless demeanor.

He rolled his eyes and continued, "Now don't nobody wanna say nothing."

"I don't know who takin' sides," Lil Bar-Dog informed. "But I don't think none of us should be. I mean, we don't even know what that shit is about. If anything, we should be trying to put a stop to it, Cuzz."

Ju-Ju nodded at him and looked at the crowd for any other input. "Anybody else?"

"I feel what the young homie just said is right," Megatron chimed in. "He pretty much summed it up."

A chorus of agreements and head nods permeated the crowd.

"This in-house war shit is fuckin' the Hood up, Cuzz."

"Yeah, it gotta end, on Nine-O, Cuzz."

Ju-Ju allowed it to simmer down a little before he went on. "I agree with everything that was just said. I think this shit is dividin' us. It ain't never just been about money with me, or power, or prestige. I've always done this for the love of the Set. As I tell niggas all the time, I'm loyal to the soil, not no individual. That's what all of us should be pushin'. I grew up from the sandbox with Lil 9 and Lil Tef—them both my brothers. But I can't condone what's going on with either side. I say all that to say, you young niggas stay out that shit. Let us try and work it out or let them work it out themselves. Either way, this not your fight."

Baby Devil chuckled lightly into his fist.

Ju-Ju gritted his teeth. "Baby Devil, you got something you wanna say? You think you bigger than the program, nigga?"

"Nah, big homie," Baby Devil said in a sarcastic tone. "However the Hood pushin', that's how I'm pushin'."

"Act like it then. Keep all that funny-actin' shit to yo'self." Ju-Ju's brows creased in anger.

Baby Devil said, "Cuzz, everybody know that Lil Teflon was my nigga, and I rolled wit him in the past. But I was young and didn't know no better. Now I'm my own man. If y'all can stop Lil 9 and them from trippin' on me, then I'm out that shit."

Lyin' motherfucka, Ju-Ju thought. He could see straight through Baby Devil's act. Whatever Lil Teflon was up to, Baby Devil knew all about it. "That's what it is then," Ju-Ju responded. "I already talked to Big 9-Lives and Big Teflon. I'm tryna get shit worked out. Just let the process happen and stay out the way." He glared at Baby Devil.

Just then, Ju-Ju caught a glimpse of Hitter emerging swiftly from a row of tall trees that camouflaged a narrow trail that ran behind the gym all the way to Western Avenue. Hitter's oval brown face was shaded by the edges of a black hood. He wore black and gray military fatigues with tan-colored army boots that reached his calves, and two Glock 40s at his sides.

Ju-Ju instinctively clutched his Colt .45. The crowd's attention veered in Hitter's direction. Some immediately reached for their weapons.

"I wouldn't draw those if I were you."

Eyes darted toward the voice. Big Wizard was positioned atop the grassy hill on the side of the gym with a black gym bag concealing a pistol grip AK-47, dressed in the same attire as Hitter. The crowd froze. Their eyes and feet shuffled, panic evident.

Big Wizard slowly made his way down the steep grassy embankment toward them. "Don't nobody make no sudden movements."

"What type of shit is this?" Megatron snapped. "This how y'all approach the homies now?"

"Calm down, Cuzz, it's just precaution," Big Wizard assured. "Everybody here not homies."

Hitter positioned himself among the crowd. The tension was thick enough to cut with a knife.

"What's up, Cuzz?" Ju-Ju still clutched his Colt .45 in his waistband. He didn't know what to expect from Hitter. They were not exactly the best of homies and Hitter was unpredictable.

Big Wizard kept his hand in the bag and glared at the crowd. "We here to see what niggas wanna do. We been hearin' all this talk about niggas takin' sides against us. So here we are. Anybody that want it with us can bust yo' move right now."

"It ain't like that." Ju-Ju eased his hand from his waistband in an unthreatening manner. "We all was just talkin' about everybody stayin' out that shit and trying to squash the whole beef if it's possible."

"Where he at?" Hitter demanded.

"Who?" Ju-Ju asked.

"Lil Teflon-Black," Hitter barked.

"We don't know. We made the meeting known, but who showed up is who you see." Ju-Ju waved his hand around the crowd.

Hitter walked toward Baby Devil. "Looka here, if it ain't the Devil." He smirked.

Baby Devil tensed up. He upped his chin at Hitter, not breaking eye contact. "I ain't trippin', Hitter Cuzz. I'm here 'cause I want my name out the beef."

Hitter stared at Baby Devil. A long pregnant pause ensued; everyone seemed to hold their breath.

Droopy suddenly moved to Baby Devil's side. "Cuhzzz, why you all in da homie's face when he said he not in da beef?" he said in his slow-witted, countrified drawl.

Hitter frowned. "What you say, you lil ugly big-lip motherfucka?" He moved closer to Droopy, putting one of his Glocks on his hip.

Droopy puffed up his chest defiantly. "I said—"

The sound of flesh-on-flesh impact resounded as Hitter viciously slapped Droopy to the ground open-handed.

"Cuhzzz, what da fuck?" Droopy sat upright rubbing his cheek. "I ain't neva in my mah fuckin' life been hit dat hard," he mumbled, dumbfounded. "Cuhzzz, y'all get dat nigga." He looked around at the Tiny Toons in confusion.

"I wish one of you lil motherfuckas would." Hitter stared all of them down.

They all stood still. Droopy gently pulled himself up from the ground, picked up his hat, and faced Hitter.

Ju-Ju stepped in. "He a youngster, Hitt, he didn't know no better. Stall him out."

"He better learn to know better." Hitter turned from Ju-Ju to all the Tiny Toons. "You lil niggas better stay in your place. Ain't none of you big enough around here to have a voice on shit." His voice rose. "Y'all better remember who laid the foundation to this shit around here. We the reason enemies tremble when they hear the footsteps of Nine-Os comin'."

Hitter then turned to Ju-Ju. "And you know the truth. The platform you got around here is one we made possible for you. You a lil homie nigga; don't ever get so big for your britches that you feel you can tell us something."

The tension was heavy in the air. Ju-Ju knew that Hitter was trying to check him, but he wasn't going to just stand by and be disrespected.

Ju-Ju stood his ground. "It ain't about tryin' to tell you anything. My aim's for the survival of the Hood, and I don't feel no one man or one clique is bigger than that. I respect y'all, Cuzz. I know what homies paved the way, but I don't fear nothin', on Nine-O."

"We don't want you to fear us." Big Wizard stepped in. "This ain't even for you, Ju, so don't get defensive. What would we want you to fear us for anyway? We don't thrive on fear; we thrive on makin' believers outta niggas that try and go against us. Like Hitt said, we just came to see who this clan is that's speaking on us. Don't wait till we leave to start the tough talk. This is your opportunity right here."

Big Wizard let the open challenge hang in the air. Ju-Ju agreed that it was time for everything to be laid out on the table. He was tired of all the backbiting and division in the Set. However, he didn't appreciate how Hitter and Big Wizard were going about it. He felt that they were always trying to put down and disrespect the homies. It was due time he gave them a piece of his mind. "With all respect big homie—"

Suddenly, the shrill of a car engine and the vibration of loud music averted everyone's attention to the convertible Mustang 5.0 that was driving up to the crowd. There were four Black men in the car.

Hitter and Big Wizard fanned to opposite sides of the area.

One passenger threw up a two-finger-and-a-thumb gang sign. "Six-tayyys!" he hollered at the Nine-Os. The big yellow *S* on their

Seattle Mariners hats came clearly into view.

"That's the Six-Os," Ju-Ju confirmed, as one car after another full of Rollin 60s pulled up and around the driveway.

"What's this all about?" Hitter asked, fully alert.

Roughly thirty carloads of Six-Os pulled up, parked, and got out, flooding the park with their presence. Lil Bam was leading the pack. His tall, wiry frame added extra distance with each step.

Ju-Ju had a sudden concern that the Six-Os were coming at a bad time with Big Wizard and Hitter being there. He knew the rest of the homies would follow his lead when it came down to how things played out with the Six-Os. But Hitter and Big Wizard would act however they felt, and they were already in kill-mode. He braced himself as Big Wizard stepped from the side into the Six-Os' path.

"What's up, Cuzz?" Big Wizard asked.

The Six-Os paused. Lil Bam held out his hands. He stared at the butt of the assault weapon poking out of Big Wizard's gym bag.

"Hold up, Cuzz, on Six-O, this how you get at us?" Lil Bam said. "I thought we was on some Nine-O-Six-O shit."

"We always on that . . . this ain't for y'all," Big Wizard clarified. "We got our own shit goin' on over here."

"Yeah, Cuzz, we ain't come for no gunplay." Lil Bam shook Big Wizard's hand. "We just here for a lil friendly Thunderdome." He smirked.

"Thunderdome? For what?"

"Nah, it's good," Ju-Ju interjected. "I knew they was comin'. Me and Lil Bam arranged this. It was an issue with one of the young homies gettin' packed out over in they hood. The homies went back and returned the favor. And so that this don't keep goin' back and forth, we just called the Thunderdome to let niggas with issues get it out the way."

"Cool?" Lil Bam looked back at Big Wizard.

"Ain't nothin' ever wrong with a lil exercise." Big Wizard smiled.

The Six-Os drew to one side of the circle, and the Nine-Os to the other. All the previous internal issues were momentarily set aside for instant Nine-O unity.

"Who's up?" Lil Bam addressed the Six-Os.

Cas walked into the middle of the circle. He had long curly hair and a brawler's face. "I am." He stared coldly at the Tiny Toons.

Before any of the Nine-Os could choose a challenger, Baby Devil pulled his 9mm pistol from his pocket, handed it to Skip, turned his North Carolina Tar Heels baseball cap backwards on his head, and stepped into the clearing to face Cas. Without a saying a word, Cas rushed forward with savage-like force; two controlled haymakers connected hard to the sides of Baby Devil's face and stumbled him.

"Six-tayyys!" The Rollin 60s excitedly cheered.

Baby Devil took a couple of steps back and shook it off. Cas came forward and swung another heavy haymaker that Baby Devil ducked and countered with a barrage of rights and lefts to Cas's face and abdomen.

Cas, a seasoned brawler, absorbed the blows, gained his footing, and let loose. Every blow he threw aimed at his target.

Baby Devil caught as many punches as he gave. It became a battle of volition, both standing their ground as each landed solid blows to the other's face in rapid succession.

The crowd was in a frenzy as they cheered each fighter on. The booming alternating cheers of "nine-dayys" and "six-tayys" became a barbarous chorus.

A sharp right cross to Cas's chin seemed to turn the tide of the fight. As he went to one knee, Baby Devil rushed in to finish him off. But with an almost inhuman force, Cas reached up with one hand and snatched Baby Devil by his shirt collar, and in one fierce motion, he pulled Baby Devil downward while pulling himself upward, launching an over-hand right that smashed squarely into Baby Devil's face. Baby Devil's baseball cap flew off as he fell backwards. Before he could hit the ground, still gripping the collar, Cas landed two more punches.

Baby Devil crashed hard on his back. The Rollin 60s crowd went wild with jubilation, shouting, "Six-tayys!"

Cas stood up and raised six fingers to the sky. The crowd roared louder.

In the next instant, Baby Devil was back on his feet and rushing Cas with all he had. The dance began again as they went blow for blow. Baby Devil darted forward and grabbed a handful of curls, then he yanked Cas's head in a downward sideways angle, twisted his hair tight, and went to work with the right fist. "Ninetieth Street, nigga," he grunted as he came down with each blow.

It was the Nine-Os turn to go wild. "Nine-dayys!" they shouted.

Cas fought back with his own blows, but they were not as effective due to the awkward angle of his head throwing off his balance.

They threw blows savagely all the way to the ground, ending with Baby Devil on top.

"That's it, Cuzz." Lil Bam separated the two.

Baby Devil got up and stumbled back to the group of Tiny Toons, his chest heaving rapidly.

Cas sprang to his feet, winded, but pushing to continue. "On Six-O, we can go again." He breathed heavily.

Lil Bam stepped over and blocked Cas. "Nah, that's it, Cuzz. Y'all got it in."

Cas nodded and took a step back.

"Who next?" Ju-Ju looked at the Nine-Os.

A tall gangly new Nine-O member stepped forward.

Ju-Ju examined the youngster's thin frame. He moved closer to him and whispered in his ear, "Young homie, you might should sit this one out."

The youngster persisted adamantly, "I got it, big homie." He cracked his knuckles in nervous excitement. "Y'all gave me the name 'Hitman', and I gotta live up to it."

Ju-Ju stepped back and nodded. "Alright, the homie Hitman got next."

Hitman took off his shirt exposing the chest of a lanky adolescent boy. He stepped into the clearing.

C-Rag, a dark-skinned, rugged-looking youngster with raccoon circles around his eyes, matched up with Hitman. C-Rag was a few inches shorter than Hitman, but he was slightly heavier.

Both threw up their fists and circled each other. With lightning quick speed, Hitman lurched forward and shot a barrage of straight rights and lefts that all connected with pinpoint accuracy. The blows were not powerful enough for a knockout but enough to send C-Rag scrambling for recovery. C-Rag was stunned. Hitman unleashed another onslaught of rapid almost mechanical punches, overwhelming C-Rag. The Nine-Os were in a crazed frenzy of noise.

C-Rag dropped his head to prevent some of the blows. He swung wildly upward, landing an occasional shot here and there. Hitman anticipated those blows; he countered by swiftly moving out then back in with his long limbs.

C-Rag finally grabbed him but the move worsened C-Rag's position. Hitman grabbed C-Rag's shirt by the shoulder, extending him with a stiff arm, and used his free hand to throw measured hard shots at C-Rag's face.

C-Rag would not give up. He threw blows back, but they couldn't connect the right way because Hitman was too tall.

Lil Bam and Ju-Ju separated them. The Nine-Os boasted loudly; the Six-Os became overtly hostile.

Hitman threw up the Nine-O in triumph, barely breathing hard.

Bolo, a tall light-skinned Six-O, stepped into the clearing toward Hitman. Bolo matched Hitman in height, a mixture of fat and big boned. "On Six-O, I want it, Cuzz."

Ju-Ju and Megatron stepped between them, "Nah, Cuzz, the homie just got through squabbin'. It don't go like that," Ju-Ju said.

"Fuck that, I wanna rumble wit' that nigga on Rollin 60s." Bolo snatched off his shirt, his massive gut pouring over his beltline.

A standoff ensued.

Hitter and Wizard moved to angle the Six-Os.

Lil Bam stepped in and held up his hand. "Hold the fuck up,

Cuzz." Everyone got quiet. "We not 'bout to let this shit get outta hand. We all homies, and if you can't accept a 'L,' don't enter the Thunderdome."

Tension filled the air. An erupting violence covered the crowd as they verged on a full-scale gang rumble.

"Johnny!" A loud voice suddenly broke through the den of noise and pushing and shoving.

Eyes darted around as the crowd faded back in preparation to scramble.

The sound of helicopter blades approached from the sky. Two plain gray CRASH cars pulled up to the back entrance of the park on Ninety-Sixth Street, and four uniformed LAPD gang officers jumped out with guns drawn. More police engines, with their distinctive sound of the accelerator being smashed to capacity, sped up the park's driveway.

The crowd scattered in every direction. Hitter and Wizard sprinted for the trailway behind the gym and disappeared through a slit in the gate leading through Manhattan elementary.

The rest of the crowd ran wherever their legs would take them. The helicopter soon hovered low over the park as the police on the ground apprehended some and pursued others. The meeting was officially over.

CHAPTER 9

A gent John Berrigan lingered with the car door open, one foot propped on the floor panel, and one arm resting at the top of the door. He scratched the top of his balding silver buzz cut as he surveyed his surroundings with bloodshot icy-blue eyes. All the foot pursuits had concluded, and the helicopter had left the scene. The taskforce had the entire drive from the indoor swimming pool to the golf course covered. Gang members were handcuffed in the backseats of several squad cars, while multiple others had clusters of Nineties and Sixties standing around the front and sides of the cars with their hands on the hood. A few of them had gotten away, melting back into the Neighborvilles and backstreets. Some officers stood at a distance, forming a perimeter, while others did the groundwork: pat-down searching and writing down information to run the gang members through the database for outstanding warrants and identification purposes. The six guns and minor drugs found were laid out neatly on one of the squad car's hood.

A young Caucasian agent dressed in blue jeans, tennis shoes, and a blue T-shirt with bold white FBI engraved on the back approached Agent Berrigan with a thick folder under his arm. "They're not here." He shook his head. "Either the intel was bad, or they got away." He handed Agent Berrigan the folder.

"Thanks, Jim." Agent Berrigan took the folder and nodded to the young agent who headed back to the flurry of activities.

"Son of a bitch," Agent Berrigan cursed. *I know they were here,* he thought. *My CI is reliable. How the fuck did we miss them?*

He looked over at the foliage that covered the gate leading to Manhattan Elementary School until he finally realized that was not going to yield any results. He scanned the other surroundings, and his focus landed on one of the squad cars about ten feet away where a group of youngsters stood wearing North Carolina Tar Heels hats or jerseys.

He made his way over to them, scrutinizing each one carefully. He slowly drew closely behind the group, sizing them up. He got to Hitman, paused, and drew closer. "Goddamn, brother, you all right?" he exaggerated.

Hitman looked at him in a dazed. The whole side of his face was swollen, and coagulated blood already formed under the skin. "I'm straight," Hitman answered.

"You sure, man? That looks pretty bad. I think you need some medical attention." The agent stepped closer to examine the damage.

Hitman leaned away. "I said I'm straight." He stared straight ahead.

"Suit yourself." Agent Berrigan shrugged and walked to the front of the car. "Would you guys excuse me just a bit?" He squeezed between two of the Nine-Os, sat the folder on the hood, and flipped through the pages. "I'm looking for a few people."

Their eyes shifted to one another nervously.

Agent Berrigan found the page he was looking for and turned it so they all could see the two medium-sized photos that were on each page. "You all know these four guys, right?" He looked around at the silent mob. "You . . ." He kicked one of them lightly on the shin.

"You know who they are, don't you?"

Silence. No one uttered a single word.

"So you mean to tell me you don't know Hitter and Wizard? Or Little 9-Lives and Little Wizard?" He turned to another youngster. "What about you? Look closely at these pictures." He snatched the folder up and held it in front of their faces. "When was the last time you saw them?"

The chubby, fresh-faced boy looked at the photos, then at Agent Berrigan expressionless. "I never seen them people before." He turned away.

"Look, I just want to talk to them. There's no warrants for their arrest. I know they were just here. If you guys can tell me where they went, you guys can go free. If not, then let's just say me and my partners saw you guys put those guns that were found over in that bush."

"Uha-uha-uha." Droopy chuckled his slow, goofy laugh.

"Something funny? Did I say something that amuses you?" The agent got in Droopy's face.

"Yeahhh, muufucka . . . you da one funny." Droppy laughed.

Agent Berrigan grabbed him by the back of his shirt and rammed his face into the hood. "Is that funny, motherfucker, huh?" He smashed his face harder into the car. "How 'bout that, huh?"

"You's a reallll bitch white boy," Droopy mocked with his face still smashed against the hood.

"I see you wanna be tough." He snatched Droopy upright, holding his wrist tightly behind his back. He whispered in his ear, "You just earned one of those pistol charges, tough guy,"

"I don't give a fuck, you white mothafucka." Droopy tugged and struggled violently. "Take me to jail, mothafucka!" he screamed, and yanked his hands away.

Agent Berrigan grabbed him in a chokehold around his neck and slammed him hard against the car. Another officer ran over to assist in subduing Droopy.

Droopy wrestled and squirmed against their aggression, yelling, "Fuckkkkk you! Fuck you, mothafucka"!

The other Nine-Os raised up from the car's hood and postured aggressively toward the officers.

"Get off the homie, nigga. Leave him alone. Bitch motherfuckas," they grumbled, circling the officer and Agent Berrigan.

"Get back," Agent Berrigan screamed over his shoulder, still trying to hold Droopy down. "I said get back."

The other officers standing nearby drew their weapons and pointed them at the group. "Get down, motherfuckers . . . get down."

"Fuck y'all, we ain't gettin' down," Baby Devil yelled defiantly.

"Get on the ground! Get down! Get on the fucking ground!" the orders resounded from multiple officers.

Unexpectedly, Droopy ripped free from their grip and burst into a deranged sprint across the open field. He screamed as he ran toward Century Boulevard.

The move surprised Agent Berrigan. He paused and stared at Droopy's disappearing figure, perplexed, not knowing if he should chase him or face the threat of the agitated mob. He snapped out of his momentary shock, deciding the mob was the immediate threat. He raised one hand in a "hold-up" motion and placed his other hand on the butt of his pistol but did not draw it. The other officer, who assisted him with Droopy, drew his pistol and aimed it at the Nine-Os.

Droopy's delirious screaming could still be heard in the distance as he ran through a narrow space in the gate and sped up Century Boulevard. "Fuck you white motherfucka . . . kiss my black asss!"

"Now hold up, just calm down," Agent Berrigan warned to the officer. "Don't make this worse than it needs to be."

The Nine-Os stirred nervously, looking at one another with uncertainty.

"Get down," a beefy, pink-faced officer screamed at them.

"Shut up," Agent Berrigan screamed back at the officer and directed a rebuke with his raised hand. "Let me handle this!" He turned to the Nine-Os. "Come on, guys, let's end this peacefully. Just calmly lay on your stomachs and spread your arms wide."

The Nine-Os were still hesitant as they looked at one another for direction.

"Come on, guys," Agent Berrigan edged on, seeing their uncertainty. "Nobody going to fuck you over. Just bring this to an end."

Baby Devil signaled to the others. "Fuck it, Cuzz. The homie already got away." He slowly lowered himself to the ground and the others followed suit. Before they fully hit the ground, a swarm of police pounced and cuffed them. Then they snatched them to their feet and threw them into squad cars.

Agent Berrigan took a deep breath and walked speedily for his car. "Spread those guns and dope between each of those sons of bitches," he called over his shoulder to the young agent.

He made it to his parked car, opened the door, and paused. "Officer McMahon," he called out to a young black CRASH officer.

"Yes sir?" Officer McMahon stopped what he was doing and faced him.

"Find that little motherfucker who got away from us and arrest him ASAP." He got in the driver's seat without awaiting a response.

"Will do," Officer McMahon responded to an already moving vehicle.

CHAPTER 10

———— ❧ ————

The Serving Spoon, a modest yet bustling restaurant in Inglewood that served breakfast until it closed at two p.m., was one of the few successful Black-owned eateries in the community. The place was packed and buzzing with chatter and laughter. Most of the patrons were middle-aged Black people who had been eating here for decades. The Black waitresses worked the room almost effortlessly, pouring coffee and orange juice, bringing trays of hot food balanced on one hand while fraternizing with the patrons at the same time. Big 9-Lives sat at a low-key corner table in the back of the dining area where he was able to watch everyone approaching and entering. This was his favorite breakfast spot. He had been coming here since he was a teenager and could order without looking at the menu. Yet he still had the menu open and looked at it absently. He paused to look at his watch again for the umpteenth time.

He was unnoticed in this inconspicuous area of the restaurant. He had long since transitioned from wearing gang-member gear to more mature, casual apparel similar to his current attire: a brown button-up shirt, matching Docker pants, Polo boots, and a plain Rolex on his left wrist with no diamonds, no flash.

He nursed a glass of cold freshly squeezed orange juice intermittently between staring at the menu, his watch, and out the large front window that gave a view of the parking lot and the traffic along Centinela Boulevard.

An attractive young waitress in a low-cut uniform approached his table carrying a silver tray with multiple plates of food on it. Big 9-Lives could smell the perfume emanating from her smooth, dark skin as she bent next to him to place the plates on the table. He lustfully checked her out from head toe, smiling with satisfaction.

She made eye contact with him after she finished putting the plates on the table.

"Anything else?" Her smile revealed perfect white teeth.

He stared at her momentarily. "Yeah . . . can you tell me the name of the perfume you're wearing?"

"I can't tell you that."

"Why is that?" He sipped from his glass of orange juice.

She put her hand on her hip. "Because a woman is not supposed to tell her secrets. If you want to smell this fragrance, you gotta come see me. If I tell you what it is, you can just buy it for another chick or multiple chicks and smell it whenever you want; then it wouldn't be unique to me." She smiled suggestively and walked off with the empty tray.

He watched her backside with a thoughtful grin as she disappeared through the kitchen swing-door.

He turned his focus to the plates in front of him. He picked up a half English muffin, buttered and put jelly on it, and took a bite. He broke off a piece of the turkey ham with his fork, put it with some cheese eggs, and ate them together. He savored his breakfast, going in and out of thought, enjoying the liveliness of the atmosphere. Patrons at the other tables laughed and chattered at all levels of conversation, as they, too, enjoyed the Serving Spoon's delicious food.

Loud vibrating music drew his attention to the gray Aston Martin pulling into the parking lot. Big 9-Lives rolled his eyes. *Why do I always got to tell him 'bout that loud ass music announcing every time he shows up.*

A few moments later, Elijah entered wearing a white button-up shirt, an ice-blue tie, dark blue suspenders, dark blue slacks, and black Armani loafers. His VVS-diamond earring sparkled brightly in the light. He was carrying a flat leather briefcase. He made eye contact with Big 9-Lives and headed over to the table.

"What up, Unc?" Elijah sat across from him, put his briefcase in the empty chair at his side, and eyed the food hungrily.

"What's up with it, Neph?" Big 9-Lives scooped up another mouthful of food.

"Same struggle, different day. What's mine?" Elijah indicated to the plates of food on the table.

"It don't matter, just eat what you want."

There was enough food on the table to feed four people. He had ordered more than enough.

Elijah pulled the meat plate toward him that was stacked with turkey ham, turkey bacon, and beef breakfast sausage. He dished out a healthy portion of each on one of the empty plates. He filled the rest of the space with cheese eggs and home-style potatoes. He grabbed the small bowl of grits, loaded it with butter and sugar, and dug into the food. "So, what's the word?" he asked between bites.

"Seein' how we need to roll with what's goin' on in the Hood," Big 9-Lives said. "I slid through Lady Rawdog's soon as I got back in town to see what's what. You heard about what happened at the meeting, huh?"

"I heard." Elijah paused to drink some cold milk. "What the fuck was Hit and Wiz tryna prove goin' to it?"

"I don't know. Wiz told me they wasn't even goin'. Probably some knee-jerk reaction type shit at the last minute." He pushed the eggs around absentmindedly with his fork. "They said that FBI motherfucka' showed up again too."

Elijah shook his head. "Motherfucka still fishin' . . . fuck 'em."

"They said he already knew Hitt and Wiz had been there. Somebody's feedin' him information." Big 9-Lives rested his fork on the plate, wiped his mouth with a napkin, and leaned back in his chair.

"Fasho, how else would he be knowin' shit? We gotta start payin' closer attention to how we movin'. I been tryna be out the way, but sometimes a few moves here and there's necessary." Elijah filled his mouth with more food.

"So, where do you stand on squashing this mess with Lil Tef? I talked to Ju-Ju, and he said Big Tef came through his house tryna see if this situation can be fixed. I ran it past Wiz, but he's bein' stubborn about even talkin' about it."

Elijah lowered his face and looked out the window for a short spell. Ambivalence and distress etched across his face. His shoulders slumped with the burdens of all the unanswered questions and looming decisions that left the fate of the Hood in his hands. This question was inevitable, but that did not make the answer any easier. "That's a hard one to just swallow. That lil snake-ass nigga tried to get me puffed." His voice elevated slightly with sudden anger. "Didn't you tell me when we was in Georgia that he's a threat and had to be dealt with?"

Big 9-Lives nodded. "Yeah, but I hadn't seriously considered if

Lil Teflon would be willin' to squash it at that time. Now that it's come up, we would be negligent if we didn't at least look at the option. My aim is to keep you safe. If we can do that without more headaches, why not consider it?"

"You make the call then. Whatever you think is best I'm gonna roll with it." Elijah threw up his hands, then slapped them on the table.

"Nah, Neph." Big 9-Lives shook his head. "You have to be a part of this decision. You know Lil Tef better than I do—you use to run with him. So the real question is: Do you honestly believe he'll honor a ceasefire if we all agree to it? His life or death should hinge on the answer to that question. When I start arranging these meetings and movin' chess pieces, I need to know what our aim is."

The waitress came back. "You guys alright here?" She smiled.

"Yeah, we good," Big 9-Lives responded smoothly, eyeing her up and down.

"Alright well give me a call if you need something." She walked off, hips swaying.

"I see you still on your old man perv shit." Elijah watched her figure as she moved through the crowded room.

"I got your old man nigga . . . I can't help that she wanna share her blackberry juice with me." He laughed.

"She is a lil fine chocolate motherfucka, ain't she?" Elijah admired her momentarily. "Anyway . . . let me think on that question about Lil Tef for a few days. Can you hold off hollerin' at anybody for right now?"

"Yeah." Big 9-Lives drank the last of his juice, slammed the empty glass on the table, and stood up. "Just don't think too long.

Our opposition not sittin' around waitin' on you to be indecisive. Make a decision and stand on it." He grabbed his keys and cellphone from the table. "Pay the tab." He walked to the front and paused to whisper in the waitress's ear. She giggled and scribbled on her order pad. She gazed into his eyes and blushed as he winked at her, then he exited the restaurant.

Elijah snickered and watched as his uncle hopped into his black Chevy Tahoe and smashed out of the parking lot. He sat in silence, staring into space, until his phone vibrated.

He answered and listened attentively. "O'right, I'm on my way."

He ended the call, looked around, and slowly got up from the table. He pulled a wad of bills from his pocket and laid a one-hundred-dollar bill on the table. He walked out of the busy restaurant with a heavy burden weighing him down.

*   *   *   *

Elise turned westbound from La Brea on to Washington, checking her rearview mirror constantly to ensure she was not being followed. She was driving her inconspicuous Buick LeSabre that no one knew about. The commercial property and old factories on the south side of the street became more and more rugged as she made her way further west. The entire span of buildings was covered with graffiti. She passed an area where there was a full city block of two-story high brick wall that ran along the back of an empty field of grass. The wall was covered with a mural that was an ode to the 18th Streets, a notorious Mexican gang that was one of the largest in the country. A big colorful block letter "18th Street" was painted from the ground to the top of the wall as the introduction piece. A collage with pictures of *cholos, cholettes*, lowriders, and names followed. The piece was a true work of art that she marveled at every time she passed.

These were once her everyday stomping grounds. The 18th Street gang had taken her in and helped when she did not have anyone or anything. The relationship with them was not all peaches and cream, but she still appreciated the life lessons she gained from encountering them. They gave her the will and drive to survive the wicked streets of LA.

She came to the corner of Smiley Drive and turned onto a residential street. A cluster of Mexican men loitered in front of apartment buildings, drinking and smoking. Cars and junkies moved up and down the block in a constant rotation. Since the 18th Streets ran the Geer Gang Crips out of the area after a long and bloody war, they completely cornered the drug market. Dealers and users alike came from all over Los Angeles to buy product. From pieces, to weight, the Smiley-Drive 18th Street had it.

Elise drove to the middle of the block and pulled over in front of a well-kept one-story house with a black security gate surrounding it. A pale Mexican teenager with a bald head covered in tattoos hung out in the front yard alertly watching everything happening on the block. She put her pistol in her purse and got out wearing a matching yellow and blue Nike miniskirt and tank top, bootie socks with blue balls, and yellow, blue, and white low-top Nike Air Max.

"What's up, Sleepy?" She approached the gate.

"*Que pasa, Mia?*" He unlatched the lock on the bar gate and opened it for her. "She's inside." He waved her through, locked it back, and resumed his lookout duties.

As soon as her foot touched the steps that led to the porch, the door opened and a young Mexican girl wearing heavy makeup stuck her head out, then backed out of the doorway to let Elise in.

The girl pointed Elise toward the back of the house, then walked over to the couch and flopped down in front of the TV. She moved the M1-carbine rifle on the cushion next to her and rested it on her lap. She was fully engrossed in her TV novellas.

Elise walked through the hallway to an open bedroom door where Diabla sat on the floor at the end of the bed getting her long black hair braided by another cute young Latina. Diabla beamed brightly, her rose-colored lipstick emphasized by the heavily caked-on pale foundation.

A warm feeling bubbled inside of Elise seeing Diabla again. Despite the curveballs life threw her way, Elise knew Diabla always had her back no matter what. They'd started out as friends and confidants in a group home as young teenagers, then partners in crime, robbing and killing for survival. They became lovers for a spell. Now Diabla was like the sister she never had.

Diabla never berated her or judged her for choosing to be with Elijah, even after Elise revealed the complicated arrangement, she, Elijah, and Lauren shared.

"Hold up." Diabla stopped the girl braiding her hair and rose to her feet to hug Elise. "What's up, Mommy?"

"What's up with you? See you still at it." Elise nodded to the pile of money sitting atop the dresser.

"That shit is chump change, girl." Diabla waved her hand dismissively at the money and sat back down to resume getting her hair braided. "I miss gettin' it in chunks like me and you used to do."

Elise walked over to the window and peeked out the curtains. "Well, that's kinda what I came over to holla at you about." She turned to face Diabla.

Diabla tapped the girl who was braiding her hair on the calf.

"Give us a minute."

The girl looked blankly at Elise and walked out.

Elise gave the girl a once over as she left the room. "Your new fling?" She smirked at Diabla with a crooked smile.

Diabla took a cigarette out the pack on the dresser and lit it up. "Something like that." She exhaled a big plume of smoke and sat on the edge of the bed.

Elise sat next to her. "She's cute."

"Yeah, she's alright," Diabla responded nonchalantly. "What's up though? I know you didn't come over here to check on my love life."

"You right, I didn't." Elise pulled her purse to her lap and opened it. "I want to test run something. If you can find a lane, you can make a lot of money." She removed a kilo of cocaine and handed it to Diabla.

Diabla rolled the tightly wrapped square around in her hands. "My bitch." Her face lit up. "You came up on a lick?"

"Nah." Elise stood up and paced the room. "I got the plug now. I can get however much I need, whenever I need it."

"So, what you need me for? I mean, Lil 9 got the network to move whatever."

"He's not in with me on this. It's all me."

A look of concern crossed Diabla's face. "Is everything alright with you and him?"

"Yeah, we're good." Elise sighed. "He just not really in the game like he used to be, so he don't want me in the game."

"It's understandable. You guys have a kid to look after now."

Diabla pulled from her cigarette.

"I get that. But at the same time, I'm not no stay-at-home type bitch. Maybe when I'm a lil older, but right now, I still crave the fast pace of the streets."

"I hear you." Diabla looked around thoughtfully. "So, what's the plan?"

"I got fifty birds right now . . . well, forty-nine minus that one." Elise pointed to the kilo now sitting on the bed. "I was runnin' the ship for him when he was bringin' things to a close. I made a few contacts with some outta-town niggas that was connected to his people down there but not directly connected to him. I can still fuck with them on business without it gettin' back to him. If we can line them up right, and if you can get a slice of the pie here in the Eighteens, we should be able to build a major ship that we both get fat off of in the next year or so."

Diabla nodded. "OK . . . OK . . ." She rubbed her chin. "What's gonna be our prices so I can know how to get at these *vatos*?"

"Just find out what your homies are paying right now. Whatever that is, we beat it by a thousand a key."

"Sounds good. You already know I'm gonna break some down and piece it out anyway, so it will all make sense price-wise at the end of the day." Diabla put the kilo in a small compartment at the bottom of her dresser.

"One more thing," Elise said hesitantly. "There is a small problem . . . that peon Lil Teflon tryna challenge the throne. He needs to go away."

Diabla grinned, looking like a beautiful Latina clown. "Nuff said. Just get me the what, where, and the rest." She moved close, hugged Elise tightly, and whispered, "That's the easy part."

CHAPTER 11

The Neighborvilles really came to life late nights. From Ninety-Second to Ninety-Sixth Street, the Nine-Os congregated in different groups. Four drug spots operated in this small stretch of land by separate and independent dealers, all from the same gang, but individuals in their economic conquest. Lookouts and defense posts were set up in three strategic locations. At the mouth of the alley on Ninety-Second Street, two youngsters stood in a darkened backyard with pistols and walkie-talkies. On Ninety-Fourth Street, two youngsters were stationed in the second-story window of the apartments directly on the corner with a set of walkie-talkies and weapons. The third lookout was in the duplex on Ninety-Sixth Street where Nine-O soldiers watched for enemies or police under the cover of darkness.

On the opposite side of Western Avenue, crackheads, prostitutes, and late-nighter civilians moved in and out of the cuts and apartment buildings. A constant flow of Nine-Os and young 10-5 Gangstas, who were just a clique off Underground Crips, bounced back and forth between the Sima Motel and the adjoining apartment next to it.

Western Avenue was like a cross between the *Twilight Zone* and *The Walking Dead* after midnight. Even the police stuck to the outskirts during these hours, unless they were on a full-scale special raid that brought out a third of their division forces. This opened the opportunity for a person to be robbed, shot, or molested with almost impunity. These were the hours that the crackheads roamed the neighborhood, stealing anything not bolted to the ground, and sometimes even if it was bolted down, they found a way to get it.

Baby Devil and his crew were holding court in a duplex unit right off the alley on the Ninety-Sixth Street end. The exterior surrounding their spot was pitch dark except for the soft yellowish tint coming from one of the apartment units.

Birdman and Mannie Fresh's "Hood Rich" played on the stereo system as they played *Madden NFL*, talked shit, and made passes at the four females from the Harlem 30s Crips hanging out with them. A MAK-90 assault rifle with a seventy-five-round drum was propped behind the front door. Multiple pistols covered the coffee table in the living room and the small round kitchen table where Droopy lounged rolling weed and nursing a bottle of Hennessy. Half the table was cluttered with individually tied clear sandwich bags containing ounces of crack in each, and a plate filled with individual rocks and a razor blade with crack residue on it. A lightweight digital scale sat on the side.

"You been rollin' that blunt for 'bout an hour…hurry yo slow ass up."

"I'm comin', Cuzz, shiddd . . . you can't rush purefection, nigga." Droopy concentrated intensely, putting the last touches on his work.

Baby Devil cut his eyes toward the kitchen, opened his mouth to say something else, but changed his mind. He glanced over at Skip sitting on the sunken black sofa with one of the Thirty-lettes on his lap, her arms wrapped around his neck as they whispered to each other and giggled.

He returned his focus to the game on the screen, then back to

Skip and the girl. He shook his head with disgust. "All these niggas wanna fall in love with these hood-rat bitches," he mumbled and continued to the next play.

Droopy came into the living room with a lit blunt in his mouth. He pulled on it deeply, coughed, and passed it to Baby Devil.

"Took yo' ass long enough." Baby Devil took a hard toke.

"Gotta take ya timeee, baby."

"Get the fuck outta here," Skip teased. "You wasn't taking your time when you was runnin' yo' stupid ass up Century, hollering like a short-bus kid."

Everyone burst into laughter.

Skip flailed his arms up, imitating Droopy's great escape. They laughed even harder.

"Fuuuck you, niggahhh." Droopy cut his eyes at the girls. "Don't let these bitches get yo ass whooped."

"Ain't nobody worried about you, nigga, on Nine-O." Skip waved his hand dismissively.

"And ain't nobody yo bitches," the girl sitting on Skip's lap chimed in.

Droopy stared at her blankly for a long pause. "Bitch, I beat you up," he retorted finally.

Baby Devil laughed. "You ain't gonna beat her up, Cuzz. You ain't got it in you," he egged him on.

"Bullllllshit . . . I'd beat dat bitch like she stole somethin'. You better ask somebody."

Baby Devil doubled over in amusement. "That's Skip girl, you can't do that."

"Ain't his motherfuckin' girl. All you bitches need to get naked around dis motherfucka." Droopy lit the second blunt.

Skip's girl sighed dramatically, but the other girls giggled.

A sharp knock at the front door got everyone's attention. "Get that, Cuzz," Baby Devil directed Droopy.

Droopy cracked the curtains to investigate, then opened the front door, letting a crack-smoking couple in. They were filthy from head to toe. The woman made a constant smacking noise with her teeth and rocked back and forth, humming a made-up tune. "Let me get a dime, baby."

"Where da money?" Droopy looked her up and down.

"I got the money. Lemme see what Imma get," she hummed.

Droopy went to the kitchen table, moved the rocks around on the plate, chose one, and brought it back to drop it in her hands.

"Ummmm . . ." she hummed, body swaying, as she rolled the rock in her hand examining it. "This kinda short, baby."

"It's a dime," Droopy snapped.

"Don't wrestle with her, Cuzz. Just give her an extra piece and let her get on," Baby Devil instructed over his shoulder.

"Thank ya, Devil," the woman said. "You always hook Momma up." She glared at Droopy.

Droopy got her another tiny piece. She dropped the money into his hand, and the couple hurried out.

"I don't know why Devil got that slow motherfucka' workin' the spot . . ." Their voices could still be heard as they faded into the night.

"I heard dat, bitch! Fuck youuuu." Droopy yelled from the door.

The room erupted into laughter. They continued their smoking, drinking, and festivities in a jovial atmosphere.

*　*　*　*

Outside on Manhattan Avenue, a dark figure slipped through the front gate of one of the residences and walked up the pathway on the side of the house to the backyard. His black Dickies, Adidas tennis shoes, hoodie, and dark skin blended him perfectly with the night.

He hoisted himself atop the brick wall and paused to survey the alley. The couple who had just left the spot walked past him, never noticing his presence. He waited for them to make it halfway down the alley, then hoisted himself over the wall. His feet landed on scattered glass and garbage. He listened to the faint sounds of the crowd huddled near the Ninety-Fourth end of the alley momentarily before moving swiftly across the clearing and disappearing into one of the set of duplexes.

As he slowly approached with roving eyes, the music and voices from inside one of the units became more distinct. He clutched the pistol against his thigh and crept toward the side door nestled in a narrow walkway in between houses. He listened intently, trying to make out all the voices. He quietly tampered with the doorknob until the door slightly cracked open.

Baby Devil walked into the kitchen. "Which one a them stupid motherfuckas didn't shut the door all the way?" he mumbled. He walked over and pulled it open. Lil Teflon stood there like Darth Vader.

"You slippin', lil nigga," Lil Teflon said. He put his pistol in his waistband and pulled his hoodie back, uncovering his damaged features.

"How's that?" Baby Devil nonchalantly walked away, preoccupied with opening a box of crackers. He popped crackers into his mouth and walked to the living room.

Lil Teflon scoffed. "I been here listenin' to y'all for a minute . . . I could've been anybody." He surveyed the drugs and money on the table as he walked behind Baby Devil. "I heard some bitches . . ." He spotted the four young women. "Hey, what we got here?" He suggestively gawked at the women as he swaggered into the living room. The girls greeted him lukewarmly.

Droopy and Skip stood and dapped him up. Tiny Looney was passed out sleeping on the floor.

"Cuzz o'right?" Lil Teflon asked, staring at Tiny Looney.

"Yeah, he straight. Nigga just tired that's all," Skip answered, sitting back down next to his female companion.

"Damn, you booed up, ain't you, Cuzz?" Lil Teflon asked Skip.

Skip smirked smugly.

"Where y'all from?" he asked the girls.

"We from Harlem Crip," one of them announced proudly.

"Aight, aight . . . Harlem in the house, huh," he joked. "Shid, we need to get it all the way crackin' then." He pulled out a baggie of powder cocaine and set it on the table. "Y'all fuck with the Montana, right?" He emptied the contents on the glass-top coffee table.

Skip's girl looked hesitant, but the others cheerfully jumped at the opportunity.

"Y'all enjoy yourselves while I holler at the lil homies for a minute." Lil Teflon signaled Baby Devil, Skip, and Droopy to the bedroom.

He closed the door for privacy after everyone entered. They each gave him their accounts of what happened at the meeting and how they personally felt about it. He questioned them, gauging their demeanors and responses until time slipped away from them. Before they knew it, over an hour had gone by and the last topic of serious conversation was about Ju-Ju.

He snuffed out the tiny remainder of the last blunt they smoked. "So, when Hitter got off on you, Droop, how did Ju-Ju respond to that?" Lil Teflon asked.

"Cuzzz didn't do shit. I meannn, nobody could really. Dat's Hitt and Wizzz; don't nobody really wanna fuck wit' 'em. But da homie Ju-Ju did tell him to stall me out afterwards. Guess dat was da best he could do," Droopy stuttered and shrugged his shoulders.

"Where y'all think Ju-Ju really stand in all this?" Lil Teflon questioned the other two.

Baby Devil spoke first, "Cuzz is just neutral far as you and them. He don't wanna see niggas at war. I know he don't like me personally, but I don't got him plottin' on us."

"I don't either," Skip added. "Ju-Ju a good homie. He don't wanna see the Hood divided."

Lil Teflon studied them with a poker face. He didn't trust anyone at this point in the game. Disloyalty could arise from anywhere, and he was looking for any sign of it in these youngsters' words and demeanor. Baby Devil had been loyal over the years and never hesitated to move when he gave the word, but Lil Teflon could detect that something was changing in him. Baby Devil was asking more questions and making decisions without running them by him first. Lil Teflon knew from his experience in the streets that when one of the young cubs started questioning too many of his calls, it was time to watch him closely. Baby Devil had become the unofficial leader of the Tiny Toon clique. So Lil Teflon's power in the Hood was tied directly to his relationship with Baby Devil. This predicament was beginning to bother him endlessly. He was supposed to be one of the head figures in the Nine-Os but instead, he was at war with most of the homies in his generation; with the G-homies because of Big 9-Lives; and now he had to tread lightly with a bunch of kids to maintain some sort of manpower in the Set. He was growing more suspicious, bitter, and dangerous with each passing day.

Finally, he nodded and stood up. "Guess we see how it play out then. Skip, who the lil bitch with the big teeth you all snuggled up with?" He laughed along with Droopy and Baby Devil.

Skip smiled sourly. "Aw, Cuzz, why you fade a nigga bitch like that?"

"Fade you like what?" Lil Teflon acted dumbfounded. "I'm just statin' the obvious. The bitch got unusually big teeth."

Baby Devil stifled a laugh.

"Ain't nothin' wrong with my bitch teeth." Skip attempted to put up some type of defense.

"Bullshit." Lil Teflon gestured dramatically with his hands. "That bitch look like she got piano keys for teeth. You hit that bitch in the mouth, them motherfuckas go all crack slowly, then fall out like thin Chinese porcelain, like the cartoon's nigga."

They roared in laughter except Skip. He mumbled incoherently and walked toward the living room. The others followed.

Lil Teflon continued to clown him, "Aw, Cuzz butthurt . . . don't act like that."

Skip flopped down on the sofa next to his date, putting his foot on the coffee table.

Lil Teflon strolled up to the opposite side of the girl. "Scoot over a lil bit, babe." He squeezed in to sit next to her before she had time to move.

Skip cut his eyes at Lil Teflon.

Baby Devil walked toward the kitchen with a knowing smirk on his face.

"So how long y'all been from the Thirties?" Lil Teflon asked.

Each girl gave a different timeframe. He leaned forward and separated some lines of coke on the table. He sniffed a line, leaned back, wiped his nose, then handed the straw to Skip's date.

Skip grabbed her arm aggressively. "What the fuck you doin'?"

"What? Why you trippin?" She pulled away. "I thought we was supposed to be partyin'?" She leaned forward with the straw.

Skip grabbed her more forcefully. "You don't need to be doin' that shit."

Lil Teflon reached over her and unclasped Skip's grip from her arm. "Hold up, nigga, if she wanna do her thing, let her do her. What, you Captain Save 'Em or something now?" He stared Skip down.

"Nah, Cuzz. I'm just sayin' . . ." Skip hesitated, unsure of himself.

"You ain't just sayin' shit." Lil Teflon rubbed her thigh gently. "Go 'head and do you, lil momma."

She smiled at Lil Teflon, then bent over the table and inhaled a deep snort of the powder. She leaned back on the sofa with a euphoric gaze in her eyes, rubbed the excess powder from her nose, and licked it off her fingers.

"You like that, lil momma?" Lil Teflon swooned softly in her ear, rubbing her thigh higher as she blushed.

"What you doin'?" Skip leaned forward aggressively.

"Fuck you mean what I'm doin'?" Lil Teflon paused.

"This me right here . . . you trippin', big homie," Skip said angrily.

The room came to a standstill as everyone watched to see how this would unfold. Droopy giggled to himself.

"Oh, this you, huh?" Lil Teflon looked at the girl, then stared at Skip. "You must think the rules don't apply to you I see." He got up and stood directly in front of her. "We gon' let her decide."

The girl stared up at Lil Teflon with lustful eyes, the cocaine already working its magic on her.

"Lil Momma, don't be shy, tell this nigga the sayin' of what Rollin Crips do when it comes to the locs and lettes," he ordered, glaring at Skip.

She stood up and faced Lil Teflon. "Shiddd . . ." She moved closer, their faces almost touching. "It ain't no fun if the homies can't have none," she purred, as she grabbed Lil Teflon's crotch.

Skip's face looked anguished.

Droppy laughed his goofy laugh. "Dat's what da fuck I'm talkin' 'bout. Niggas wanna be all lubby dubby and shit." He grabbed one of the other girls and led her over to him.

She straddled Droopy and wrapped her arms around his neck. "Let's get it crackin' then."

Lil Teflon placed his hands on Skip's girl and gently lowered her to her knees in front of him. She undid his belt, snapped open the button of his pants, and undid his zipper. He smiled as she took him in her mouth. "Ooh, watch the teeth baby, watch the teeth . . . don't need no accidents."

Droopy's laughs and groans came from across the room.

Skip's eyes popped in horror. He stood abruptly and stormed out the front door, slamming it behind him.

Lil Teflon watched Skip go as she continued her slow motion of pleasure. A satisfied smile washed over his face as he closed his eyes in ecstasy.

CHAPTER 12

A fat, furry brown cat jumped down from the kitchen counter after licking old stale milk from a metal bowl next to a cluster of plates, cups, pots, and pans that appeared to have been sitting there for weeks. Flies and gnats buzzed and hovered over the parcels of old food still stuck to the dishes. The cat walked from the kitchen nonchalantly into the living room-bedroom area of the small bachelor apartment and hopped into the kitty litter positioned by the door.

Lil Wizard opened his eyes in the nearby couch bed to the smell of cat litter and old food. A light film of perspiration dotted his forehead from the heat in the windowless stuffy apartment. He stretched and reached for his bifocals on the nightstand. Pushing the cotton blanket back, he sat at the edge of the bed, eyes glued to the floor as he gained his bearings. He tried to remember when he fell asleep; his mind was blank.

The small color TV sitting on a ragged wooden crate was still on. The voice of the weatherman delivering the day's forecast loomed in the recesses of his mind. Snapping out of his daze, he looked confusingly around the room. He scratched his head; dry flakes fell from the scalp of his unkempt hair. The cat nestled against his ankles. He stared down absently at her for a short spell, pushed his glasses up the bridge of his nose, and got up slowly headed for the bathroom.

After relieving himself, he washed his hands and face, loaded the toothbrush with toothpaste, and scrubbed with unnecessary vigor. He walked back to the living room still brushing his teeth as the red breaking news banner at the top of the TV screen caught his attention. A news reporter stood in front of the liquor store on Forty-Sixth Street and Western Avenue at an active crime scene. Yellow caution tape sectioned off the entire northwest corner. Numbered cones surrounded a 1994 yellow four-door Cadillac, and two bodies lying under white sheets on opposite sides of the car.

He turned the volume up.

"Three people are reported dead at the scene, not two as was earlier reported. There is another victim inside of this liquor store who also has died from gunshot wounds…" the newscaster said.

He moved closer to the screen, squinting to get a better view. "That look like Baby Dee-Dog car."

"According to witnesses, a lone gunman exited from the alley right here behind us, walked up to the victims, who were sitting in this yellow vehicle, and opened fire, killing the driver and passenger. The third victim managed to make it out of the car after suffering multiple gunshot wounds, but as I just stated, he, too, has succumbed to his wounds after running inside."

His phone rang. He spat inside a wastebasket overflowing with trash, placed the toothbrush on the nightstand, and wiped the toothpaste from around his mouth with the back of his hand.

"Hello," he said. A dark cloud came over his face as he listened intently. Baby Dee-Dog, Tiny Dee-Dog, and Tiny Rip-Dog were dead. He shook his head. "That's fucked up. Baby Dee-Dog was my nigga. I mean one of my real Six-Os niggas. Imma park something for Cuzz on Nine-O. Who they say did it?"

He listened somberly as he got the street version of what happened, the real version that the news stations knew nothing about. He knew the guy who did it. "Yeah, that slob nigga who mom's live in the Hood on the Western side," he said. "We been givin' that nigga a pass all this time. Nuff said."

He hung up the phone and moved around the apartment with purpose. After getting dressed, he went to a side area that served as the closet. He pushed a pile of clothes to the side, exposing a portion of the lower wall that had an inconspicuous groove to one side. He cuffed the groove and slid it sideways, exposing a silver safe. He spun the combination, opened the safe, and pulled out a large stack of bills. He carefully removed one twenty-dollar bill from the bundle, put it in his pocket, and returned the rest to the safe. Next, he removed four different pistols from the safe, admiring each one—the .44 Bulldog Revolver, the .38 Supra with an extended clip, and another two pistols. He made his choice. He locked the three pistols back in the safe and tucked the .44 in his waistband. He grabbed a handful of bullets from a box on the top shelf and shoved them into his pocket.

He walked back to the living room and examined himself in the full-length mirror to make sure the pistol could not be seen through his tight multicolored T-shirt. He pulled at his conservative-fitting Wrangler jeans to adjust the waistband so the pistol snugged in perfectly. He looked down at his large brown orthopedic sport shoes, raised the heel on one shoe, and rotated it side to side as if they were Gucci loafers. Satisfied with his appearance, he grabbed a flimsy fake leather jacket, his keys, and headed out for the day's adventures.

*   *   *   *

Dusk was beginning to settle over Western Avenue when G-Bill poked his head out from a cut between two storefront properties. He looked both ways before stepping onto the sidewalk and darting across the street to the bus stop on Eighty-Ninth Street. He pulled his light gray hoodie further down his face to shield his grisly beard and dark beady eyes.

An elderly woman clutched her purse and moved a few steps over when his stocky six-six frame made its way to stand next to her at the bus stop.

He noticed her apprehension at his appearance. "How you doin', ma'am?"

"I'm doing fine." She continued eyeing him cautiously.

"Nice weather, ain't it?" He lit up a cigarette.

"Yes, it is, young man . . . well, it was." She looked at the RTD bus pulling from the bus stop on Ninety-Second that was heading their way.

G-Bill took one last drag from the cigarette and thumped it to the ground as the bus pulled up. Both readied their bus passes as the air compressor hissed with the opening of the bus doors. He allowed her to board first.

An old rust-brown LTD sitting a half-block away pulled slowly out into traffic behind the bus. When the bus made its next stop on Manchester Avenue, the LTD cruised past it on up Western Avenue.

G-Bill sat near the backdoor, head bobbing rhythmically to his Discman. The bus made a few more routine stops before it reached Florence. It halted in front of the Burger Palace to let some passengers off. The driver closed the door and was about to pull off when someone tapped on the door at the last minute. The bus driver hit the brakes and slid open the doors. G-Bill noticed the young man with bifocals and a multicolored shirt, who appeared to be a little out of breath, as he dropped a few coins in the fare box, then walked toward the back of the bus.

"Damn, blood almost left you, didn't he?" G-Bill joked as the guy approached.

The newcomer chuckled lightly, vaguely staring at him, before turning to stare out the window as he held on to the top support rail that ran up the aisles of the bus.

As the bus neared Sixty-Ninth Street, the man leaned over and pulled the wire that was running the length of the bus. A distinct ding sounded, notifying the driver that a passenger was getting off at the next stop. The driver pulled over at the Sixty-Ninth Street stop. The man walked to the back door where G-Bill sat directly on the opposite side.

G-Bill removed one of his earphones. "Have a good one, homie."

The man stepped down one step into the door's exit. He straightened his bifocals, spun around swiftly, and aimed a .44 caliber revolver at G-Bill's chest. "You too, blood," he responded menacingly.

G-Bill's street survival instincts immediately took over. He sprung from the seat and attempted to kick the gun from the man's hand. Before his foot could reach its target, the gun went off, sending G-Bill flying backwards into the hard plastic bench seats. The deafening explosion permeated throughout the bus, causing an ear-piercing ring.

"Aaahhh," the elderly woman screamed in horror, and the other passengers followed. The bus driver jumped from the driver's seat and sprinted out the front door like a world-class track star. The bus idled as he disappeared into the fish market. Passengers scrambled for the exits in panic.

G-Bill lay on the bench sideways gripping his stomach, writhing in agony. "Ahh, Blood, this nigga done shot me." He panicked as the stranger stepped back and stood over him. "What did I do to you? Please don't kill me, man," he pleaded feebly between death coughs of blood.

"Too late." Lil Wizard calmly squeezed the trigger three times at point blank range in G-Bill's face. The shots rocked the bus with each cannon-like sound, and then it was quiet.

He glared at G-Bill's contorted corpse with a sadistic smile, then exited the bus and fled up Sixty-Ninth Street toward Harvard Boulevard where his car waited.

*　*　*　*

Long after midnight, the RTD bus still sat in the same spot on Sixty-Ninth and Western. The entire corner was taped off, as detectives and medical examiners scurried around the crime scene performing various duties. The front and back doors to the bus hung open as they combed it, dusting for prints, taking photographs, and logging everything that might be evidence. A few local news teams waited outside the police perimeter to report the latest on the incident while crowds of onlookers gathered on opposite sides of the streets gossiping.

Agent Berrigan pulled up to the edge of the tape, slammed the car in park, and got out. He walked under the yellow tape and headed for the bus. He entered from the back door and wandered over to the body under the white sheets soiled with blood splotches.

Jim Holland, one of the detectives looked up from taking pictures. "Hey, John, how's it going?" he greeted jovially.

"I was doing alright till I got this call." Agent Berrigan moved closer to the body. "So, what do we got here?"

"The usual around these parts: young black male in his early twenties—"

"I don't need his profile, I need specifics: who and why. No disrespect, but I'm not a murder detective. I'm working a specific case, and my CI tells me this murder may be connected to it."

The detective considered Agent Berrigan briefly. He pulled the sheet back, exposing the victim from the waist up. "Is this specific enough for you? A Blood called 'G-Bill' on the streets."

Agent Berrigan looked down at what was left of the victim's face, folded his arms, then used one hand to shield his mouth to camouflage the laugh that involuntarily slipped out.

The perplexed detective continued, "Say he got on near Manchester. His killer got on a few minutes later, a couple blocks from here. Witnesses say there was no hostilities between the two. The perp rang the bell to get off, walked to the back exit here, and turned with a gun." He demonstrated holding an imaginary gun. "Bang, bang, everyone scatters, and finally our guy stands over the victim. The curtains close." He moved the sheet back over the victim. "A couple of the passengers say the assailant called the victim 'blood' or something to that extent before he shot him."

"So the perp knew this guy was a Blood." Agent Berrigan scanned the crime scene. "That confirms he got on with the intentions to whack this guy."

"Looks that way. We had three Rollin 60s killed early yesterday by a Blood. If history is a true indicator, this was just retaliation."

They left the bus and stepped out into the cold night air.

Agent Berrigan furrowed his brow. "It may not be a retaliation." Detective Holland cocked his head. "The victim got on the bus back toward the Nineties. Even though the Nineties and Sixties get along, it's unusual for an actual hit on a rival gang by the Sixties would originate in the Nineties, and I got this tip from an incredibly good source to look into this one."

"We definitely won't leave any stones unturned." The detective paused to scribble something in his notepad. "But I've been working this area a long time, and I can tell you that the Rollin 60s are a treacherous lot."

"Believe me, I'm aware. But this was on a public bus, Jim—a fuckin' public bus. It takes a different brand of killer to do some shit like this. And the Nineties have a group over there right now that fits this brand."

"Don't read too much into it," Detective Holland said. "It's just your average everyday senseless gang violence." He bent under the yellow tape and strolled to his car. "Gonna head to the station for some follow-up interviews."

"Do me a favor and keep me posted. I know you've been doing this a long time, but I have a hunch about this one. It's going to lead back to the Nine-Os." He stepped close to the detective's car and grabbed the door before it closed shut. "Jim, take my word, these guys—the Nine-Os—they have the making of a new Sicilian mafia. We got to stop these guys. Whatever's needed to get it done, let's do it." He stared at the detective with an expression of obsession and desperation.

Detective Holland nodded and gently tugged at his door.

Agent Berrigan was unaware that he was holding the door. He slowly stepped aside allowing the door to be shut. The detective got into the car and drove away without another word.

Agent Berrigan stood there for a moment looking up and down Western Avenue. He closed his eyes and inhaled deeply. "These murderous gang-bangers have to be stopped," he mumbled. "I'm coming for you Nine-Os . . . I'm coming." He casually strolled to rejoin the crime scene workers.

CHAPTER 13

Elijah rolled over in his California king-sized bed to the morning rays beating at his eyes. He shielded them momentarily, allowing his vision to adjust. He was stretching when his attention was drawn to Lauren's naked body standing in front of the mirror as she brushed her hair. The scent of her perfume permeated the air. He smiled at the thought of their activities last night. Their lovemaking always felt fresh and adventurous. It wasn't that he loved Lauren more than Elise, he just loved each one uniquely. Both had been pivotal in his rise to the top. The three of them were more than a family, they were a team.

She spotted him watching her through the mirror and smiled. "Good morning, handsome." She stroked her hair.

He grumbled an inaudible response and rolled over to stare out the window.

"Don't be grumpy with me." She crawled on top of his back. "You wasn't grumpy last night when you were trying to take advantage of me." She kissed the back of his neck.

Her soft skin pressed against him, instantly giving him thoughts of a morning quickie. He raised her weight and shifted to lay on his back. He moved her back slightly so he could admire her face and firm breasts. Her piercing blue eyes studied every inch of his face. He pulled her to his chest and stroked her long black hair that cascaded from her shoulder to his chest.

"You better stop this before I quit work so we can lay here like this all day every day," she purred.

He kissed the top of her head and eased her up.

"You right, we don't need to start again . . . not right now. We'll be snowed in for the rest of the day. You gotta make that meeting, it's important." He got up and walked naked toward the bathroom.

She watched him with longing. "Noooo," she protested. "Don't . . . I can still make it on time . . . just a quick one."

"Stop being a pervert and get ready for work."

She giggled and walked to the bathroom. "I'm not the pervert, you asshole. Told you, you better stop calling me that."

He finished relieving himself, flushed, reached inside the glass-encased shower, and turned on the water. The steam slowly filled the bathroom. He pecked her on the lips and stepped under the hot water.

She smirked and attempted to step in the shower.

He grabbed the door. "Nope."

"What? I just need to take a shower." She acted innocent. "Let me." She tried to pry the door open, but he wouldn't let her.

"You just took a shower," he said with a laugh. "I know what yo' ass tryna do."

"Why do you always think I'm trying to do something?" She giggled mischievously. "Just let me in."

"No way Jose," he joked. "Don't make me scream rape." He cupped the corners of his mouth with his free hand. "You know I will."

"You better not, you fucker." She blushed. "I told you don't ever do that again. You got Ms. Raheema thinking I'm some type of sexual deviant or something."

He roared in laughter. You gotta admit, that was a good one though, wasn't it?"

"No, it wasn't. That woman was looking at me sideways for a week." She gave up on her attempt to get in the shower. She wiped a section of steam from the mirror and brushed her hair. "Don't come looking for me later—off limits for you, buddy."

He rinsed the African black soap from his face and stared at her from his peripheral as he soaped up his body. The hair resting at the small of her back, leading to perfectly spread hips, and a fat but firm ass hypnotized him. He was fully erect.

"Looks like you're changing your mind, huh?" she said seductively.

She looked down at his erection, then back into his eyes. She gently set the brush down on the marble countertop and stepped into the shower.

He kissed and caressed her voluptuous breasts. Unexpectedly, he turned her around and gripped her throat as he moved close to her neck, inhaling her fragrance.

She moaned in ecstasy. "That's right, Daddy, let the beast out for Mommy." She closed her eyes and braced her palms against the wall of the shower as the piping-hot steam engulfed their bodies into blissed obscurity.

*   *   *   *

Elijah woke up groggy a few hours later. Lauren was already gone. He shook his head at the thought of her, knowing he would have to hear her bragging about putting him to sleep like a baby. *Just still tired from all the traveling, rippin' and runnin',* he justified to himself.

He got up and dragged himself to the bathroom, threw on a wife beater, cotton sweatpants, socks, and tennis shoes, and headed downstairs. He grabbed the pitcher of orange juice from the refrigerator and poured himself a glass.

"I left you some breakfast in the oven there."

He turned around. Sistah Raheema stood in the doorway sipping from a cup of tea.

"Appreciate it. I'm not really hungry right now. I'll get to it after I work out. Where's everybody?" He drained the glass of orange juice.

"Elise was heading out with both the boys on my way in. Said she was taking them to the doctor for checkups. Lauren just left for the office about an hour ago."

"Alright, I'm goin' out back." He grabbed an apple from the basket of fruit sitting on the counter and headed outside. He stepped out on the spacious patio and took a deep breath. The air was crisp, and the bright midmorning sunrays washed over his face. This immediately invigorated him. He strolled off the patio, walking past the infinity pool, to a side gate shaded by thick shrubbery on both sides. Passing through the gate, he entered an expansive, well-manicured green lawn that was dotted with an assortment of lush fruit trees and rose bushes. A large white bungalow loomed impressively all the way to the back. It was meant to be the guesthouse, but Lauren turned it into her official quarters. She and Toussaint did all the daily functions in the main house but retired to their own slice of peace most evenings.

In an area of the yard west of the bungalow, a quarter acre of fenced-off land contained a row of gated dog kennels, chicken coops, and an eight-by-twenty walk-in pigeon cage.

Before he could fully enter the animal enclosure area, an all-black, cropped-eared, muscular Pitbull began barking, spinning in circles, and jumping high in the air repeatedly as he approached the kennels. The two Rottweilers caged on each side of the Pitbull barked in excitement, arousing the birds and chickens in their cages.

"Hey, boys . . . hey." He made air-kissing sounds and snapped his fingers at the dogs, making them more excited.

He went to the Rottweilers' cages first, petting and greeting each one separately. They leaped on his chest. He scuffed their necks and head playfully. They ran freely as he replenished their bowls with food and water. The Pitbull barked and whined at the attention the other dogs were receiving.

"Hold up, Cannon," he said to the fussy Pitbull. He finished up with the Rottweilers and put them back in their kennels, then he released the Pitbull, who burst out of the kennel like a horse out the gate. He ran to the edges of the enclosure at full speed, then bee-lined for Elijah.

"Hey, Cannon, come here, boy" He egged him on.

Cannon jumped onto his chest, nearly knocking him down. Elijah ruffled his neck and cropped ears. Cannon nipped playfully at his hands and wrist as his tail wagged. Elijah grabbed him by both sides of his jaws and wrestled him onto his side. Cannon shook out of it and jumped on top of him. They roughhoused for a while until Elijah led him out of the kennel area into the yard. Cannon ran the yard, sniffed the bushes, pissed to mark his territory, running back and forth to Elijah's side repeatedly.

"Come on, boy." They walked to another area close to the swimming pool. A painted concrete slab with a few dumbbells ranging from twenty to fifty pounds, jump ropes, a trampoline, yoga mats, and a few metal chairs comprised his workout spot. He began his stretching routine followed by ten minutes of jogging in place. Then he went into a strenuous workout of burpees, push-ups, squats, and curls with the dumbbells in a fast-paced circuit. By the time he reached his one-hour mark, he was drenched in sweat, exhausted.

He grabbed a clean dry towel off a rack in the corner, sat in one of the chairs, hunched over trying to catch his breath. He draped the towel over his head, his eyes pinned to the ground.

The door opened and light footsteps came his way. He raised his eyes; Sistah Raheema approached him carrying a big bottle of cold Gatorade and a couple granola bars.

"You're a life-saver." He took the items from her.

"Knew you needed something; you haven't eaten at all." She looked at him with concern. "Gotta take care of yourself and stop worrying so much."

He looked at her somewhat perplexed. "What makes you think I'm worrying?"

"Because your eyes tell it. You know the old saying: 'The eyes are the window to the soul.'" She sat in the chair next to him and gazed at the beautiful yard.

"I'm alright. Just got a lot on my mind. Tryna get a lot accomplished, that's all." He washed the granola bar down with Gatorade.

"Just remember that life's not a sprint." She gestured to the property with a wave. "Allah gives us the things of this world as blessings. But in these blessings, there are often tests. Don't become consumed by the rat race of this world and forget about the divine reason you are on this journey."

"Yeah, I hear you. It's just a little cloudy at times, far as what the reason and purpose is. Sometimes it feels like the harder I run, the more I'm pulled backwards."

She chuckled. "*Shaytan* is always going to make it cloudy, that's his job. But wisdom and patience are your safeguards; and staying appreciative and faithful is your weapon. So sometimes it's not all about how hard and fast you run the race; it's about knowing this is a long-distance run that requires times for you to stop, rest, and replenish in order to be efficient and effective on the next leg."

He studied her curiously. She did not usually speak much about matters outside of taking care of the boys and the house. He could count on one hand how many personal conversations they have had since the day he met her in front of the mosque selling fish dinners after Jumu'ah.

"You know . . ." she continued. "The prophet Muhammad, *sallallahu alaihi wasallam,* had multiple wives," she continued. "His youngest was Aisha, may Allah be pleased with her. Many say that she was his favorite. I don't know if that is true, but I do know that she spent a lot of quality time with him, even accompanying him until he took his last breath. A lot of hadith came from her. But upon the Prophet's death, she was one of the main ones to take up arms against the Prophet's little cousin, Ali, and his daughter, Fatima, may Allah be pleased with them." She turned and faced him. "Even after learning all she did from God's own prophet— after all of his care and protection and wisdom—she still became one of the bloodiest and divisive forces in the world of Islam."

He stared at her, waiting for the moral and purpose of the story, but none came.

She patted him on the leg affectionately and stood up. "I'll warm your breakfast." She walked to the house without looking back.

CHAPTER 14

B ig Teflon sat at the dining room table with his mother, Virginia, his son, Akili Jr., and Akili's mother, Keisha. He tried to find normality in the family dinner that he knew was far from normal. Virginia had just finished another stint in rehab a few weeks prior, and he could already see the telltale signs that she was itching to relapse again. It had become a recurring theme in his life: him rescuing her off the streets, cleaning her up, getting her to rehab, and she would do well for a few months, but then she'd return to what she had been doing since he and his siblings were young.

His relationship with Keisha was also turbulent. He never got over the feeling that she had "trapped" him by getting pregnant. Her attitude toward him after the pregnancy had been extreme bi-polar to say the least. If he gave her material things and gave her his time, she acted nice for a period. But when he wanted to have quality alone time with Akili, she became irrational and sometimes violently psychotic. Keisha's rationale was that she and Akili came as a package. If he wanted to play a father's role in Akili's life, he had to be a part of her life too. There were times, like this evening, when he had to bear with her pettiness and accept her presence for Akili's sake.

The entire dinner was awkward, filled with silent tension. The two women collaborated on preparing the meal, which turned out to be a sloppy display of mush and grease. The fried pork chops were coated with a crust golden brown in some spots and charcoal black in others, bathed in lard. The canned vegetables were mushy, and the rice was clumped together and soggy.

Virginia, Keisha, and Akili ravished the food as if they were eating from a five-star restaurant. Poor five-year-old Akili did not know any better. Virginia and Keisha were accustomed to eating like this most of their lives. Big Teflon's taste in food changed when he started getting real money with Big and Lil 9-Lives. It was hard to return to Virginia's train-wreck cuisine after eating quality food prepared the right way.

He toyed with the food on his plate absently, waiting for them to finish. He occasionally nibbled at one of the less burnt parts of the pork chop and made forced conversation for appearance's sake.

"This pork chop is the bomb, Ms. Vee," Keisha smacked through greasy lips.

"That's right, girl. You got the recipe now so you can make it whenever you get ready," Virginia boasted.

Their voices irritated him. *Damn, I wish they'd shut the fuck up. I can't even think straight with all they yappin'.* He stood up from the table, his plate barely touched. "I gotta make an important call."

"You haven't even really ate nothing," Virginia protested.

"I'm takin' it with me." He grabbed the plate. "I really got to be on this call." He was already making his exit.

Keisha shot daggers at him. "He always got something important goin' on, let him tell it." She gestured unapprovingly to Virginia.

Virginia raised her hands and shrugged her shoulders. "I don't know what his problem is."

Big Teflon ignored them as she walked out the backdoor and into the driveway. He tossed the remaining food to his Pitbull chained to the post in front of the garage. The dog immediately went to work on the disgusting scraps. He set the plate near the backdoor and walked to the enclosed drive-in garage. He looked both ways before slipping into the small side door. He fumbled for the light switch in the dark and flipped it on. The garage lit up in a dim yellow haze. There was an old primed-up, dust-covered Chevy Impala parked to one side of the garage, and the other side was cluttered with tools, a lawnmower, dirt bikes, cans, and other miscellaneous items.

Toward the back of the garage there were hanging chainsaws, a heavy generator, and a huge propane tank. He lugged the items out the way, revealing a small door. He twisted the tiny inconspicuous knob and gave the door a hard push; it groaned and creaked, granting entrance to a walk-in-sized space.

He stepped in and pulled a tiny metal chain hanging from the ceiling. A bare light bulb blinked twice and jumped to life with a light humming noise. Four assault rifles with extra clips were mounted to the wall. He opened a metal chest in the corner. An array of pistols, two Tech-9s, and a sizable supply of ammunition still in factory boxes glistened under the gleam of the light.

He put one of the Tech-9s, the .45 semi-automatic pistol, and ten boxes of bullets into an oversized gym bag he'd picked up from the floor. He studied the assaults on the wall, reached for the AR-15, changed his mind, and grabbed the AK-47 with two extra banana clips, completing the package with a black bulletproof vest. He secured it all neatly in a bag, then busied himself putting everything back like it was. After he did a last-minute security scan on the room, he turned the light off, secured the door with all its camouflaging items, and exited the garage quietly. He placed the padlock on the garage door.

"What you doin'?"

He jumped at the unexpected voice and spun around. Keisha stood there, craning her neck to see what was in his hand.

"What you got in the bag?"

He drew the bag closer to his side. "None-a your fuckin' business," he snapped. "Why the fuck you creepin' around tryna spy and shit?" He bumped her hard as he walked past her toward the house.

"Damn, you gon' run me over, motherfucka? Ain't nobody spying on you. I was comin' to see if you was alright." She trailed behind him, still trying to get a glimpse of the contents in the gym bag.

"Yeah right. Stay out my business, nosey ass." He hurried to his bedroom and slammed the door.

She pounded on the door loudly. "Open this damn door! Don't be treating me like one of yo lil hoodrats, nigga." More pounding. "I'm yo' motherfuckin' baby momma…"

He swung the door open and grabbed her by the throat with one hand, silencing her as she clawed at his wrist in a desperate attempt to unclench the death lock that quickly cut off her air supply.

"Stop it, boy." Virginia came out of nowhere, grabbing his arm violently. "Leave her alone."

He struggled with them until he heard Akili's cry. Akili stood at the end of the hall yelling hysterically. Seeing his son snapped him back to his senses. He released Keisha; she crumbled to the floor, gasping for air.

He rushed to console Akili. "I'm sorry, lil man. It's okay . . ." He picked him up, bounced him, and rubbed his back.

"Give me my fuckin' son," Keisha yelled, panting heavily. "You black son of a bitch, give me my goddamn son." She charged Big Teflon and attempted to rip Akili from his arms.

Big Teflon resisted her.

Akili screamed at the top of his lungs as his parents played tug-a-war with him.

Big Teflon relented, realizing they were traumatizing Akili. He released him to Keisha. He hurried back to the bedroom, grabbed the gym bag, his keys, and other travel belongings, and rushed out of the house to the sound of Akili crying and his mother and Keisha cursing at him.

Virginia rushed behind him. "Don't come back here with that shit, you stupid motherfucka."

Keisha pushed past Virginia, holding Akili on her hip. "You ain't never gon' see him again!" She rubbed Akili's head vigorously. "You no good, black motherfucka."

Akili screamed as tears and snot covered his little face.

Big Teflon jumped in his Lincoln Navigator and slammed the door. He tossed the bag on the backseat and grabbed his head with his hands. "Aaahhh," he screamed. After a few seconds, he took a couple of deep breaths and calmed himself.

He took out his cell phone. "A nigga can't never win," he mumbled as he dialed a number. Someone finally picked up. "It's me . . . I'm on my way. 'Bout two and a half out." He put on his seatbelt and started the car.

Virginia and Keisha continued their barrage of cursing from the porch, as Akili continued to bawl. He flipped Keisha the bird as he backed out of the driveway. He smashed the gas and sped off to South Central.

*   *   *   *

Lil Bar-Dog navigated the K5 Blazer in the Sunday night traffic on Sunset Boulevard. Ju-Ju was riding shotgun, bobbing his head to the Gap Band's "Outstanding." Cars were bumper-to-bumper, as many people were out and about, the Hollywood nightlife was in full effect. An array of partygoers, onlookers, and weirdos filled the many restaurants and nightclubs on the strip. The crowded sidewalks buzzed with cheerful festivities.

Lil Bar-Dog gawked, mesmerized by all the Bentleys, Lamborghinis, and Ferraris that meandered along the busy thoroughfare of Hollywood. Entertainment and sport celebrities had their weekend toys out on full display. The police patrolled the strip in force but that did not stop Ju-Ju and Lil Bar-Dog from blowing their weed and blasting music like it was legal. It was their night to parlay like the big boys.

They finally arrived at the Roxbury, a high-end three-level club where the rich and famous partied. A block-long line of fashionably dressed partygoers anxiously awaited their turn to enter. Cars crowded the front parking lot next to the club. Valet handed out parking stubs, jumping in and out of luxury vehicles as they came and went. Crowds of people streamed back and forth with the bulky security teams working the busy doors.

Lil Bar-Dog pulled up to the valet station. He and Ju-Ju hopped out, giving the attendant a fifty-dollar bill and the keys for a ticket stub in return. They had ditched the gang attire for the night and opted for the fly-casual apparel. Ju-Ju flaunted his pieces: a blue-faced presidential Rolex watch peppered with a diamond band and dials, a diamond embezzled pinky ring, and a three-karat diamond stud in his ear. His long, freshly done cornrow braids stretched to the middle of his back.

It was a known fact in LA that nobody shined harder on these occasions than the street captains with black market money. The ball players, entertainers, and execs had a lot more money, but the city's nightlife belonged to the young, rich, and dangerous rather than the famous.

Ju-Ju had invited Lil Bar-Dog to tag along to get his first real experience of how the upper echelon of the Nine-Os moved outside of the Hood. He followed Ju-Ju as they walked past the crowds of people in line and those congregating out front. Music boomed from inside the club. They made it to the red velvet rope that blocked the opened door. Four burly Black security guards were posted with no-nonsense looks on their faces. Ju-Ju approached the head guard who was holding a clipboard and gave them his name. The security guard quickly scrolled down the list, nodded, and opened the rope for them to enter.

They slowly made their way through the packed club of sexy women and hungry-eyed men. The dance floor was packed shoulder-to-shoulder with patrons dancing to the beat of what the DJ was spinning. They reached a set of stairs that led up to the third level and were met by another set of security guards at the VIP section at the top of the stairs.

Ju-Ju raised his voice to match the blasting music, "I'm with the Bang Side Enterprise crew."

Before the security guard could respond, a voice called out from across the room, "Ju! Over here, Cuzz."

Ju-Ju looked past the guard to Elijah waving him over. His whole face lit up.

The guard looked at Elijah and stepped aside for them to enter.

"What's up with it, Crip?" Ju-Ju smiled, wrapping Elijah in his signature bear hug. "Missed you, nigga."

"Missed you too, bro. Been busy as hell tryna make it happen." Elijah returned Ju-Ju's affection.

Lil Bar-Dog hesitantly approached Elijah. "What's up, big homie?" He extended his hand.

Elijah stared at him, then gave him a lukewarm handshake.

Ju-Ju noticed Elijah's apprehension and tried to break the ice. "This Lil Bar-Dog . . . he straight. This my lil nigga."

"I know who he is."

"This motherfucka jumpin' tonight." Ju-Ju tried to break the tension "What time yo' artist go on?"

"Around midnight, a lil before. Let's get a drink and chop it up." Elijah led them to a cordoned off section set up with plush red leather couches and tables.

A group of men and women occupied a part of the section, having a good time. Weed smoke and drinks flowed continuously.

Elijah gestured for Lil Bar-Dog to follow him as he approached the group. "This my artist." He pointed to a young dark-skinned man who was the center of attention. "You can pull up with them for a bit while I holler at Ju." He turned to the man. "Kazi, this my lil homie from the Set. He gon' lounge with y'all for a bit."

"Nuff said." Kazi waved Lil Bar-Dog over to take a seat. Lil Bar-Dog nodded to Elijah and joined the party happily.

Elijah and Ju-Ju moved to the empty area next to them and sat across from each other. Elijah grabbed a bottle of champagne from a bucket of ice sitting on the glass table. He unsealed it and popped the cork, then drank straight from the bottle. He passed it to Ju-Ju who did the same.

"I'm happy to see you doin' your shit." Ju-Ju looked around the room. "Moms woulda been proud of you."

It had been a few years since Ju-Ju's mother, Brenda, died from cancer. She loved Elijah like a son. She had become like a second mother to him after his mother, Fatima, committed suicide. Brenda always saw the best in Elijah and encouraged him to be a successful leader.

"Yeah, I wish she could have been here to see some of it." He took a pre-rolled blunt from his pocket. "You just don't know how much she inspired me to do a lot of the shit I'm doin' now." Elijah lit the blunt and hit it.

Ju-Ju drank more champagne from the bottle. "Where the hell you come up with the name 'Bang Side' for your record label?"

Elijah laughed. "Because that's us. For years niggas been screamin' what side you from: Eastside, Westside. Then within the Hood you got the Orchard side, the Western side, the Budlong side. But with all this shit with Lil Tef, it's like the unity of the Budlongs and what we stood for is fading. We all used to be family. It wasn't crippin' just for the sake of Nine-O; we was crippin' for the love of us. But now the lines are blurry. All the sides in the Hood can't be separated. These young niggas joining the Set because they mesmerized by the money and cars. It was never about that when we was growing up. We joined the set because we was the Set—it was our family lineage. So I'm pushin' something now that's only us: the family. We not Eastside or Westside; we from that small strip of land where niggas bang the hardest. That's why we come from the Bang Side."

Ju-Ju nodded and smiled. "I dig that. The Bang Side Ridahs." He pulled from the blunt, letting that sink in. They had to survive hell to make it to where they were. They were in a class by themselves and the name defined that. "That's what it is then. So what we doin' with the Tef situation? I'm quite sure Unc hollered at you."

"Yeah, he hollered at me." Elijah slouched back on the couch. "I mean, we could never be friends again."

"We all know that, Cuzz." Ju-Ju leaned forward. "But it ain't 'bout being friends at this point. Me and you are bros because we roll like that. Big 9-Lives is Unc because that's who he is to me. Mostly everybody else in the Set is just homies—Nine-Os—and that's how I treat 'em. I don't play friends with niggas. We function on this Nine-O shit and that's it. With you and Lil Tef, it would be the same thing—a ceasefire and niggas do they own thing."

Elijah studied him. "From what you sayin', I take it that you think I should squash it."

Ju-Ju paused for a moment, taking an extra-long drag from the blunt. There wasn't a simple answer. He thought about the situation for countless hours since Big Teflon came to see him. But he knew something had to be done to stop the madness. "I just don't want us dyin' at the hands of each other out here," he said. "Cuzz did what he did, and y'all responded. If we can stop it here, I think we should." He decided he had to be the voice of reason; however, he'd made up his mind earlier that morning that even though he still had love for the Teflon brothers, his loyalty was always going to be with Elijah and Big 9-Lives. "Make no mistake about it though, homie, if this shit crank back up, I'm in the trenches with you off top."

Elijah nodded. "Do you think we can count on Lil Tef keepin' to the ceasefire if that's what we all agree on?"

Ju-Ju was unsure. He knew Lil Teflon was selfish and untrustworthy. "Nothing is a hundred percent. But I think if we got everybody in the same room to air their grievances and hash this shit out, it's a good chance he'll play ball the right way. Especially if all of us are on the same page, including Big Tef, otherwise he would be on an island by himself."

"We been knowin' that nigga since kids, so we both know he won't mind bein' on his own island." Elijah laughed.

"Yeah, but beyond all the cut-throat shit Cuzz be on, nobody wants constant war, not even him. That shit is stressful, having to look over your shoulder all the time. We already got the Snoovas and Tramps at our heads, but to have niggas on your head in-house is a whole 'nother ball game."

Elijah looked around the room, gathering his thoughts. He drank deeply from the bottle and set it back on the table with a loud thump. "Fuck it . . . go ahead and set it up. I'll talk to Unc, Hitt, and Big Wiz to let them know where I'm at with it. Unc been waiting on my decision. Hitt and Wiz probably gonna need convincing, but I think if I'm good with squashin' the beef, they'll come around."

"What about Lil Wiz?" Ju-Ju asked with a hint of concern.

"Lil Wiz is just an extension of Big Wiz. He go off the rails sometimes, but for the most part, wherever Big Wiz leads, he follows."

"O'right, fasho. It's settled then. You work yo' end, and I'll work mine. We try to get this shit worked out," Ju-Ju said, clearly relieved.

Just then, 50 Cent's "In da Club" came on and the club went nuts. The entire VIP section turned up a whole nother notch. Some women found guys to dance with, while others danced with one another. Kazi sicked a trio of gorgeous Ethiopian women on Lil Bar-Dog and he danced cheerfully.

A thick, longhaired red bone flirted with Ju-Ju as she danced with her girlfriend. She looked like she just stepped off the pages of a *Stuff* magazine. He winked at her suggestively; she blushed and continued her sensual flirtation.

"I think I got a fan." Ju-Ju stared her down.

Elijah followed his gaze to the beautiful woman. "My God," he exclaimed.

"My God is right." Ju-Ju grabbed the bottle of champagne, hit it, and passed it back to Elijah. He watched her with lustful admiration. "She on the Loc, gotta give her what she lookin' for." He made his way over to her.

Elijah watched as he squeezed between the two women and danced.

"Don't you even think about it," came a woman's voice from behind him.

He turned around. Elise stood there shining like an exotic gem. Her lush, curly black hair cascaded over her bare shoulders, slightly grazing the top of her sleeveless royal blue and emerald green Versace dress. Her caramel skin glistened under the lights. Her six-inch stilettos complemented her perfectly pedicured feet and accentuated her petite legs. She strolled casually toward him; her full glossed lips curved in a pouty smile.

"Don't think about what?" he mimicked jokingly.

"You know what I'm talkin' about, nigga, don't play." She snuggled up against his chest and wrapped her arms around his waist.

"You the one bet not play. I'm already feelin' a lil adventurous tonight." He kissed her forehead and squeezed her tightly.

"I bet you are . . . in here lustin' off all these women."

"Ain't nobody lustin'. Shut up." He knuckled the top of her head.

"Uh-huh, I bet." She pulled his waist in to her. "It's okay. I know you miss your little slut nights with the bimbos."

"Bimbos? What, you a white girl now?"

"Nope. But whatever your adventurous fantasy is, I can be it. You want a slut bimbo? I can be her tonight." She stared into his eyes seductively.

He looked around the room secretively. "Meet me in the VIP bathroom stall in five minutes."

"Oooh, you do wanna be bad tonight." She stroked his lips. "I'll be there." She took the bottle from his hand, gave him another seductive glance, and swayed off.

He smiled as he watched her ass. He reached into his pocket for another blunt and lit it. He smoked and watched the crowd, bobbing to the music for a few minutes. He snuffed the blunt out and headed over to the bathroom. Looking around to make sure the coast was clear, he twisted the knob, entered, and let the door close behind him.

CHAPTER 15

Big 9-Lives tidied around the family home on Ninety-First Street. With him living in Georgia and Elijah busy with his company and real estate ventures, the family house they all grew up in was starting to look worn. The furniture and appliances were top of the line, but with no one there for daily upkeep, dust and cobwebs had built up throughout the three-bedroom dwelling. The front and backyard grass were overgrown and dried up. Wild weeds sprouted everywhere with the slightly rusting bench and weights surrounded by it.

Dressed in a wife beater, cut-off khakis, long white socks, corduroy house shoes, and elbow-length yellow rubber gloves, he went from room to room wiping, sweeping, scrubbing, and waxing. He opened all the blinds and windows, letting the house air out. "Can't believe he let the place get like this. He ain't that damn busy," he cursed under his breath.

His eyes landed on an old family photo in a small brass frame as he wiped the living room mantle. He set the rag down and picked it up. A tinge of sadness ran through him looking at his sister Fatima and brother Cannon. He studied their eyes and the innocent smiles. He remembered the day they took the photo. Fatima could not have been more than nine years old, so beautiful and full of life. Cannon was sa tall, gangly youth at the time, a goofy Mamma's boy. Big 9-Lives was the only one not smiling in the photo; he was mad that day. He wanted to go roller-skating with K-Mike and some other friends, but their mother wouldn't allow it.

He chuckled at the thought of his childishness and sat at the edge of the couch clutching the picture. Looking around the house, he shook his head. "So many bad memories here." He looked again at the photo of his siblings. Visions of Fatima's lifeless body with a bullet hole in her head, slumped over in this living room, and Cannon's bullet-riddle body on the sidewalk raced through his mind. "I should've done better to protect you guys." He teared up. He quickly caught himself before the tears fell, stood up, and returned the picture frame to its place on the mantle.

He composed himself and continued cleaning. "It's too damn quiet in here," he grumbled. He walked over to the stereo system and turned it on. The Isley Brothers' "For the Love of You" immediately filled the house with loud soul-soothing music. He mixed in a little two-step and sang as he went about his chores.

After hours of oldies-filled cleaning, he wheeled two big trashcans to the curbside. As he opened the lid on one of the trashcans, a dark-skinned crackhead riding a pink low-speed bicycle with two bags of cans tied to the sides rode up.

"Big Nine, my nigga." He parked the bicycle on its kickstand like it was a car. "Man, I missed ya, baby." He beamed an egg-yolk-yellow-teeth smile, extending a fist dap.

"What's up, Lotto?" Big 9-Lives gave him a fist pound and replaced the lid on the can.

"Man, it's been fucked up around here without you." Lotto rattled off in his fast-clipped speech, looking up and down the street uneasily.

"You ain't been holdin' it down?" Big 9-Lives joked.

"I been tryin', man. But these young dudes, man, they don't respect nothin'. They won't even lookout for a nigga."

"Ju and them been keepin' you straight, ain't they?" He walked back into the yard with Lotto trailing.

"Ju-Ju?" Lotto asked with an incredulous expression. "Man, you talkin' 'bout a bullshit nigga. Ju-Ju a real bullshit nigga. He wanna run a nigga to death, then give you some lil shit you can't do nothin' wit. I told him he need to stick to shootin' at motherfuckas and shit—he good at that. But he need to leave the hustlin' to somebody else."

Big 9-Lives burst into laughter.

Lotto still had not changed throughout the years. He had been a real player before the crack came in, running a prostitution ring that extended from California to Missouri. Rumor had it that Lotto had had a stable of twenty-five women. He dabbled in powder cocaine a little back then, a few lines here and there, but then one of his hoes introduced him to crack. It was downhill for Lotto ever since, but Big 9-Lives still treated him with decency. Lotto had served as his entertainment and company on many late nights in the trenches with his outlandish stories and personality. He was like the Hood comedian.

"You know how it go when the OGs ain't on deck. But it's the youngsters' time now." Big 9-Lives walked toward the garage. "I need you to help me with the yard. I'll look out for you."

"You ain't even gotta say that. I know the OG gon' lookout. Where my nephew Lil 9 at?" Lotto followed him inside the garage.

"He out the way." Big 9-Lives pulled out the lawnmower and other gardening tools. "He'll probably slide through later."

Lotto assisted with all the tools. "I miss Nephew. He knew how to run shit when you wasn't around. You got gas for the mower?"

"Yeah. Over there." Big 9-Lives pointed to an old gas can in the corner of the garage.

Lotto picked up the can. They toted all the items to the front yard. Big 9-Lives set about giving him instructions on what he wanted done. Lotto went to work under the cool morning sky.

Big 9-Lives relaxed on the porch, enjoying the weather and view of the block. He missed these mornings. There was no place like the Set. He waved at some of the neighbors who were outside in their robes with cups of morning coffee in hand, talking about the latest news, putting their trashcans out to the curb.

Just then, Big 1-Punch pulled up in a black cherried-out 1988 Chevy Nova. "What's up with the Loc?" Big 1-Punch yelled as he got out of the car smiling.

Big 9-Lives got up to meet him halfway. "Salute, my nigga," he greeted, hugging Big 1-Punch.

"Man, it's been a minute." Big 1-Punch looked him over. "Still lookin' young and sharp."

They carried their conversation to the porch and caught up on old times and the latest events. The hours passed quickly as they reminisced and commemorated about the Hood.

"It's crazy, Cuzz, how shit changed so much 'round here." Big 9-Lives stepped off the porch and stretched.

Hell yeah, but I ain't changin' with it. I'm always gon' be Big 1-Punch from Nine-motherfuckin'-O." He threw up the Nine-O hand sign.

Big 9-Lives chuckled. "I'm already knowin', homie."

As the sun beamed brighter in the midmorning sky, two more OG Nine-Os pulled up in front of the house, followed by another and another. Word had spread through the Hood like wildfire that Big 9-Lives was back at the family headquarters. Within no time, cars lined the block on both sides of the street. Homeboys and homegirls packed his backyard, drinking, smoking, listening to music, fellowshipping, and enjoying themselves.

He looked around at all the happy faces. *It's good to be home.* He smiled. *This is how it's supposed to be.*

*   *   *   *

Big Teflon parked near the corner of Vermont and watched as the last batch of homegirls entered Big 9-Lives's driveway and walked to the backyard. He started the car and drove past the house slowly to get a full view. Torn as to what his next move should be, he turned right up Budlong, drove to Ninetieth, and made another right back to Vermont. His head was spinning too fast, and he needed something to calm his nerves. He headed up Vermont and pulled into the parking lot of Kites Liquor Store. He quickly dashed into the store, exiting with a fifth of Hennessy and a box of Blacks. He sat in the parking lot breaking down the cigar and filling it back up with weed.

The weight of the situation was heavy on him. This was his neighborhood and the people he'd been around all his life. Now he had to tiptoe around, debating if he should pull up or not. He loved Big and Lil 9-Lives, and although he hadn't done anything to make them enemies, his brother did, and that made him an enemy by association. But would Big 9-Lives have him killed if he dropped by to talk things out? Did Big 9-Lives consider him that much of an enemy or threat?

He lit the blunt and pulled hard, choking, before chasing it with a strong drink from the Hennessy bottle. "Why did my stupid-ass brother even get all this shit started?" he grumbled in frustration. "Everything was goin' right for a change. We wasn't wantin' for shit. He still had to go fuck it up." He pulled from the blunt again. What was he supposed to do? Let the homies kill his brother, or would he have to kill them instead? The more his mind drifted, the more frustrated he became. He stared into space for a moment. "Fuck it."

He drove back around the block, parked a short distance from Big 9-Lives's house, put a pistol in his waistband, and got out. One homie was posted on security detail near a bush across the street from the house, and another was two doors down sitting on the neighbor's front porch. All their eyes were on him.

"It's too late to turn back now," he mumbled, chin-upped them, threw up the Neighborhood fingers sign, and walked through the front gate. One of the lookouts across the street raised a walkie-talkie to his mouth and spoke into it.

By the time he reached the backyard, one of the OGs had an M-1 Carbine aimed at his chest from the garage roof. Everyone in the backyard ceased all movements and stared at Big Teflon.

"Hold up, Cuzz . . . damn." Big Teflon spread his arms out wide to show he did not have a weapon in his hands. "I just came to talk." He looked around the yard for an understanding face.

"Stand down," Big 9-Lives ordered the shooter on the roof. "What you doin' here?" He approached Big Teflon with a mean mug.

"I just came to talk to you, Unc." He tried to keep his voice steady.

"If you wanted to talk, why didn't you reach out to me first?

Matter of fact, pat him down."

One of the young homies jumped on the task. He pulled the pistol from Big Teflon's waist and held it up. Big 9-Lives held out his hand, and the youngster handed it to him.

"That's just for protection. It ain't for no homie. It's for the enemies," Big Teflon explained.

Big 9-Lives ejected the clip, slid the shaft back to eject the bullet in the chamber, and handed the gun back to him, empty of rounds.

Big Teflon looked around anxiously as he put the pistol back into his waistband.

Big 9-Lives examined his face closely. "You say you come to talk, so go ahead and say what you need to say."

It was so quiet you could hear a pin drop on the grass. Every eye bore into Big Teflon.

"I'd rather me and you holla one-on-one, not like this." Big Teflon gestured to everyone watching.

"With everything that went on—and still goin' on—it's G-homies here that wanna know what you and your brother got to say. It's been too many secrets in the Hood, and some of this shit needs to be said in the open so it ain't no guessin'." Big 9-Lives sat in one of the old yard chairs and opened his arms. "So speak."

Big Teflon pivoted uncomfortably on his feet, silently cursing himself for walking into this predicament.

"Cuzz . . . I'm . . . I'm just tryna see how we can get things back to where they used . . . well, not used to be, but put all this animosity behind us." Big Teflon straightened his back, determined to get his point across. "It's no secret like you say, of all the shit that happened, and we can't change it. I'm here to see how we can change the now. None of what's happenin' need to keep goin'. This shit crazy . . . we homies."

Big 9-Lives nodded. "Since we bein' candid, you know yo' lil brother is the cause of all this, right?"

"You ain't tellin' me something I don't know, big homie. And believe me, this shit keeps me up at night. But at the end of the day, that's my brother. And niggas ran they play on him already. So it ain't like he just gettin' a pass. He almost lost his life for whatever it is he supposed to had did. Can't we just leave it at that?"

Big 9-Lives considered him.

Big 1-Punch chimed in, "If you know he did wrong, why didn't you bring him to the table or deal with him yourself? Fuck him bein' your brother. Right is right, wrong is wrong. You niggas ain't bigger than the Hood. Niggas think it's all about them—that's how shit got fucked up." His open animosity toward Big Teflon was apparent. "Y'all niggas don't never supposed to go against no righteous G-homie."

Big Teflon turned to 1-Punch. "Shit gets fucked up too because motherfuckas always wanna put they two cents in where they ain't got no business."

"This Nine-O business—" Big 1-Punch started.

"This Budlong business," Big Teflon cut him off.

"Nigga . . ." Big 1-Punch started walking up on him. Big Teflon clenched his fists, ready for the rumble.

"Nah, hold up, Cuzz." Big 9-Lives stepped between them. "This not the time and place for this."

"You gotta stop lettin' these young niggas think they gotta voice. Talkin' 'bout Budlong business. Fuck all that side shit, nigga.

This Nine-O," Big 1-Punch growled angrily.

"I got it, Cuzz." Big 9-Lives raised his hand to calm him down.

Big 1-Punch respected the call and simmered down. He and Big Teflon continued to mad-dog each other.

"This the reason why I didn't wanna do this here." Big Teflon looked around at the faces. "We tryna get something worked out. It's enough egos involved as it is, and doin' it like this is just adding fuel to the fire." He was nervous and wanted to get out of there, but it was too late for that. So he had to stand up to whomever and get matters sorted out with Big 9-Lives.

Big 9-Lives looked around thoughtfully. "I dig what you sayin', Big Tef, but like I said before, we not doin' no more secretive shit when it comes to this situation. The homies got a right to know what's goin' on. So this what we gon' do. Once I talk to the circle, *if* they willing to come to the table to see about straightening things out, we'll set up a roundtable and have a few solid, neutral homies to be a part of it."

"That's cool," Big Teflon agreed. "Hopefully, we can get this done."

Big 9-Lives nodded.

A long pregnant silence ensued.

"O'right, you dismissed." Big 9-Lives smirked arrogantly.

Big Teflon hesitated. "Can I get my clip?"

"No." Big 9-Lives responded coldly.

Big Teflon backed his way toward the exit under hard stares and eerie silence.

"Oh, and Tef?" Big 9-Lives called out.

Big Teflon paused at his exit route, startled.

"If we call this meeting, and you don't bring your lil brother, I advise you not to even show up."

Big Teflon nodded his understanding, picked up his pace, and got out of there as quickly as possible.

*   *   *   *

The earlier festivities were over and everyone had cleared out. The crisp sounds of Miles Davis jazz streamed through the now-peaceful house. Big 9-Lives sipped from a quarter-filled glass of Crown Royal, recounting all the events of the day, specifically the Big Teflon encounter. He chuckled with the thought of how much he relished the moment. He could not have asked for a better situation; it was almost like a gift had fallen from the sky. One of the things he had been trying to figure out was how to accomplish squashing the beef without showing weakness. It was imperative that they negotiated from a place of strength. But that was now settled. Big Teflon had unknowingly brought the perfect solution, and the homies were there to witness it. He came bowing down, practically begging for peace. It showed everyone that their side was the right side, and they did not initiate the turmoil, as rumors had insinuated throughout the Hood. The homies in attendance now knew without question that Lil Teflon had initiated the war, and now the Teflon brothers were clamoring to call it off. The heat had gotten too hot for them to handle. He read straight through Big Teflon's feign toughness.

He chuckled again with satisfaction, knowing he had played the whole situation to his advantage. He was firm but allowed Big Teflon to leave humbled but still with his dignity, so that he would be more inclined to get his brother in line and not feel that he would have to retaliate to save face.

Yes, it was indeed a major piece in the puzzle of realigning the Hood under his terms. He swallowed long and hard from his drink, snapped his finger, and vibed to the smooth, relaxing sounds.

CHAPTER 16

Elijah walked into the mosque on Jefferson and Fourth Avenue just as Friday's *Jumu'ah khutbah* was winding down. The building was a typical storefront commercial property that had been hollowed out on the inside. The freshly painted white walls were decorated with prayer rugs with various designs and Arabic calligraphy of Quranic verses.

The floor was covered with a thick plush green carpet with two large white emblems of the Kaaba on either side of the curtained petition that separated the men and women during services. A bald elderly man wearing a white *jilbab* and a cream *kufi* that matched his brown skin delivered the *khutbah* to the congregation from a simple wooden podium.

Elijah looked around the room and spotted Big Wizard and Hitter sitting in their usual place in the back. They were shoeless and sitting cross-legged as they listened attentively to the Imam. Elijah went to sit next to them.

"The *dua* I just recited specifically asks Allah to save me from the evil of myself," the imam said. "Think about that, ponder it as you go through your day. It is a deep thing to seek refuge in Allah from the evil of oneself. Not from *Shaytan*, not from the *dunya*, but from the evil of your own mind." The imam paused, allowing his words to resonate through the room. "*As Salaamu Alaikum. Qad quamatis salah.*"

The muezzin called the *iqamat*, a call to prayer, and everyone in attendance stood to perform two *rakats* in congregational prayer. Once the prayer was over, Elijah, Big Wizard, and Hitter let the crowd file out, leaving them alone except for a few people who were offering additional supplications or make-up prayers.

Big Wizard, Hitter, and Elijah huddled together and spoke in hushed tones. Big Wizard led the conversation. "What's the word?" he directed to Elijah.

"I've been thinking over everything. I know Unc talked to y'all . . ." Elijah looked around before continuing. "I think it's best we squash it."

Hitter and Big Wizard gazed at him with unreadable expressions, then looked at each other in silence.

"So just like that, you ready to wave the white flag?" Hitter asked.

"It's not just like that. In reality, we won. From the jump, I smacked the niggas who tried to slide on me. Then the homie damn near blew half Lil Tef's face off."

"But that don't change the fact that he made the effort to kill us. That makes him a threat still," Big Wizard pushed back.

"Yeah, he tried, but he failed," Elijah responded. "Think about all that we have goin' on. Why risk it for some miserable nigga with no goals and vision? We dealt with Cuzz; it's not like he got away scot-free with what he did. If he wanna bow down and ask us for peace, I say we put it behind us. They already ridin' around the Hood with pictures of us. Now they sayin' it supposed to be a warrant out on Lil Wiz. We don't even know what that's about yet. This war is just an added pitfall."

"If we did squash it on our part, how can you be certain he'll honor it?" Hitter said. "He might just use our guards down as an opportunity to strike again."

"That's just a risk we take. Ain't none of us 'bout to have our guards down anyways. Dudes don't know our moves as it is, and whenever we do come to the Hood, we strapped and ready to go at all times. Security is built into our daily lives, so I don't think that part is even worth sweatin'. We know niggas is tellin'. We can give them the word that the beef is over to go tell the pigs. That in itself would be wise on our part." Elijah looked at them, hoping for agreement.

"I don't know about this." Big Wizard stared an Elijah skeptically. "If he showin' his face again, this might be our opportunity to get rid of him once and for all before he go underground again."

"Lil 9 got a point though." Hitter surprised them. "We gotta always remember war is not personal in most instances. This is one of those times where it's just business. And from a purely business standpoint, the unnecessary attention this war brings isn't good."

Big Wizard scoffed. "The Quran tells us that when there is an open enemy, we are to slay them whenever we shall find them, for war is sometimes required as a test to see who will remain obedient."

Elijah nodded. "Yeah, but it also says to inflict blows that are equal to what was inflicted on you and not to transgress boundaries. When the steeds of war have been laid down against you in sincerity, turn back in compassion toward those who once fought you. Verily Allah rewards the righteous and those who don't transgress in war, these are the limits that has been set by Allah for the believers." Elijah quoted verbatim from the Holy Quran.

Hitter and Wizard were both shocked and amused that Elijah

knew the Quran enough to quote it.

Hitter laughed. "Looks like he got you on that one, Wiz."

Big Wizard smiled and extended his hand to Elijah. "Well said, soldier." He bowed his head slightly as they shook hands.

The tension left Elijah's body as he realized he had just overcome the first real hurdle in getting past this mess.

CHAPTER 17

E lise watched from the loading dock of a warehouse as one of Guzman's workers guided a box-truck slowly toward them. The constant beeping from the reverse warning light and squeaking brakes filled the otherwise empty alleyway. The back of the truck tapped the rubber-protected loading dock. Then the driver put it in park and hopped out. Both Mexican men wore dark blue Dickies work-suits with "Lopez's Air Conditioning Services" patches on the back and an embroidered nametag on the front shirt pocket. The driver unlatched the back and let the slide door roll upward, revealing the holding compartment filled with neat rows of boxes. They spoke in rapid-fire Spanish as they brought out a dolly and began unloading the boxes into the warehouse.

Elise waited until the last set of boxes were unloaded, then sealed the heavy iron door shut. She walked over to the small refrigerator, took out two cold Coronas, and handed them to the workers. She grabbed one of the boxes from the top of the stack, placed it on the floor, and cut it open with a switchblade.

Diabla came from the back office and joined them. Her long curly hair with blue highlights at the tips matched her blue Fila tracksuit and sneakers. She hovered over Elise as she removed one of the kilos of cocaine from what appeared to be an air-conditioning part. Elise handed the kilo to her over her shoulder, still kneeling.

Diabla went over to a different area that had a few work tools. She grabbed a box cutter and worked through all the vac-seal bags and packing tape that was used to preserve, conceal, and transport the cocaine.

Elise rummaged through some of the other boxes to get an accurate count of the kilos so there would be no discrepancy. She cut a rectangle hole at the top of one of the kilos and brought it over to Diabla.

Diabla examined it. "Yeah, this is A-1 quality." She beamed at the pearl marble texture and smelled it. "Strong and potent." She used the box cutter and dug into the open section of the brick for some powder. She put it on top of one of the boxes and used the butt end to crush it. She lifted some of the powder on the edge of the blade and said, "Allow me." She put it to her nose and inhaled deeply. She looked around the room with a new twinkle in her eye as she wiped the excess dust from her nose and sniffed in deeply to get the residue all the way through her nasal cavity.

"*Ven aquí y toma un poco,*" she offered the two workers. They rushed over, scooped out some cocaine, and snorted their own portion.

Elise watched them indulge. "*Uno momento,*" she told the two men and walked to the back office. She sat behind the brown wooden desk as Diabla followed her in, closing the door behind her.

"The tall one, Eduardo, is cool." She sat across the desk from Elise. "I can bait him in. He's just a worker, but he can give us all your connect's moves. We can take down a couple of their trucks. What you think for old times' sake?" She grinned wickedly.

"That's not even an option. The man they work for is my people. He's been good to me and my family. What, the money you're making isn't good enough for you?" Elise snapped.

"No, no, no . . . that's not it," Diabla retracted. "Didn't know they were your people like that. Just thought, maybe you know—"

"Don't think." Elise walked to the storage closet in the corner of the office. She opened it and wrestled with a large black duffle bag and slid it toward Diabla. "Take that out to them." She took a second duffle bag from the closet.

Diabla dragged the first bag across the floor back out to the two men.

Elise followed behind her dragging the other bag. They set the two bags in front of the men and unzipped them so they could see the neat stacks of bills.

"No need for dat," Eduardo said in broken English. "Boss says I good." He zipped the bags back up. He and his partner each grabbed a bag and headed out.

Elise and Diabla walked them out and watched from the loading dock as the two men loaded the duffle bags into the back of the truck and locked it shut. They climbed into the truck and slowly drove away from the loading dock.

Once they were out of sight, Elise sealed the loading dock door. They walked back into the warehouse.

"Let's get everything resealed and call the drivers," Elise directed. "Make sure each box has the same amount, so we don't mix up the count."

They went to work silently, removing the kilos out of the square air-conditioner compartments, and putting them in smaller UPS boxes in batches of fives. When they were finished, twenty professionally packed boxes lined one of the walls.

Diabla grabbed two cold beers from the fridge, and they kicked back in Elise's office.

Elise drained half the bottle in one swig. "It's a relief when all this shit is safely in hand."

"Tell me about it," Diabla agreed. "It's like you really accomplished something great when you get past all the so-called 'best police in the world.'" She laughed.

"Hell yeah. So are you gonna be able to handle a few more this time, or is the twenty-five going to be enough?" Elise directed the conversation back to business.

"Look, whatever you need me to handle, I can get them gone. My *tia* went up to Pelican Bay and got it cleared with one of the big homies to give me the supply chain for the homies from West LA all the way to Baldwin Park. I give him a weekly cut, and I'm good to go." She sipped from her bottle.

"Cool. I'll give you thirty of them this time then. I want you to split up the other seventy, thirty-five, thirty-five, and send one half to Iowa and the other half to Arkansas. Make sure they're packed and shipped right, no corner cutting."

"I got you, don't worry. Everybody knows what they supposed to do, and I stay on their ass to make sure they do it."

Elise nodded. "Any progress on what I got at you about on Lil Teflon?" She reached for her phone sitting on the desk.

"You know how we work. We gettin' our homework done first. Once everything is in place"—she bounced one hand off the other like an airplane taking off— "it'll be smooth sailing." She smirked.

*   *   *   *

Elise watched from the driver's seat of her Range Rover as the last driver drove away from the warehouse. Diabla, having orchestrated the loading of the stash cars and giving the drivers' their instructions, walked to her late-model white Corvette. She flashed Elise a big smile and a thumbs-up, then took off.

Elise smiled as Diabla burned rubber out the alleyway leaving a trail of Reggae music from her stereo system. Elise waited behind. She reflected on how far she had come in life and all the unexpected twists and turns that came with it, even her relationship with Diabla.

She knew she would eventually have to tell Elijah what she was doing. A part of her knew it was wrong to jump back into the drug game against his wishes, but that life was what she was good at. It made her feel alive. At times, she felt inadequate trying to function in the square world. She had not gone to college like Lauren. Hell, she did not even finish tenth grade. So when Lauren and Elijah were engrossed in their conversations about corporations, real estate, and such, she just listened quietly, feeling inadequate. The routine of her giving Lauren money to invest and waiting on the returns was beginning to feel like dependency. The new legal business ventures gave Lauren and Elijah much more time together; it appeared to her that their bond was growing deeper.

Being back in the game was her lane. She was able to control her investments how she saw fit. Elijah would be angry when he found out, but he would eventually get over it, she figured. It was just a matter of finding the right time and place to tell him.

The thought of that conversation sent a shiver up her spine, rattling her back to the hard reality of the present. The sun was setting. She needed to get home before her baby went to sleep.

* * * *

The sun was a dull orange globe as it descended for the evening. The streetlamps blinked on as Elijah turned onto Ninety-First Street. The street buzzed with activity; old women on their porches fanned themselves with paper fans and gossiped; the working-class residents pulled into their driveways or walked from the nearest bus stop returning home for the evening; children got their last dose of street football and Double Dutch in before curfew. The neighborhood addicts went about their business amid what seemed like a small black Utopia.

He loved South Central during these moments; there was no place on earth like it. Even with all his newfound wealth and the big house in Malibu, it still took real effort not to return to his childhood stomping grounds on a regular basis. But he found a way to stay out of the Hood as much as possible because deep down inside he knew that these peaceful moments were an illusion. The city could change courses in an instant. It was like an unseen dark evil spirit resided over this stretch of land, feeding off pain and sorrow, grief, death, and destruction. The streets were soaked with the blood of the youth. Many of the elders who came from the South to find work in the factories and a better life in LA had instead become a part of the nightmare. Even the drug-free hard-working Blacks had to deal with their sons and daughters being strung-out on crack, alcoholism, and stray bullets; no one was immune. Yet, many refused to leave; it was home.

He pulled into the driveway of his childhood home. There was a homie posted on the porch. He appeared to just be enjoying the fresh air, but Elijah knew better. There had to be an assault rifle, or some other weapon concealed close by. Big 9-Lives was not taking anything lightly.

He parked and turned off the engine.

The homie on the porch stood up and surveyed the block.

Elijah gathered his belongings from the passenger seat, tucking his pistol in his waist. He took a deep breath and exited the car.

"What's up wit' it, homie?" the brown-skinned, brawny youngster greeted Elijah.

"What's the deal?" Elijah approached him with a dap and a hug.

"Same shit. Just on deck."

"Hey, Elijah," a female voice came from the next yard over. Carmen, a girl he used to have a crush on in elementary school, smiled brightly and waved at him.

"Oh, what's up, Carmen. How you been?" Elijah flashed her a smile. She did not give him the time of day back then. She was the prettiest thing in the world to him: a smooth, dark-chocolate beauty with high cheekbones and full lips. Now, after twenty years, a few children, and a few kegs of beer too many, she was a worn out, obese shell of her former self.

"Shidd. I'd be a whole lot better if I had you around here more." She looked him up and down, thirsty.

"Watch out now; don't get yourself in trouble." Elijah obliged her bullshit for the fun of it.

"Um, I think I'd like that type of trouble," she shot back.

The homie on the porch chimed in. "Bitch, take yo' dusty ass back in the house somewhere. Don't nobody want you." He rolled his eyes, shaking his head.

"Fuck you, nigga. You just hatin' 'cause don't nobody want yo ass," she fussed with full ghetto-attitude.

"I don't want yo' nasty ass to want me—all them damn kids, wit' a million baby daddies. That pussy ain't no good no mo', it's trash."

Elijah burst into laughter at the exchange. "Y'all are burnt. I'm gone man." He rubbed the tears from the corner of his eyes, trying to compose himself. "Where Unc?"

"He in the garage." The homie gestured toward the back.

Elijah walked toward the back of the house and opened the door to announce his presence inside the home-style boxing gym. "Hey, Unc."

Big 9-Lives was already busy. "What's up, Neph?" He added weights to the bar.

"Same shit." His eyes roved over the gym's equipment. "See you gettin' money." He indicated to the sweat dripping from Big 9-Lives's brow.

"You know it. A nigga gettin' old and gotta stay fit to keep up with y'all crazy young motherfuckas."

Elijah chuckled. He scanned the space. Being here with his uncle was like déjà vu or being in a space frozen in time—nothing had changed. He could tell Big 9-Lives had given the place a thorough cleaning recently. The smell of bleach and Lysol mingled with perspiration filled the air. The same beat-up gray mat spread throughout the exercise area. A heavy punching bag hung from the ceiling in the corner; the accuracy bag suspended between two straps made for jabs and footwork; the speed bag, jump ropes, and free weights were all in their original place. Even the posters and autographed memorabilia, though a little worn, were still in place, just as his uncle Cannon had placed them.

His eyes lingered on the large photo of him as a kid in sparring gear with Cannon. The picture always sparked an array of emotions in him. He thought about all the times they had spent there together; Cannon teaching him not only about boxing but many lessons he would utilize throughout his life. There were still moments when he daydreamed about Cannon squeezing him in his signature bear hug and roughhousing with him as a kid. And even though the dreams were not as frequent, there were still times when they were so real that he felt like Cannon was visiting him. The thoughts were becoming too overwhelming. He averted his eyes.

Big 9-Lives rested, watching him. "Sup?" He worked his fingers into a pair of leather gloves with thumbtack holes.

He watched in disbelief that the gloves still fit Big 9-Lives's huge hands after all those years. "Aw, nothing. 'Bout to get some of this money with you." He undressed down to his wife beater and a pair of gym shorts. He grabbed his old pair of boxing shoes and tied them up tightly. He removed a roll of tape and wrap from a wooden box and brought them over to Big 9-Lives.

He wrapped Elijah's hands. This used to be their routine at least three times a week before they moved away.

Elijah slipped his heavily wrapped hands into the Spartan-padded mixed martial arts gloves, then moved into the sand-loaded heavy bag and went to work.

Big 9-Lives shook his head. "I done told your hard-headed ass a thousand times not to use those gloves on the heavy bag." He returned to his own workout. He lay back on the bench, braced his arms under the bar laden with heavy pig-iron plates on each side, and lifted it off the hooks. He pumped out ten hard reps bouncing off his chest.

The tapping of leather on leather and the clinking of weights was therapeutic in their silent sanctuary.

After a twenty-minute pounding on the heavy bag, Elijah stopped to take a water break. He took a bottle of water from the pack Big 9-Lives had sitting out.

Big 9-Lives finished another set, sat upright, and flexed his tight muscles. "So what's the deal?" He broke the silence.

"I talked to Hitt and Big Wiz," he responded between deep breaths. "We on one accord; it's time to squash this shit."

Big 9-Lives nodded. "Was it your call or theirs?"

"Mines. I mean, at the end of the day, smacking Lil Tef don't put no money in our—"

Big 9-Lives held up his hand and stopped him. "No need to explain." He grabbed a bottle of water. "I told you whatever you decided, I was with you. If this what makes more sense to you, then that's what it is." He poured a little water over his head, then took a small sip before twisting the top back on. "We tell Ju-Ju to get word to Big Tef that him and his brother's presence is wanted in the Set for a sit down. Big Tef been waitin' on our response since we had his ass hemmed-up over here last week. So I don't think it's gonna be a problem with him showin'. The question is Lil Tef."

Elijah sat down on the floor mat. "When and where you wanna have the sit down?"

Big 9-Lives paused for a minute. "What you think about doin' it up at Peso's shop over in Leimert Park? It'd be a neutral location, and I think Lil Tef would trust comin' to a spot where Peso is in control over rather than one of ours."

"I think that's a good call. When we aimin' for?"

"Next weekend."

"Nuff' said. I'll get on my part ASAP." Elijah lay on his back, eyes focused on the ceiling. A momentary silence filled the room. "Unc, I think we doin' the right thing."

Big 9-Lives lay back and lifted the bar off the rack. "Let's hope so," he said, and started another set.

* * * *

Agent Berrigan reclined in the passenger seat of a Buick with deep tint parked near the corner of Ninety-first and Budlong. He watched the verbal exchange between the young Black man, who was sitting on the porch of the Hassahn property, and an overweight woman on the other side of the fence. A few moments ago, Elijah Hassahn, a.k.a. Lil 9, had disappeared into the garage. He lowered the high-powered binoculars and checked his watch. He picked up his notepad and scribble rapidly in it.

His partner, sitting in the driver's seat, cut his eyes at him. "How long are we planning on being here?"

Agent Berrigan refocused his attention back on the Hassahn house. "However long it takes, buddy." He raised the binoculars again.

His partner reclined his seat, leaned back against the headrest, and closed his eyes. It was going to be a long night.

CHAPTER 18

The late evening traffic on Crenshaw was bumper-to-bumper. The fly guys were out in masse, showing off their old-school lowriders and new foreign cars, hunting for the women who circulated the Crenshaw strip in abundance. The Black-owned barbershops, art depots, clothing stores, and food spots were buzzing with foot traffic. The Leimert Park business district was one of the few remaining successful endeavors that the Black community called their own. The affluent elders from surrounding communities continued to hold on to their properties and circulate their Black dollars here. Now, many of the young Black aspiring entrepreneurs flocked to the area for their share of the pie. It was an unwritten rule that this was a neutral zone for the business owners who were former or active gang members. For this reason, gang members and hustlers, from all factions, businesses functioned here with hardly any problems; no one brought their beef. The underlying stabilizing force was the original Muslim and elder's presence.

Big 9-Lives and Peso stood in front of his communication shop on Forty-Third and Crenshaw, catching up on old times and the latest drama. Even with this being a neutral zone, Big 9-Lives had already set up a hidden security net that even Peso didn't know about. He was not going to let Elijah walk into this meeting without knowing for sure they were all walking out.

Big 9-Lives had Little Wizard sitting across the street in a café.

A briefcase containing a fully automatic MAC-11 rested at his feet as he enjoyed coffee and a sandwich. Big 1-Punch and two young Orchard block killers were staked out in a windowless van parked up the block a short distance away on the same side of the street as Peso's shop. They had a clear view from the front windshield of both sides of the street.

In the alley that ran behind the storefronts from Forty-Third to Vernon, Baby E.C. was given the task of laying low in the backseat of a tinted minivan with an assault rifle at ready. He covered the parking area in the back, watching everything coming and going from both ways with a clear view of the backdoor to Peso's shop.

A black Suburban SUV pulled next to the parked cars in front of Big 9-Lives and Peso. The SUV held up the already-jammed traffic as six individuals got out. The driver nonchalantly pulled off and headed to the alley to park.

Megatron and five Nine-Os hugged and dapped, exchanging polite greetings and small talk.

Back in the alley, the driver of the Suburban did not see Baby E.C. as he parked a few cars away. The extremely obese driver exited the car, moving swiftly for a man of his size. He halfheartedly attempted to pull up his gigantic Dickies to cover the top half of his exposed ass crack. The pants slid back down as he disappeared through the walkway that led to Crenshaw.

He joined the others at the front of the shop.

"What's up, Big Red?" Peso cheerfully greeted him.

"Ain't shit up, just the same ol struggle 'round this motherfucka," Big Red drawled in a barely audible tone. His smooth baby face gave him the appearance of a happy giant toddler, but that was a façade. Big Red was an OG Nine-O, one of the coldest killers and best fighters South Central had ever seen. This seemingly jolly stuffed teddy bear could turn into an over-sized real-life Chucky doll in an instant.

As they joked and jested, a five-man group appeared out of the McDonald's parking lot and waited on the corner of Forty-Third Street.

Big 9-Lives watched as they crossed the street. He recognized the Teflon brothers immediately. There was no mistaking Lil Teflon with his pronounced limp, even under the camouflage of his hoodie. Baby Devil and their usual crew flanked Lil Teflon on both sides. Big Teflon led the pack.

Their approach was met with silence and hard stares. The Teflon crew returned the sentiment with hard stares of their own. The air was thick with underlying animosity.

Peso broke the silence. "What's up, Cuzz?" He stepped forward and shook hands with both Teflon brothers.

The brothers' eyes did not stray from Big 9-Lives and the others as they shook hands with Peso.

"Y'all don't have to worry," Peso assured. "Nothing's gonna happen here but talk." He turned to Big 9-Lives and the others. "Look, this my place of business. I'm lettin' you niggas do this here as a favor because I know it's for the betterment of the Set. But I'm tellin' y'all now, don't disrespect my shit. If anything go down here, you better make sure I'm dead afterwards." He looked at each one of them, making sure his point was well taken.

"Don't trip, Loc, I gave you my word. We not gonna fuck up what you got goin' here," Big 9-Lives vouched for the group.

"Good. We goin' inside, but for the record, everybody gotta turn they straps in. I'm responsible for security here."

Everyone but Lil Teflon nodded. He was hesitant to give over his weapon. He lingered behind as they filed into Peso's shop.

Once inside, Peso's two brothers waited on both sides, collecting the weapons from everyone who entered. Peso's uncle, Knuckle, posted behind the counter with an eighteen-shot twelve-gauge street-sweeper clutched to his chest like a sentential guard.

Lil Teflon paused and looked around suspiciously. "Where's Lil 9 and them?" he called out to Big 9-Lives.

Peso answered before Big 9-Lives could respond. "I told you, man, you straight. The rest of the homies is comin'. Don't start makin' this more complicated than it already is." Peso held out his hand for the gun.

Lil Teflon looked from Peso to Big 9-Lives with uncertainty. Big Teflon had already turned over his own weapon, and he nodded at Lil Teflon to do the same. Reluctantly, Lil Teflon handed his gun over and walked further into the shop.

Peso signaled to one of his brothers, who walked outside and pulled the shutters on the front windows of the shop to obscure the view of passersby. He re-entered and locked the door behind him.

*   *   *   *

Elijah, Big Wizard, and Hitter sat at a table in the back of the nearby Coley's Jamaican restaurant having lunch as updates came through to them from a walkie-talkie discretely covered by a hat. Their plan was to only show up once they were certain the Teflon brothers were inside. After the message came that all the expected attendees were there, they finished eating, paid for their meal, and left.

Hitter took the lead, Big Wizard closely by his side, and Elijah covering the rear. They moved in sync as they cut through the parking lot, nodding to Baby E.C. in the van as they stealthily passed by. Hitter approached the back door to Peso's shop first, pulled out his pistol, and checked it. Big Wizard and Elijah followed suit. They scanned the parking lot. When it was all clear, Hitter tapped lightly on the door.

Ju-Ju opened the door discretely and nodded as he let them in and shut the door behind them. He pointed to the open doorway that led to the front of the shop. Chattering voices spilled from the front.

Elijah, Hitter, and Big Wizard tucked their pistols in their waistbands, making sure the weapons were concealed. They stepped inside and headed to the front.

The talking ceased and all eyes fell on them as soon as they entered the room.

Elijah immediately locked eyes with Lil Teflon. Seeing Lil Teflon's face after all these years incensed him. All the emotions that he thought he had rationalized away reared up again. A white rage washed over him. It wasn't simply the fact that Lil Teflon tried to kill him; it was the fact that Elijah once loved him like a brother. The betrayal of it all twisted the knot in his stomach into pure hatred. It took everything in him not to snap. His adrenaline pumped wildly. He wrestled with the urge to shoot Lil Teflon in the face right there in front of everyone. As Hitter and Wizard exchanged greetings with some of the homies in attendance, Elijah and Lil Teflon seemed to exist outside of the chatter going on around them, locked in the grips of their shared animosity. Elijah's hand unconsciously moved toward his hidden pistol.

"You straight, Neph?" Big 9-Lives gripped his shoulder.

Elijah snapped back into the reality of the full room. He stared at his uncle momentarily, bewildered. "Uh . . . yeah. Yeah, I'm straight, Unc."

"Let's get this thang goin' then." Big 9-Lives gestured to Peso. He walked over and sat down in an empty chair in a corner section of the shop that was cleared out for the meeting.

Peso got everyone's attention. "Hey, y'all, let's get the show on the road. Everybody grab a seat."

Each group took up seats except Hitter, who elected to stand near a case that held an array of phone accessories.

Peso stood in the middle of the circle. "As everybody here know, I'm not on nobody's side. I'm just here to give y'all a safe place to talk. If you need my opinion or input on some shit y'all talkin' about, I'm cool with doin' that. But don't ask me if you don't want my unbiased truth. So this how its gon' go: Nobody talk over the next man. Let everybody that got something to say have an opportunity to say it without niggas interrupting. Let's keep it civil and respectful." With that, Peso took a seat.

After a silent pause, Big 9-Lives pointed to Big Teflon. "The floor's yours first, youngin'."

Big Teflon looked around the room nervously. "Well . . . I mean . . . shit. Just like, I don't know. I just want all of us to come together to get this shit over with." He looked at Elijah then to his brother. "Y'all need to work this shit out."

"Lil Teflon, I wanna hear what you got to say," Big Red said through labored heavy breathing. "From what I've been told, you the one set all this bullshit in motion. So what's up with you?"

Lil Teflon studied Big Red with a glint of amusement in his eyes. He cleared his throat and started slowly, "I'm the one who ended up with bullets to the face. So I don't know why everybody automatically think I was the one who started all the bullshit. To me, Lil Wiz the one who started the bullshit I'm on. And I don't think it's a coincidence that Cuzz not here today."

"What you insinuating?" Big Wizard asked. "That Lil Wiz scared to be here or something? Because we can get him in here right now if that's what you really want." He did not try to disguise the implied threat.

"I don't give a fuck if he do come," Lil Teflon shot back.

"So what you sayin', nigga?" Big Wizard stood up aggressively. Hitter straightened up, ready to lean in.

Elijah and Big 9-Lives stood up.

Big Teflon stood up and tried to diffuse the situation. "Bro, chill."

Lil Teflon was ready for action. "Whatever you want me to be sayin', nigga. It's whatever with me." His brother placed a hand on his chest to stop him.

"Hold up, niggas!" Big 9-Lives stepped in. "Y'all better pull yo' motherfuckin' selves together. We gave the homie our word that we wouldn't disrespect the shop, and that's what it's gon' be, period!"

Both sides calmed down and reeled it back, but they shot daggers at each other from across the room.

Big 9-Lives continued, "Lil Tef, you actin' like you came here lookin' for static. If that's the case, why did you even come? We can end this talk right now and niggas go for what they know when they leave here."

"I ain't lookin' for static, big homie. I came because Bro said niggas wanted to squash the animosity. But I feel like I'm gettin' verbally attacked from all sides. I'm with settling shit, but niggas ain't gon' treat me like I'm a bitch though."

"Ain't nobody tryna treat you like no bitch. But, nigga, you did get this shit started. Bottom line, you was dead wrong." Big 9-Lives dressed him down. "You and Lil Crip from U-G pulled some bullshit. You got with a nigga from another Hood to move on a homie—a real one. That's my nephew nigga." He pointed to Elijah. "How fuckin' dare you try to move against one of mine. I'm one of the reasons that Nine-O even exist, nigga. I raised you lil punk."

"Let's keep it respectful, big homie—" Peso began.

"Nah, fuck that," Big 9-Lives cut him off, his anger now overruling his reason. "Lil nigga, I oughta snap yo' fuckin' neck." Big 9-Lives loomed over Lil Teflon. "The only reason this talk is happenin' is because my nephew asked me to reconsider it. So don't walk in here with this tough-guy act like niggas don't know the full extent of what you did. You got yo' face pushed in because you forgot who the fuck you was dealin' with. I'm Big 9-Lives, the Loc around here, nigga. Nothing moves with the Budlongs unless I say so. So whatever beef you got toward Lil Wiz, aim it at me because I'm the one who gave the word to peel yo' fuckin' cap," he spat with venom.

Shock ran through the whole room. Even Elijah, Hitter, and Big Wizard were surprised by this revelation. Elijah had always assumed Lil Wizard tried to snuff Lil Teflon for his own personal reasons. Lil Wizard was a loose cannon who often acted as a lone wolf. The fact that his uncle sanctioned the hit without telling him stunned him.

Lil Teflon's face froze; his eyes wide like a deer caught in headlights.

Big 9-Lives composed himself and walked back to his seat, letting his words sink in. He crossed his legs and stared at Lil Teflon casually. "So the ball's in your court. Is this something you gonna be able to get over and we put this thing behind us, or do you wanna try your hand at the title again?"

"Wait, wait, wait, wait." Big Red held up his hand to speak. "Just so I can be sure I know what y'all sayin', because this the first time a lot of us hearin' all the details. It's been all these rumors and shit, but I see niggas been keepin' what's really goin' on under wraps." He put his hand on his chin and cocked his head to the side. "So you mean to tell me that a Nine-O plotted with an Underground to kill a Nine-O?" he asked no one specifically.

Lil Teflon squirmed under the scrutiny of his actions.

"That's 'bout the sum of it," Big 9-Lives answered, still staring Lil Teflon down.

Lil Teflon and Big Teflon turned their attention elsewhere and shifted in their seats.

"If that's what really happened," Big Red continued, "I don't know how you let Cuzz get away with that. The Hood didn't know all the details, but now that this part is out, this is the ultimate violation."

"It is. But they shot Cuzz up for doin' it, ain't that enough?" Megatron chimed in.

A chorus of grumbling filled the room, some agreeing, some disagreeing.

Megatron continued, "I'm just sayin', if we say this the ultimate violation and do something more to Lil Tef, then we gotta do something to Big Tef and the niggas that fuck with them. Where would be the end? And just to keep it all the way real, it's a lot of niggas in the Hood who feel like the niggas with all the money ain't lookin' out enough. Maybe he went about it a little extreme, but he might was just feelin' some type of way. I say each side wipe the slate clean and let's start over. Homies gon' make mistakes, that's just how it is."

Hitter leaned from the wall and put in his two cents. "Don't nobody give a fuck about niggas feelin' like they not gettin' enough from us. We don't owe none of you niggas shit. Y'all broke asses wanna sit around gettin' high and drunk all day and lay up on your fat bitches waitin' on their county checks, that's your fault. Tell all the niggas that feel some way to go get a motherfuckin' job or sell some ass or something. We work hard for ours; nobody gave us shit. So you can miss me with all the we-owe-the-hood shit. Take that to some niggas that ain't punchin' they clock. It ain't no nigga in the Set with more enemies under they belt than us."

"I'm just sayin' Cuzz…" Megatron tried to stand his ground.

"You ain't sayin' shit nigga." Hitter cut him off.

Peso stepped in. "Let's not get off course. Megatron, you goin' into a whole 'nother topic. This is about squashing a beef. It ain't about airing out Hood grievances about money." He turned to Elijah. "At the end of the day, only you and Lil Teflon can make this shit end or continue, and we haven't even heard nothing from either of you really. Lil 9, where you at on this?"

Elijah gritted his teeth as he stared at Lil Teflon. *The nerve of this ugly motherfucka sittin' in front of me like he the shit,* he thought. He glared at the disfiguration and burns on Lil Teflon's face. He momentarily couldn't bring himself to speak. Gradually, his sense of reason came back. He had to set his ego aside and put on his politician's hat for the betterment of all. "Where you at with it, Cuzz?"

"I thought me bein' here said where I'm at. If we gon' squash it, I'm with it," Lil Teflon replied, stone faced.

Elijah studied him intently. "I don't wanna keep draggin' this meeting out with all these different opinions. What happened or didn't happen in the past is really not the point right now. It is what it is. It's about how we rollin' forward. You struck at us, we struck at you, so let's leave it at that. It's no secret that we can never be friends, or even homies, ever again. But we can stay in our own lanes and not have to look over our shoulders for each other."

"I'm with that." Lil Teflon nodded.

"If these two good with it, then that should deaden it," Peso added eagerly. "Big 9-Lives, we good here?"

"If Neph good, then I'm good." Big 9-Lives stood up and walked over to Elijah. Everyone took that as an indication that the meeting was ending. The group stood up and moved around the room, handshaking, sealing the Nine-O truce.

"Unc, I hope this shit for real 'cause it took everything in me not to do something to that snake-ass nigga."

Big 9-Lives nodded. "I know," he whispered. "All we can do is wait and see how this shit play out. But I will say this, if them niggas go back on they word and try some funny shit, Imma flood these LA streets with they blood . . . and that's on Hood."

CHAPTER 19

———— ❧ ————

Drinks floated around, weed smoke filled the air of the dimly lit room, and lines of cocaine-covered plates sat on the coffee table. Voices and laughter mingled with the music blasting from the stereo system in the Neighborville hut. Lil Teflon and the youngsters were in full party mode for the night.

He snorted a line of cocaine and flopped back on the couch. His attention drifted over to Baby Devil who was dancing flirtatiously with Murder-Min. She laughed and moved suggestively as he touched her. He whispered in her ear; she giggled, smile beaming, a rarity for her.

"Baby Dev," he called out, waving Baby Devil to come sit next to him.

"What's up, Cuzz?" Baby Devil drank from his bottle and sat down.

Lil Teflon put his arm around his shoulder. "It's about that time again, lil homie," he slurred with a smile.

"Time for what?" Baby Devil's attention was focused on Murder-Min.

"For another big lick. What you think? I been havin' my eye on this bank in Canoga Park. It'll be a piece of cake. All we—"

"Nah, my nigga." Baby Devil stopped him in his tracks. "Me and the homies off them banks. That's old shit. We boomin' off the work. Only licks we hittin' is if we catch a nigga slippin' with some bread, jewelry, or dope."

Lil Teflon clenched his jaw. He knew he had to stay calm and not show his irritation, but Baby Devil's constant opposition was eating him up. "Damn, since when you start speakin' for Droopy and them? And I'm talkin' that real money. Getting it in chunks like we used to. Not this nickel-and-dime shit you got goin' here."

"The game safer than bank robberies. You see how all the Sixties and Four-Trays got wrapped up by the feds with football numbers for that shit? And I'm just sayin, if I'm not gon' do it myself, I wouldn't ask the homies to do it."

"Is that right?" Lil Teflon looked at Murder-Min in the corner talking to one of the homegirls from the Hundreds. "I see you got it all figured out now."

"I ain't got it all figured out, but I'm not a lil kid no more either."

"What's that supposed to mean?" He squinted his eyes at Baby Devil.

"Just that I'm not that same crash dummy I was before. If it's something that makes sense to me, I'm with you ten-toes-down. But if it don't make sense, then I'm not with it." Baby Devil glared back, unflinching.

Lil Teflon stared at him with no emotions. A smile slowly creased his lips. "I feel you. Look at my nigga, he done grew up on me." He turned back toward the activities. "You gotta do what you feel is right to you."

"Fasho, and Murda's what feel right to me tonight." Baby Devil laughed and pushed up from the couch.

Lil Teflon grabbed his wrist. "Hold up my boy, damn. You

wanna take my bitch too?"

Baby Devil looked at Lil Teflon's hand gripping his wrist, then up at him. "Yo *bitch*?" He grinned. "I thought she was the homegirl? We been flippin' Murda. What, something changed?"

Lil Teflon loosened his grip on Baby Devil's wrist. "Nah, I mean, ain't nothin' changed but . . ." he stuttered.

"Come on, Cuzz, not the infamous Lil Teflon-Black." Baby Devil laughed in his face. "I know you ain't forgot, me and Murda was out here ridin' for you when you was laid up. Me and her got close over that period. But damn, that didn't make me wanna try and cuff her. You ready to cuff her now, my nigga? Say it ain't so."

"Hell nah." He let out a fake snicker. "If she with it, I ain't go never save a bitch. Nigga, what you thought?"

"Say no more then." Baby Devil swagged over to Murder-Min. He whispered in her ear and caressed her ass. She blushed and rubbed up against his crotch. He grabbed her hand and they walked toward the backroom. He looked back at Lil Teflon sitting on the couch and smiled. "You said it ain't no fun if the homies can't have none, right my nigga?" He threw his head back in laughter as they disappeared down the hallway.

Lil Teflon watched with a sour smile until they were out of sight. His smile melted into a disfigured scowl as he continued staring at the empty hallway.

"What's up, baby? You partyin' by yo'self?"

Lil Teflon gazed up at the sexy, young cutie wearing a miniskirt and a short halter top showing off her midriff. He smiled and pulled her onto his lap. "Nah, baby. The party just started." He ran his hand up her skirt as she giggled and wiggled on his lap. "The saga continues . . ." He grinned ominously.

CHAPTER 20
SIX MONTHS LATER

———————— ❧ ————————

Droopy, Skip, Lil Bar-Dog, and P-Nut, a new Nine-O recruit, pulled into the liquor store parking lot on Ninety-Second and Western in Skip's baby-blue 1977 Cutlass supreme on Daytons. They all hopped out of the car. Skip quickly reached under the seat and retrieved a pistol. He handed it to P-Nut as they hurried to make the last liquor run of the night before the store closed.

The crackheads and winos loitered near the side entrance drinking and telling old war stories of their past glory. The four youngsters passed them, exchanging a few words before entering the store. They headed to the refrigerated glass cases with the cold liquor. Skip selected the drinks while Droopy and Lil Bar-Dog argued back and forth about who was the best LA Lakers' player, Shaq or Kobe. P-Nut waited silently near the counter, observing more than doing.

Skip set the bottles of beer and wine on the counter and looked past the cashier to the hard liquor on the shelves behind him. "Let me get a fifth of Seagram's gin, and a fifth of Hen." He pointed out the bottles to the cashier.

The cashier grabbed the bottles, put them on the counter, and rung up the items.

"Get a couple bags of chips too," Skip told Droopy.

"What kind?"

"It don't matter, nigga, some Doritos or something."

Droopy walked to the potato chip rack and surveyed it for a moment. "Nigga act like I'm da muda-fuckin' chip-getta or somethin'," he mumbled, and settled on the Cool Ranch Doritos. He brought the bags of chips to the counter and tossed them next to the liquor.

The cashier added them to the tab. Skip pulled out a wad of bills, peeled a fifty off the top, and handed it to the cashier. Droopy and Lil Bar-Dog went back to their debate as Skip collected his change.

They walked out the side door that led straight to the parking lot, shooting the shit as they walked to the car. Skip chirped the alarm from his keychain and walked to the driver's side. The others went to the other side of the car.

Out of his peripheral vision, Skip saw the crackheads and winos scattering.

P-Nut attempted to reach for the gun in his pocket, but he never got a change to pull it out. "Watch out—" P-Nut shouted.

A single shot to the head swept P-Nut off his feet. He landed between the Cutlass and the car parked next to it.

Skip spun around and saw a dark-skinned man with a perm, who was wearing a Texas Ranger baseball cap and blue bandana tied around the bottom half of his face.

A succession of rapid shots rang out as the shooter wielding the .9mm aimed his next shots at Droopy and Lil Bar-Dog, who were on the passenger side of the car next to P-Nut. They immediately fled, attempting to dodge the barrage of bullets. Lil Bar-Dog dipped low between the cars, running for Western. Droopy ran left toward Ninety-Second. A bullet pierced his back before he reached the edge of the lot. He hit the ground and crawled under a parked car.

Skip dropped the liquor bottles and bolted between cars toward Ninety-Second Street. The resounding blasts from the gun followed him through the night as the bullets whizzed past his head. He zigzagged, ducked, and dodged until he was able to open into a full sprint down Ninety-Second and up Hobart.

After Skip disappeared around the corner and the shooter saw no more movement, he turned his attention back to P-Nut. He walked over to the motionless body and aimed the pistol at his face.

"Nacho-ass, nigga, Eighty-Third Street." He emptied the rest of the clip in P-Nut's face. The killer's face contorted into a sinister grimace as he turned and fled through the dark alley behind the liquor store.

*   *   *   *

A large group of homeboys and homegirls watched from the corner of Ninety-Second Street as the paramedics loaded Droopy's wounded body into the back of the ambulance on a stretcher. The EMTs hopped in and sped off with the sirens blaring and the emergency lights flashing. The parking lot was being taped off as a succession of black-and-whites and detectives arrived on the scene.

Cones were set up near the empty shell casings. Pictures were being taken of P-Nut's sprawled-out body with a nearly unrecognizable partially blown-off face. Skip took in the carnage with tears in his eyes. This was like a bad nightmare that he wanted to wake up from. It could not be real. He wanted to walk over to P-Nut and tell him it was okay; he could wake up now. They had just been talking and laughing together—how could this be? He thought of the Eight Tray gangster who was holding that gun, and rage surged through his veins. He pounded his fist into his hand and cried tears of sorrow and vengeance.

"Fuck that, Cuzz!" he screamed as he walked toward the cluster of police behind the yellow tape surrounding the body. Lil Bar-Dog stopped him before he breached the perimeter and wrapped his arms around him to support and restrain him.

"Nah, Cuzz, nah. Don't do that to yourself," he spoke into Skip's ear through broken sobs.

"We gotta get the homie, Cuzz, he gotta wake up." Skip dropped his face into Lil Bar-Dog's shoulder and bawled. "Them bitch-ass niggas killed the homie."

Baby Devil sped up on the scene in his Chevy. He slammed it into park and jumped out. "What happened, Cuzz?" he asked the crowd. "Who's that over there?"

"That's young P-Nut," a homegirl responded. "They just took Droopy to the hospital. He got shot in the back."

Baby Devil shook his head. "Who did it?" he demanded, enraged.

"Skip said the Tramps," her voice cracked.

Baby Devil spotted Skip and Lil Bar-Dog and bee-lined for them. He embraced them in solidarity and shared grief.

"The Tramps caught us slippin' . . . killed the homie," Skip uttered through sobs.

"We gon' fix this shit, Cuzz; we gon' fix it," Baby Devil assured.

Skip tried to gain his composure. "Come on, let's go get them niggas." He wiped away tears.

"Not right now. Let's get to the hospital first to make sure Droop straight." Baby Devil led the way back to the crowd. They gathered around him for instructions.

"Everybody with cars go get 'em. We 'bout to caravan up to Killer King to make sure Droop straight." He called over to a baby-faced Nine-O who was walking toward the vehicles.

Baby Devil pulled Baby Grape to the side. "Take two or three homies with you and y'all go through the Tramps and lay something down before y'all come to the hospital," he whispered.

Baby Grape nodded his understanding, ready to earn his stripes.

"Go to the spot and tell Yo-Yo to give y'all the M-1 and the Tech."

"Got it. I'm finna have Lil Kaos go get the g-ride and meet me over there." Baby Grape eagerly started on his mission.

"BG?" Baby Devil stopped him in mid-stride. "Not no drive-by shit. Make sure some of them niggas is stiff before I see you again."

"On Ninety Crip," Baby Grape responded, and trotted off up Western Avenue.

Baby Devil turned to the rest of the crowd. "Let's roll out," he shouted.

They piled into the cars scattered around the crime scene. Baby Devil led the caravan, each vehicle falling in line, as they headed to Martin Luther King Jr. Hospital a.k.a. "Killer King."

CHAPTER 21

A tap on the conference-room door stopped Elijah in midsentence. The secretary eased in quietly holding a tray with cups of hot coffee. She set the tray on a small table in the corner and left the room.

"Where was I?" Elijah paused and studied the dry-erase board covered with illustrations of his business plan.

Big Wizard, Hitter, and Big 9-Lives lounged in the soft leather seats around an elongated table positioned to give a spectacular view of Downtown LA from the floor-to-ceiling glass wall.

"You was just gettin' to the real estate part." Big Wizard glanced over his written notes.

"Oh yeah." He pointed at the diagram marked "REAL ESTATE." "The real estate is the cornerstone because the ultimate future goal is to buy back the Hood. But we all know it takes a ton of capital. So that's why each of these has to come into play." He pointed to the other diagrams on the board. "We got entertainment and music here, corporations and LLCs, and small businesses."

"And each of us supposed to start these specific businesses?" Hitter rapidly scribbled notes on his pad.

"Nah," Elijah responded. "To start, us in this room will put up two hundred thousand a piece to start an LLC—that will basically be an investment corp. I'll put some of it toward my music projects with my existing company. I'm already in talks with some of the majors, and if that take off, I'll have our new company down as an investor which could give us a nice amount of bread from an established source. With all what we got and get in the LLC, we'll start buying multiunit rental properties, commercial properties, and we create a nonprofit community center."

"OK, I'm gettin' what you sayin.'" Hitter nodded.

"But is eight hunnit bands really gon' do it?" Big 9-Lives interjected. "I mean, when you start talkin' about apartment buildings and commercial properties and shit, you talkin' about tickets not thousands. And we damn sure better have solid accounts and sources where we can show where this start-up money came from."

"Believe me, Unc, I've thought about all that. I'll make sure all the I's are dotted and T's are crossed. And we don't have to buy everything cash. There'll be banks and lenders lining up to approve us for credit lines, especially when we start making that initial bread bubble right before their eyes over a period of time. I already got accountants and the right people on deck to make it all flow." Elijah smiled smugly.

"Gotcha, gotcha." Big Wizard jotted down another note.

"So you say you eventually want to involve others. How'd that work?" Hitter asked.

"This is where the shit gets big." Elijah excitedly rubbed his hands together. "We start gettin' with hood captains from other hoods after we prove the success of our model. We get with niggas, not based on some bullshit ceasefire or trying to corner the drug market, but on a real alliance. We show them how to set up LLCs of their own. Then we use the homies who aren't the hustlers, but the shooters and squabblers to be enforcers. All the businesses in the

Hood that aren't run by the appointed and approved heads of the agreement, the enforcers will make them pay taxes or force them to sell to the corporations. This way, the money will go in a circle and everybody will eat. If we start redirecting the focus, we can put an end to all these stupid-ass beefs that we been in for decades because all the heads throughout the city will be on one accord."

Big Wizard raised an eyebrow. "I'm gettin' us four working together, but you gonna have to go into a lil more detail with how you plan on bringing all these other cats into play."

"Alright, look . . ." Elijah erased a portion of the board, then picked up a marker and drew a diagram with three connecting boxes. "The corporations will be in tiers—five men to each one, for as many as it takes." He tapped the top box. This would be a holding company, the parent company for the companies to come. We'll have to get with the real power players to form this one. It'll be created by millionaires, and million-dollar moves will be made with this company. This company will dribble down to these . . ." He tapped the middle box. "The middle tier. Each company on this tier will be formed by five people with a hundred bands a piece. A half-million is a nice start-up company under the right guidance, and we'll provide that." He tapped the last box. "In the final tier, these can be done by groups of five with twenty-five bands a piece. All of these businesses—from the top to the bottom—will exchange goods and services with each other. I'm tellin' y'all we'll kill 'em. The shit can transform a whole generation. This is just a general explanation." He put the cap on the marker, tossed it on the table, and sat down. He had spent a lot of time on the plan and had worked out all the details. He knew that if they could execute it, it'd be beyond big.

Big 9-Lives sipped his coffee as he thought over the prospect.

"Where did you come up with this idea, Cuzz?" Big Wizard

asked, intrigued.

"Man, brainstorming." Elijah sat back and folded his arms. "It's like, being part of both worlds. The legal and the streets gave me this opportunity to see how money flows through both and how they could connect. Then, you know I ain't super religious, but I really take my lil interactions with the Nation serious. A lot of the Dogma I ain't really with, but they got a lot of game when it comes to community-building. I be sucking that shit up. Every book he's given me I really study it."

The minister at Temple-27 had given Elijah a series of books on Meyer Lanski and Lucky Luciano. At first, he didn't understand why the minister gave him that type of literature, but then it dawned on him that it was all relative to what he was trying to accomplish.

Elijah continued. "For the street element, we can't do no peace and love, get-a-job shit; it's not gon' work. We got to organize with a combination of force and solid economics, where everybody can play a part and see the progress."

Hitter scribbled on his writing tablet. "All the business stuff as far as us here in the room, I see how that can maybe work as long as everybody egos stay in check." He set his pen down. "But this mass movement, with a bunch of different hoods and personalities, that's a tall task, lil bro. You know P-Nut got puffed last night. How can you tell them young niggas at a time like this that we cease-firing with the Tramps? You wouldn't have been able to convince me of that when we was knee deep in the wars and before we had the opportunity to chip a bunch of 'em."

Elijah sighed. He knew this would be a hard sell, but the vision was there. He just needed the right people to buy into it, and that included other hoods, even some that the Nine-Os considered their enemies. "I know this not gonna be some just wave-the-magic-wand

and everything happens overnight. It's gonna take a lot of planning and politicking on our part. And of course, it got to be right timing. As far as our initial company and egos gettin' in the way, this not no street shit. We'll set up a board with members who have voting power. Nobody's gonna move on their own accord. All decisions will be made by a majority vote. All finances comin' in and goin' out will be transparent. So that's not even an issue. When it gets to the rest of the plan, it won't be easy; but it's not impossible either. Shit, y'all already do it on the street level with your Muslim comrades—you got Bloods, Gangstas, and Rollins all in the same room based on family ties. This is just takin' the next step."

Big Wizard nodded. "Yeah, that's a part of the secret sauce that keep things flowin' smooth on our end."

Elijah rested his clasped hands on the table. "At the end of the day, power and organization moves the world. We wouldn't start off tryin' to build with our immediate surrounding enemies. We start off with tightening up our alliances we got now. It's this new thing where it's not just the Rollin car from the Forties to the Hundreds no more. Everybody startin' to emphasize 'Neighborhood Crip' now. It's all these lil sets hoppin' on board throughout the city. So we use this model with the neighbors first. At the same time, we build with people we already got in our circles from different sets. Now we just get them to start tryin' to bring parts of their sets on board to the program."

Elijah sat in silence as he let his words to sink in. He wanted them to get on board with his plan. He knew that if he couldn't convince them, it would be almost impossible to convince the others.

Big 9-Lives broke the silence. "Like I told y'all before. It's y'all time to take this thing to the next level. I'll lend my support where you need it, but for the most part, I'm out ya way. I believe this is a helluva blueprint. But like Hitt said, it's gon' take a lot of work to implement it. You gotta remember, Neph, you not just dealing with Black people; you dealing with Black people from the Hood. You'll have some jump on board, but some will oppose it just because. Somewhere along the line, we been taught as a people not to respect the leadership of our own. Everyone think they're qualified to be leaders and always wanna voice they dumb-ass opinion."

"The Willie Lynch doctrine," Big Wizard chimed in.

"Exactly." Big 9-Lives nodded. "It's become second nature to be jealous and envy each other. We are our own worst enemy."

Elijah got up and walked to the window. "I know all that. But everybody evolved at some point in their history." He stared out at the city. "The Italian and Jewish gangs in New York back in the day didn't stay doin' the same shit. Like I said, they ain't no better than us. All it takes is a little vision and the nuts to carry it out."

Big Wizard stood. "It goes without saying that you got us wherever we needed. But I wanna shoot something at you real quick."

Here it come, always a negotiation with Wiz, he thought. "Shoot."

"Well, you know it's been a minute since we been gettin' down." Big Wizard walked around the conference table, sat on top of it, and folded his arms. "But we feel it's time again. We kicked back and let some of the heat die down, and now it's time to get back to the loot."

"You ready to get back in the game?" Elijah was perplexed at the notion. Big Wizard and Hitter were millionaires. They didn't need to hustle anymore. Why would they take the risks with all the madness going on in the streets? The feds were already sniffing around, and they needed to stay out of the way as much as possible.

"Yep. Just like you got your goals, we got ours." Big Wizard smirked.

Anger swirled through Elijah. "Why would you wanna go back to that route when I just spelled out some shit that's gonna get us paid the legal way? On top of that, it's no possible way we can be in business together running a corporation with y'all fuckin' with coke. It can crash everything I've been workin' toward."

"You right. That's why me and Hitt's name will never be on any of the paperwork to the company. We'll just be ghost investors. You let my niece sit on the board or give her some phony title, CEO or some shit, I don't know." He waved dismissively.

Elijah shook his head, trying to make sense of the request. "I guess, man. Anyway, how does y'all wantin' to get back in the game have anything to do with me?"

"We want the plug," Big Wizard responded bluntly.

He laughed and grabbed the eraser from the table. "I haven't dealt with my guy in years." He erased the content from the board.

"But you still speak to him?" Hitter asked.

"Yeah, I do. That don't mean we do business." He and Guzman maintained a friendly relationship, although they no longer did business together. Elijah had tremendous respect and admiration for Guzman for giving him the opportunity to make millions, and the man didn't begrudge him when he was ready to get out of the game. When Guzman visited the States, they did the occasional dinner together and caught a boxing match in Las Vegas once or twice yearly.

"Well, I need you to holla at him. Just open the door for me."

Big Wizard gathered his belongings. "This can help what you tryin' to accomplish too."

"How's that?" Elijah asked, skeptical. He considered Guzman a friend. Big Wizard had to come up with something good for him to even consider the request.

"Because once we start tryin' to bring niggas into the fold, it would be a extra incentive for them if we got the pipeline to all the dope and guns. You would never have to associate yourself with that part of it—I'll orchestrate that end. You can have a stash out of every shipment that will go to making sure your agenda gets pushed."

Elijah thought for a minute. "Let me sleep on it. I'll let you know something soon."

"Don't sleep too hard or too long." Big Wizard laughed, and hand signaled to Hitter, "It's time to roll, bro."

They all dapped and hugged.

Big Wizard and Hitter hurried out the room.

Elijah and Big 9-Lives watched them leave, then stared at each other in silence.

CHAPTER 22

Baby Devil led a group of thirteen Nine-O Tiny Toons through the sliding doors at Martin Luther King Hospital. A couple of weeks had passed since the shooting at the liquor store. They did not bother to stop at the reception desk; they walked straight to the elevator. As they waited, others in the area gawked at them with wary eyes. A security guard started walking their way, but he abruptly stopped and pulled out his walkie-talkie, rethinking his stance. He spoke into it, watching them closely.

The elevator arrived. Baby Devil and the rowdy group joked and laughed loudly as they waited for the elevator to empty out. After an apprehensive older Mexican woman timidly exited, they all filed in. They continued their raucous until they arrived at the sixth floor. As the elevator door parted, four security awaited them. Baby Devil mad-dogged them as he brushed past. "Excuse me, sir, you have to check in with the receptionist." One of the security guards stepped forward attempting to stop him.

"For what? We know where we goin'," Baby Devil responded over his shoulder.

"Yeah, but they have to log in all visitors, and there can only be two visitors in at a time," the second security guard added hesitantly.

Baby Devil stopped and walked up to the first guard. "Do it look like we give a fuck about the visiting policy? You already know what it is. I'm sure you been workin' here long enough to know how the Crips do it when we come up here. Don't try to act brave today. We comin' to see our homie. Give us thirty minutes and we out, no problems."

The nurses at the nurses' station watched nervously. The security guards postured, ready to challenge the group. "Don't y'all come up here with no mess now." An older Black nurse got up and walked around the desk. "Who y'all here to see?" She made her way to Baby Devil.

"Donte Williams," Baby Devil answered in a respectful tone.

"Oh, that little hurt boy in 608." She looked him up and down. "That's your brother?"

"Nah, that's my homie."

"What the hell do that mean . . . homie?"

"My friend," he corrected.

"I'm gon' let you in for fifteen minutes."

"Ma'am?" the security guard attempted to protest.

"Un-un-un." She raised her hand to silence him. "I got it. They not gon' give any problems. Let them see their friend and leave. We don't need to cause any fuss, disturbing the patients with the police and all that." She turned back to the group. "Y'all don't give me no problems now. Go in and check on him then get outta here before you get me in trouble." She walked back to her seat. "And pull up y'all damn pants," she added.

"Yes, ma'am," the group intoned, some chuckling.

They walked silently toward room 608. The gravity of where they were set in. They passed by rooms occupied by incapacitated patients—tubes and wires running through their nose and mouths, machines beeping the only signs of life. The hospital was nicknamed "Killer King" for a reason. It had the highest rate of DOAs by gunshot wounds in the city. The trauma unit was considered one of the best because they treated so many mortally wounded patients. It was short staffed, with some of the meanest Black and Hispanic nurses. The recovery stay was often a nightmare. But the poor and uninsured did not have too many options, so they had to deal with it.

They walked through the door to Droopy's room. He lay in the bed on his back, weak and semi-conscious. His head tilted toward them and a faint smile flashed across his face. A large white tube ran from a machine into an incision a little below his armpit. Small clear tubes ran from his nose, and a metal stand with two IV bags dripped fluids into his veins.

Baby Devil walked over and stood by his bedside. "How you feelin', Loco?"

"Fuckkkked up." Droopy was barely audible.

"I know, Cuzz. It's gon' be alright though. We got back at them niggas the first night shit happened. We tried to get in here then, but you was in surgery. Yo' gramps and them was trippin', so we just fell back. We been on them niggas though nonstop."

Droopy looked up at him and tried to speak, but the words caught in his throat.

They took turns hugging him.

"Did . . . did Peee-Nut . . . make . . . it?" Droopy drawled out in a whisper.

Skip teared up and squeezed his arm. "Nah, Cuzz, the homie didn't make it."

Droopy shook his head and looked up at the ceiling.

"What they sayin' with you though? When you gettin' outta here?" Skip quickly switched the topic.

Droopy shrugged his shoulders. He tried to speak again but it was inaudible.

"What you say, Cuzz?" Skip leaned in closely to him.

"I . . . I can't . . . feel . . . my . . . legs," he drawled just audible enough for Skip to hear.

"What he say?" Baby Devil asked.

"Cuzz say he can't feel his legs." Skip hung his head and stared at the floor.

Baby Devil grabbed Droopy's ankle and shook it. "Don't worry 'bout it, champ, ya body just need time to heal. You'll be back on ya feet in no time."

The rest of the group added their sentiments and encouragements.

They spent the next hour talking and laughing like they were out on the block. This was their way of showing love and support to one of their fallen comrades.

The nurse finally came in. "It's time for y'all to wrap it up. I gave you an extra thirty minutes. It's time for him to get his dose of medication. He'll be sleep after that." She moved to the side of his bed and checked his IV.

"Is it alright if we stay until you give him his meds?" Skip asked. "That way he can go to sleep before we go so he won't have to watch us leave."

She stared at Skip, considering his request. "I guess it won't hurt." She took a new syringe out of the package. She shook up a small vial with a clear liquid in it, poked the needle through the top of it, and turned it upside down to draw it into the syringe. She twisted a dial on one of the IV bags and injected the medication into it.

Within no time, Droopy began to fade. He raised his hand and waved uncharacteristically on the brink of unconsciousness. Sleep overtook him. Skip kissed him on the forehead. "Sleep well, homie."

They filed out of the room one by one leaving Droopy in his drug-induced rest. They headed out into the wicked streets of South Central to reign another night of terror and death on their enemies.

*   *   *   *

Elijah walked into the house and threw his keys on one of the end tables. The house smelled of roasted lamb chops and baked bread. He loosened the knot on his tie and walked toward the kitchen. To his surprise, Elise was there, helping to prepare dinner. He greeted Sistah Raheema, then walked behind Elise and wrapped his arms around her waist, kissing her on the cheek as she stirred the contents in the large stainless-steel pot on the stove.

"What you in here tryna do?" he joked. "Sistah, you tryna give her some lessons?"

Elise rolled her eyes. "Don't play with me." She smiled.

Sistah Raheema laughed. "Don't get me in y'all mess." She checked on the bread in the oven.

"You know I don't need no lessons, I'm the chef of the family." Elise gently elbowed him in his stomach.

"Yeah right." He took the spoon from her and scooped out a

spoonful of oxtails and vegetable stew from the steaming pot. He inspected it.

"Just a lil something to go with your lamb," Elise boasted.

"Interesting, lamb and oxtails in the same meal. Never did that one before." He blew on the spoonful and then put the bite in his mouth, savoring the taste. "Add a little water to kill some of the salt. You were a little heavy-handed with it."

"Get your ass outta here." Elise took the spoon back and popped him on the arm. "Thinking you the damn chef."

Sistah Raheema burst into laughter. "Now you know you can't be talking about a sistah's cookin', boy." She shook her head.

"Daddy!" Amaru ran into the kitchen and jumped in his arms.

Elijah kissed him on the cheek and walked toward the living room. "I'm gonna go shower and chill for a bit. Let me know when dinner's ready." He headed upstairs with Amaru.

Elise added some more spices to the pot and stirred absent-mindedly. She caught Sistah Raheema watching her. Elise smiled awkwardly as she put the top on the pot and set down the spoon. "Excuse me, I'll be back in a few minutes."

Sistah Raheema grabbed her gently by the forearm. "Sweetheart, I noticed your peace has been disturbed lately." She studied Elise closely. "Is everything okay?"

"Um, what do you mean? I'm good." She averted her eyes.

"I'm not trying to pry, just concerned. It seems like something is weighing you down. I want you to know I'm always here if you need to talk. I do more than cook good meals." She smiled.

"No, I'm alright. Trying to figure out some things, that's all."

"Come sit down, have a cup of tea with me." Sistah Raheema led her to the kitchen table. "This will only take a minute." She poured two cups of tea. "You know I'm old and like to ramble sometimes, but I won't keep you long."

"You don't have to say that. I like to get your wisdom when you feel like sharing it."

Sistah Raheema studied her for a moment. "You know who you remind me of? Hagar of the bible. You know the story of Hagar?"

Elise shook her head. Sistah Raheema told her the story . . .

Hagar was the mother of Abraham's first son Ishmael. Hagar was originally the handmaiden of Sarah, Abraham's wife. Sarah couldn't have children and was getting up in age. She wanted Abraham to have an heir, so she suggested that he have a child with Hagar. Abraham already had an affinity toward Hagar, who was a beautiful Egyptian woman. So he took her into his bed, and they bore a son.

In the beginning all was well. Sarah was happy for her husband and their household. But Sarah soon began to feel resentful toward Hagar. After some time, Allah was merciful to Sarah and he sent her glad tidings that she would bear a son because her desire to have a child of her own was so powerful. Sarah thought it would never happen because of her age and barrenness. But lo and behold, she gave birth to Isaac. The two brothers loved each other, but out of her own selfishness, Sarah demanded that Hagar and Ishmael be expelled from living among them. Abraham obliged Sarah. He gathered some things together for Hagar and Ishmael. Then he sent them out into the desert wilderness, prayed to Allah to care for them, and left them there to fend for themselves.

Elise's eyes were wide. "Why would Abraham do that to them when Sarah was the one who suggested it in the first place?"

"Abraham's reasoning is not made clear in the story. Of course, the preachers and scholars have come up with their own theories, that Abraham was privy to God's will, that it was his test, blah, blah, blah. That's not the important part though. The women and children are the lesson in this. Anyways, Hagar was a strong woman, a warrior. She and Ishmael wandered the scorching desert on the brink of starvation and dehydration. But again and again, Allah provided them with sustenance just when they needed it most. They say water gushed from a dry rock to quench their thirst. As we all know, Abraham went on to become known as the father of many nations. Through Sarah, the Jewish line of succession began. Through Hagar, the Arab nation. In essence, Hagar is the mother of Al-Islam. There is even a re-enactment ritual that commemorates her during the Hajj. To this very day, the Arabs and Jews are mortal enemies, with a hatred and violence for centuries. Sarah didn't realize that her son, and her wife's stature, was a test to her. Everything became about her. She chose a woman to bear a son for her husband when that wasn't her place to do so. She should have let him make that decision. The divine man is head of the household for a reason. Then after making that decision, she let her jealousy cause her to push another woman into a horrible situation unjustly. She didn't understand that her actions would have ripple effects for thousands of years."

Sistah Raheema peered at Elise over the rim of her cup as she let her words resonate.

"I don't understand. What about me reminds you of Hagar?"

"Your beauty and your strength." She set the cup down. "But I didn't say you *were* Hagar, just that you remind me of her and that particular story. You see, you have the potential to be either of these women, Sarah or Hagar. It's all based on the decisions you make when you are confronted with the test of Allah and the whispers of

Shayatan." She gently patted Elise's hand. Elise was perplexed for a moment.

"And Elise?" Sistah Raheema continued. "As uncomfortable as it may be sometimes, Elijah has been given the test of leadership. Let your strength complement him, not make his task more difficult."

Elise opened her mouth to question but caught herself. She chose to simply respond with a nodded. An akward silence simmered between them.

"Execuse me. I'm going to see what Amaru and Elijah are up to," Elise finally said, getting up from the table and walking out of the room. As she made her way through the living room, she thought about what Sistah Raheema had said. *Sometimes I wish she'd just say what she means in plain language . . . always talking in riddles, tryna tell me how to deal with Elijah.* She headed up the stairs and entered the master bedroom where Elijah was lying on his back with Amaru on his chest, both half-dozing.

She sat next to them on the bed and rubbed Amaru's back, smiling at them.

Elijah put his hand on her thigh. "Dinner ready?" he asked in a hushed tone.

"Not yet, probably about thirty minutes or so." She cuddled up next to him. "Do you still love me?"

"Where that come from? Why would you even ask that?"

"I don't know, guess I just need to hear it sometimes. I know I'm not perfect and have my moments where I do and say fucked-up shit, but it's not on purpose. I just can't help it sometimes."

"Nobody's perfect. Don't trip that. Our love ain't built on the superficial. We are one machine, and that's what it'll always be." He kissed her on the forehead.

Amaru popped up and smiled at them. She tickled his belly. "You are so nosey, ain't you? Always wanna be in the know," she teased.

Amaru buried his face in Elijah's chest and giggled uncontrollably.

Elijah smiled in amusement.

She peeled him from Elijah, rolled him on his back, and tickled his ribs, smothering his chubby face with kisses.

Elijah got up and made his way to the bathroom. "I'm gonna need you to do me a favor too," he called out over his shoulder.

"What's that?" She continued playing with Amaru.

"I want you to call Guzman when you get a chance."

Her heart dropped. "Um . . . okay . . . what's up?"

"Had a talk with Wiz. They wanna start back gettin' down. I'm not gettin' myself involved. But I told them I'll see if Guzman will be willing to deal with them directly. If so, I'll plug 'em and get out the way."

The toilet flushed. Her heart pounded as she willed herself to remain calm. "Alright," she responded unsteadily. "I'll tap in with him tomorrow."

He walked back in the room and flopped down on the bed. She put Amaru back in his arms. "I've been wanting to talk to you about something."

"What's on ya mind?"

"Well, let me show you." She got up and walked out of the room. She returned with the envelope that Guzman had given her in Mexico. She handed it to him and sat on the bed next to him.

Elijah sat up and carefully opened the seal. "What is this?" He pulled out the two-page document. He slowly read the contents, then looked to her for an explanation.

"It's my father. I've had it for a lil while now, just couldn't bring myself to open it."

"I know who it is. The question is how did you get this? This look like some government shit."

"It's a long story. I'll tell you, just not right now."

"You keepin' secrets now? How is it—"

"Please," she cut him off. "For once don't fight me on this. I'm trying to ask you what to do, not argue with you."

He considered her, then refocused on the papers. "I apologize. I know this is important to you."

She nodded.

"Well, you went through the effort. What you plan to do now you know where he is?"

"I don't know, that's why I'm asking you. I'm torn." She looked down at the floor as a somber mood came over her. After her mother died, she'd wished and hoped that her father would show up and get her, but he never came. She was adopted by her aunt Maria and Maria's husband, Thomas, which eventually turned into the nightmare of her life. Thomas began molesting her at a young age and continued to do so into her teens. The sexual abuse finally ended when she snapped and stabbed him to death after he raped her one evening. She ended up in juvenile hall, then a cycle of abusive group homes where she suffered degradation and violence. She longed for her father to find her, to save her, to love her. She was so lost and alone in the world at that time, longing for him to come and rescue her. The painful memories stabbed at her heart.

She looked at Elijah with misty eyes. "I mean, a part of me wants to see him, to know who my dad is. But there's all this other shit in me that's filled with anger toward him for not being there for me when I needed him. He left me in this world by myself to go through all this hell. I don't have to tell you; I know you feel the same way about your dad."

"Nah, not really."

"Not really what?"

"I mean, I don't feel anger toward my pops. I used to when I was a kid, after my moms passed. But I got over it. I fought too many battles, had to deal with too much shit, to even lend energy to being mad at that nigga. My uncles was my pops and I'm cool with that. Honestly, I don't even think about him much. Every now and then I wonder what aspects of myself I got from him or his side of the family, just small stuff like that. I guess curiosity."

"I wish I could have the same attitude as you. Guess women wired differently. We care more about things like this."

"It's not that I don't care, I just don't burden myself with all the extras no more. And besides, it's two sides to every story. We don't know why our fathers wasn't around. I've come to learn that in life shit happens. It ain't as black and white as we think it should be. Don't be mad at him before you know what the situation was. You got the info for a reason." He handed her the papers. "Go see him."

She stared at the papers with uncertainty. "Will you go with me?"

"Jamaica?" He rubbed his chin. "Amarrrru, you want to go to Jamaica, mon?" he joked in a fake Jamaican accent.

Amaru excitedly nodded his head. "Daddy go . . . Daddy go."

"Guess it's settled them." Elijah lay back and grabbed the remote.

"Really?" Elise asked with a hint of excitement. Elijah's casual confidence and reason always had a way of strengthening her. These were the moments when his love and support made her love him more than she thought possible.

"Yep. Just let me know when you ready to connect the dots."

"Okay" was all she managed to say. "I'm gonna go finish up in the kitchen." She stood up and headed for the door. She stopped and looked at him as he played with their son. She eased the door shut behind her and leaned against it to compose herself. After a moment collecting her strength, she walked downstairs full of anxiety.

*   *   *   *

Baby Devil signaled for the two cars driven by Lil Bar-Dog and Lil Kaos to park near the corner of Budlong and Ninetieth Place. He then drove off to catch up with Skip's car. They drove up Budlong to Ninety-First, made a right to Normandie, then circled around the same path. A group of Back West Eight Tray Gangsters and their homegirls hung out on both sides of the street drinking and smoking.

Skip lowered all four windows in the old Buick Skylark. The passenger in the front seat and the two in the back readied their pistols. Four cars-lengths behind them, Baby Devil and his passengers did the same thing.

Just as Skip reached the first crowd on the north side of the street, one of the Eight Tray gangsters spotted them. "Shooter!" he yelled. A gunman stepped out from the side of a bush and opened fire on Skip's car. The front seat passenger in Baby Devil's car fired his .40 Glock at the shooter to get him off Skip's car.

That gave Skip and his passengers a window of opportunity to get in on the action. Both passengers on the right side leaned out the window and let off a barrage of shots. Skip and the back-left passenger fired at the crowd running for cover on the opposite side of the street.

The group split in every direction, running, screaming, and diving as bullets blew out windows of parked cars, chipped paint, and shattered glass of nearby homes. Skip slammed on the breaks, getting a better aim at his running targets. He hit a youngster in the back as he ran up the stairs to one of the front doors of a house.

Out of bullets, he let up off the brake and the car rolled slowly down the block as his passengers continued their rain of fire until they ran out of bullets.

"Go, Cuzz go!" one of them screamed.

Skip floored it. Baby Devil followed right behind him. They sped to Budlong and made a right, signaling Lil Kaos and Lil Bar-Dog with the thumbs up as they smashed off.

The Eight Trays who were not injured scrambled out of hiding and checked on the wounded. They gathered around the youngster who laid at the foot of the steps, bleeding profusely. A homegirl gently picked up his head and cradled it in her lap.

"Call the ambulance!" someone yelled.

Suddenly, another round of gunshots rang out. An Eight Tray attending to the youngster dropped to the ground. The homegirl screamed at the top of her lungs as another barrage of bullets rained down on them from another surprise attack by Lil Kaos and Lil Bar-

Dog driving in the opposite direction toward Normandie. Once more, the deadly drumbeat of the shots, screams, and shattering glass echoed like a symphony from hell. The assault vehicles burned rubber out of sight leaving carnage and confusion.

CHAPTER 23

Neighborhood Crips from the Forties to the Hundreds filled the block on Fortieth Place, between Menlo and Hoover, for P-Nut's repass. Cars lined both sides of the street; lowriders and new foreign cars competed to make the biggest statement. Young, dusty Crips hopped out of old buckets, satisfied with being the soldiers in the trenches. Blue flags hung from nearly every pocket and car antenna in attendance. Blue khaki suits, Chuck Taylors, Charlie Brown shirts, Pendletons, and dark sweatshirts with big, bold white letters of what Set the individual was from, and "O-I-P P-Nut" stamped on them were the attire worn to send off one of their fallen soldiers.

Two cars were parked side by side in the middle of the street blocking any traffic from coming through. Music blasted from multiple cars; the sad occasion was turning into a block party. Forty-plus Tiny Toons hung out in front of the two-story housing complex where P-Nut's grandmother lived.

Ju-Ju and Lil Bar-Dog carried two crates of liquor to the front porch and handed it out freely to the homies. They all popped caps, gathered in a circle, and poured liquor on the ground. "For young P-Nut," Ju-Ju proclaimed.

"For P-Nut." They all turned their bottles up.

A black Infinity pulled up to the roadblock with Lil Teflon in the passenger seat. He stepped out of the car wearing blue Ben Davis shirt, painter pants, some shiny black Romeos, with braided pigtails, and a pair of Locs. He glared around the crowd and mad-dogged everyone, knowing all eyes were on him. Murder-Min was in the driver's seat. He deliberately reached back into the car and pulled a Tech-9 from the front seat and stuff it between the small of his back and pants for all to see. He covered it with the back of his shirt and walked to the crowd of Tiny Toons. He was welcomed with daps and hugs.

A black Chevy Suburban with super dark tint pulled up to the corner of Hoover with music blasting loud enough to wake up the entire community. The baseline vibrated car windows along the block. It turned on to Fortieth, followed by four old-school classic cars. Elijah drove the all-white 1953 Belair; Hitter the 1955 Chevy; Big Wizard the 1957 Chevy; and Big 9-Lives a 1956 Chevy. The candy paint from the vehicles glistened under the bright sun. The block stopped and watched as they crawled at a snail's pace toward the house.

Lil Cannon drove the Suburban. He and five of his young homies hopped from the truck, all business. They wore beige army fatigues, boots, and Locs. On the back of their jackets, "Bang-Side 90th Street" was etched in black embroidery. They approached the crowd gathered around the cars blocking the street and talked to one of the drivers. The man nodded, gave Lil Cannon a dap, got into one of the cars, and backed up, letting their caravan pull through.

Elijah parked first and got out, followed by the rest of the crew. They all wore small round derbies and were cripped down from head to toe like it was the 1980s. They were decked out in blue-and-gray Charlie Brown shirts with "Bang Side 90s" stitched into the left breast, and "O-IN-PEACE P-NUT" on the back of their collars. The spectators gawked. OGs and Lil Locs from different sets mobbed the five Hood stars to pay respect.

Lil Teflon's face twisted, and his fist clenched involuntarily when he saw Lil Wizard get out of the car with Big Wizard.

Lil Wizard had not attended the funeral, nor did Hitter. They were making their first appearance of the day. Lil Wizard let his circle do all the socializing as he scanned the crowd. He saw Lil Teflon watching, pushed his glasses up his nose, and smiled brightly at him. He threw up the Nine-O hand sign directly at Lil Teflon.

Lil Teflon seethed as he accepted a bottle of Silver Satin and Kool-Aid from Baby Devil and turned it up.

Big 9-Lives walked toward the Tiny Toons. A crowd trailed behind him into the yard. Greetings and pleasantries were exchanged among the group. It seemed like the whole block followed.

Elijah ignored Lil Teflon and greeted Baby Devil and his crew of youngsters.

Lil Wack and Fat Jack from the Underground Crips walked up and embraced Big 9-Lives and Elijah.

"What's up with this new Bang-Side thing y'all flying?" Lil Wack asked.

"This what we pushin' now. This ain't everybody though. Bang Side just ridahs from all sides. No bustas allowed." Big 9-Lives made sure everybody heard him.

Lil Wack looked amused. "Y'all niggas keeps some new shit rollin'. What's crackin', Lil 9? It's been a minute."

"Same shit. Tryna get to the next level," Elijah said.

The crowd grew thicker around them. Elijah observed the effect they had on the homies. They hung on every word Big 9-Lives spoke even though it was just casual conversation. The homies treated them like Hood celebrities.

Elijah felt the energy and it filled him with a burst of clarity about leadership. He thought back to a book he had read about Aristotle's philosophy. One of the themes was that the capable leader should be allowed to rule. The republic was best served when it followed the lead of benevolent and wise rulers. At this moment, it made sense to him. The reason so many homies wrecked themselves and did foolish things was because the leaders were inexperienced, uneducated, and reactionaries, not thinkers. In most Crip circles, going to school was uncool. Listening to the advice of older square people in the community was shunned. Fighting, shooting, and sexing as many women as possible was applauded.

This is what they mean by man living according to his lower self. Probably ninety-eight percent of the homies here, including me, hadn't graduated high school and didn't see anything wrong with it, he thought.

He decided to capitalize on the unexpected opportunity. He turned to Big 9-Lives and said, "Shit, since we all here, let's build with the homies on what we been talkin' about on the program."

"It's your vision. Go ahead, put it on the table." Big 9-Lives turned and got everyone's attention, "Hey y'all . . . listen up real quick. Neph got something he wanna holla at y'all about."

The crowd moved to gather around them. That drew curiosity from others down the block. They flocked to the yard to see what was going on.

Elijah shared a short version of his vision with them. He tailored it to focus on the economic program and the benefits for everyone involved, purposely leaving out language that would turn them off, sticking to organizing and pushing the Neighborhood Car forward. He made it a point to be inclusive and steer it toward the others who were there from other gangs, detailing how they could push the same program in their hoods.

Elijah captivated the crowd. They were openly intrigued by the vastness of his plan and all the possibilities and benefits it could bring. Even if it was just for that moment and they were caught up in the excitement, at least he got their attention and they listened.

Lil Teflon watched Baby Devil, who appeared to be transfixed by Elijah's philosophy. He tapped Baby Devil on the shoulder, rolled his eyes, and mouthed "bullshit."

Baby Devil looked at him, irritated, and turned his attention back to Elijah.

When Elijah was done, many of the homies nodded and voiced their approval, while others just allowed it to sink in. "Just a lil something for y'all to think about," he concluded. The older homies dapped and hugged him.

"Man, that was some well thought-out and positive shit that'll help the Hood. Whatever role you need me to play, I got you," 1-Punch expressed.

"Fasho. Nine, we need this. It's time for all the small-minded shit to stop and niggas progress," Big Red added.

Baby Devil waited until some of the crowd cleared out. Then he walked up and shook Elijah's hand. "That's some good shit, Lil 9. Can I ask you a couple questions real quick?"

Elijah looked around. "Grab us a bottle from Ju and let's rap."

After Baby Devil grabbed a bottle, he and Elijah moved over to the neighbor's unoccupied porch, out of the earshot of others.

"What's up?" Elijah pulled a blunt from his pocket.

"Just wanted to ask . . . like, you know, with all the shit that happened, if niggas start pushin' this program, will I be able to be a part of it? I mean, I don't know shit about no legal businesses and property and all that. But I wouldn't mind learning and just doin' my part. I wanna see the Hood do shit like these other hoods be doin'."

Elijah lit the blunt and took a drag. "I never faulted you for none of the things that happened. You was just young and tryna be loyal to what side you was on. It was business, that's all. I ain't never fuckin' with Lil Tef again, but I don't put you in that same box. What we 'bout to build trumps all these little, petty gripes. You a solid, young homie with some influence in your circle. Long as you ain't on no bullshit, we gon' fuck with you."

"What about Wiz 'n' them? I know they still hate a nigga." Baby Devil gazed in Big Wizard and Hitter's direction.

"Don't worry about that. One thing that's for sure, Wiz and Hitt are real veterans in the field. They understand the concept of business over personal better than me. They don't even hate the Tramps, and they killed their big brother. They ride on 'em because it's just business at this point. The lil scrimmage you was part of with us, they don't even give it thought no more. So when everything comes together and names get put in the hat, when yours come up to play a part, they ain't trippin."

"That's what's up." Baby Devil smiled.

They continued to smoke and talk as the festivities went on around them. Nobody really paid them much attention . . . except one person. Lil Teflon nursed a bottle of liquor and scowled at them as Elijah continued to engage Baby Devil in deep conversation. He seethed with hidden rage at the sight of Baby Devil and Elijah's newfound connection.

CHAPTER 24

Elijah drove up in front of Ju-Ju's house and blew the horn. Ju-Ju walked out pulling a shirt over his head with one hand and balancing a half-eaten sandwich in the other. An extremely attractive, brown-skinned woman with braided hair followed behind him holding a little boy's hand.

Ju-Ju spoke something to her as he walked toward the car, eating his sandwich.

Elijah spotted the little toddler and stepped out of the running car. "Is that Brendon?" he called out.

"Yeah, that's his lil bad ass." Ju-Ju approached the car.

"What's up, lil man?" Elijah smiled and held out his hand. "Give me five."

The little boy put his head against his mother's thigh, acting shy.

"What's up, Jada?" Elijah greeted her.

"Hey, Nine." She looked down at Brendon. "Give 'em five, man-man."

The little boy shook his head. "Boy, give yo' uncle five," Ju-Ju said.

Brendon looked at his dad, then to Elijah's outstretched hand,

and suddenly slapped his hand hard and clumsy.

"That's right," Elijah chided, and rubbed the top of his head. "Man, he done got big. Time flies." He shook his head.

"Hell yeah it do, he'll be three next month."

"Alright lil man, see you later." Elijah waved at him.

"Say bye," Jada said, and the little boy waved.

Elijah and Ju-Ju got into the car. Ju-Ju looked around the car interior as he fastened his seat belt. "This motherfucka like a spaceship." He admired the Lamborghini Diablo.

"It is a spaceship." Elijah smiled, put it in gear, and blasted off down the street, Frankie Beverly and Maze bumping through the speakers.

Elijah tossed Ju-Ju an ounce of weed. "The Phillies in the glove compartment."

Ju-Ju broke down the weed, then rolled it up in the tobacco shell. He sang along to "Before I Let You Go."

Elijah hit the 110 freeway north and opened the Lambo up, darting in and out of lanes. The early morning weekend traffic flow on the highway was perfect. They bobbed their head to the music. Elijah cracked the windows to let out the smoke from the blunt.

Ju-Ju gazed out the window, enjoying the whole vibe.

After a few moments, the Hollywood sign in the distance looked close enough to touch. The Lambo continued its smooth trek through the light traffic. Elijah turned the music down. "Has things quieted down any with the Tramps?"

"Nah, not really. The young homies ain't stoppin'. I guess,

just the way it was done right in our backyard, with Skip 'n' them being there; they took it different. Even though P-Nut was a new recruit, they liked Cuzz. Then you know, Droop in a wheelchair for now and don't know if he gon' walk again. So it's all bad. And the Tramps ain't gon' stop either. I don't see this quieting down for a while."

"Who's leading the charge for us? Who's gettin' the shine in this one?" Elijah changed lanes to get past a slow-moving vehicle.

"You know everybody givin' it to Baby Devil. But for real, it's really been young Skip. Cuzz been goin' non-stop."

"I already figured their lil crew was the ones. Them lil niggas always had big paws as pups but they just under the wrong guidance."

"You hit it on the nose. Now that the cloud startin' to lift from the shit Lil Tef was feeding them, I think they gon' be straight."

"Fasho. What's been up with you though, otherwise?"

"Man, I'm good, can't complain. I got a roof over my head and food to eat. Everything else don't really matter that much at the end of the day."

"It's way more to life than food and shelter, my guy. You don't have no goals you tryna accomplish? It's about tryin' to thrive and be happy, homie."

"I don't really think about goals and shit. I just try to survive day to day, tryna make sure Jada and Brendon get what they need and be a solid homie. I don't think happiness and all that is for niggas like me or you. Think about it: when have we ever had the time to be genuinely happy? It's been one battle after another all our lives. All our people dyin', goin' to jail, don't know where they next meal comin' from, so they doin' all type of wicked shit. It's crazy, Cuzz.

To tell you the truth, I fear lovin' anything or anyone too deeply anymore. It seems like when a nigga let that happen he just settin' himself up for heartache 'cause something wicked bound to happen."

"I feel you." Elijah paused. "But we can't give up seeking and trying. We gotta plan for the future—for our sons' futures. You right, this whole shit was designed to crush us and give us hell, but look, nigga"—he gestured to the Lamborghini—"we still here. We still makin' the most happen. We still solid. That should inspire us daily."

"Yeah, I guess. Maybe one day it'll all make sense. Till then, you already got enough goals and moves to do for all of us. So I'll let you use all your brain power and I'll ride along." Ju-Ju laughed.

Elijah joined in the laughter. "You never told me what you felt about what I got at the homies about after the funeral." He passed Ju-Ju back the blunt.

"I think it's genius, homie. We need ridahs like you. A lot of us don't know about all that. We just Crips. Most of us don't even know what real organizing look like. Shit, it's hard to even put a simple barbeque together with these dudes, so listening to what you was poppin' the other day was mind-blowin' for a lot of niggas. You gon' have your work cut out for you though. It's haters that's gonna try and sabotage it just because. Not to mention, the greed and snakes you gon' have to deal with. But if anybody can do it, it's you." Ju-Ju blew smoke toward the small crack in the window. "I know we don't say it much, but I love you, my nigga. You always was the best out of us. I'm not ashamed to admit that. Lil Tef and them knew you was the best; they just too prideful to accept it. That's not me, I accept it. And wherever you leadin', I'm with you."

Elijah nodded. "For death though."

"For death," Ju-Ju concurred.

Elijah turned the music back up as they arrived at the exit to the Universal City Walk. Elijah pondered over what Ju-Ju had just expressed as he exited. He knew in his spirit that this day was significant in some unknown way.

CHAPTER 25

B ig Wizard pulled into the parking lot of Simply Wholesome on Slauson and Overhill. He spotted Elise sitting in her Range Rover in the back of the parking lot. He pulled up next to her and parked.

"What's up with you?" Big Wizard greeted as he climbed into her passenger seat.

"Same ol', how you been?"

"You know me, forward marchin'."

She dug in a bag and handed him a sandwich, then pulled out another one for herself.

He examined the sandwich closely. "What kinda meat in this?"

"It's turkey breast. I don't mess with swine either."

"Alright." He unwrapped the sandwich and took a bite. "So what's the word?"

"I connected the dots for you. But you won't be meeting him."

He stopped chewing. "Why not?" He looked at her with disappointment.

"The best that's gonna happen is you let me know how much you're spending, how many birds you can handle, and in what timeframe. From there, I'll tell you what the ticket gonna be and how he wants everything to work."

Big Wizard examined Elise suspiciously. "But Nine said—"

She cut him off, "I know what Nine told you, but I'm telling you what my guy in Mexico is telling me." She turned and faced him. "Look, if you tryna work, don't make this difficult. There's other shit at play that don't need you prying and making waves. I'll make sure whatever you trying to do happens, but I need you to fly low and quiet without pulling at my man." She locked eyes with him.

A spark of understanding flashed in his eyes. He nodded hesitantly. "Alright I got you."

This was not their first rodeo working together. He understood her ways more than she realized. And even though there were times where he wanted to smack her for her slick mouth, he respected and admired her ruthlessness and business savvy.

"When will you be ready to give me the details?" she asked.

He grabbed her mango juice from the middle console. "I'm ready now." He twisted the cap off and took a long chug. "I buy fifty, he front fifty. Let me know the price, when, and where, and I'll be there." He opened the door and hopped out.

"Where you goin' with my juice?"

"You rich, you can buy another one." He slammed the door in her face. He jogged over to his car, laughing as he got in. He took another log chug and waved the empty bottle at her. He cracked a smirk and drove off.

"Bullshit-ass nigga," she called out as he drove away laughing.

*　　*　　*　　*

The sun glowed like an orange globe setting beyond the horizon as the modest chartered boat sailed through the calm waters of the Pacific, a stones-throw from the Catalina Island coastline. Ju-Ju leaned against the rail sipping a margarita, taking in the beautiful scenery, thinking about the conversation he had had with Elijah about goals and dreams. Before, he never really considered those aspects of life; they seemed so far out of reach. With all the tragedies they suffered being from the Hood, hopes and aspirations were a waste of time because the odds were never in their favor. Yet, the way Elijah spoke sparked something anew within him.

Can I actually do something else with my life beyond the Set? he thought. *Nine make it seem possible, even for me.* He looked down at his son, Brendon, who was hugging Ju-Ju's leg, his thumb in his mouth, looking out at the ocean in curiosity. *I gotta try and make a better way for him . . . at least give him a fightin' chance to do better than we did and endure a lot less sufferin' than we had to. I owe him that as his father. I owe that to Jada too, she deserves that.*

"This look bomb, don't it?" Jada walked over with a margarita in her hands, jarring him out of his thoughts.

Ju-Ju admired her with a bright smile on his face and a twinkle in his eyes. "Yeah, this is creation at its finest." He turned back toward the setting sun.

She snuggled up next to him. He wrapped his arm around her neck and kissed her on the cheek. Brendon looked up at their affectionate interaction, still holding on to Ju-Ju's leg. He scuffed the top of his son's head. "What you lookin' at, lil nosey man?"

Brendon giggled and buried his face in Ju-Ju's leg.

"You know I'm on to you," Ju-Ju chided him. "You always tryna watch what me and your mama doin.' She not yo' girl, she's mine." He laughed at him.

"No," Brendon spurted, and hit him on the leg.

Ju-Ju and Jada laughed. "His lil ass don't like that."

"No!" he retorted again, making them laugh harder.

The boat docked in the harbor just a short walk away from the restaurants and shops lining the boardwalk, leading to the cobblestoned streets. This small piece of paradise was a hop, skip, and a jump away from the ghettos of LA, but it seemed like a world away.

They made their way up the boardwalk with Brendon walking between them. Every few steps, his parents lifted Brendon up by his hands, lifting both his feet off the ground, and he giggled as if he was on a ride at the carnival. They had figured out a while back that this was his enactment of flying.

"Boy, you starting to be too heavy for me to hold you up," Jada said. He promptly put his feet down, walked a few more steps, then up went his feet again. "This boy is crazy." She chuckled.

It did not take long for them to reach Lobster Trap, a quaint, colorful local restaurant on Catalina Avenue and Third Street. The aroma of deliciously prepared food greeted them as they entered and gave the host the name on their reservation. They were immediately seated in the cozy nautical-themed dining area. It was busy, but not overly crowded. Jada got comfortable in the old-fashioned cushioned leather seats. Ju-Ju placed Brendon in a booster seat.

"We got to start doing this more often." Jada smiled over the menu at Ju-Ju.

"I knew that was comin'," he snickered.

"I'm serious. We gotta experience a different way of life. The

Hood is gonna be there, and they'll be there doing the same old things. It's more to life," she said.

"I know, our time will come." He was still trying to make up his mind on what to order.

"We can't wait for our time to come, we gotta make it come."

He set his menu down and looked at her. "Don't think I'm not tryin' to make things change for us. It's just not as easy as I thought it would be. What my moms used to say? It's hard to teach an old dog new tricks."

"Well, you not an old dog and it ain't a trick—it's just about doing. Look at everything you say Lil 9 doing now, and even Big Tef. If they can make the transition you can too."

Ju-Ju loved that Jada saw the best in him. They had been together for six years and during that time Jada added a spark of light to his life. She was a great mother to their son and didn't burden Ju-Ju with undue expectations. He knew she simply wanted him to be his best and was always there to assist him in any way she could. His commitment to the Set was their biggest obstacle, but they were going to get through and make it work. It had been that way with them since they met. When he first laid eyes on her walking from her college campus, he knew she was special. He was never the cool kid growing up; in fact, he was the punching bag and do-boy for his homies. The neighborhood girls always seemed to sense that and treated him with disdain. It wasn't until he did his stint in juvenile hall that the girls started being attracted to him. At that point, he only wanted them sexually because he assessed that they were more attracted to the image of who he had become and not who he really was. But Jada was different. She didn't care about his street persona; she wanted the real him, Julius. And although he had his casual flings with other women, Jada was his heart and he would never leave her for another.

"I know it can be done. I mean, I don't know to the extent that Nine doin' it. Because he's just a smart-ass nigga. Even when we was kids, it was like he was already grown in the mind. But I'm slowly tryna get some things in the mix where we can do better things. The problem is, I love the Hood too much—it's hard to get away from it."

"You can't love the Hood more than it love you though." She stared at him intently. "And don't sell yourself short, you're just as smart as any of them when you put ya mind to something. And whatever we need to figure out—whether it's real estate, business, whatever—I'll help you learn it. I don't know much about it right now, but it's nothing for us to get on the grind and learn it. They're books on everything we need to know."

"You right." He shook his head, taking in everything she said. "If I can give all this time and effort to the Set, I can do the same for me and my family."

Ju-Ju paused for a moment. He reflected on his childhood and how different things were back then. Out of all his friends, he'd grown up the most normal. He had a mother who cared for him. His father didn't live with him, but he was around and never let Ju-Ju go without. His friends had it rough. Elijah's mom killed herself, and he didn't know his father. Big Teflon and Lil Teflon didn't know their father either, and their mother, Virginia, was a stone-cold crackhead who didn't give a damn about what her kids did. Ju-Ju went to school regularly and made good grades until he went to juvenile hall. He was a normal, good kid.

"You would think I'd been the one to already had businesses and doin' the things they doin'," JuJu said after contemplating. "Everyone else had it worst. I had a pretty decent childhood. So it's like, with all the crazy shit that went on in my homies' lives, how did they get further away from the Hood than I did? I somehow got rooted to the soil so deep that it's hard for me to even see anything outside of it," Ju-Ju said.

"I know how it goes. You been through your shit too, just like we all have—"

The waiter stepped up to the table ready to take their order.

"Can you give us a few more minutes?" Jada responded politely.

"No problem. Can I get you something to drink while you decide?"

"Two margaritas and a Coke," she told the waiter with finality.

"Can I at least get a extra shot of Patron in mines?" Ju-Ju looked at her.

"Alright. Give him a shot of Patron in his." She gave Ju-Ju a side-eye.

The waiter left with a resigned grin.

"Always tryna be the boss of something," Ju-Ju mumbled.

Jada smiled. "Back to what I was saying. We all been through our own struggles and we all respond in different ways. But we got this. Let's start making that change."

Ju-Ju stared at her seriously. "Change, huh?" He cut his eyes to the waiter, who was standing at a distance, and nodded.

The waiter made his way back over with their drinks. He gingerly lifted the saucer from the tray and placed it in front of Jada. She looked around, confused.

"The envelope is for you." The waiter smiled, bowed, and

walked back toward the kitchen.

She picked up the small envelope. Still perplexed, she carefully opened it before letting out a low screech and putting her hand over her mouth in surprise.

"Is that change enough for you?" Ju-Ju smiled at her.

"No . . . you didn't!" She laughed in delight. "Does this mean what I think it do?"

"Yeah." Ju-Ju sat back and folded his arms across his chest. "You gon' be my bitch for life."

She burst out in a loud laugh. "Damn boy, that's a helluva way to ask me to marry you!"

"You know I don't do all the mushy get-on-one-knee shit. We keep it Hood."

She excitedly slipped the rock on her finger. She hopped over to him and smothered him with kisses. "I love you, Julius."

"I know, I know," he said arrogantly.

"Stop it," Brendon yelled with an attitude.

They both looked at their son, then laughed uncontrollably at his jealousy.

The waiter brought a bottle of champagne, popped the cork, and filled the two accompanying glasses. "Congratulations." He set the glasses in front of them and walked away cordially.

Ju-Ju raised his glass toward Jada for a toast. "To our future." He smiled optimistically.

"To our future." She was flushed with joy.

"Yeyyy." Brendon giggled and clapped his tiny hands as if he understood everything that was going on.

They laughed, clinked glasses, and sipped champagne as they stared into each other's eyes with an unspoken vow that it was them against the world.

CHAPTER 26

The plane made its descent over the sparkling, clear water of Jamaica. Elijah looked down at the beauty of the Caribbean Sea in awe. A giddy excitement tingled in his stomach. This was his first time traveling outside of the United States, other than his business trips to Tijuana, and he wondered what took him so long. Elise sat next to him in silence. He knew she was wrestling with a lot of emotions, facing the prospect of meeting her father for the first time. The old pictures that she had seen of him holding her as a baby was too far back for her to recollect being in his presence. She tried to act as if it was not that big of a deal, but her silence and intensity over the last few days had told him otherwise. He wanted to bring Amaru with them to meet his grandfather, but Elise overrode him on that. Her argument was that she wanted to meet her father, Miguel, first, to determine if he was worthy enough to meet her son. Even though Elijah felt otherwise, he decided not to fight her on it. This was her trip, her life experience, so she had the right to decide how it unfolded.

They descended onto the landing strip in Montego Bay. After a brief wait, they exited the crowded plane into the airport. Festive traditional-costumed dancers and singers greeted passengers as they made their way toward Customs and Immigration. They cleared all the formalities and headed to the outside area with the assistance of a jovial skycap. A hot, sticky, humid breeze gripped them as soon as they walked through the doors of the airport and stepped outside.

Elijah had dealt with the dry heat on many occasions when he went to the Mojave Desert to ride his quads and horseback ride, but this was different. This was a Florida summer day on steroids. They headed to the area where the itinerary stated. A driver holding a sign reading "Hassahn" was waiting for them.

"My name is Tweety, your driver," the man stated as they approached. "Welcome to Jamaica."

Elijah suppressed a laugh at the sight of the robust dark-skinned young man bearing the name of the tiny yellow bird cartoon character. "What's up, Man," he greeted.

The humidity seemed to wrap a blanket of steam around them as they waited for Tweety and the skycap to load their bags into the Toyota minivan. Elijah thanked the skycap and handed him a fifty-dollar bill. The skycap beamed and uttered his appreciation in Jamaican Patois, the local dialect.

They welcomed the air-conditioner in the back of the darkly tinted, plush van as they pulled out into the hectic Jamaican traffic. The highway was only two lanes, with cars going in both directions. The steering wheel was on the right side and cars drove on the left. This was disconcerting for Elijah, along with the extremely fast pace that all the vehicles were driving at, including their driver. Reggae music blasted through the stereo system. Tweety honked and cursed in Patois at the other drivers. Elijah was certain that they were going to crash at any moment. Elise seemed to be thinking the same, as she reached over and interlocked her arm to his.

After a few miles of observing all the beautiful scenery and the local sites, they relaxed and allowed Tweety to give them his tour of the north coast of Jamaica. Craft and fruit vendors, local eateries, anglers and so much more lined the highway. At one point, Tweety stopped along the roadside by the ocean where there were a cluster of stalls and makeshift eateries with food being cooked over open flames so they could sample some of the local fares. They purchased and drank from big green coconuts, shaved, and chopped by a Rastafarian with a sharp machete. They ate roasted breadfruit and fried fish prepared over an open fire and got cold Red Stripe beer from a little shop made from plywood. They marveled at all the contrasts between all the majestic resorts, huge homes on the oceanfront and hillsides, and the little shanty houses and animals wandering the busy streets. They passed multiple tourist attractions, including the famed Dunn's River Falls, which they would more than likely be visiting in the coming days.

They were exhausted by the time they arrived at their four-star all-inclusive resort in Ocho Rios, Couples San Souci. Elijah tipped Tweety and arranged for him to be their personal driver for the stay. They were greeted by well-groomed, smiling, uniformed staff, waiting with glasses of rum punch when they were escorted into the lobby area. They checked in and settled in their exquisitely decorated cottage villa that overlooked the breathtaking azure ocean. Their villa was nestled on a cliff surrounded by exotic flowers and greenery in a secluded hideaway. They lounged in the spacious living room with French doors opening to the private balcony and outdoor Jacuzzi.

Elijah had already placed a room service order for drinks and a light lunch. Elise leaned her head against his chest as they enjoyed the view. A tap at the door interrupted the shared daydream. He let the worker in and had the food set up on the table on the balcony. By the time he tipped him and closed the door, Elise had gotten in the shower. He lifted the metal covering off one of the plates and sampled a piece of the jerk chicken. He had to force himself to cover it back before he ate the whole plate without her. Impatient, he got two shot glasses from the bar and poured some Jamaican white rum and headed to the bathroom.

The hot steam filling the bathroom had a natural floral scent from the soap Elise had lathered on her body. He opened the glass door to the huge walk-in shower and extended her the shot glass.

"It's too early to be drinking. I'm not gonna be any good tryin' to go out later." She chuckled.

"You'll be alright. This our first shot of Jamaican rum together."

She smiled and rinsed the soap from one of her hands and took the glass.

"Salute." He held up the glass, then drained it.

"Salute." She did the same and choked a little when the liquor hit her chest. She handed the glass back to him.

Elijah set both glasses on the sink, sat atop the marble counter, and watched her shower. He observed every sensual move and caress as she soaped and rinsed.

"You not gonna shower now?"

"Nah, I'm enjoying the view." He smirked.

"Boy, stop being a stalker and get your sweaty ass in this water."

"I'm cool . . . I want you to smell my sweat. You be the beauty and I'll be the beast," he said.

"Uh-hmmm, I knew you was tryin' to give me alcohol to try and take advantage of me."

"That's enough."

He hopped down from the sink and opened the shower door. She came to him, wrapping her arms around his neck. He lifted her up by the back of the thighs, and she wrapped her legs around his waist, kissing him deeply. Water soaked his clothes and dripped to the floor as he carried her from the bathroom to the four-post king-size bed in the lavish bedroom, where he laid her on her back.

She melted into the comfort of the bed as he kissed her softly from her neck down to her breasts and stomach. She rubbed the back of his head, moaning in the pleasure he brought to her body.

He expertly guided his lips to her inner thigh, licking and tasting her flesh with his tongue. He worked his way to her other thigh, making her burn with anticipation of what she knew was coming.

Her back arched as his tongue slid into her wetness. He probed and licked gently, but then grew more aggressive with his technique as she craved for more and urged him to eat it like his favorite snack. Her juices painted his face; he licked and sucked on her fiercely, slipping two fingers inside her to work simultaneously with his tongue. This always drove her wild.

She grabbed the back of his head and grinded with his movements in ecstasy. Her moans and pants grew louder. "Eat this, motherfucka" became her mantra as she, too, grew more aggressive.

He raised up suddenly and lowered his body onto hers. She licked her juices from his lips as he entered her. She let out a scream of pleasure, feeling his hardness deep inside of her. Their bodies caught a fierce rhythm as they competed in a synchronized battle of passion, love, and lust.

After their energy was drained from their erotic lovemaking, drenched in sweat, they dozed off for a couple of hours. When they awoke, still a little buzzed from the rum, they showered and enjoyed a brunch of jerk chicken, red peas and rice, and plantains.

By late afternoon, they were making their way through Fern Gully, then the hilly countryside of Jamaica to Kingston. The near two-hour-long drive gave Elijah and Elise the opportunity to chill and take in more of the sights, sounds, and smells of the island. Tweety played a constant cycle of old and new reggae music that Elijah had never heard before but found himself bobbing to the rhythm. The traffic and winding roads were even more treacherous than the trip from the airport—with narrow pothole-filled dirt roads and absolutely no traffic rules whatsoever—but they were much more prepared for it this time.

As they arrived in Kingston, the atmosphere became more vibrant. Aside from the fast-speaking dialect and the opposite-side driving, this could have been any metropolitan city in America. Old and late model cars filled the streets, blasting music and honking horns continuously, some with the drivers hanging out the windows as they drove erratically. The public "taxis," which were regular vehicles licensed to carry passengers, littered the streets along with the passenger minibuses. KFC and Burger King stood alongside street vendors and traditional Jamaican restaurants. Pedestrians battled with vehicles for walkways as sidewalks were nonexistent.

Elijah loved it. "Hey, Tweety, turn down the music a little so you can tell us more about Kingston."

Tweety was more than happy to oblige. He rambled in broken English-Patois that they had to strain to understand. They caught a few words here and there that allowed them to keep up with the conversation.

Tweety exaggerated with extra emphasis on every topic from local politics to the history of the island, to who were the big-time gangsters. Some of his stories were so overly dramatic that they knew he had to be lying, but they liked his energy, so they kept the conversation going back and forth, relishing in the atmosphere of Kingston, home of the Don Dada and the Original Rudeboys.

After a lengthy escapade in the city area, they veered off into an upscale residential area with various architectural-styled homes. The sun was beginning to set as they parked in front of an iron-gated yellow two-story house with two older, but well-kept cars parked in the driveway. Bright lights surrounded the property with people moving around visibly inside the house. Tweety turned off the engine and got out to open the door for them.

Elise stared at the house without moving. She had been apprehensive about this whole endeavor since they arrived. So much so that Elijah was the one who called Miguel from their resort to let him know they had arrived on the island and arranged the visit. He clutched her hand for reassurance and led her out of the car.

A teenage girl appeared on the veranda, looked at them inquisitively, then called out something inaudible over her shoulder. Within seconds, a middle-aged, light-brown-skinned man of average height and weight stepped out onto the porch followed by a lovely slender dark-skinned woman. He and Elise locked eyes, and for that moment, they were the only two people in their world. He moved involuntarily toward her, tears filling his eyes with each step closer. His resemblances to Elise was undeniable: the same black wavy hair, smooth tan-brown skin, and piercing blue-green eyes. This was her father, Miguel.

Elijah released her hand and stepped aside to watch the encounter. Elise stood there bewildered.

"My Leesy," Miguel exclaimed, wrapping her up in a tight hug, lifting her off her feet. His tears flowed as he squeezed her tighter. She had no choice but to hug him back. "*Mi Dios*, my God, my baby, I missed you suh badly," he expressed repeatedly in Spanish and Patois.

The girl and woman watched with tear-filled eyes. By now, a group of people poured out of the house and joined them. A young woman about Elise's age immediately caught Elijah's eyes, so much so he did a double take. She could have easily passed as Elise's twin except for slightly tanner skin and a more voluptuous body. She was the only one who stopped at the foot of the steps and watched from a distance. Her style and dress were of any urban American fly girl, wearing a pink and white Baby Phat shorts set, white sandals, big gold earrings, and bangle bracelets. Her thick curly hair pulled back in a ponytail. Two small children ran out of the house and stood shyly next to her.

The crowd rushed over and surrounded Elise, all taking turns hugging her and marveling at her beauty. They showered her with affection as she cried tears of joy.

The woman on the porch came rushing over. "This is your stepmother, Dawn." Miguel ushered her in front of Elise.

Dawn took her hands gently. "Welcome, Elise, welcome." She pulled her into an affectionate embrace. "I'm so happy to finally meet you and have you here."

"Thank you," an overwhelmed Elise uttered.

Miguel approached Elijah and gave him a firm handshake. "You must be Elijah." His heavy Spanish accent mingled with Patois.

"Yeah. Nice to meet you."

"Nice to meet you too. I'm so grateful that you brought her

here to me."

"She brought herself, I just came along." Elijah smiled at Elise, who was trying to be social with the rest of the clan.

"Either way, I'm just happy. Come on, everyone, let's go inside." Miguel whisked Elise away toward the house. "I have a lot of explaining to do to you," he whispered.

They all made their way to the house. Elijah remained outside, sitting on the hood of the car. He lit a Cuban cigar he'd purchased at one of the duty-free tourist shops in "Ochi," as the locals so favorably call Ocho Rios, and engaged in small talk with Tweety. The young woman was still standing by the steps, gawking at him. He puffed on the cigar and blew smoke in the air, not breaking eye contact.

Without provocation, she suddenly walked over. "Who are you?" she asked in a heavy Patois accent.

He smirked and stared at her a moment. He knew without having to be told that this was Elise's sister. He started to say something slick for her rudeness but changed his mind. "I'm Elijah."

"Meh don't wan kno your name. Meh wan kno who yuh are to da gurl." She pointed toward the house.

"Damn, you aggressive, ain't you?" He looked over at Tweety. "Is all Jamaican women mean like this?"

Tweety threw up his arms and laughed.

"Like I said," Elijah continued. "My name is Elijah. And the 'girl' is my woman and son's mother. Who are you?" he asked in the same blunt fashion.

"Meh name Princess." She looked him up and down.

"And you're Elise's sister?" Elijah sized her back up.

She rolled her eyes, kissed her teeth, and walked back to the house. "Come." She called out without looking back.

Elijah looked at Tweety, confused about what she meant.

Tweety caught on. "She wan yuh to guh inside." He indicated to the house.

"Ohhh, okay." Elijah chuckled and hopped off the hood. "Yeah, they definitely sisters," he mumbled as he headed to the house.

He stepped into the spacious house and surveyed. Elise was sitting on the couch with two little girls on her lap. One stroked Elise's hair while the other just stared at her longingly the way children do.

"Come meet my nieces." Elise waved him over. "This is Shauna and Tishna." She smiled at them.

Elijah introduced himself to them and the rest of the household. He met her two brothers, Junior and Garry, and her teenage sister, Bria, along with some cousins.

Dawn gave him a big motherly hug. "Why yuh don't bring yuh son?"

"We were gonna bring him." He looked at Elise briefly. "But things changed at the last minute. We'll bring him next time."

"Okay good." She smiled. "Princess? Come se yuh sistah," she called out.

Princess came from the kitchen with an attitude. "Meh tryin' to get tings ready."

"Wat yuh mean? Yuh come talk to yuh sistah now," Dawn insisted.

She approached Elise stubbornly. Elise had been so occupied with everyone else that she hardly paid Princess any attention when she passed her on the way in. Now, looking at her directly for the first time, she could not believe their resemblance.

"Come hug meh gurl," Princess practically demanded.

Elise stood up and hugged Princess.

"Meh ah yuh sistah, Princess." She squeezed Elise tightly.

"I'm Elise."

"Meh know." Princess held Elise back to give her a good onceover. "Meh daddy can't stop talk 'bout yuh since him know seh yuh ah come."

Elise smiled uncertainly. "You look like me."

Princess laughed loudly. "No, yuh look like meh." She abruptly turned and walked back to the kitchen.

Elijah watched in amusement, now holding Tishna on his hip.

"Come now, everybody come tuh deh back. Let dem have time alone." Dawn indicated to Miguel and Elise, as she herded everyone including Elijah to the back patio.

Once everyone cleared out, Elise and Miguel sat in awkward silence momentarily. He leaned forward with his elbows on his knees, head downcast, searching for the words and the courage this moment demanded. "I know there are a lot of questions you have." He raised his head and looked into her eyes.

Elise only nodded to him. She was so nervous and full of questions. She didn't know where to begin. When she saw him earlier, her heart fluttered because he was a physical piece of her creation. She had been so angry with him for abandoning her and leaving her in a cold world to fend for herself. All the hell she suffered and he wasn't there to protect her. Now, as he sat before her, she felt like a vulnerable child in his presence. It was all surreal and overwhelming.

He dropped his head again and sighed.

"First, I just want you to know that I did not abandon you." He raised his head to face her again. "I never stopped thinking about you."

"Then why didn't you come for me after Mom . . ." She could not bring herself to say the word.

"It was a while before I found out that your mother died. Me and her were not on good terms when she left Belize with you. We kept in contact; I sent money when I could. I never wanted her to take you to America. She insisted and left without telling me she was leaving. Once she got there, she wrote me a letter and we exchanged phone calls. The plan was for me to come there once she was settled. But things did not go as planned. I was caught trying to cross the border illegally and was deported back home. I was young and wild back then. I ended up getting into some trouble once I got back home and had to go away for a while."

"Go away . . . you mean jail?"

"Yes. I'm not proud to say it, but that was the case. Your mother wrote and sent me pictures of you for a while. Then suddenly, the letters stopped coming. I wrote and wrote trying to find out what was going on, but nothing came. I never got a response. I figured she must have gotten a new man and did not want me around. The letters never came back to me, so I did not know if they were being received. Anyway, when I got out of jail, I went to your grandmother's house in Belize City to ask what was going on. That's when I found out about your mother's sickness and that she had died."

He dropped his head again and slumped his shoulders heavily. "They told me that you were with your aunt Maria. I got her phone number and called her. She refused to let me speak to you. She told me that you were hers now, and I did not deserve to be in your life because I had abandoned you and your mother. She did not know the situation between us before your mom died. I didn't know why Maria acted that way to me. I never did anything to her for her to treat me like that." He shook his head.

"You . . . you tried . . . to come for me?" She teared up.

"Of course, Mia. I would have never left you intentionally. I was in an impossible situation. I had no way to get to America to take you, and I did not have money for lawyers to help me. I didn't know what to do. I even had your uncle, who is still in Belize, call Maria and ask that you be returned to me. She would not hear nothing of it. All I could think was I had to get myself together, get some money, and then I could come for you. I worked day and night in Belize, then to here in my uncle's construction company. By the time I got stable and tried to reach out again, none of Maria's numbers were good anymore. Even her family in Belize said she had stopped communicating with them. I got an investigator to look for you, but it was like you fell off the face of the earth."

Tears flowed down Elise's face. "I had so much hatred and animosity toward you for all this time, thinking that you didn't love me and had abandoned me, not knowing that you had been searching for me all along." She wanted to say so much more to him, to tell him all the things that had happened in her life, all she had to endure, but the words would not come out, only tears.

Miguel took her in his arms. "I love you, Mia. I love you and I missed you so very much." He kissed the top of her head and rubbed her back as she cried like she never cried before.

CHAPTER 27

E lijah rode in the passenger seat of Garry's late-model white Honda Accord, rolling up weed in a big dried-out tobacco leaf, jamming to Buju Banton. Garry had taken him to some of his Rastafarian friends that sold him handfuls of weed for twenty US dollars. Elijah was set to meet Elise and Princess for dinner in the next few hours or so. He had been playing the background for the past week, giving Elise time alone with her family to get to know them better. His time was mostly spent with Garry, who was like one of the homies except he was Jamaican. He was a few years older than Elise and was from a previous relationship Miguel had before he got with Elise's mother. He moved to Jamaica with Miguel, adapted, and fit in just like one of the locals. Garry was a younger version of Miguel: tall, athletic, handsome, deeply sundrenched tanned skin, wavy black hair, and the same blue-green eyes.

Elijah grew tired of all the touristy activities fast. He zip-lined, went horseback riding, white river rafting, parasailed, rode dune buggies, climbed waterfalls, and ate like a hog at an array of the touristy restaurants. They had decided to leave Ocho Rios and stay closer to Elise's family in Kingston. The two-and-a-half-hour drive was too tedious. Miguel found them a charming villa, owned by one of his business colleagues. Even though he wanted them to stay at his home, they did not want to impose, so they rented the villa.

Staying in Kingston was perfect for Elijah because he was ready to see the other side of Jamaica, the part that was not shown on brochure advertisements and postcards. The part where the ruthless Jamaican posses back home came from. Where elections were hashed out with assault rifles and machetes, and where poverty reigned supreme. Garry was the perfect tour guide for that element; he knew and loved the ghettos and street life of Kingston.

Elijah was blown away when he went through the ghettos of Kingston: Trench Town, Waterhouse, Rema, Jungle, seeing how the locals lived. The poverty back home could not compare to the social conditions there. Children ran the street barefooted, with clothes that looked like they had been passed down for three generations. Families were packed into shacks in dilapidated tenement yards, some with no running water or electricity. For lack of a better word, they were the lower class of the island that had to scrap daily for necessities, barely enough to live on.

Garry gave him the history on each neighborhood: how they came to be, who ran them, and what happened there. Elijah learned that the only real jobs for the locals were mostly the ones fortunate enough to work in the hospitality industry. Those were not high-paying jobs but at least they put a little food on the table. Outside of these workers, there was only a small percentage of government workers, professionals, and business owners that were well off. Most of the prosperous businesses were run by foreigners who got a lot more incentives than the locals for doing business in the country. The middle-class was almost nonexistent, and they worked endlessly to stay above the poverty line and maintain a decent lifestyle. If you did not fall into one of those categories, you had to get it any way you could.

In America, low-income people could get assistance from the

government through the welfare program, which provided some modem of housing, food stamps, and health care. Here the lower class was relegated to the slums and forgotten about. It was literally survival of the fittest. Everything on the island cost an arm and a leg, but the average wages were crumbs.

He could not understand the structure of it all. He came to the notion that, just like any other black population, the Jamaicans were dispensable pawns in the white man's game. The descendants of the slaves had basically been relegated to servants on the island. They were able to get just enough to live on so they could keep the island going for the mostly white tourists who came to kick up their feet and be waited on by the smiling negro populace. But regardless of all of that, Jamaicans loved their country. To them, nowhere was better than *yaad*.

Elijah smoked from his tobacco leaf spliff as he stared out the window at the housing projects of Tivoli Gardens, origins of the infamous Shower Posse. A large group of kids played with a battered football (soccer ball) in the middle of a common area. His heart melted for them even though he did not know them. He felt some deep connection to their struggle. They were him and his circle as kids, just in a different ghetto . . . a different hell.

"Pull over," he suddenly told Garry.

"Wha?" Garry asked, surprised. Although they had been through many of the ghettos, Garry was usually the one to choose when and where they went, according to his alliances in those areas. Tivoli Gardens was not one of those areas.

"Pull over real quick. I wanna get out and walk for a bit," Elijah repeated, staring out the window.

"Wha yuh mean? Of all de odda areas weh guh, yuh wan stop yah suh?" Garry stared at him, incredulous. "Yuh mussy rassclaat mwad. Ah meh responsible fi yuh. If anyting hapen tuh yuh, meh fadah and madah gwan kill meh."

"Don't worry about it, just pull over, I got this."

"Dis Jamaica my yute, yuh nuh—"

"Pull over, G," he demanded more forcefully.

Garry considered him long and hard, then shook his head, and kissed his teeth. "Ah'rite suit yuh'self." He pulled the car over.

Elijah got out with the spliff dangling from his lips. Garry got out, walked to the trunk, and pulled out a huge machete.

All eyes fell on them immediately. They got hard and curious stares from the rude boys who were hanging out like the homies back in the Hood, smoking ganja and drinking. Women and children, who were going about their daily chores, gawked at them. Elijah knew he was in the jungle and loved it. His adrenaline spiked as he started walking up the street toward the group of children playing near the corner. He always felt a certain power and connection among the wolves; killers and robbers did not scare him. Where the average dude would be nervous in certain environments, danger excited him. Maybe because he was not scared to die, and it seemed that others sensed that about him.

He made eye contact with the roughnecks on the block and gave the occasional head-up gesture as he passed. Garry followed closely behind, unflinching, feeding off Elijah's energy. They approached the band of kids.

"What's up, youngins?" Elijah greeted them.

They looked at him like he was an alien.

"Deh Yankee Boy wan talk to uhnuh," Garry rolled off in Patois and smiled.

The kids laughed and gathered around him in curiosity.

"What's yo name, lil man?" Elijah asked a tall, skinny dark-skinned boy who he assessed to be the dominant male in the group by the way all the others crowded behind him.

"Meh name Malik, who yuh?"

"My name 9-Lives."

"Wah . . . wat yuh seh?" he asked in confusion.

"Nine Lives," Elijah mouthed it carefully.

All the kids tried to mouth it out. He had to say it a few times before they began to get some form of his name right.

"I got something for y'all." Elijah dug in his pocket, and their hungry eyes followed in anticipation. He pulled out a wad of bills, peeled a fifty, and gave it to Malik. The rest of the children went into a frenzy, crowding him, reaching, pushing, and yelling. Elijah peeled off bill after bill feeding their greedy hands.

Garry looked up the block at the ragamuffins who were now pointing their way trying to see what all the ruckus was about. He shifted from foot to foot nervously, gripping his machete.

Some of the women passing by saw what was going on and made their way over. Elijah gave them bills also. Once he felt he had touched all their hands with bills, he took the remaining bills and threw them in the air as hard as he could. The bills fluttered back down to the ground in all directions. The street went wild as the locals scrambled for the money. The roughnecks hurried their way for a portion of the spoils.

"Let's roll," he hollered to Garry and headed for the car.

The crowd was so occupied with getting the money that no

one paid attention to them leaving until they were almost at the car. All the bills had been picked up and now the kids were looking for the man who just made it rain US dollars. They spotted him getting into the Accord. Malik pointed in his direction and yelled something; they all ran for the car in excitement.

Garry hopped in the driver's seat as Elijah smiled and got in the passenger seat. By the time he put it in drive, the crowd was up on the passenger window.

They screamed, yelled, and reached out to Elijah. He leaned out the window to give as many daps out as he could as Garry pulled off slowly. The kids ran alongside the car for a half-block. Once he was sure they were clear of the kids, he punched the gas.

Elijah turned in his seat and watched them through the rear window as they faded into the distance. He turned around and caught Garry looking at him.

"My yute yuh bad nuh rascloot. Meh neva se nuting like dis. Big up yuh'self, meh general." He shook his head at Elijah and focused his attention back on the road.

* * * *

Elijah arrived late to meet Elise and Princess at Gloria's Restaurant in Port Royal. They were already seated at a table in the crowded dining area with a tall, slender Jamaican man with long, thick dreadlocks.

"Hey, y'all, sorry I'm late. Garry had me on some Jamaican adventures." Elijah laughed, pulled out the chair next to Elise, and sat down.

"Adventures?" Elise looked at him suspiciously. "I can't wait to hear all about it later." She smirked. "Anyway, this is Raz,

Princess's boyfriend."

"Dis Elise's baby fadah, Elijah," Princess added.

Raz continued punching numbers into his cell phone, not acknowledging Elijah. He did a half-wave toward him and mumbled inaudibly in Patois without making eye contact.

Elijah sized him up, and intentionally did not speak, making the moment awkward. Raz finally looked up with an attitude expression. Elijah continued to stare at him with a challenging posture until Raz caught on and reluctantly acknowledged him respectfully.

"Wha ah gwan, meh general?" Raz extended his hand.

Elijah hesitated briefly, then gave him a strong handshake to let him feel his strength. *This arrogant, cocky motherfucka. I oughta break his fuckin' fingers.*

Elise watched their interaction with nervous anxiety, hoping Elijah would not ruin the evening by beating up Princess's boyfriend. She knew Elijah could go from zero to a hundred in a split second if he felt disrespected.

After the tense introduction and they ordered drinks, Elijah let down his guard and enjoyed the atmosphere. The place was lively; patrons talked and laughed loudly over plates of lobster, fish, and other Jamaican cuisine. The alcohol flowed freely as music played from an outside area.

Elise and Princess talked non-stop about everything from childhood to fashion. They had become almost inseparable throughout the visit. Princess was teaching Elise all about Jamaican culture and acquainting her with her life. She was actually an accomplished and goal-focused young woman. She was in her final year at the University of the West Indies studying international business, ran a high-end salon/spa, which she owned with Raz, and was an avid traveler who had been to many countries, including the US multiple times. Elise loved spending time with her and getting to know her. She was sincerely enjoying her newfound family.

"You enjoying yourself, babe?" she asked Elijah over the music.

"Yeah, I'm straight. You know I can blend in any mix." He smiled at her and looked around at the others. He had caught both Princess and Raz sneaking glances at him when they thought he was not looking. It started to irritate him; he did not like the feeling of being under observation while he was trying to enjoy himself. "Imma go get some air for a minute." He picked up his drink and walked outside into the night air.

The lights on the island under the warm night sky were majestic. From the moment he had stepped off the plane in Montego Bay, he never felt like a tourist. There was something familiar about the island that resonated in his soul. It felt like more of a return home than a vacation.

He heard footsteps behind him and turned to see Raz walking his way. He stood next to Elijah and looked out at the lights. Elijah had already assessed that Raz was some sort of a hustler. His flashy Versace suit, jewelry, and slinky, carefree style reminded Elijah of the Rastas back in the States who ran the marijuana trade in most of the larger metropolitan cities.

Raz turned and looked Elijah up and down. "Yuh ah gangsta?" he asked bluntly.

"What?" Elijah was caught off guard by the question.

"I say, are yuh a gangsta, mon. Sumting wrong wit yuh ears?"

Elijah stared at him for a minute, trying to decide if he should answer the seemingly unnecessary question. After a long pause he responded, "Nah, I'm a hoodsta."

"Hud-stah . . . wat yuh mean?"

Elijah had to remind himself that a Rasta man in Jamaica would have no idea what the hell a "hoodsta" was.

"It means I'm bigger and harder than a gangsta."

"Wah yuh mean harrrdah? Edah yuh gangsta, are yuh not? Meh ah real rude-boy gangsta, yuh kno?"

The idea that he was standing there bantering with a Rastaman about who was more gangsta made him chuckle unexpectedly.

Raz smiled for the first time. "Oh, deh Yankee Boy tink meh funny, huh?"

"Nah, man." Elijah laughed again. "It's good. You a gangsta, I'm a gangsta . . . it's good," he conceded good naturedly. *I don't wanna waste energy goin' back and forth with this dude. He probably don't even realize he's bein' rude and obnoxious. It's probably just how he is*, he thought.

"Meh ah gangsta, yuh ah bomboclaat hud-stah." He held up his bottle of Guinness Stout.

Elijah tapped the bottle with his glass and they both drained the last of their drink.

"Yuh kno," Raz began, "I tek yuh to meh hometown tomorrow—deh realll ghetto, kno wat I mean? Meh introduce yuh to deh realll ragamuffins and Don Dadas, yuh kno? Yuh tink yuh can handle dat?"

"I handle whatever comes my way."

"Wah yuh can handle?" Princess asked as she and Elise walked up.

"Meh ah guh tek im to Trench Town. Let im se deh realll ghetto." Raz laughed.

"Yuh nah gwine tek im deh? Dem whe eat im alive," Princess joked.

Elise wrapped her arms around Elijah's waist and squeezed up against him. "You must not know who you dealin' with. This is a real lion. We don't get ate, we do the eat'n."

Princess smirked and gave Elijah another once over. "Yeh, im look like im duh de eatin ah'rite." She laughed loudly.

"Yeh, we guh tomorrow. Weh kill ah goat; eat an drink gud, yuh kno." Raz pulled Princess close to him.

"Sounds good, we'll slide through." Elijah nodded.

"Ah'rite den. Meh wan tek unu tuh Club Asylum latah. Ah dancehall nite tonite. Now yuh can see ow we partey in Jamaica."

"Let's bounce then. I been hearin' all the hype about dancehall. I wanna see what it's all about." Elijah smirked at Elise. "You ready for some whining?"

She laughed. "Are you ready for some whining?" She wiggled her ass against his groin area.

"Ah shit." Elijah grabbed her by the waist.

"Guh get sum more drinks." Raz leaned down and spoke directly into Princess's ear. "We wah tuh be nice for tonite."

Princess smiled and broke free from his grasp.

Raz chuckled. "Meh ah guh roll up a spliff ah de car." He walked off toward the parked cars.

"Come." Princess waved for Elise to follow her. "We guh get

de drinks dem feh de road. Yuh gwine like Club Asylum, it nice."

As they walked away, Elijah instinctively noticed Princess's thick brown thighs, hips, and ass, killing her tight Dolce & Gabbana mini-dress. She looked like she just walked off a hip-hop video set. *Goddamn,* he thought with a broad smile. *That's sis; get your mind out the gutter.* He shook his head and strolled over to Raz who was standing by a Black 840i BMW, already smoking a gigantic spliff, vibing to Elephant Man's "Pon Di River Pon De Bank." Yep, it was going to be an all-night party in Kingston, Jamaica.

CHAPTER 28

———————✦———————

"And you say Cuzz got the work in there right now?" Baby Devil walked toward the back room of the spot on Western.

Lil Teflon trailed behind him dialing a number in his cell phone. "Nigga, I just said I was over there a couple hours ago." Lil Teflon put the phone to his ear. "I coulda upped on 'em right then, but it was too many neighbors and shit outside." He spoke into the phone, Hey, I need you to do me a favor. Drop the G-Ride off for me in front of Green Eyes's house." He listened to the person on the other end. "I'll be there in 'bout twenty minutes or so. Just leave the tools under the seat." He hung up and turned back to Baby Devil. "Like I was sayin,' if it wasn't so many people around, I woulda just did my thing. But we slide through now that it's night, we good."

Baby Devil grabbed clothes from the closet as Lil Teflon talked. He sat on the bed, slipped on some black jogging pants, put on some black and white Nike Cortez, and a black zip-up hoodie.

"Are they strapped up and gon' buck, or you think we can get in and get out without no gun play?" Baby Devil pulled a duffle bag from under the bed.

"Them niggas pussy. Taggers turned Crips type dudes. Long as we draw first they gon' do what the fuck we say with no problems, trust me."

Baby Devil took the Tech-9 from the bag and an extra clip. He walked back to the living room. "Let's get to it then. You say around ten birds?" He sat on the couch next to Skip who was playing a video game.

"Yep, we go down the middle with everything," Lil Teflon assured.

"Fasho." He finished up the last touches on the blunt. "You rollin' with us, Skip?" He leaned back and lit up.

"Nah, I'm straight," Skip responded without bothering to look their way.

"You don't wanna get none of this money, my nigga?" Baby Devil elbowed his arm, offering him the blunt.

Skip looked down at his hand, grabbed the blunt, then turned back to the game, moving the game controller around vigorously. "I got some shit to do tonight."

"That's what's up. We 'bout to get this loot." Baby Devil stood. "Don't think I'm givin' you a portion of my shit when I get back." He laughed, snatching the blunt from Skip's mouth.

"Come on, Cuzz." Lil Teflon shot Skip an ominous look and walked to the door.

"Love you, my nigga." Baby Devil headed toward the door.

"Dev?" Skip called to him just as he reached the door, and Baby Devil stopped and turned around. "All money ain't good money, homie," Skip warned.

Baby Devil smiled. "Nigga, you just trippin' 'cause the homie fuckin' on yo lil bitch. Get over that shit. Pussy come a dime a dozen." He laughed and slammed the door behind him.

Skip stared blankly at the door, then resumed his game.

*   *   *   *

Big Teflon read a *Forbes* magazine as he waited for the bank manager in the spacious lobby of the Bank of America in an upscale area of San Diego. Most of the patrons were white, and aside from a few cursory glances, no one paid him any mind. The bank was minimally crowded with customers conducting their various forms of business—some with window agents, while others sat at the cubicle desk area.

His thoughts shifted to how his life had normalized lately. He was finally able to breathe easy again. After all the drama dealing with the Hood and his brother, after finally ending his toxic relationship with Keisha and putting Virginia on a Greyhound bus back to LA, he could now focus on himself and the things he wanted to accomplish without all the unnecessary distraction. He was at a positive place and things were looking much brighter. A surge of joy shot through him. He smiled and exhaled deeply.

"Mr. Smith?" The bank manager, a gangly Ivy-league type Caucasian man, approached him with an outstretched hand.

Big Teflon was jarred out of his reverie. He hastily closed the magazine, stood up, and shook his hand. "Yes sir. How are you?"

"I'm fine. Sorry to keep you waiting. I'm David Bailey by the way."

"No problem." He picked up his briefcase.

"Right this way." David led him to an office adjacent to a row of open cubicles.

The office was small but comfortable. A nice brown mahogany desk separated the manager's plush black leather chair from two chairs on the opposite side. Big Teflon took a seat and admired the family photos and plaques that adorned the desk and walls.

"So, what can we do for you today?" David sat back and folded his hands.

"Yeah . . . well," he stumbled on his words. This was his first time being in a formal business meeting. "Uh, I'm trying to get a small business loan. Um . . ."

"Is this a loan on an already existing business or a start up?" David cut him off abruptly.

"Existing. I've been in business for a year already. Just want to expand some and upgrade my machinery."

"You have your bank statements, tax-filing for the year, and business operation plans?"

He opened his briefcase and produced all the paperwork. "Here they go." He handed them to him.

David looked over the documents with a neutral expression. "Hmph." He mumbled as he read. "How much of a loan are you trying to get?" He kept reading the documents, not looking up.

"Thirty thousand dollars."

"Hmph." He flipped the page. "Have your business accounts been with us since you've been in business?"

"Yes sir." Big Teflon shifted uncomfortably in his chair.

"Will you excuse me for a few minutes. I need to check some things." David stood up and gathered the paperwork.

"No problem. Take all the time you need."

David left the office and disappeared through another door

leading further into the building.

Big Teflon gazed around the office, looking at the pictures of what he assumed to be David's wife and children. He giggled at the pictures of David hunting and fishing. *I need to try some of this shit one day*, he thought, and laughed at the idea of him dressed in rubber boots, a hunting vest, and a fisherman's hat. He turned to the plaques and framed accolades, reading them one by one, wondering what it would be like to have such accomplishments.

David finally returned with a few documents in his hand, snapping Big Teflon back to reality. He sat down. "I have a few questions for you. I see that you currently have forty-six thousand dollars in your business account. That's quite a sum for a landscaping business to accumulate in a year." He looked at him with unspoken accusation written across his face.

"I work hard; I advertise hard." He met David's gaze.

"Hmph. I see that you keep the secured credit card and the five-thousand-dollar credit line we gave you in good standing. I want to be blunt with you, Mr. Smith. With this amount of money you already have in your account, and the relatively low overhead it takes to run a landscaping business, I don't think you are hard-pressed for a loan. And to be completely honest, with this loan application, I should have run you out of here before you even sat down. But I respect your entrepreneurial spirit and would like to help you. Tell me why exactly you need this money?" He leaned back in his chair.

Big Teflon considered what to say. *He basically tellin' me the application not gon' fly as it is. So fuck it, what I got to lose. Two nos is the same as one.*

"Alright here it is . . . ." Big Teflon sighed. "You're right, I do have all the funds to do all the things I want to do with my business.

But this is the thing, I come from nothing. I don't have parents or family to help me establish credit or show me how to run a business. Hell, I didn't even know what credit was a year ago. I came from a place where I got my first debts at eight years old because my mom put utilities in my name that I knew nothing about. Now as an adult, I'm having to clean all these things up and trying to build myself at the same time. So to your question, I want the loan so I can pay it back in a timely fashion so that it will be credit history attached to my company and help me to build it up."

David rubbed his chin thoughtfully. "I see." He nodded. "You want the credit line more so than the loan."

"Exactly." He started putting his documents back in his briefcase. "But now that I've told you, I know you won't be able to do it at—"

"Hold on now." He waved his hand. "I haven't given you an answer yet."

Big Teflon leaned back in his chair.

"I might be able to work something out for you," David continued. "I know what you're trying to do. For the sake of this conversation, your money comes from your landscaping business. Should your landscaping business generate more money, you become eligible for the larger credit line. You follow me?"

He nodded his understanding.

David looked around and lowered his voice. "I have a friend who's a financial advisor. You hire him and these things will become much easier for you."

"Got you. Say no more." Big Teflon confirmed that he fully understood what he was alluding to.

"Leave me your direct contact number," David He raised his voice back to a normal level. "Let me make some adjustments on this loan application for you. It's a little too early for this right now. But I'm sure I can get you fourteen to fifteen pushed through with no problem. Let me play with the paperwork and I'll fax it over to you for your signature when I'm done."

"Sounds good." Big Teflon smiled broadly.

David stood up and extended his hand. He took it in a strong grip, and they shook.

Big Teflon gathered his things and walked out of the office. The sun seemed to be shining much brighter when he exited the bank. The light breeze from the Pacific Ocean shimmied through the trees and washed refreshingly over his face. For the first time in a long time, he knew in his soul that his fortunes were changing. Life was looking up, and a new chapter was beginning for him.

* * * *

Night fell over the city as Lil Teflon and Baby Devil turned the stolen Nissan Maxima into a dark alleyway off Eighty-Seventh and Avalon. Lil Teflon killed the headlights and drove slowly until they reached the back of an apartment complex sitting midway between the opposite ends of the alley. He made a turn through the sliding black security gate and backed into a parking space facing the gate opening. The alley and the apartment complex were dark except for the few lighted windows at the back of the building.

"Come on, Cuzz," Lil Teflon whispered as they exited the car.

Baby Devil looked around nervously. He walked to the back of the car where Lil Teflon waited near the trunk.

Lil Teflon popped the trunk and grabbed some duct tape, ropes, and a bulletproof vest. He immediately slipped the vest over his head and strapped the Velcro tight. "Put the other vest on." He gestured to the trunk.

Baby Devil reached inside the trunk and rummaged for it. "Where that mothafucka at—"

Just then, the sound of scurrying feet approached as Baby Devil turned around. Lil Telfon was running and disappeared around the building.

"What the . . ." Baby Devil exclaimed as he grabbed the Tech-9 from the trunk.

More movements came from the opposite side of the building.

Bang!

Baby Devil felt a dull thump in his shoulder as his entire left arm went numb. The Tech-9 hit the ground and Baby Devil scrambled to retrieve it. Three more slugs skimmed into the car near his head. He hugged the ground and stretched out for his gun. He reached it and swung it aimlessly toward the direction of where he believed the shooters were. He let off shots in rapid succession. Most of the aimless slugs went into the second story of the apartment building's exterior.

Suddenly, a fast-moving shadow emerged from the opposite end of the car behind Baby Devil. He saw the figure a split second too late. As he tried to swing the Tech-9 toward the new threat, his attacker quickly closed the gap between them accompanied by five shots into Baby Devil's torso and face.

Baby Devil lay on his back, mouth open, staring blankly at the sky with his gun at his side. A slow pool of blood formed beneath and around him as his killer faded into the darkness, a distant chorus of barking dogs piercing the deathly silence.

*   *   *   *

Lil Teflon pulled away from the curb as the last barrage of shots rang out. He made it to the stop sign on Eighty-Eighth Street, made a right, and smashed the gas toward the 110 freeway. He checked his rearview mirror constantly to make sure he was not being followed. He had parked this stolen car at the front of the apartment building earlier that morning and ensured that no one saw him when he walked through the apartment building to the alley where Murder-Min had been waiting for him.

By the time he entered the on-ramp of the 110-North, he heard sirens wailing in the direction he just left, followed by the distant chopping of approaching helicopter propellers in the sky. His heart raced more at the sounds. He merged into the fast lane and sped toward the downtown lights.

He exited on Olympic and pulled onto a residential side street where his truck awaited. He parked the stolen car and double-checked it to make sure he was not leaving anything inside it. He was not worried about fingerprints; he made it a rule to never get near any stolen car without gloves. He rushed away from the car and speed-walked to his truck, turning to scan the area one last time before hopping into the driver's seat and pulling off. He drove cautiously to the '76 gas station and pulled on the side of the building next to two glass-encased payphones. He got out, stepped up to one of the phones, dropped in a quarter, and dialed a number, anxiously surveying his surroundings as it rang.

"Hello . . . Skip?" He spoke and paused for a second. "Hey, just wanted to see if you heard from Baby Dev." He put on his best act of concern.

"Nah, I thought he was with you," Skip responded nonchalantly.

"Nah, we went on that lil mission earlier, but that shit was a bust.

Too many neighbors and shit so we just called it off. I came to the house, and that nigga said he was gonna go holla at Lil 9 on some business shit or something. I just don't trust them niggas. I told him he shouldn't even be fuckin' with 'em. But you know, Cuzz gon' do what he gon do. I was just checkin' in on him. He ain't answering his phone so I was seein' if you rapped to him."

"I ain't heard from him since y'all left. When he get here, I'll tell him you tryna holla' though."

"That's what's up. Ninety minutes."

"Yep." Skip hung up.

Lil Teflon got back in the car and just lingered in a daze. Reaching a place of inner resolve, he started the engine and drove off.

*　　*　　*　　*

Early the next morning, the Hood was ablaze with the news of Baby Devil's murder on the Eastside. The rumor mill churned many different accounts of what happened: Baby Devil had gone to visit a girl and the 8-7 Gangsters mistook him for a Hoover and killed him. Baby Devil was trying to rob one of the 8-7 Gangsters' drug houses and they killed him. Lil 9-Lives had called Baby Devil to a meeting and ambushed him upon arrival. The rumors changed by the hour. They grew more and more outlandish as answers were sought for this blatant and vicious violation.

The entire Tiny Toon clan was in an uproar. Baby Devil was their champion, their leader, their brother, friend, homie. Even those who did not see him as such still respected and admired his gangsta-hand. Revenge was the battle cry. Somebody had to pay; bloodshed was the alleviation for their grief.

By ten a.m., they were strapped up and deep on the Eastside at the murder scene. His body had already been taken away and the crime scene cleared except for a few detectives and one black-and-white who was tying up some last-minute loose ends.

Skip stared at the spot where Baby Devil's dried blood painted the concrete, grief stricken in disbelief. "This can't be," he mumbled repeatedly.

They pressed over to Green Meadows Park to do some investigation. The 8-8 Avalons and the 8-7 Gangsters were clueless about the details surrounding the incident. Both sets claimed that they only became aware someone had been killed when they saw the police and yellow tape. A few people heard some shots during the night, but that was a regular occurrence, nothing out of the ordinary.

"I expected to hear as much coming from them niggas. If they smoked Baby Devil, they not gon' admit it. I just wanted to see they body language and hear whatever stories they had to tell. If it didn't sound right or feel right, like I told y'all before, we was gon' smoke a couple of them just for good measure. I believe them niggas tho." Skip paced back and forth, looking aimlessly at the pavement. He was having the discussion with himself more than the group.

"Cuzz, everything about them niggas said they don't know shit about who did this to the homie," Lil Bar-Dog added.

Skip clenched his teeth in angered frustration. "I told y'all that Lil Teflon said Dev was supposed to be goin' to meet Lil 9 on some business or some shit like that."

Grumblers voiced their suspicions of it being an in-house killing. "It's been so much animosity and gunplay between Lil 9 folks and Lil Teflon-Baby Devil's folks, that nigga Lil 9 probably was on some secret revenge type shit, someone speculated.

The chorus of agreement with the speculation grew louder and louder as individuals added their take on the event. A few of them openly voiced their disagreement with the baseless theory, but they were cowered by the masses who had already convinced themselves that they had the motive and perpetrator.

The group made it back to the Nineties. They gathered at the back of Jesse Owens Park for an important meeting. Skip's brain was scrambling to try and connect the dots of everything that happened on the last day he and Baby Devil were together. "I can't put my finger on it, but I know I'm missing something."

Time-Bomb was advocating for the Tiny Toons to be their own entity within the Nineties. "Fuck them ol' niggas. We need to start our own shit. And if one a them responsible for what happened to Baby Dev., I don't give a fuck who he is, we handle that motherfucka."

"Hold up, all that ain't necessary right now. We don't even know for sure any of the homies was involved," Lil Bar-Dog argued. "Not to mention, it's them OG homies that paved the way for us. How we gon' just spit in they face like that?"

Skip got tired of hearing all the back and forth. "Y'all niggas need to shut the fuck up for once." The bickering ceased. "Let's figure out what's goin' on first before we start sayin' what we gon' do. We all fucked up over the situation but runnin' around like chickens with they heads cut off ain't gon' fix nothin'."

"That's what I'm sayin'," Lil Bar-Dog added.

Skip clenched his jaw. "Don't think I'm agreein' with everything you sayin' on this." He walked up to him. "All the shit about they paved the way . . . I don't care about none of that. If we find out them niggas killed the homie, we gon' extinct them niggas like the dinosaurs."

"That's where I'm at with it," Time-Bomb said. "And when that time comes—if it comes—who side you gon be on, my nigga?" He directed at Lil Bar-Dog. "Are you with the Toons or them cats?"

Lil Bar-Dog did not shrink back. "I'm a Toon, but at the end of the day, I'm from Nine-O first and foremost. I don't know who the fuck you think you is all of a sudden. Niggas can't press me 'bout nothin'." He assumed an aggressive posture, facing Skip and Time-Bomb down. "I understand y'all hurt; we all hurt. But y'all ain't 'bout to start dictatin' and talkin' crazy to me. You can do that to these other niggas, not the Loc though."

Just as the tension was reaching its peak, two cars drove up to the area.

Skip looked at the group. "Don't nobody speak on who we think mighta had a hand in this," he spoke quickly. "We don't know nothing. Listen and watch everything. If the homies did it, they'll tip they hand eventually, got it?"

They nodded their silent assent.

Ju-Ju exited from the lead car. He approached Lil Bar-Dog with a dap and a hug. "What y'all hear, Cuzz?" he asked Lil Bar-Dog.

Lil Bar-Dog glanced at the group. Skip and the others stared, awaiting his response.

Lil Bar-Dog dropped his head and sighed. "Nothing." He raised his head. "Just that the homie dead."

The Toons let out a proverbial collective sigh of relief as they all moved in for condolences, hugs, and daps with the newcomers.

Skip and Time-Bomb discretely faded to the sideline and silently watched them all.

CHAPTER 29

B ig 9-Lives was finalizing some rental agreements for a couple of his tenants when the phone rang in his home office.

"Salute, G-Homie," Big Wizard greeted him on the other end.

"What's the word?" Big 9-Lives continued signing the applications.

"Man, you heard about Baby Devil?"

"Nah, what's up with him?" Big 9-Lives asked nonchalantly.

"Cuzz got smoked last night on the Eastside."

This got Big 9-Lives's undivided attention. He set the pen down and leaned back slowly. "What happened? Who done it?" he asked in disbelief.

"Nobody knows right now. Just a bunch of rumors, you know how it go."

"Damn, Cuzz, that's fucked up." He shook his head. "Regardless of all the shit with Lil Tef and him, I slick liked that lil nigga."

"Me too. Cuzz was a young ridah, was just misled early on. They say whoever did it fucked him off too, all face and chest shots."

"That's wild. Seems like every time I leave, way-out shit happens, bro. Is it some type of sign or something?"

"Might be. But really, LA streets is like this fuckin' island . . . an island where a big-ass tsunami comes through every couple years, and a big-ass wave wipes out everything in its path. Just think about it, damn, yo' whole generation gone, dead, in jail for life, or smacked out on dope. It's only a couple of y'all that got families and shit, living normal. You and niggas like Big Punch is relics. I know you live most of your life out there in the 'A,' but maybe it's time to just stay there. Fuck comin' back to the Hood; you don't need to. You did yours already—missed many of the tsunamis. Grow old with yo' family now, big bro. Niggas will take care of the affairs of the Hood; it ain't goin' nowhere."

"I feel you. It's hard though to just walk completely away. I be feelin' like in certain situations, I'm needed. Then with my nephew and you and Hitt still being in the mix to whatever degree, I feel like it's a duty to make sure y'all stay ahead of the pitfalls."

"Don't worry 'bout us, we good. And Lil 9 don't be over there much no more no way. Speaking of, how he likin' Jamaica?"

Big 9-Lives chuckled. "Nigga over there thinkin' he a Jamaican gangsta. I talked to him last night. He tellin' me 'bout goin' to the ghettos there and how much he felt at home."

"That's cool. Don't even tell him about what's goin' on right now. Let him enjoy his trip."

"Yeah, fasho. I'll put him up when he gets back."

"O'right big homie. I'm 'bout to get in traffic. When I get confirmation on the who, what, and why, I'll tap in with you."

"Yessir. You be careful out there!" Big 9-Lives emphasized.

"No doubt . . . ninety minutes." Big Wizard signed off.

Big 9-Lives reclined back and stared out the window at the Georgia pines that skirted the edge of his property. A light rain began to fall. He pictured Baby Devil's face. Not the gang member or the ridah Baby Devil, but the young Black man that he was. The kid who used to be an innocent boy before the streets turned him against his true nature. A kid just like Elijah, or even himself, for that matter. Visions of all his loved ones and homies rolled through his head. K-Mike and Cannon smiling; Fatima with her beautiful face; Big Fonn, Big Too Sweet, Big Micron, Big Hike, Lil Disco and Baby Disco . . . the procession went on and on until it became too painful to continue in his reverie.

He brought himself back to the present moment, wiped the tears from his eyes, and gathered himself. The rain fell harder, patting against the window ledge. He slowly picked up the pen and went back to his work.

*   *   *   *

Big Teflon worked under the hot sun with his team of six Mexican employees who he hired for the day from the front of the local Home Depot. These undocumented workers were just as skilled as licensed landscapers but at a fraction of the cost.

They were in the process of laying sod and transplanting shrubbery around a soon-to-be daycare center when his phone vibrated on his hip. He answered and listened to his homegirl, Coco, in silence, his arm propped on the digging shovel. His stomach fluttered at the news about Baby Devil, his thoughts immediately going to his brother's well-being. He handed the shovel to one of the workers and walked to his truck. A weight lifted off his shoulders when he heard Lil Teflon was not there when it happened.

Coco gave him an earful concerning Baby Devil's killing. Most of it was conjecture and speculation, but that did not stop her from spilling it like it was the gospel.

He knew that the killing was going to start a new chapter for Lil Teflon. He would not let Baby Devil's death go without extreme repercussions; Baby Devil was his protégé. His gut reaction urged him to get on the highway immediately, drive to LA, and gear up for the war.

He sat in the truck bed and reflected on his memories of Baby Devil. His thoughts drifted to Lil Teflon. *Why ain't he called me by now to give me the scoop on what happened?* Although he and his brother were not as close as they once were, he should have been in contact immediately when something this big was concerned. He stared at his phone. "Maybe I should hit him up," he mumbled, then dialed the number.

Lil Teflon answered on the third ring. "What's up?"

"What's the deal?"

"Man, same shit," Lil Teflon answered dryly.

"What happened with the young homie? Why you didn't let me know?"

"Cuzz, my mind been all over the place. Just tryna figure out who did the shit. It's been hectic; I figured you knew already. Who ended up tellin' you?"

"Coco just hit me, you straight though?"

Lil Teflon sighed. "Yeah, I'm good; I guess. What Coco tell you on who she hearin' did it?"

"She don't know; she just goin' off whatever she hear in the streets and that everyone's a suspect but nothing concrete."

"That's pretty much the situation right now. But I'm gon' get to the bottom of it. Look, I gotta take care of somethin' real quick. I'll tap in wit' you a lil later."

"That's what's up. I'll holla at you later."

"Ninety minutes." Lil Teflon hung up.

The phone lingered at his ear momentarily after the line went dead. He closed the phone and set it next to him. If he did not know anything else, he knew his little brother, and he knew he just rushed to get off the phone. *Why was he being so evasive? Baby Dev was his lil road-dog, he didn't wanna talk about specifics; he didn't sound too fucked up about it. And that nigga was in too much of a hurry to get off the phone. Something ain't right, it ain't addin' up.*

He lingered in thought, replaying the situation repeatedly. *I'm doin' good for me and my son. I can't risk myself for all that madness no more. Ain't that why I moved all the way down here to San Diego? I got that lil nigga outta the situation with the homies, and I told myself that was it, my service to the Hood and my brother was finished. None-a that shit back there in the city is any of my business and Imma stick to that. Period.*

He hopped down from the truck bed, retrieved his shovel from his worker, and began digging up soil with renewed vigor.

*   *   *   *

The weeks passed; Baby Devil was laid to rest, and there was nothing concrete as to who killed him. Usually when mystery killings happened in the Hood, the Set conspiracy theorists ran rampant, and Baby Devil's murder was no different. Whispers circulated around the time of the funeral about Elijah not being in attendance. It did not make the situation any better that Lil

Wizard and Hitter did not attend either. Big Wizard and Big 9-Lives had shown up, but that was not enough for those who wanted to believe that their crew was somehow responsible.

The Tiny Toons were growing more and more susceptible to all the rumors. Young minds were easily influenced, and Lil Teflon was the master at planting seeds in subtle ways. He was not screaming from the pulpit that Elijah and the others were responsible, but a nudge here and a whisper there in the right ears was enough to ignite the fire and stoke it gradually until it became big enough to burn down mountains.

The Tiny Toons' own divisions within their circle started to become more pronounced, although they kept it mostly among themselves. Skip had taken a step back to try to clear his head. This left Time-Bomb and others to be the voice of retaliation as Lil Bar-Dog and a small band of detractors continued to call for restraint.

Their most recent meeting about the issue almost resorted in a gunfight, with Lil Bar-Dog and Time-Bomb facing off. Time-Bomb accused Lil Bar-Dog of being a traitor, claiming his loyalties lay with Ju-Ju, which meant they lay with Elijah. Time-Bomb had the numbers on his side, and he used the advantage to try and force an ultimatum on Lil Bar-Dog: either he was with the Toons, or he was against them.

Lil Bar-Dog held his ground, standing firm on the principle that unless hard facts were presented that the homies did Baby Devil in, he was not supporting any actions against them.

A few level-headed Tiny Toons intervened between Time-Bomb and Lil Bar-Dog to stop it from escalating to violence right then and there. But it was obvious that the winds of change were in the air at every level of the Hood. Just when everyone thought they had put the divisions behind them with Lil Teflon and Elijah squashing the beef, chaos was brewing at their front door again. And this time, the players knew that if the powder keg blew, the damage would be irreparable.

* * * *

Ju-Ju and Lil Bar-Dog rode from Jesse Owens Park together, heading to Ju-Ju's house. The nighttime traffic was easy on Century Boulevard. Lil Bar-Dog passed Ju-Ju the blunt, who was bobbing to Evelyn Champagne Kings "Heartbeat" playing low on the car stereo. Ju-Ju pulled on the blunt, watching the passing scenery from the passenger window.

"Cuzz, with all this talk goin' around, what do you think about the fact that Lil 9 didn't show up to the homie funeral?" Lil Bar-Dog asked.

Ju-Ju looked over at him. "Are you serious, Cuzz? You gon' really ask me some dumb shit like that?"

"Nah, not me, Cuzz. I'm just sayin'. That's what some of the homies been sayin' like, he didn't show—"

Ju-Ju cut him off. "I don't give a fuck what them niggas sayin'. Any nigga tryna say Lil 9 had anything to do with Baby Dev gettin' killed can come holla at me. The homie not even in the country right now. Where's this bullshit comin' from anyway? How did that even become a topic?"

"Shit, I don't know. Guess niggas just tryna figure it out, and somehow Nine's name was thrown into the mix. Guess 'cause of that beef niggas had in the past. You know how it go."

"Yeah, well, I know how it ain't gon' go. Niggas ain't 'bout to smut the homie name up. When we go back to the park tomorrow, point out who talkin' that shit. And anybody else you hear sayin' something about it, just let me know. I'll deal with this myself. Nip this shit in the bud right now."

"That's what's up." Lil Bar-Dog cut his eyes nervously at Ju-Ju, then back at the road. "Hey, did you fuck that bitch China Doll the other night? I saw her all on you." He laughed lightheartedly.

"Hell nah." Ju-Ju hit the blunt again and passed it back. "The Forties can keep that pussy. I don't even like fuckin' on our homegirls, and I damn sure don't want theirs. I like square bitches, not no bitch bangin' as hard as me."

"I feel you. But me, I'd take her ass down. She kinda cool for real tho."

"Yo young ass just at that age where you want to fuck everything. Better stop trickin' off ya dick."

Lil Bar-Dog laughed as he pulled in front of Ju-Ju's. "Just tryna enjoy my youth." He parked. "Is it cool if I come in and take a leak real quick?"

"It's good." Ju-Ju got out of the car.

They walked to the front door. Ju-Ju fumbled with the keys, finally inserting the right one that unlocked the door. He stepped in and flipped on the light in the living room. Lil Bar-Dog followed him in and closed the door.

Ju-Ju set his pistol, phone, and keys on the coffee table. "You know where the bathroom at." He walked to the refrigerator and opened it.

Lil Bar-Dog walked toward the bathroom on the right side of the hallway.

Ju-Ju stood in front of the opened refrigerator trying to decide what he wanted to snack on. He grabbed the jar of Miracle Whip and reached to the lower shelf to grab a variety pack of turkey lunch meat. As he raised up, his entire world went dark.

* * * *

Lil Bar-Dog's heart raced as he stepped into the darkened hallway toward the bathroom. Instead of entering, he pivoted to the left and retrieved a small, five-shot .22 revolver from his pocket. He took a quick, deep breath and reversed course back toward the living room. His hands and legs trembled as he tiptoed through the living room lightly. Panic gripped him as he entered the kitchen where Ju-Ju was bent over grabbing something out of the refrigerator. It was too late to turn back; he steeled himself and raised the pistol. As soon as Ju-Ju stood up, he moved to where the barrel of the pistol was mere inches from the back of Ju-Ju's head. Time stood still as he squeezed the trigger. His senses heightened. He saw the cylinder spin as the hammer went back with a menacing, faint clicking sound. A slight "pop" erupted. Black soot and a tiny tongue of flame reached out and licked Ju-Ju's head, right behind the ear.

The shattering sound of the Miracle Whip jar crashing to the floor snapped him out of his slow-motion daze as Ju-Ju's body fell limp, head hitting the hard linoleum with a thud. He stepped back in a panic as a pool of blood expanded from Ju-Ju's head toward him. He knew instantly that a second shot was not necessary, seeing the damage of the slug and the lifeless body. Ju-Ju was gone.

He backed out of the kitchen on rubbery legs and peeped out the living room window. Time-Bomb had suggested using the .22 because it would not make much noise. If someone on the block did hear it faintly, they would probably figure it was a car backfiring or an exploding firecracker.

Everything outside was going on as normal. He turned out all the lights in the house, waited a couple minutes just to be sure the coast was clear, then exited out the side door. He stealthily crept to the front and looked both ways before speed-walking to the car. He hopped in his car, beads of sweat dotting his face and shivers running up and down his body. He started the car and casually drove off at a moderate speed so as not to draw any unnecessary attention.

He turned onto Vermont, drove to Century, and headed east to the 110 freeway. As he rounded the ramp heading north to the Valley, the reality of what he did hit him like an avalanche. His eyes blurred with tears. He'd just killed his big homie Ju-Ju and left him in a cold, dark house bleeding on the floor. His conscience questioned him: Did Ju-Ju deserve that? He was not so sure.

But Baby Devil did not deserve what happened to him, he reasoned. It was war with Lil 9-Lives, and Ju-Ju made it clear that whoever went to war with Lil 9-Lives had to go to war with him. Ju-Ju was more of a presence in the Hood than Lil 9-Lives, so that made Ju-Ju the bigger threat. They would see Lil 9-Lives coming, but not Ju-Ju, because he was ingrained in the fabric; so he had to go.

He wiped his eyes. "A soldier for a soldier, a brother for a brother," he mumbled. "Toons against the world." He loudly repeated the mantra that he, Time-Bomb, and a chosen few of their circle had come to terms on in a meeting earlier in the week. They had put to rest their animosity toward one another and aimed it against what they perceived to be a common threat to them. As much as it pained him, he had to pick a side. He chose his own generation: the Tiny Toons.

CHAPTER 30

E lijah took another bite from a half-eaten Juici Patties beef patty as he waved goodbye to the two elderly white tourists. His driver was not available for the night, so he decided to drive himself around the island. Sizzla's "Solid as a Rock" boomed from the stereo as soon as he started the car.

Elijah stuffed the last piece of the patty into his mouth and pulled out into traffic, bobbing his head. He soon transitioned from the pothole-filled road onto a narrow, two-lane highway that stretched along the coastline. The radiant sun was just beginning to fade as the waves tumbled onto the soft, white sand. A couple rode horses along the shore, a picturesque scene of beauty and calm. He drummed his thumbs against the steering wheel to the music as he took in the spectacular scenery.

Suddenly, an ominous row of black clouds rolled in, covering the sky. In an instant, the beautiful, orange dusk that illuminated the beach fell to night. The car accelerated slightly without him pressing the gas. The cars going in the opposite direction were now moving exceedingly fast as well. "What the fuck?"

"It's o'right, just roll with the flow, Cuzzo," a familiar voice came from the passenger seat.

Elijah swung his head to the passenger side; Ju-Ju sat there, smiling at him.

"Damn, Cuzz, where you come from?" Elijah asked, shocked.

"I just came from the Hood." Ju-Ju continued to smile.

Elijah was confused. "It's good you here. I'm gonna take you to this lil food joint; the patties is bomb. And the women here . . . my God! They exude sex. They wear all this super-tight shit that you see the thighs, ass cheeks, everything."

He glanced at Ju-Ju again and noticed the smile seemed pasted on his face.

"You straight, Ju?" Elijah's eyes darted back and forth from the road to Ju-Ju; the car moved faster.

"I'm good, Cuzz. I'm just on my way home and wanted to see you before I go."

"You goin' home?" Elijah looked at him with concern. "You just got here; ain't even had time to do nothing yet."

The car was now moving so fast that he had to dart into the oncoming traffic lane to prevent running into the car in front of him. He tapped the brakes, but that did nothing to slow them down. "Damn, Cuzz, the brakes not working!" He swerved back into his lane, barely avoiding a head-on collision with an old truck whose horn rang in his ears as it flew past. He looked back at Ju-Ju, who was now smiling again, staring straight ahead at the speeding road before them.

"All gas no brakes, my nigga!" Ju-Ju laughed.

"Huh?"

"All gas no brakes, my nigga . . . all gas no breaks, my nigga," he repeated as he laughed hysterically.

"What's going on with—" Elijah had to dart in and out of the lane again.

"No brakes, my nigga . . ."

The gas pedal was all the way to the floor, the car moving in a blur. The highway elevated at some point in the drive and the ocean was about seventy feet below them. Elijah knew that if he could not get the car under control, it was only a matter of time before they plunged into the ocean.

"All gas no brakes, my nigga . . ."

Elijah put the car in neutral, figuring that once it was no longer in drive, it could not accelerate anymore. It did not do any good; the speed continued accelerating. He panicked, pressing the brakes, steering in and out of traffic like a NASCAR driver, knowing that one miscue spelled certain death.

They sped toward the bumper of the car in front of them and the oncoming headlights were too close to use that lane to pass. The only options were to run into the back of the car in front of him or try to squeeze through the gap, which was really a pedestrian lane. He decided the better option would be to hit the rear of the car in front, hoping it would slow his car. He braced for impact.

"All gas no brakes, my nigga . . ."

They moved rapidly toward the car, their headlights illuminating the trunk and back window. They made impact; a loud boom sounded as the car spun out of control and slid across the freeway through the oncoming traffic.

Ju-Ju laughed hysterically, then suddenly disappeared, leaving Elijah alone to feel the impact.

Elijah tried to wrestle the steering wheel in the opposite

direction, to no avail. The car hit a patch of gravel, then flew airborne off the side of the mountain, plunging slowly toward the dark ocean below.

"Ahhhhh!" Elijah screamed right before impact.

The front of the car pierced the ocean, and Elijah shot up in bed with a start. He looked around the hotel suite as beads of sweat poured from his forehead and his heart raced. Elise was sound asleep beside him. The soft glow of the rising sun touched the thin curtains; the birds chirped their morning songs. He laid his head back on the soft pillow and stared at the ceiling. It was not long before sleep overtook him again.

CHAPTER 31

JuJu's death was an unexpected blow to the entire Hood. Baby Devil and now Ju-Ju, within such a short period of time. This was unprecedented for the Nine-Os. It sent shockwaves from San Diego to Atlanta. His body was found by Jada the day after he was killed. She had gone over to see what was going on after he did not show up to pick her up to go house hunting and look at some investment properties.

Since their engagement, they had put plans in motion to start moving their lives in a direction out of the Hood. She'd stocked up on all sorts of reading material about real estate and other investments and enrolled in a real estate program to get her license. Ju-Ju had a sizeable stash from hustling, and with her job at the bank and good credit, they were on a solid financial path. For the first time since they got together, she saw a different side of him—one of optimism for a better life, one of hope. Now all that was gone, taken away by a ruthless act. She was devastated, beyond consolation. All their hopes, dreams, and plans for a better future for their little family had been stripped away.

Agent Berrigan was on the scene as soon as the news hit the airwaves. It did not take long for him and the LAPD detectives to surmise that Ju-Ju's killer was someone he knew due to the manner of his murder. He had to have been acquainted with whomever killed him to let them in his house and turn his back on them. There was no forced entry, no sign of a break-in or robbery, nothing disturbed. He was willing to wager that it was one of Ju-Ju's Set members who punched his ticket.

He and the LAPD scoured the neighborhood searching for clues and questioning anyone who saw or heard anything. One of the neighbors claimed that they thought they heard a car backfire the night before, but that was about it. He knew someone had to see something but was not talking. This murder bothered him. For Ju-Ju's son's mother to find him the way she did was unthinkable to him. He saw the pain in her eyes, heard the deep sorrow in her cry. Regardless of who Ju-Ju was, he did not see that in her; he only saw a broken young mother of a now fatherless child. Another statistic.

* * * *

The birds chirped their dawn awakening outside Agent Berrigan's window as he laid on his back in the semi-darkness, his hand under his head, staring up at the ceiling. Ju-Ju's crime scene was the first thing on his mind after a long, unsettling night. A thousand scenarios played over and over in his head as to who may have pulled the trigger. But beyond the whole whodunit aspect, something about this crime went beyond his job.

His thoughts went to when he first got to the scene. To see Ju-Ju lying face down in front of his open refrigerator, knowing he was getting something to eat or drink, shot from behind in the comfort and safety of his own home by someone he obviously believed to be a friend. To Berrigan, that was the ultimate treachery and violation of basic humanity. *They're a bunch of fucking animals, killing one another for ego and sport. This makes no sense.*

His mind jumped back to Jada. Her standing there, eyes puffy and red, with Ju-Ju's dried blood still staining her clothes, her small son clinging to her leg trying to understand what was going on. She had practically begged him on hands and knees to find the people responsible. He was usually numb to all emotional hysterics from family members. He had dealt with more crime scenes than he could count, and they all seemed to be the same, for the most part. Yet, Jada had reached him.

He reached over to the nightstand and grabbed a pack of cigarettes and a lighter. He lit the cigarette and threw the pack back on the nightstand. He lay back down, blowing a plume of smoke toward the ceiling. "I have to find a way to lean on my informants harder." He spoke softly. "It's time. It's fucking time." He sat up abruptly, threw off the covers, and stood up naked.

He made his way to the bathroom, pissed, then jumped in the shower. Feeling reinvigorated, he toweled off and ambled to the kitchen. He put on a pot of coffee and dropped a couple slices of bread in the toaster. He grabbed the *LA Times* from the counter, sitting down at the table and thumbing through it.

A thin, naked, unattractive dirty-blonde dragged in from the bedroom, looking half-asleep. "Why didn't you wake me?" she asked in a southern, country twang.

"I didn't know I was supposed to," he responded without looking up from his paper.

She rubbed sleep from her eyes, then scratched her ass as she walked over and opened the fridge. "You don't have any more Donald Duck orange juice?" She bent over and rummaged through the refrigerator.

"Do you see any?"

"Well damn, you don't have to get your panties in a heap; I was just asking a question."

"And I was just answering." He folded the paper and looked over at her. "And speaking of panties, why don't you try putting some on?" He got up and poured a cup of coffee.

"You wasn't worried about no panties when you had your nose up my ass last night." She uncorked a bottle of apple juice and drank straight from the container.

The toast popped up. He put them on a small saucer, grabbed his cup of coffee, shot her a disgusted look, and walked to his office at the back of the house. "Airheaded bitch," he mumbled. He shut the door and sat down at his desk, setting down the items in his hands and pulling his black "R'90" folder in front of him. He flipped it open and jotted a few notes while eating his toast.

A knock at the door. "I'm gonna get ready to go. Can we fuck one more time before I leave?" she screamed from the other side of the locked door.

"Go away!" he yelled, irritated.

"Yeah . . . fuck you too!" she called back.

He paused, listening if she was still at the door. He heard her soft footsteps padding down the hallway. He returned to his work. "Unfucking believable." He shook his head, reached for the phone, and dialed a number.

"Bill?" He spoke eagerly into the phone. "Gonna need some big favors. Tap every contact you have over at the DA's office and over at CRASH. We need search warrants for as many Rollin 90s' houses and drug spots as possible. We need to make as many arrests as possible. And on our guy, the 'Silver Fox,' see if there's something we can arrest his ass on. We've been playing too nice. He's given us good leads but that's not enough. It's time for him to play ball fully or he's out."

He paused and listened intently to Bill's response.

"Probable cause? Fuck all the red tape. Make up some fucking probable cause. Listen, Bill, playing it by the book is over. That book is in the fucking trashcan as far as I'm concerned. We've been running this rat race for too long and haven't stopped this shit. Either you're with me or you're not. Tell me now so I'm not wasting no more goddamn time on this phone."

"Fine," Bill snapped. "I'll piece together what we already have and come up with something we can work with."

"Thanks, Bill. I knew I could count on you." He hung up the phone and leaned back in the chair. A hint of a smile crept across his face.

* * * *

Big Teflon cried like a baby when he heard about Ju-Ju's death. He ripped his entire garage apart in a fit of rage. He vowed that whoever was even remotely responsible would pay the ultimate price, no matter who it was.

He loaded his trunk with enough artillery to supply a small army and jumped on the freeway. He cried off and on all the way from San Diego to LA as visions of Ju-Ju's face flashed before him in a montage of experiences, from buying candy and ice cream from the ice cream truck to the first real mission they went on together.

When he arrived in LA, he could barely see through the smoggy sky. It heightened his mood of sorrow. He cursed God as he beat on the steering wheel, threw his head back, and let out a wail of pain that verged on madness.

* * * *

Elijah's eyes were bloodshot-red with puffy bags beneath as he searched the rack for the keys to his low-profile Ford Taurus. He and Elise cut their trip short when they heard the news. He moved around in a nostalgic daze since their return from Jamaica. Elise, Lauren, and Sistah Raheema tried to console him, but to no avail.

With every passing moment, he slipped further and further into an unreachable zone.

He packed a bag filled with all the attire he would need for the trenches. Sistah Raheema came into the kitchen as he searched aimlessly through the keys on the rack. She looked him up and down, noticing the black Chuck Taylors, black Dickie pants, and black-and-gray Charlie Brown shirt he was wearing.

"You seen the keys to the Taurus?" He continued staring at the key rack.

She walked over to the rack and found them instantly. "Here you go." She handed them to him.

He took them from her, picked up the bag of clothes, and walked toward the back door adjacent to the kitchen.

Amaru ran in. "Daddy!" He jumped in Elijah's arms.

Elijah held him in one arm, staring closely at his face as if he were trying to etch it in his memory. He kissed Amaru on the cheek.

"You know Daddy loves you, right?" Tears filled his eyes.

Amaru nodded his head enthusiastically.

"Here you go." He handed him to Sistah Raheema. "Stay with Aunty; Daddy gotta go." He started back to the door.

"Elijah?" Sistah Raheema called out to him.

He stopped and turned to her without saying a word.

She held up three fingers to him. "Three," she said. "The Quran says you have three days to mourn the dead. After that, the affair is between that person and his Maker." She concluded with a knowing look.

He nodded and walked out the door.

CHAPTER 32

E lijah pulled into the driveway of his childhood home. The sky was an ash-gray and the neighborhood was uncharacteristically still, like the atmosphere itself was in mourning. He grabbed his bag of clothes and a big duffle bag from the trunk, slamming it shut. He then headed up the steps to the front door. He entered the dark house and dropped the bags near the door. No one had been there for weeks; the stale smell was blatant testament to that.

He pulled the curtains to let in some light, then walked to his bedroom. The house was eerily quiet. He felt an unseen presence there with him as he sat on the bed, looking around at the pictures on the wall. He stood up and grabbed an old Polaroid picture encased in a thin plastic covering from among them.

It was a picture of him, Ju-Ju, and Big and Lil Teflon in their early teens. Ju-Ju was the only one smiling as they posed for the shot. A tear slid down his cheek and hit the plastic. A pain rose from his stomach up to his chest, an emotional response so pronounced that it manifested as a physical pain that squeezed his heart and made his breath come in dry ragged snatches. His eyes poured tears in endless streams; he fell to his knees. He held his chest as a rhythmic, hoarse chorus escaped his lips. He rasped forward like he was straining to get it out. Someone watching him would have thought he was having a stroke. But this was not a stroke; this was grief so deep, so ancient, that its release threatened to shatter him from the inside out. A grunt caught in his throat for what seemed like an eternity, then he abruptly let out what could only be described as a feral animal-like howl that could be heard a half-block away.

*   *   *   *

Hours passed before he finally regained his composure. He washed his face but could not wash away his bloodshot eyes. He spread the contents of his duffle bag out on the bed. Inserting banana clips in the AK-47 and the AR-15, he locked and loaded them before stuffing them in the closet. He double-checked both .40 Glocks before putting them on the sides of his hip. He pulled his puffy Raiders starter jacket from the closet, looked at himself in the mirror to make sure it still fit, pulled the hood onto his head, and tightened the drawstrings to further conceal his features.

It was still relatively early as he walked out the house to a cut that led to the next block over. He leaped the fence the same way he had done so many times as a youngster. Within a few minutes, he was in front of a set of duplexes across the street from Ju-Ju's house. The homies and some of Ju-Ju's family crowded the outside, parked cars completely blocking the street.

Elijah walked into view and approached the crowd. Lady Rawdog rushed over to give him a big hug. The other OG homeboys and homegirls also gathered around to console him.

Elijah then approached Jada and Ju-Ju's cousins to offer his condolences.

"Where did it happen?" he asked Jada.

She led him inside the house to the kitchen, where remnants of his dried blood could still be seen on the floor. She pointed to the spot in front of the refrigerator. He stooped down and put his hand on the spot where his brother had taken his last breath.

Thoughts of Ju-Ju's mother, Brenda, crossed his mind, paining him even more. He had promised her that he would take care of Ju-Ju, and he failed her. He looked up at Jada.

"Who did this? I mean, was he beefin' with somebody who could get this close to him? Ain't no enemies from outside the Set could come in here and done this."

She shrugged her shoulders. "He didn't say anything about having problems with anybody." She started to tear up.

He stood up and hugged her. "Don't worry, I'm gonna find out who did it. And when I do . . ." He caught himself.

She eased him back, holding him at arm's distance. "Kill all of them motherfuckas." She looked up at him with flowing tears.

Elijah nodded and walked away before he broke down in front of her. He stepped out onto the porch and surveyed the block, considering what his next move should be.

Across the street, two doors down, he spotted Ms. Alice, an old woman who had been living in the neighborhood all their lives. She locked eyes with him and gestured with her head for him to come over, then walked back into her house.

He looked around, making sure no one else noticed the exchange between him and Ms. Alice. He exchanged a few more greetings, then discreetly slipped away to the house next to Ms. Alice's. He walked up the driveway, checked his surroundings, then hopped the gate, landing in her backyard. She was waiting with the door open.

"Hey, Ms. Alice." They embraced.

"Hey, baby." She stepped back and looked him over. "I'm sorry about Julius." She shook her head and led him into her house. "I know he was your friend. It's such a shame."

"Yeah, it is." He followed her to the kitchen. "Ms. Alice, I need to know if you saw anything."

"Have a seat." She motioned him to a chair at the table. She sat opposite him. "You know I don't get into you young folks' business . . ."

"I know, Ms. Alice, and I promise, whatever we talk about is between me and you."

"I know that, boy. I wouldn't have called you over here if I thought you would go run ya mouth. I'm not tellin' nobody else but you because I know you and him loved each other. I didn't even tell the police when they came by here askin'." She leaned forward and whispered in conspiratorial tones, "I saw that boy leaving out of Julius's house that night. He didn't think nobody saw, but I saw 'im, yes I did . . . um-hm." She nodded.

"When? Who was it?" He was barely able to contain his eagerness.

"It was the young boy I see him with all the time. The boy with that fancy car; only that night, he was in a different car."

"What young boy? What type of car? Why do you think he was the one who did it?" He rattled off the barrage of questions.

"I don't know his name. That lil, fat, brown-skinned boy. In one of them new cars y'all be driving. I know it was him because I was sitting in my living room watching *COPS* when they drove up. I watched them go in the house. A couple minutes later, I heard what sounded like a firecracker or something. I looked out the window, but everything seemed okay. A few minutes later, I saw that boy come out of the driveway and hurry to his car. It was a lil strange that he didn't come out the front door, but I didn't pay it much mind. It wasn't till the next evening when all the police and stuff came, and I heard what happened, that it hit me of why that boy was moving like a ghost in the night."

Elijah leaned forward. "Can you give me some more details of what he looked like? Is he somebody that grew up with us?" He pressed for any information he could get.

"No, he not one of the boys that grew up with y'all. He a new one; I can't believe you don't know who I'm talkin' 'bout, he used to be with Julius all the time."

He put his hand on his chin, trying hard to think of whom she was referring to. "If he come over, or you see his face, can you point him out to me?"

"I sho can." She sat back with her arms crossed.

"Alright, let me figure out how to make it where you can see them, but they don't see you. For right now, while people is comin' and goin' from the house, keep your eye out and let me know if he shows up. I'll leave you my number."

"Okay. All I ask is that you keep me safe. Don't want none of it coming back to my front door."

"Don't worry, I got you." He stood up. "You have a pen and paper so I can write my number down?"

She shuffled over to one of the drawers and brought him a pen and small writing pad. He scribbled his number down and handed it to her.

"I'm right around the corner at the house. Call me, and I'm here in no time."

She nodded and looked at him. "I known you boys for a long time." She patted his arm gently. "I don't want to know the details, but don't let them get away with doing that to Brenda's boy."

"They won't, Ms. Alice." He kissed her cheek. "They won't." He walked out the back door and jumped the gate, returning to Ju-Ju's house. The crowd was much larger than when he left. He approached the crowd with new suspicions. Anyone there could be involved. Ju-Ju's killer could be right there in front of him. It did not make sense; Ju-Ju loved the Hood and the everyday front-liners loved him back. *Who from the Hood would want to see him dead, and for what?*

Big Teflon drove up, parked, and hopped out of his truck. He mean-mugged everyone in the crowd, the butt of his pistol sticking out of his pocket in plain view. Elijah saw the devastation on his face as he paced back and forth like an enraged bull. He did not see Elijah standing with Lady Rawdog aside from the crowd. "Hold up a minute, Aunty." He walked off and headed over to Big Teflon.

Big Teflon hugged him and sobbed. "These niggas killed our bro, Cuzz." His tears streamed onto Elijah's jacket. "Why they kill him? Why they kill him?"

Elijah's tears poured freely. All animosity disappeared; none of it mattered anymore. The only thing that mattered was the bond of shared grief for their friend, their brother.

Big Wizard and Hitter walked up just as Elijah and Big Teflon separated from their embrace. Big Teflon wiped his eyes and turned to the entire crowd. "I don't know who killed the homie!" he yelled. "But when I find out, you dead, nigga! You hear me? Imma kill yo' whole family, you bitch-ass niggas!" He reached for his pistol.

Elijah grabbed him. "Come on, Cuzz, not here." He half-pushed, half-carried Big Teflon back toward his truck. "His family's here," he whispered in his ear.

"Fuck that, Nine. They killed my nigga!" Big Teflon started bawling again. "They killed my nigga, Cuzz!"

"I know, I know, just not here. We gon' handle it." He held Big Teflon near the truck until he got himself together.

"I gotta go, Cuzz." Big Teflon wiped the tears and snot from his face. "I can't be in these niggas' presence. I know they did it; I know it." He reached for his door. "I'm here, Nine. I ain't goin' nowhere until I find out what happened and make these niggas pay."

He put one foot in the truck, turning around and addressing the onlookers again. "Remember what I said. Remember my face, niggas. It's gon' come out, and when it do, I'm comin' for you, any of you!"

He looked back at Elijah. "Don't trust none of these niggas. I'm here, Cuzz, I'm here." He jumped in the truck, started it up, and sped off.

When Elijah turned around, everyone was watching him in stark silence. He considered them all for a moment, then turned and walked away, disappearing back through the cut that he had emerged from earlier.

*   *   *   *

Skip watched Elijah go with mixed emotions. He hated what had happened to Ju-Ju and did not approve of the move. He was not aware of what was happening until it was already done. It was agreed that no moves would be made until they were sure who was responsible for killing Baby Devil before he left to lay low at his family's spot out of LA. But while he was not around, Time-Bomb and Lil Bar-Dog came up with the ill-advised plan. He did not care much for either one of them, but he was not going to sell them out in case they turned out to be right. And if they were right, it went without saying that Lil 9-Lives was next on their list.

He watched Big Wizard and Hitter walk over and join a group with Lady Rawdog, Big 1-Punch, and other older homeboys and homegirls. He discreetly eased closer to eavesdrop on their conversation.

"Yeah, I know he fucked up about this, they been road dogs for forever," Lady Rawdog was saying. "Y'all make sure you don't let him crash out."

"We got him," Big Wizard responded. "Life is a trip. He went to Jamaica, enjoying life, now come back to some shit like this."

"Tell me 'bout it," Hitter added. "But at the end of the day, this the life we live."

The tidbit about Lil 9-Lives just coming back from Jamaica caught Skip's attention. This was not the first time he'd heard that. He dismissed it before, but this could not be a coincidence that he heard it again. Was it true that Lil 9-Lives was in Jamaica when Baby Devil was killed? If that was the case, then Lil Teflon lied about Baby Devil telling him he was going to meet Lil 9-Lives.

His mind raced back to the last day Baby Devil was alive. He remembered the uneasy feeling he had when Baby Devil and Lil Teflon left to go hit that lick. He wanted to ask questions to try and figure out when Lil 9-Lives left for Jamaica, but how could he inquire without raising suspicions? They were not on terms where it would make sense to be asking about Lil 9-Lives' vacation. Skip gauged those in the conversation to see who would be the best one to approach later.

"Somethin' you want?"

Skip was startled by Hitter's unexpected question. He had not realized that Hitter noticed him there. "Uh . . . nah, um . . . I'm good." Skip stumbled on his words.

"You sure?" Hitter asked with venom in his voice.

"Yeah. A nigga's mind just fucked up right now. Too many losses."

"Um-hm . . . alright."

Skip lingered for a moment longer, then made his way over toward another crowd of homies. *Now may not be the time. These older niggas 'bout to go on one for sure. They suspect us.*

He engaged in a couple meaningless conversations for appearances, and as soon as he saw a clear opening to leave without drawing attention, he got the hell out of there.

*   *   *   *

Lil Teflon sipped from a cup of hot coffee on the balcony of his condo off the Las Vegas strip, watching the busy traffic below. He was usually an early riser, but it was already afternoon and he was just waking up. In fact, he could have slept longer, but dragged himself out of bed. For once in his life, his conscience was eating away at him and depression engulfed him like a dark cloud. He had gone too far, and an unintended consequence had come out of it: the death of Ju-Ju.

The Tiny Toons had not told him that they planned to kill Ju-Ju. But he'd played cutthroat politics for so long it was not hard to put two and two together. He fueled the flames on the Baby Devil situation, knowing it would fester hate in the heart of the youngsters for Elijah. He never considered that some of them would have the balls to start killing any homies they thought were close to him, especially Ju-Ju. Everyone in the Set knew that even though Ju-Ju loved Elijah, his loyalty was to the Hood; he was fair.

I shouldn't have even wacked Baby Dev, but the nigga had gotten too big for his britches, tryin' to take my crew, fuckin' my bitch, goin' against my calls, and rubbin' elbows with niggas that he knew was my enemies. He tried to reason with himself. *I just had to get my position back, righten the ship. Was tryin' to kill two birds with one stone, getting him and Lil 9 out the way at the same time. They couldn't have thought I was gonna let them niggas get away with shootin' me in the face. But damn, Ju-Ju?* He shook his head as visions of Ju-Ju's face flashed in his mind. Eventually, tears that he did not even think he had anymore flowed down his cheeks.

"Damn, Ju, I fucked up," he whispered to Ju-Ju's invisible presence. "I'm sorry, homie . . . I'm sorry." The floodgates burst and he openly bawled.

CHAPTER 33

B ig 9-Lives's phone rang in the middle of a set of bench presses. He considered not answering. He was spiraling into a black hole; he withdrew from everyone. Ju-Ju was like another nephew to him. he'd raised all those kids, even the Teflon brothers. The phone stopped ringing, then immediately rang again. He resigned himself and answered it.

"What's up, OG? How you doin'?" Lady Rawdog greeted.

"Just here." He sounded deflated.

"I'm already knowin'. That's how we all feel right now."

"What's the word though?" He cut to the chase.

"I won't make this long. Just wanted to put you up on what's goin' on right now. Shit is crazy. You know Nephew is back livin' at the house . . . or should I say, he been there for the last week or so straight."

"Nah, I didn't know that. We haven't been talkin' much. Niggas just kinda in they own world. I'll catch up with him though to see what's up."

"I think you should. He's over there and niggas is shook up. Between me and you, the G-homies from the Orchard side and Western side had a little powwow among themselves. They didn't wanna tell you because they feel our side is the source of the problems . . . say we fuckin' the Hood up."

"What the fuck they mean?"

"It ain't no secret at this point; they sayin' Nephew did Baby Devil in. And that supposed to have led to what happened to Ju. They feel that Nephew moving back to the Hood is to take the homies to war. They was talkin' stupid at the meeting, like they wanna smash us or kill the problem. But Big 1-Punch nip that shit in the bud, at least for now. This shit is a problem though."

"It is. I don't know where they got this shit that Neph flipped Baby Dev. He wasn't even in the fuckin' country! That's why he didn't make it to the funeral. Niggas is stupid as fuck."

"Maybe that should be addressed then. Show the ticket or something, I don't know."

"Let me get on top of this. Keep your ears open for me."

"All the time. And make sure you holla at Nephew. He not listening to no one else, and I see it in him. He's on the verge of tearin' some shit up or gettin' himself in a twist. He's too important for that."

"I'm on it." Big 9-Lives ended the call.

He lay back on the bench and gripped the bar but did not raise it. He suddenly felt exhausted. He sat up and reached for his towel to wipe the sweat from his brow. He looked around his home gym and sighed. "No more wars. I'm tired of this shit."

*   *   *   *

Elijah sat on the steps of the front porch of the family home nursing a forty-ounce bottle of Old English 800 under the night sky, the AK-47 propped up behind the bannister out of sight. He was becoming accustomed to being alone, where he was free to wrestle with the demons in his mind. It was obvious to him that this life would never afford him peace. He could never be "normal," a regular Joe with a family and nice career. All his life he was cursed; death, destruction, and sorrow followed him wherever he went, no matter how good he tried to be. So he would not run from it anymore. Since the world wanted war with him, war was what he would give it. He would dance with death until it carried him off as its captive.

He immediately noticed a familiar figure when he hit the block. The bald, stout-built man walking like he had bad feet was unmistakable. It was not long before he entered the front gate. His face became clearly visible as he drew closer. He pushed his bifocals up the bridge of his nose and squinted down at Elijah on the steps.

"You ready?" He took the bottle from Elijah without asking, turning it up for a big chug.

Elijah stood up, pulled his hoodie tightly over his head, and grabbed the AK. "Let's go huntin'." He led them out into the night.

CHAPTER 34

Big 9-Lives and Big Wizard sat across from each other at Roscoe's Chicken and Waffles in Atlanta. Big 9-Lives picked over his breakfast of three wings, one waffle, and cheesy eggs. Big Wizard ate ravenously from three different plates of fried chicken gizzards, a chicken breast, a stack of waffles, and sides of grits and eggs.

"So, what you want me to tell 'em?" Big Wizard shoveled a spoonful of eggs and gizzards into his mouth.

Big 9-Lives sighed. "I don't even know." He set the fork down on his plate. "Between me and you, lil homie, I'm tired."

"Understandable."

"It's like, I called myself leaving shit in y'all hands before, but somehow I find a reason to get pulled back in."

"You not findin' a reason." Big Wizard wiped his mouth with a napkin. "You have a reason: your nephew. As long as he's in the mix, it's natural that you gon' try and protect him as much as possible."

"Fasho. I thought that burden was off. Neph been doin' so good; he been on his shit, not even really in the Hood like that. Now Elise and them been callin' me sayin' he ain't been home in weeks. He barely even responding to my calls. I been gettin' info that he in the Hood on a daily, back to his old ways."

"You know how that goes; some shit hit harder than others. He been off the grid with me and Hitt too. Him and Lil Wiz is rollin' together right now."

"Yeah, and that makes it even worse." He leaned back in his seat, shoulders slumped. "Lil Wiz is a wild card. With Neph bein' in this fucked-up state of mind right now, I don't think that's a good mixture."

"Lil Wiz is who he is. Lil 9 know it's a time of war, and who better on the battlefield with him than the lil homie?" Big Wizard leaned forward and set his fork on the plate. He lowered his voice. "Look, you can't keep stressin' yourself out. Lil 9 ain't a rookie, and you can't have an arm around him on every situation. This is one of those times where you gotta let him get it out of his system. You already know that Ju-Ju wasn't one of my favorite homies, but that was Lil 9's brother, regardless of the shit that happened in the past. He not gon' sleep right until he flip something over this. I was over at Ju-Ju's visual when everybody slid through. I saw it in Lil 9's face; he's in a zone, and I know that zone all too well. You gotta face it; the Hood has changed forever with this shit. We had our scrimmages and beefs in the past with homies. But this situation is way different, big bro. It ain't no turning back. Nine-Os about to die at the hands of each other until one of the parties is gone. It got leaked to me before I left the city that them young Tiny Toon niggas supposed to ran the play on Ju-Ju. Even if it ain't true, it won't matter after the empire strikes back." He picked up his fork and got back to finishing off the last of his grits.

"The Tiny Toons." Big 9-Lives shook his head. "Who would even be tryin' to lead them lil niggas into something this big?"

"Who knows who's the puppet master behind them. But I know Time-Bomb and Skip 'n' them lil circle is the dominant crew over there. So you know how the sayin' goes, 'When in doubt, air 'em out,' and figure out if you was wrong later."

"Fuck. This shit is wicked, Wiz."

Big Wizard wiped his hands with a napkin. "My flight leaves at nine forty-five tonight." He dug into his pocket and pulled out a wad of bills. "Sit this one out, big homie." He peeled a few bills from the stack and set them inside the black bill folder. "It's alright to live your emeritus status. When your spirit not into something no more, don't force it. And I see your spirit not in this one. Lil 9 will be alright. You trained him well; trust that he can handle it. I'll give him your best regards and love."

He stood up and put on his jacket, then smiled down at Big 9-Lives. "You and Big K-Mike created some monsters. Let those monsters out into the wild now. This is all part of y'all history bein' made. One day, you niggas' faces gon' be on the Crip Mount Rushmore and it's gon' read on the plaque: 'The Big Homies'." He spread his arms expansively, laughed, and walked briskly from the table.

*   *   *   *

Elijah and Lil Wizard jogged through the Hathaway Golf Course located in the back of Jesse Owens Park under the cover of darkness. The park was closed hours before, so the entire golf course was a pool of blackness in which the two, dressed in all black, moved like ghosts in the night. The west gate of the course led to different residential streets from Ninety-Seventh all the way to Century Boulevard, depending how far you traveled up the course. The only thing separating the golf course from these side streets was the common chain-link fence.

They made it to the section of the gate that led to Ninety-Eighth Street and dropped to one knee, breathing heavily. Lil Wizard laid his pistol-grip pump twelve-gauge shotgun next to him and unslung a black backpack from his shoulder that contained a pair of wire cutters, zip ties, duct tape, and rope.

"You sure Cuzz live here?" Elijah asked in hushed tones.

"Yeah, nigga, I told you that already," Lil Wizard whispered as he clipped links in the fence. "I been following all these niggas for months. First Baby Devil before he died, then figured why not just get all the info I could on these new niggas in the Hood in case a day like this came."

Elijah looked around nervously, hoping no one could hear the wire cutters at work. "So what, you just been randomly following niggas around?"

Lil Wizard paused and stared up at Elijah. "Yes," he answered with no further explanation. "Can I finish now?"

Elijah nodded.

Lil Wizard returned to work. He finished cutting a four-foot vertical line in the gate and pulled at it quietly, making the gap in it big enough for them to pass through. He took the zip ties and duct tape and handed them to Elijah, then looped the rope around his shoulder and picked up the shotgun. "You lead in, I run clean up." He zipped the wire cutters in the bag and set it on the opposite side of the gate as a marker during their anticipated fast getaway. He held the gate open while Elijah stooped and squeezed through.

While Lil Wizard squeezed through, Elijah double-checked his two Glocks to make sure they were ready to go and that the tape and zip ties were secured in the pocket of his hoodie. He could have sworn he saw a hint of a smile on Lil Wizard's face as he came through the fence, but his expression was blank by the time he gathered the shotgun and turned to face Elijah.

They swiftly put on ski masks and hurried to the gate of a green house. The block was empty and quiet. Their footsteps and breath were all that pierced the night air as they picked up speed.

The porch light suddenly illuminated their presence as they rushed through the gate and closed in on the front door. Without hesitation or delay, Elijah kicked the front door with all the rage and violence within him. The door groaned and the hinges splintered under what sounded like a small explosion.

*　　*　　*　　*

A heavy-set, elderly Black woman lounged in front of the TV in an oversized muumuu and worn house slippers, watching *Jerry Springer*.

"Jerry, Jerry, Jerry!" She laughed hysterically at the dwarf fighting a full-sized man.

Time-Bomb passed through from the kitchen back to his bedroom with a glass of milk in one hand and the other holding the phone to his ear.

"Nah, that's my aunty watching that bullshit," he spoke into the phone. "All she do is sit in front of that fuckin' TV watching *Jerry Springer, Judge Judy*, and all them stupid-ass shows all day, laughing like it's the funniest shit in the world." He shut the bedroom door behind him.

His aunt cut her eyes at his back as he disappeared through the hallway. *Bastard act like I can't hear him or somethin'. Betty should have swallowed that little ornery motherfucka and spit him out while he was still sperm.* She turned back to her TV show just as a stripper came out and started twerking for the crowd.

"Ooooh, look at her shakin' her narrow lil ass. She know she shouldn't be—"

The front door suddenly exploded; the words caught in her throat. Terror froze on her face as ski-masked Elijah and Lil Wizard burst in with weapons drawn. Her instincts sprang her to her feet even though she was too old and too fat to run from anyone.

Elijah aimed his pistol and screamed in her face, "Where's your son? Where's your fuckin' son?"

Frantic and in a state of confusion, all she managed to do was scream at the top of her lungs.

"Shut up, bitch! Ain't nobody gonna hurt you, we just want your son!"

"Ahhh! Ahhhh!"

"Shut the—"

Boom! The blast from the shotgun was so loud, the entire house went quiet except for the continuous ring lingering in their ears.

Elijah nearly jumped out of his skin at the sound and impact of the unexpected shot at close range to the torso that sent the lady flying across the living room, landing her in a heap in front of the old, floor-model TV. She laid contorted, blood spewing into the carpet beneath her. He momentarily paused in shock.

Lil Wizard did not skip a beat. He racked the pump-action, dislodging the used shell casing, putting a fresh round in the chamber and sprinting for the hallway toward the bedrooms. Elijah quickly snapped out of it and ran to catch up with him.

The noise from the kicked-in door had alerted Time-Bomb in the bedroom. When he heard the yelling, he assumed it was the police raiding the house. He dropped the phone and ran for the window to attempt his escape. That was when he heard the shot and the silencing of his aunt's scream. He changed course and ran for the clothes hamper in the corner of the room. He flung off the top and frantically pulled out dirty clothes to get to the pistol he stashed there.

The bedroom door flew open. He turned just as Lil Wizard charged in. Time-Bomb swung the 9mm in his direction and squeezed off a shot as the shotgun went off.

Lil Wizard dove right to avoid the shot. Elijah paused at the gunfire exchange, then rushed into the bedroom, gun drawn, after no more shots were fired. Lil Wizard was already back on his feet.

Elijah cautiously surveyed the room. He noticed Time-Bomb's legs sticking out from the side of the bed. He moved slowly toward the bed with the gun leveled. When he reached in full view of the bedside, he saw Time-Bomb was shot in the side but was still alive. His pistol lay near the head of the bed frame as he struggled to reach it.

Elijah reached down and grabbed Time-Bomb violently by the shoulder and flipped him over on his back. With no need for saying something cold or asking questions, just the primal need to inflict death to soothe the spirit of revenge, he forcefully thrust the barrel of the pistol into Time-Bomb's mouth, chipping and breaking some of his teeth in the process. He pulled the trigger. Time-Bomb's head thumped against the floor and the back burst open like an exploding watermelon, sending brain matter, flesh, and skull splattering in every direction. Blood splatter painted the edges of the bed covers, the drawers, and Elijah's shoes and pant legs. Time-Bomb's eyes bulged, locked in a glassy stare at nothing.

He cut his eyes at the corpse, brushed past Lil Wizard, and sprinted for the front door.

Lil Wizard lingered for a moment, staring at a motionless Time-Bomb. He smirked, turned, and sprinted in the same direction as Elijah.

By the time they emerged outside into the night air, many of the houses on the block had their lights on. A few neighbors had ventured out with their phones in hand, trying to see what was going on, calling 911. Elijah descended the porch steps with one leap, taking off in an all-out sprint as soon as his feet touched the ground.

Lil Wizard hurried out, hot on Elijah's trail. He anxiously scanned the block, perplexed by the gawkers. An elderly man on his phone across the street, trying to hide behind a bush, caught his attention. He aimed the shotgun in his direction and let off a shot. All the neighbors scattered. "Nosey motherfuckas," he mumbled, taking off toward the golf course at a comfortable trot.

Within seconds, Elijah and Lil Wizard snatched up their bag, squeezed through the slit in the gate, and were in a race through the darkened, empty golf course toward the getaway car parked on the opposite side. They made it to the car and hopped in. Lil Wizard dropped the shotgun on the backseat. They removed their ski masks, put on their seatbelts, and looked around, paranoid.

Elijah stared over at Lil Wizard as he put the keys in the ignition, started it up, and pulled off with the headlights off. He drummed his fingers against the steering wheel as if a tune were playing that only he could hear. He turned on the headlights as they waited for the stoplight to change at Western Avenue. He began a festive hum that accompanied the continuous tap on the steering wheel. He glanced at Elijah, who was still glaring at him.

"You all right?" Lil Wizard asked with a clueless expression.

"The question is, is you alright?" Elijah snapped.

Lil Wizard continued to stare at him blankly. "What you mean?" He looked at traffic, then back at Elijah.

"I mean why you flip the old lady is what I mean, nigga."

"Oh, her?" He waved his hand dismissively. "Old bitch was makin' too much noise." The light turned green and he turned left on Western.

"We could've shut her up. That's what the tape and ties was for," Elijah reasoned in frustration.

"No time for that." He pushed his glasses up and shot Elijah another hard glance. "Do this bother you or something?" His eyes darted between him and traffic. "'Cause if it do, you shouldn't have never called me to the hunt. This is what I do. If you don't want death, don't call the reaper." He turned his attention back to the road, mumbling, "Niggas always wanna get tender and shit."

"Ain't no tender-shit nigga. Fuck you mean?"

Lil Wizard looked at him again and laughed. Elijah shook his head at him, leaned back, and stared at the passing lights.

Lil Wizard began to hum and tap his fingers against the wheel again as they made their way back to headquarters.

CHAPTER 35

S kip circled the block three times before pulling into Lady
Rawdog's driveway. He looked at his watch again for the
tenth time in the last thirty minutes. Lady Rawdog was expecting
him by seven a.m., but he was intentionally forty-five minutes
early as a security measure to canvas the area ahead of time,
making sure it was not a setup. He, like everyone else in the
Hood, was on edge. Paranoia and fear were setting in on all sides.
Time-Bomb and his aunt's murders removed all pretense; there
was an in-house war within the Nineties and everyone was a
suspect; no one was safe.

A rooster's crow pierced the early morning air as he stepped
from the car and looked around. His only company out on the
block was a few stray dogs rummaging through garbage cans for
food. Morning dew dampened the grass and left films of moisture
on nearby car windows. He had a fleeting thought that someone
might be camouflaged behind the frosted windows, watching
him. He clutched the pistol in his pocket tighter and hurried up
the steps to Lady Rawdog's front door. He knocked and turned
his back to the door, keeping an eye on his surroundings. After a
pause, he knocked again, louder. He heard footsteps inside.

"Damn, nigga, hold the fuck up. Who the fuck is it?" she
barked.

"Young Skip."

"Nigga, why the fuck"—she unbolted the door and swung it open—"you at my door so early? I told you after seven." She held a .357 Python in her hand; hair matted, with sleep in her eyes.

"I was already this way handling something so figured I'd swing on through."

She stepped back to let him enter, then pushed the door shut and locked it. She lazily joined him on the couch, setting her pistol next to her for easy access.

"So what's up?" she asked with an attitude, picking the crust from the corner of her eyes.

"Tryin' to figure this shit out—"

"Nah, nigga," she cut him off. "Don't start hittin' me with no bullshit, roundabout political talk. Why you need to know this info and who else waitin' on you to get it?"

"What you mean? Ain't nobody waitin' on me to get nothin'. This something for me. Like I told you on the phone, this shit in the Hood is wicked right now. If I can figure some things out in my own head, I can know what I can do on my part to try and help the situation."

"How can you help something that's beyond helping? Whoever killed Ju and whoever was behind it or know about it—it'll never be forgiven." She stared at him with accusing eyes.

Skip threw his hands up. "I promise, big homegirl, on Nine-O, on Baby Devil, I didn't know that was gon' happen and didn't have a hand in it, period, on the dead homies."

She continued staring at him, probing, and assessing in silence.

"My word, I'm keepin' it all the way straight up with you. I need to confirm that Lil Nine didn't have a hand in Baby Devil gettin' killed. It would clear up a lot for me. I think all this shit, Ju, Time-Bomb . . . It all stems from some foul play from somebody, and if I can connect the dots to prove it, we can root out the cancer."

"Who you think ran the foul play?" She sat up straight.

"Come on now, Raw, don't ask me that question right now. I don't wanna be responsible for starting some rumor that might not be true. That would only make matters worse. Let me figure out what I need to, and if it turns out to be what I think, on Nine-O you'll be one of the first to know."

She paused in thought. She nodded, stood up, and walked to the bedroom.

He stared toward the bedroom.

She returned shortly, handing him two photos and a piece of paper. Skip studied the pictures closely. One was of Elijah in front of the Bob Marley Museum in Kingston, posing with Elise and Tweety. The other was of Elijah and Raz in front of Club Asylum on the night of their outing.

Skip shook his head. He set the pics down and held the paper out toward her. "What I'm lookin' for on here?"

"That's my phone bill, nigga."

"I see that. It still don't tell me why I need to be lookin' at it."

"Because it's even more confirmation that Lil 9 was in Jamaica when Baby Devil got killed." She grabbed the bill and pointed at a number on it. "You see that phone number? See the eight-seven-six area code? Now look at the date."

Skip scanned the bill, nodding. She got up and walked to the kitchen. "That's my nephew. I helped raise him." She reached in the fridge and pulled out a pitcher of red Kool-Aid. "He knows my house number been the same for twenty years. Wherever he go, whatever he doing, he always gon' make sure he check up on me. And he gonna call my house phone, not my cell, unless it's an emergency and I'm not home." She raised the pitcher to her mouth and drank straight from it.

Skip picked up the pictures again and glanced from them to the phone bill repeatedly. He finally set them down and stood up. "I've seen enough. I really appreciate you doin' this for me." He took out a cigarette and lit it.

"I did it because I know it relates to my nephew. So, was it enough to let you know what you should do?" She strolled over to him.

"For the most part. Let me check out a couple more things, then I'm gon' need you to connect me to Big 9-Lives so I can holla at him."

"Ain't no need tryna talk to Big-9 on this one. It ain't no secret; this Lil 9's war. If you tryin' to address anything, it has to be to him. He's local, you know; you can pull up on him."

"Nah, this ain't the right time to just be pullin' up on niggas. Everybody on edge right now. Everybody know that Cuzz is posted up at the family headquarters. They not makin' it a secret. But nobody even ridin' up that block. Really ain't nobody even deckin' the Hood period now but him and Lil Wiz. Niggas is spooked."

"As they should be."

"So would you be willin' to arrange for us to talk in a neutral, safe spot for both of us when the time comes?"

She nodded.

"Cool. I'll hit you when I'm ready." He walked to the door with her trailing. He put his hand in his pocket and looked both ways when he stepped outside. Seeing everything was clear, he high stepped it to his car, hopped in, and pulled off in a hurry.

Lady Rawdog watched him drive away.

"He gone?" a male voice came from behind her.

"Yeah, he gone." She continued staring in the direction Skip's car drove in.

Elijah walked up next to her in the doorway. "That was interesting. Niggas wanna talk now all of a sudden when demos start gettin' laid down."

"Um-hm. Tell me 'bout it."

"I'm about to head back to the house. Let me know when he hit you again." He brushed past her, heading out.

"I will. Stay safe and stay dangerous, young nigga."

"All the time." He headed to the cut at the back that led toward the next block.

*   *   *   *

Sade's "No Ordinary Love" played as Elise's SUV crawled in bumper-to-bumper traffic on the 110 freeway. Her eyes were puffy and red; stress worn into her features. Elijah had not been home for weeks. They all figured he just needed some space to grieve for a while, then he would make his way back home. Now, her patience and restraint worn thin, worry took over, and it was time to go and get him.

He barely answered or returned her calls. When she did manage to get him on the line, he was distant and vague. To make matters worse, the two recent killings were a hot-button topic in the LA streets. Elijah and Lil Wizard's names were ringing throughout the city as the factors strong-arming the Rollin 90s back from their peers and the younger generation. Elise felt he was losing control, disregarding everything that they worked for and were working toward.

She merged over and exited at Manchester Avenue. Her anxiety grew stronger as she made the right turn, heading for the family house in the Hood. A gray cloud of smog hung densely over the palm trees in the area like an ominous sign of dark evil. She cursed Elijah silently. *How could he move back to an environment like this? It's so out of place at this point in our lives. Visit yes, but why're you back living over here recycling bullshit that we have long moved past?*

Within minutes she was pulling up in front of the house. Lil Wizard was sitting on the front steps eating a box of Lemonheads as if he did not have a care in the world. He called over his shoulder into the house as she parked.

She took a deep breath and got out. Elijah came out just as she was walking through the front gate.

"What you doin' over here? It ain't good for you to be here." He was obviously not happy by the surprise visit.

"We need to talk." She stubbornly ignored his objection.

He looked up and down the block, then hurriedly waved her inside.

"You can't be over here; it's a lot goin' on." He closed the door and led her into the bedroom.

"I know it's a lot going on; that's why I'm here," she retorted, peering around the bedroom at the arsenal of weapons lying about. "Why do you have all this shit out like this? If the police run up in here, this a fed case."

"That's why you shouldn't be here." He sat on the bed, staring at her stoically.

"Elijah, when're you coming home? You need to come home."

He inhaled deeply and turned away with a hint of sadness painted on his face. "I will . . . I don't know when. But I'll be home."

"What do you mean you don't know when? It's time to come home now. We need you; your children need you. What, you just gonna give up on us? I know this has been hard for you. I know you loved Ju-Ju and Brenda, but you can't stop living. Your family that is here and alive needs you. You've done enough. If you kill a thousand people, it won't bring him back." She teared up.

His emotions stirred. All the grief and sadness were raising their heads again. Elijah teared up also, but he caught himself before they spilled from his eyes. "I just need some time," he said in a sad tone. "It's too much goin' on in my head right now . . . still shit I gotta handle out here."

"You don't have to figure it all out. Let me help you; that's what I'm here for. Don't block me out; don't block *us* out." She rubbed his head gently. "Come home, babe," she whispered softly. "We're gonna get through this."

"They got to pay though; they did my nigga like that." A tear rolled down his cheek.

She grabbed him in a tight embrace. "They will pay, all of 'em," she whispered in his ear. "But you don't have to be the one to do it. Guzman gave me his word that whoever we need dealt with, just give him a name and location and it's done."

Elijah tensed slightly and pulled away. "Guzman? When did

you talk to Guzman about this situation? How does he know that we're having issues with niggas right now?"

She averted her gaze. "I was talking to him and just mentioned . . . I've been hollering at him lately. I was gonna tell you. I just didn't think it was the right time."

His demeanor flipped aggressively. "Tell me what? And I don't want to hear about now ain't the time."

"Don't start trippin', it's not that deep."

"It's deep enough. Spill it." His eyes bored into her.

"I mean . . ." She paused, then finally resigned herself. "I've been hustling again."

"Hustling? You mean dope? You been sellin' dope?"

"Yeah." She exhaled. "I grabbed some birds a few months ago for Diabla to work. I was just feeling like my life was at a standstill, like I wasn't me. I just wanted to—"

The loud sound shook the room and next thing she knew, she was on her back seeing little bright lights dancing above her. Elijah had slapped her so hard and fast that she had not even seen it coming.

"You traitor bitch. How dare you smile in my face every day while doin' some snake shit that I specifically told you not to do! Come here." He grabbed her by the hair, enraged.

"Wait!" she screeched as he pulled her from the floor by her hair with one hand, grabbing her purse from the bed with the other. She tried to pry his grip from her hair as he pulled her bent over toward the front door. "Please . . . stop. Let me explain, please!"

"Fuck yo' explanation, you ungrateful bitch. You go against my word to conspire with some other motherfucka to do some shit I told you not to do? That's treason, bitch."

"No. Wait!" she pleaded, stumbling forward, trying to keep from falling. She pounded at his hand. "Let go of my hair!"

He kicked the screen door open and dragged her outside. Lil Wizard laughed as Elijah dragged her past him down the steps by her hair, kicking and screaming.

Neighbors stared in amusement at the spectacle; domestic squabbles were the norm in the ghettos. It went without saying that no one was going to try and interfere or call the police.

Elijah dragged her all the way to the front gate, then slung her off the property. The heel on one of her Gucci stilettos broke in half as she tumbled to the sidewalk.

Lil Wizard laughed even louder.

"Get yo' motherfuckin' ass outta here. And whenever I do come home, you bet not be there!" he screamed. "Go get all yo' shit and get the fuck out. And you bet not take my son when you leave!" He threw her purse at her head and walked back to the house.

"Fuck you, motherfucka!" she screamed and cried. "You gonna do me like this in front of everybody? Fuck you!" She reached for her purse violently.

"Whoa, whoa, whoa," Lil Wizard warned Elijah, pointing her way, still chuckling.

Elijah turned as she was reaching inside her purse. He knew her all too well, so there was no mistaking what she was going for. He rushed back toward her with a deadly glare in his eyes. "You pull that out, Imma make you eat that motherfucka bitch."

She paused with her hand in her purse gripping the pistol. She hesitantly removed her hand. "Why did you do me like this? You didn't have to . . ." She broke down sobbing.

"Get outta here." He turned around and walked toward the house without looking back.

Lil Wizard chuckled as Elijah brushed past him.

"Shut the fuck up, nigga. Shit ain't that motherfuckin' funny." Elijah went into the house and slammed the door behind him.

"Yes, it is!" Lil Wizard hollered after he was gone, gawking at Elise hobbling to her vehicle.

She crawled into the driver's seat, crying tears of hurt, shame, and embarrassment. She clumsily sped off, disheveled and broken.

CHAPTER 36

Lauren sat on the living room floor wearing leggings, a T-shirt, and no shoes, surrounded by an array of colorful plastic toys, playing with Toussaint and Amaru. She looked up as Elise appeared at the top of the stairs. Elise wore a heavy cloak of sadness; her hair was a mess, her eyes puffy and red. She had been moping around the house in sweatpants and T-shirts for over a week, refusing to speak much about what happened between her and Elijah.

Lauren had spoken with Elijah shortly after the incident. He told her what Elise had been up to and about the fight, but she did not let on to Elise that she knew anything. She gave Elise her space, knowing that at some point they would talk about it when the time was right.

"Hey," Lauren greeted cheerfully.

"Hey." Elise sat on the floor next to her, sounding deflated.

Amaru and Toussaint excitedly brought their toy trucks over to her. Elise took the trucks and ran them across the carpet, making truck noises. They giggled and laughed with delight.

"You alright?"

"Yeah, I'm good," Elise answered without looking her way.

Lauren studied her for a minute, holding back what she really wanted to say. She figured Elise playing with the boys for a bit could do her some good. She joined in their playtime for a while, hoping that it would loosen Elise up a little, giving her the opportunity to broach the topic.

After a few bouts of rolling around and playing with their various toys, the boys ventured off in a footrace toward the den area where Sistah Raheema usually watched TV. That gave Lauren the time and open opportunity she needed with Elise. She scooted closer to her. "You know you can't keep all this shit in, right?" She rested her hand gently on Elise's shoulder.

"I'm good." Elise stared at the floor with sad, downcast eyes.

"No, you're not." She leaned in closer and gripped one of her hands. "It's okay that you're not. We're all going through a hard time right now. Elijah is dealing with his demons and it's affecting everyone. But this is a time when the family must dig deep for him. This is the only way we'll be able to pull this thing back together."

"I fucked up," Elise whispered softly. "I fucked up and he doesn't love me anymore."

"That's not true. He loves you, he's just angry right now. He's angry, sad, and everything else. He just needs time to come out of it."

Elise shook her head. "You didn't see him; you weren't there. I've never seen that side of him. I saw hate in him toward me. I mean, I fucked up, I know. But it wasn't meant to hurt or disrespect him. I was just trying to feel like myself again, doing a little hustling on my own. It wasn't like I did something that bad for him to call me a traitor and do me like that in front of people."

"I've always kept it one-hundred percent truthful with you, and I'm not going to start sugarcoating it now. I don't know what you meant or what your intentions were when you made those moves, but it was disrespect to him, to our household, doing what you did. You jeopardized all of us when you kept us in the blind on something like that. You didn't even give us the opportunity to move right, or to give our opinion on how you should move so that what we've built is protected.

"Outside of all that though, Elijah is the head of our household. If he gives final word on something that he feels is best for the family, we follow that, period. I don't like everything he does or how he does it all the time, but I know he has my best interest at heart, so I fall in line. This is what we signed up for. So yeah, for you to do that, you hurt him. In his eyes, it was the ultimate disrespect. What you saw in his face was his response to those feelings.

"So whatever embarrassment you felt or pain for him putting you out there in public, you just got to drink that and let it go. Bottom line, you were out of line and that was the consequences. It didn't kill you, so you're straight."

"I know." Elise took a deep breath. "I just don't know what to do right now."

"What you're going to do is pick yourself up and shake it off." She stood up and grabbed Elise's hands, raising her off the floor. "You're going to go take a shower and get fly. We're going out for drinks. After we get fucked up tonight, you'll get up in the morning, call him, and apologize. Then we figure out how to get him back home. You with me?"

She nodded, a faint smile creasing her lips.

Lauren kissed her on the cheek and hugged her around the neck. "Come on, girl, let's get out."

They headed up the stairs to get ready for their outing.

Sistah Raheema stepped out of the hallway as their footsteps faded. She shook her head. "O Allah forgive us our frailties and our ignorance. For only you are the best of knowers," she whispered.

*   *   *   *

Elise closed her bedroom door and leaned against it. Her mind mulled over what Lauren said. It was funny how she always seemed to have the right things to say and know how to say them, at times when you really did not want to hear it. *One thing's for certain, I did jeopardize the family by not thinking deeply enough. I'm gonna make this up.*

She moved over to her huge walk-in closet and rummaged through it, selecting various pieces, then putting them back. She paused browsing, retrieved her phone, dialed a number, and rested it on her ear.

"Bueno," Diabla answered.

"What's up, Mami?"

"Same shit. What's wrong? You sound down."

"I'm good. Just got some stuff goin' on the home front."

"I hear you. What's up though?"

"Wanted to know what's up with that situation with Lil Teflon. Has there been any progress with gettin' up on him?"

"You already know I'm on it. Have I ever let you down?"

"Nah, you haven't." Elise pulled out a blue mini-dress and examined it. "It's just that time now, thought we had it solved with him, but now it doesn't look that way."

"No sweat. I already did all the homework on him. I'll go ahead and press it through," Diabla assured excitedly.

"Keep me up as you connect the dots." Elise held the dress up to her body and posed in different angles in the mirror.

"Say no more. Let your girl work her magic."

"Without a doubt. Handle your business then. Love ya."

"Love you too, Mia."

Elise hung up. She took the dress off the hanger and laid it on the bed. She smiled for the first time in what felt like forever. *I'll forget all my problems tonight and enjoy myself . . . and Lauren.* Her smile broadened at the thought. She collapsed on the soft California king-size bed, flared her arms, and stretched out her limbs.

* * * *

Dusk was falling as Lady Rawdog wheeled the Buick into an alleyway off Fifty-Fourth and Avalon, with Skip riding shotgun. His nervousness was obvious as they pulled into a parking space at the rear of an abandoned-looking warehouse.

"You sure Cuzz and them gon' keep their word that I'm safe for this meetin'?" Skip scanned the area nervously.

"Yeah, nigga." She parked the car and removed the keys from the ignition. "I told you that you was good. If Lil 9 give me his word on something, that's what it's gon' be." She opened the door and got out.

Skip fumbled with the door handle, then hesitantly got out. He continued looking around him, his hand clutching onto the pistol in his pocket.

"Come on, nigga." She waved him over to a rusted metal door she had just knocked on.

He plodded his way over to her, fidgety. Footsteps echoed on the other side of the door. The lock rattled with a loud clank, and the door groaned as it slowly opened. Lil Wizard appeared in the doorway.

Skip's eyes bulged at the sight of Lil Wizard. He attempted to keep a cool poker face as Lil Wizard stared at him with an unreadable expression.

"What's up, tramp?" She pushed past Lil Wizard to enter the warehouse.

He did not respond, simply stepped slightly to the side, making just enough space for both to enter. He continued glaring at Skip as he brushed past.

The back part of the warehouse was completely dark. A pale, yellowish glow from a light in another part of the warehouse spilled over into an open walkway a few feet away. Their figures were barely visible after Lil Wizard closed the door behind them.

Lil Wizard led them toward where the yellow light was coming from. A narrow hallway right where the lamp hung from the ceiling came into view as they got closer. They stepped into the light. Lil Wizard stopped abruptly. "You gotta get searched."

Skip paused and took an involuntary step back.

"It's cool," she assured him. "It's just protocol, you know how it goes."

Skip nodded and stepped forward.

Lil Wizard gestured to Lady Rawdog with his free hand. "He's considered your guest. You make sure he clear before we go in."

She reached out her hand to Skip. "Give me the burner."

Skip hesitantly took the pistol from his pocket and handed it to her.

"That's the only one he got." She walked down the hallway toward an open door at the end.

Lil Wizard gestured with his hand for Skip to follow her. Skip did, and he brought up the rear. Skip turned and watched him after every couple of steps. Lil Wizard kept his hand tucked in his pocket the entire time.

They entered the room at the other end of the hall. Elijah sat behind a desk and Big Teflon stood against the far wall with his arms folded against his chest.

"Have a seat." Elijah indicated the seat across from him without any other formality.

Skip sat in the empty chair nervously.

"Imma let y'all get to it." Lady Rawdog exited the room. Lil Wizard closed the door behind her and locked it, posting up right behind Skip's chair.

"So, the homegirl said you wanted to tell me something." Elijah's voice was extremely calm . . . too calm.

Skip cut his eyes at Big Teflon, then looked back at Elijah. "I do, but . . ." His eyes kept darting back and forth between Elijah and Big Teflon.

"What's wrong? You keep lookin' at Tef. Would you rather not speak in front of him?"

Skip was careful in his answer. "I . . . I just think what I got to say . . . that only you should hear it first." He stared intently at Elijah with pleading eyes.

Elijah studied him for a moment. After some consideration, he raised his hand. "Y'all give us a minute alone." He looked from Big Teflon to Lil Wizard. Lil Wizard opened his mouth to protest. He held up an open palm. "It's good, Cuzz, I got it."

A look of irritation crossed Lil Wizard's brow but he turned, unlocked the door, and stepped out into the hallway.

Big Teflon slowly followed, mean-mugging Skip on the way out.

Elijah waited until the door was shut before he turned his focus back to Skip and nodded for him to speak.

Skip sat forward in his chair. "I want you to know, big homie, on the dead homies, on my grandma, rest in peace, I didn't have nothin' to do with what happened with Ju. I didn't even know it was gonna happen." His voice cracked.

"But now you know what happened, I'm assumin', or you wouldn't be here, right?"

"Yeah, I know because they told me and because the shit I put together on my own, on everything leading up to that."

Elijah folded his hands in front of him and gestured silently with a head nod for him to continue.

Skip lowered his voice to a whisper. "All this shit got started by Lil Teflon. That motherfucka smoked Baby Devil."

Elijah edged forward instantly. "What you mean? How do he play a part?" he asked anxiously.

"Cuzz killed Baby Devil, then put it out there like you had a hand in it. The night Baby Dev got killed, he left the spot with Lil Teflon. I had a bad feelin' about it when they was leaving. Lil Tef talkin' about he had some lick up or something. Shit just didn't feel right. Well, later that night, the nigga called the spot askin' the homies if they talked to Baby Dev, sayin' Baby Dev left him 'cause he was goin' to see you 'bout some business shit you was lacing him on. So when Baby Dev came up dead the next morning, it was all this whispering goin' around that he was supposed to meet you that night, and now all of a sudden, he dead. With all the past animosity and shit, the rumor just started takin' on a life of its own."

Skip swallowed a lump in his throat. "I'm not gonna front, I was mad too, and tryna figure out who had done the shit. But everybody had agreed that no one was to do anything based on no rumors. If it wasn't no real facts, niggas was supposed to stand down. I left outta town to my folks' house and then heard about the homie Ju. I was sick about that shit, Cuzz. Ju was one of the homies that raised me." He dropped his head, sadness washing over him.

"So who killed him?" Elijah pushed, unmoved by Skip's sentiments.

Skip slowly raised his head and looked at him with the pained anguish of having to betray the culprit. Finally, he blurted it out, "Lil Bar-Dog."

The news rocked Elijah. "Lil Bar-Dog?" he asked in disbelief. "That was his lil dude! Nah." He shook his head.

Skip lifted his hands and shrugged his shoulders. "Hard to believe, I know, but it's true. Him and Time-Bomb plotted the whole thing and Lil Bar-Dog pulled the trigger. They told me they did it and why. They felt like somebody had to pay for Baby Dev, and if they couldn't get to you, they had to go after one of your circle."

"And you held all this information till now, why?" Elijah glared at him.

"You know how it is, Cuzz; I couldn't just run and blurt all this shit out. It was all those mixed feelings; my loyalties to the Tiny Toons, to Ju-Ju, to the Hood. I was just pulled in all these different directions." He sighed, looking up at the ceiling, then around the room trying not to look directly at Elijah. "It was hard for me to bring myself to come tell you all this. I could've kept my mouth shut and just let shit play out and left you in the dark. But I'm here because I feel it's the right thing to do. I feel like we got to kill the cancers in the Hood, no matter what clique or generation they a part of. If not, Nine-O gonna fall from the inside out."

Elijah sat back, resting his elbows on the armrests. He clasped his hands under his chin momentarily. "You know if this info ain't what it's supposed to be, you not leavin' here, right?"

"I don't know how you gonna confirm it. All I know is that it's the truth."

"And you sure Lil Bar-Dog was the one who actually did it?" Elijah studied him closely.

"Nine-hundred percent."

Elijah nodded. "Hey, Lil Wiz!" he called out.

Lil Wizard stuck his head through the door.

"Tell Raw to come here for a sec."

Lil Wizard disappeared back out the door.

Skip stirred anxiously.

A few seconds later, Lady Rawdog came in. Elijah indicated for her to come around the desk.

She walked around to him and leaned in closely.

"Get Lil Cannon on the phone," he whispered in her ear. "Tell him to take them set of Hood pictures to Ms. Alice, the ones I got labeled 'Tiny Toons.' Let her study all of them carefully and tell us if she sees the person that came out of Ju's house that night. Make sure he include a couple with Lil Bar-Dog. I never showed her one of him because I never even considered . . ."

She stepped back in shock.

He raised his hand. "Just chill for now and take care of that," he urged. "Tell him to go immediately and call me as soon as she give her feedback."

She exited the office, practically running.

Elijah turned to Skip with a deadly grimace. "Now we wait for the moment of truth." He slouched in his seat, getting comfortable while Skip sat in awkward silence.

*   *   *   *

After what seemed like an eternity of anticipation, Lady Rawdog tapped on the door and entered. A mixture of sadness and anger filled her eyes as she walked around the desk, placing a hand gently on Elijah's shoulder. She bent over and whispered in his ear. She raised up, shot an unreadable expression at Skip, and left the room.

Elijah stared at him for a long moment.

"Well?" Skip asked nervously.

Elijah leaned forward, grabbing an ink pen, and twirled it with his fingers. "The most important piece of your info pans out." He set the pen down slowly as his mind raced. "The problem is, what do I do with you now?" He locked eyes with Skip.

"What you mean? I told you the truth; I did my part. So I don't know what you mean what to do with me. Let me get up and walk the fuck outta here."

"I know it seem like an easy call to you, but I'm conflicted. First off, you are, or were, at some point, a part of the circle that killed my brother. Secondly, I don't know how to feel about you only now comin' to tell me all this; I gotta consider your motives. And lastly, you know what happens to Lil Bar-Dog now, and that's a dangerous piece of information for you to be walkin' around with in your pocket."

Skip was panicked. "Look, Cuzz, I don't know how to make you feel comfortable about any of this shit. But one thing for sure, on the dead homies, I'm solid. I ain't 'bout to pass no info along to nobody . . . period. You don't have to worry about that. And whatever you wanna do, however you want to handle these niggas, I'm with you. Lil Bar-Dog and Time-Bomb wasn't my circle; Baby Devil and Droop was my circle. Them other niggas just Tiny Toons; that's the connection I had with them. But I'm with the program that weed out all of these foul niggas. I know Lil Bar-Dog priority for you. Lil Tef is for me. Speaking of." He leaned forward and lowered his voice. "Why you got that nigga brother over here with you? On Nine-O, them niggas ain't straight." He rested back in his seat.

"Let me worry about that part. We gotta figure out your situation first and foremost. What assurances can you give me that you won't become a liability down the line?"

"My assurance is that I ain't going nowhere. I'm in the Hood if you ever wanna get me. I'll give you my people's addresses in Compton where my aunt 'n' them been living all my life, just to let you know. If I fuck up and you can't get to me, you know where the people I love stay. On top of that, I'm here to be your gunner. Just point me in the direction and I'm goin'."

Elijah sat in silence, mulling it over. Skip was so still, he could have been mistaken for a statue. The uncertainty in the air was unbearable.

Elijah finally leaned forward and lowered his voice again. "Don't discuss any of this with anybody—and I mean nobody, not even my uncle. You don't report or take marching orders from nobody but me, you got it?"

Skip nodded his understanding.

Elijah looked at the door. "Lil Wiz, y'all can come back in!" he called out, then shot Skip another quick glance. "Silence," he mouthed with a cautionary look.

Lil Wizard and Big Teflon came back into the room and took up their positions.

"Cuzz confirmed that Time-Bomb was the trigger-man on Ju-Ju. So our hunch that Time-Bomb was the voice callin' shots for the Toons was right. Skip here gon' function through the Set and figure out who all, if any, gave any type of voice or assistance to Time-Bomb. He's gon' let us know."

"How you know this nigga tellin' the truth?" Big Teflon spewed. "He could've been the one who did it, now blamin' Time-Bomb 'cause he know Cuzz already smoked. We should kill this nigga on GP. Fuck all these lil niggas."

Lil Wizard remained quiet with a blank stare, studying everyone in the room.

"Nah, Cuzz." Elijah rejected the idea. "He wouldn't have brought himself here, in our hands, if he was gon' lie to us. He's tellin' the truth."

"I'm tellin' you, Nine, this lil mothafucka—" Big Teflon started.

"I said he tellin' the truth." Elijah's voice raised as he stood up aggressively from his chair. "Nobody's gon' fuck with him, and that's that on that."

Big Teflon stared for a moment, wanting to protest some more, but finally backed down. "Alright Cuzz, it's your call."

"Wiz, let him out. Tell Raw to give him back his burner once they out the door," Elijah instructed.

Lil Wiz nodded and opened the door.

Skip stood up, cut his eyes at Big Teflon, and extended his hand to Elijah.

Elijah studied him momentarily, then slowly reached out for a firm handshake.

Skip turned and walked out, with Lil Wizard trailing.

Elijah sat back down and looked over at Big Teflon. "If he don't bring us what we want in three days, we kill him."

Big Teflon grabbed his coat off the hanger and slipped it on. "Just let me know when it's time." He checked his pocket as he walked for the door.

"For sure," Elijah calmly stated.

"Be safe and watch yo back." Big Teflon headed up the hallway.

Elijah stared after Big Teflon. "You too," he whispered. "You too."

CHAPTER 37

———————❦———————

B ig 9-Lives tossed back a shot of tequila and slapped the thick, voluptuous stripper on her ass. He fluttered a handful of bills at her as she bent over in front of him and wiggled it.

"Yeah, that's what I love about you Atlanta hoes; y'all make that thick shit do what it do." He bobbed his head to the Ying-Yang Twins, gripping her ass again, salivating over it.

His phone vibrated. He ignored it again for the umpteenth time. He made it a point not to be bothered with anyone for a while. He just wanted to drown himself in alcohol and strippers and forget about all the madness that was haunting him.

He looked at his diamond-encrusted Rolex and saw that it was two a.m. He pulled the stripper on his lap and whispered in her ear, "I'm 'bout to roll up outta here . . . you fuckin' with the kid tonight?"

"Yeah, you gotta give me time to cash out and do what I need to do though." She continued to grind on his lap.

"How long?"

"'Bout twenty, thirty minutes."

"Alright, meet me out front."

He eased her off his lap and watched her jiggling ass as she sauntered out of the dimly lit booth. He poured another shot, swallowed it down, and exited the booth. The strip joint was packed with patrons, male and female. Music blared, strippers hung from poles, cash flew, drinks flowed. It was Magic City Monday in full effect.

He moved at a crawl, greeting a few acquaintances, trying to make it to the exit. By the time he stepped out into the refreshing Georgia night air, his phone was ringing again. "Fuck. Why do motherfuckas keep callin'?" He peeped at the phone and saw Lauren's number again. He had been dodging her calls specifically. He did not want to hear any bad news about Elijah. Over the past few months, there had been enough bad news to last a lifetime. The phone continued to ring. He took a deep breath and finally answered.

"Yes," he barked with an attitude.

"Damn. I been trying to call you all day. What's up?" Lauren spoke with her own sense of frustration.

"Been busy."

"Yeah, whatever," she shot back. "Anyway, I'm calling because you need to come and check on your nephew. He's over there and still hasn't come home."

"Elijah's a grown man. Whatever he's goin' through, he'll have to be the one to work it out. He's straight. Raw keeps me up on what's goin' on with him. I'm sure when he's ready to come home, he'll come."

"That's bullshit. You know he's not thinking straight right now. And he's not listening to no one else. It's time for him to get the fuck back from over there."

"Don't start bitchin' at me. I got enough problems. I can't keep sticking my hand in everything that goes on over there. I'm tired of that shit . . . I'm just tired."

"Well, you don't have the option to be tired. That's your fuckin' nephew . . . more than that, he's your son; you raised him. And you're the one who taught him all this shit. You're the reason he is who he is. You owe him to get your ass out here and talk some sense into him. You owe it to your great-nephews to try and make this right. So I don't want to hear that tired shit." She sounded furious, on the verge of tears.

"I don't know what you want me to do. I—"

"I want you to get out here!" she yelled. "I want you to help us get him home. So don't think, just fuckin' do it!" She hung up.

He held the phone to his ear for a minute, processing that she had just hollered at him, then hung up in his face. He finally lowered the phone and put it in his pocket. His mind scrambled as he slowly made his way to the BMW parked in the back of the lot. He got in and turned the key to access his stereo system. He reclined the seat back, resting against the headrest, as Marvin Gaye's "Distant Lover" soothed his weary mind.

*   *   *   *

Big Teflon walked into a busy M&M's Soul Food Restaurant on the eastside. The lunch rush was on in the low-key but popular South Central LA eatery. Chatter filled the atmosphere as customers feasted on the variety of delicious delights. Fried chicken, smothered steak, greens, mac and cheese, cornbread, and other favorites filled plates, an array of flavors permeating the air.

He surveyed the place until he spotted Lil Teflon sitting at a table all the way in the back area. He made his way over and sat down. "What's up with it?" he greeted as he made himself comfortable.

"Same ol'," Lil Teflon responded dryly.

Big Teflon looked at his brother closely, noticing the dark bags under his eyes. He looked like he had not slept in days. His eyes were a sickly yellow with bloodshot veins.

"You alright Bro?" Big Teflon inquired, concerned.

"Yeah, I'm straight."

Big Teflon was not convinced but picked up the menu and changed the subject. "I was with Nine and them the other day."

"Is that right? What them niggas on?"

"We jammed that lil nigga Skip up. Pressed him about Ju."

"What you mean y'all jammed him up. What he say?" He sat up straight.

"It was weird. I'm thinkin' we gon' smoke the nigga. But he came and Nine decided to have a one-on-one with him. Once we come back in the room, he pretty much confirmed Time-Bomb killed the homie and that Skip was gon' keep his ears open to see who else might've had a hand in it. Then he was like we lettin' Skip go. Shit was strange because the nigga Skip kept lookin' at me like he didn't wanna talk in front of me. It was already weird bein' there with Lil Wiz. But it was for Ju, so I sucked it up. Then Skip, he didn't want to talk in front of me specifically. Once we left out and came back, the whole atmosphere seemed different. Nine tried to act like everything was cool. But I know him . . . I know how he is. Something was off, just can't put my finger on it." He set the menu down and looked around for the waitress.

Lil Teflon shook his head. "Bro, you can't go around them ducks no more."

"Why you say that?"

"You just can't." He picked up the glass of water and took a big gulp. He set the glass down and looked at him with pleading eyes. "Just go back to San Diego and don't look back on this place. It's complicated—too many bad politics, too many mistakes."

"What you tryna say but not sayin'? Did you have a hand in any of this shit?"

Lil Teflon took a deep, defeated breath. "Just leave, bro." His voice was so low it was practically a whisper.

Big Teflon's hands trembled slightly as he leaned forward and lowered his voice. "Not Ju-Ju . . . don't tell me you . . . say it ain't so."

"Hell nah, nigga. Ju was my nigga; I could never do no shit like that. And if I had the chance, I'd kill the motherfucka who did it personally. If it was Time-Bomb, I wish I could bring him back to life so I could cut his throat."

"So if that ain't the case, why you trippin'? What's really wrong?"

"I can't . . . just take my word. Get outta here while you can. Just because I didn't have nothin' to do with Ju, don't mean I ain't responsible in other ways." Tears moistened his eyes. "We all fuckups . . . me, you, Nine, all of us. Since the day we was put on earth, all we done is fuck up. And I'm the biggest fuckup of all."

"You confusin' me. You need to stop talkin' in riddles and tell me what's going on." He searched his brother's face for some understanding.

"The time is here," Lil Teflon continued. "We all gonna die. You'll die too if you don't leave and never come back. Don't you see it? Ju-Ju is dead. Lil 9 gon' die before long. I'm gon' die . . . all this shit over with." He wiped a tear from the corner of his eye.

"You losin' me. You gotta tell me what's up. If you feel you gonna die, you need to go too then."

Lil Teflon shook his head. "I'm not runnin' from death no more. I'm gon' face the music. Maybe death'll be my escape from all this shit." He stood up and attempted to compose himself. He walked around the table and raised Big Teflon up from his seat, hugging him tightly. "Get out, bro. Lil 9 gon' kill you if you stay. Take my word on this." He kissed Big Teflon hard on the cheek. He stepped back and stared at him intensely. "I love you, nigga." He wiped away another tear, turned, and rushed out of the restaurant.

CHAPTER 38

L il Bar-Dog turned off Hollywood Boulevard onto Whitley Avenue. He loved the nightlife in Hollywood with all the weirdos, tourists, and drug addicts. He had not been to the Hood in a while. He figured he would lay low out of sight and give things a chance to die down. None of the Nine-Os knew about his new stomping grounds, outside of the few young homies that he trusted. He met a few people in the area, which allowed him to start an ecstasy-selling ring that was beginning to become quite lucrative.

Whitley was a dark residential street just off the strip, lined with multiunit apartment buildings. It was quite different from the blocks in the Hood, a lot less tension, more peaceful, even though it was only a few feet away from all the happenings of the strip. He pulled into a six-story apartment building and pressed the button on his handheld gate remote. The black cast-iron gate hissed and slowly slid open, granting him access to a well-lit underground parking area.

He pulled in and drove to the rear, then parked in a space near the elevator. He checked his rearview, the surroundings, and got out of the car. He cautiously moved around to the trunk, opened it and bent over, gathering some bags.

A dark figure rolled from under a car two parking spaces away as he grabbed the bags. The sound startled him. He looked around uneasily in paranoia, dropping the bags, gripping his pistol on his hip. He did not see anyone.

A gray cat suddenly appeared, walking toward the storage area. Lil Bar-Dog shook his head and went back to what he was doing. He used his forearm to close the trunk after scooping the bags back up in both hands. When he turned around, Lil Wizard was there aiming a 9mm Beretta with a silencer attached. Lil Bar-Dog dropped the bags in fright.

"Don't do it," Lil Wizard cautioned, indicating to Lil Bar-Dog's right hand fidgeting toward his hip.

"Aw, Cuzz . . . I'm . . . what's this about?" he stuttered.

Elijah scooted from underneath a blue van wearing a ski mask, dressed in all black. He creeped like a crouched cat around the front of the car up to Lil Bar-Dog's back. "What's up, Bar Dog?"

Lil Bar-Dog jerked his head around to the unsuspected voice.

As soon as he turned toward him, Elijah swung a powerful, hate-filled haymaker that connected to Lil Bar-Dog's temple. He crumpled to the concrete like a fallen tree, unconscious before he hit the pavement.

Lil Wizard moved instantly toward Lil Bar-Dog, removing the pistol from his hip. He speedily and effortlessly zip-tied his wrists and ankles in the matter of a few seconds.

Elijah took out a roll of duct tape and quickly wrapped it around his mouth a few times, plastering it shut. They lifted and carried him over to the blue van. Elijah slid the side door open and they tossed him in like a sack of potatoes. Lil Wizard hurried to Lil Bar-Dog's car and grabbed the gate remote. He rushed back and jumped in the passenger seat of the van.

Elijah fired up the engine and sped out of the garage.

*   *   *   *

Lil Bar-Dog looked around wild-eyed as Elijah and Lil Wizard hovered over him. He was tied to a massive tree by a thick strand rope. Darkness cloaked them except for the small visages of lights from the city peeking through the thick, surrounding brush. Lil Bar-Dog had pissed on himself multiple times in fearful anticipation of what was to come; his whimpers and groans stifled by the duct tape.

Elijah stood in front of him. "Don't cry now, nigga. You thought you did some tough shit when you killed the homie, didn't you? Stay tough now, nigga." He turned to Lil Wizard. "The spot ready?"

"Yep," Lil Wizard responded, pushing up his bifocals. "He won't be found for a while, if ever. The animals won't leave much of him after some weeks."

Elijah took his gun from his hip and turned to Lil Bar-Dog.

"Hold up . . . hold up." Lil Wizard stopped him.

"What?" He paused.

Lil Wizard approached, removing a large hunting knife from his pocket. He handed it to Elijah. "This is a special one, no gun. Let's see if you got the stomach to get up close and personal on this one."

Elijah accepted the knife, a little uncertain. He looked at Lil Bar-Dog, then back to Lil Wizard, who had a distant, psychotic twinkle in his eye.

"What's wrong? Hand not strong enough?" Lil Wizard practically taunted. "I learned anybody can pull a trigger. But to snatch your enemy's life with the strength of your hand, that's an art form. Yeah, you not ready." He stepped closer and held his hand out for the knife back. "Step aside and let a real killa work. You a lil tender—"

Elijah turned and swung the knife with a primal speed and power so great that the blade pierced Lil Bar-Dog's cheek and crushed his jawbone with the ease of snapping a twig. As if the feeling of inflicting pain on Lil Bar-Dog unleashed some savage dam, Elijah pulled the knife free and jabbed him repeatedly in the face, from forehead to mouth. The squishing sound of steel entering wet flesh and the crushing of bone and tendons played like a sickening symphony as Lil Wizard looked on with a blank stare.

He stabbed him until he was out of breath. He left the knife protruding from Lil Bar-Dog's neck as he backed away on rubbery legs, a blood-soaked mess. "Is that art form enough for you?" he spewed at Lil Wizard, chest heaving and out of breath. He did not wait for a response. He turned and stumbled toward the parked van.

Lil Wizard shrugged his shoulders and stooped down to examine Lil Bar-Dog face-to-face. He grabbed the hilt of the knife firmly, used his other hand to grab Lil Bar-Dog's shoulder to hold him in place, and ripped the knife horizontally across his neck in fits and starts as he tore through the windpipe. Satisfied with the finishing touch, he stepped back, cocking his head curiously down at the corpse as he wiped the blood from the blade with a bandana. He put the blade in his pocket and grabbed Lil Bar-Dog by the ankles, dragging him deep into the brush.

Elijah already had the van running by the time Lil Wizard finished and climbed in the passenger seat. Lil Wizard put on his seat belt, pushed his bifocals up, looked at him, and nodded.

Elijah nodded and put the van in drive. He eased out of the camouflaged trail onto the narrow road leading out of the eerily quiet Hollywood hills.

CHAPTER 39

E lijah roughhoused with his pit bull in the front yard of the family house. The dog locked onto a thick log Elijah paraded before him in their game of tease tug-of-war. He paused and took a moment to take in the environment. It was one of those mornings that reminded him of his early childhood, before he became Lil 9-Lives, when he was just Elijah. When the music from the ice cream truck sent his heart racing; sweet Red Vines, Lemonheads, and Jolly Ranchers tickling his tongue, a wishbone-shaped slingshot and marbles in his pocket; a time when LA was as close to paradise as his young mind could imagine.

The city sparkled after the unseasonably early spring showers. The morning air was crisp, the sidewalks washed clean of leaves and debris, and the snowcapped San Gabriel Mountain peaks were visible for a change. Yet, despite the day's beauty, a deep depression gnawed at his soul, as it always did after the act of murder. As a veteran of the killing fields of South Central, he told himself numerous times that only murder could stir the deep settlings within him, an unconditional urge to kill his enemies with no strings attached. But he was coming to the realization that this, too, was a lie he had convinced himself to believe. There was always an emotional consequence when it came to life and death. After the adrenaline of the moment settled, there was always the feeling of emptiness. When he looked at himself in the mirror, he could not help the question that fluttered through his mind: *Was he a monster?* Then there was the reality that the act of revenge never improved his life in any way, it only chipped away at his soul even further.

He thought about the Teflon brothers. He had already made a call to Big Teflon, telling him to come down for a meeting later that night. That prospect was weighing on him. Would he kill his old childhood friend for the sins of his brother? He blamed himself for not taking care of Lil Teflon as soon as he resurfaced. His indecision and failure to act had cost Ju-Ju his life. So the dye was cast; Lil Teflon had to go, and in his heart, he knew that meant Big Teflon had to go also. To do otherwise would be to leave an enemy in his backyard.

Knowing all this and being justified in his stance still did not make the reality of the situation any better. The four of them had done it all together growing up. Now they would all be dead except for him. And in one way or another, he would be responsible for all their deaths. If not for the tug of feeling like he owed it to Ju-Ju and Brenda to make them pay, he would probably have already walked away from it all, but his honor would not allow him to do so now.

He tossed the stick across the yard. The dog scrambled to go retrieve it. At that moment, two army-green Hummers turned off Budlong, heading his way. He casually walked toward the house without making any sudden moves, mounted the steps, and positioned next to the AK-47 propped behind the concrete post. He strained to see behind the dark-tinted windows as they drew closer.

One of the trucks turned into the driveway, stopping at the closed gate. The other pulled to the curb directly in front of the house. The door to the truck parked in the driveway opened and Big

9-Lives got out. Elijah dropped his shoulders in relief at the sight of his uncle. Lil Cannon and Big 1-Punch got out of the truck and took up security positions at opposite ends of the property.

"That's what you doin' now? Out here slippin', giving niggas the opportunity to come kill you?" Big 9-Lives approached the house with an authoritative air.

"Ain't nobody slippin', I'm straight." He returned his attention to the other Hummer. "What you doin' out here? Who's that?" He pointed at the truck.

"Yo family, nigga. It's time to go home," Big 9-Lives commanded firmly.

*   *   *   *

Elise, Lauren, and Sistah Raheema anxiously watched Elijah and Big 9-Lives from inside the second Hummer. The only sound was their breathing as they waited in silence for a sign that things were progressing in a favorable direction.

Elise broke the silence from the backseat. "This is taking too long. I'm tired of waiting." She tucked her pistol in her Chanel clutch bag. "You ready?"

Lauren grabbed a .380 pistol from her Louis Vuitton purse and put it in the front pocket of her USC hoodie. She looked around at their surroundings and nodded to Elise.

Both were on edge coming to the Hood. They were aware of the war taking place and Elijah's role in it. The streets were ablaze with the gossip about Elijah and Lil Wizard cleaning house and taking the land back as their own. They were a one-two wrecking crew, and retaliation was inevitable. Big 9-Lives anticipated it as well; that was why he insisted on renting the two bulletproof Hummers and they all strapped up like the Mob before they came over.

Just as Lauren and Elise prepared to exit, Sistah Raheema reached over and touched Lauren's arm gently from the passenger seat. "Hold on, baby."

"Yes, ma'am?"

She looked at them with eyes filled with a mother's wisdom. "I would like to be the one to do this. I . . . I just think it's best that I get a chance to talk to him alone first." She continued before any protest. "I need you to trust me on this now. Do you trust me?"

"Of course," Lauren answered. "But we'll at least get out with you and escort you in."

Sistah Raheema waved dismissively and reached for the door handle. "I don't need no escorting. I got something greater than those guns with me. I walk with the might and protection of the Creator. I've been a soldier longer than you both been alive." She opened the door, and with a little effort, exited the vehicle.

Big 9-Lives hurried over to assist her. He held her arm and led her toward the house.

"Sistah Raheema?" Elijah asked, incredulous. "What you doin' over here?" He nervously scanned their surroundings, fearing for her safety.

She determinedly made her way to the porch. "I need to talk to you, brother." She ambled up the steps one at a time and approached and embraced him in a warm hug.

"Come on, let's go inside." He moved to the side, allowing her to walk in before him. He gestured to Big 9-Lives, indicating the assault rifle leaning against the post.

Big 9-Lives followed the gesture and glimpsed the rifle. "I got it," he mouthed.

Elijah walked in. He and Sistah Raheema sat on the couch. She looked around the house. This was her first time being there. She admired the family photos lining the mantel and living room wall.

"What you doin' here?" He broke the silence respectfully.

"I'm here because your three days of mourning is long overdue and it's time for you to return to your family."

"You didn't have to come all the way over here. I'll be home . . . I just . . . just got things I have to do." He averted his eyes.

"Can I talk to you honestly right now?" She leaned forward.

"You don't even have to ask that question."

"Okay." She relaxed a little, not breaking eye contact with him. "You are giving up."

"What you—"

She raised her hand and closed her eyes, indicating for him to be quiet and listen. He caught himself and sat back in silence.

"I said you are giving up. I hold you to be greater than this, stronger. A man's virtue is tested and judged by how he reacts in times of adversity. You believe that by coming here to a place where you don't belong anymore, getting in the mud with people who are not on your level and engaging them in war, somehow makes you strong, makes you brave. But it doesn't. It's making you lose control. And for a man to lose control is weakness. Your spirit has told you that you don't belong here. But you are suppressing the voice of the spirit. You can't do that. You are a soldier of God, not a soldier of evil and darkness. Outside of your obligation to God, your priority and obligation is to your family. Not to these streets and not to the dead. I know you loved your friend, and you miss him. I know it hurts like hell what happened to him, but that bad situation can't consume your thoughts, causing you not to make sound decisions."

Tears formed in his eyes as he kept them focused on his lap, listening to what he knew was the truth, but not wanting to let go and submit to it.

"The reason the Quran says we are given three days to mourn," she continued, "is because death is a matter between him and his servant who has passed. That's not our domain; we don't control life and death, no matter how much we may want to. Our duty is to feel the loss, honor the memory, and correct whatever we can if the situation calls for it, then return our focus back to the living. When you mourn and rage excessively, you are telling Allah that he doesn't know what he's doing. Don't be that ungrateful soldier. You have been given too much; have too much to live for. Do you know that Amaru asks for you every night before he goes to bed?"

The thought of his son squeezed his heart. He had refused to think of his babies since he had been away. The thought of them was too painful, so he suppressed them altogether. Now as both their faces filled his mind, he began to shed tears quietly.

Sistah Raheema drew closer to him, cradling him in her arms. "It's okay, brother, let it out." She rocked him back and forth, rubbing his back. "This is good for you. Yeah, it's good for you. Let that pain and grief out that the Shaytan is trying to use to control and destroy you. Let it out." She whispered short *Surahs* in Arabic from the Quran in his ear.

His shoulders shuddered as he sobbed deeply against her chest. He allowed the floodgates to open freely until he was able to regain a sense of calm composure.

She retrieved a silk handkerchief from a pocket in her *jilbab* and handed it to him. "*Al hamdullilah*," she repeated over and over. "This was a cleansing that you needed."

He wiped his face with the handkerchief and sighed deeply, shaking his head.

"I have something for you." She dug back into the slit pocket in her dress, drew out a sealed envelope, and handed it to him.

Elijah slowly took it from her. "What's this?" He turned it over in his hand.

"Open it and read it." She sat back with a smile plastered on her face.

Elijah inspected the tiny, neat Arabic script on the front of the envelope. He hesitantly tore it open. He took out a tri-folded letter with a photograph inside of it. He examined the picture of the Middle Eastern man dressed in a *jellaba* with a *kufi* on his head, standing in front of the sphinx in Egypt. He frowned in confusion. He set the photo down and unfolded the letter. As he read, his look of confusion slowly transformed into one of increased understanding.

He finished reading the letter and set it next to the photograph on the coffee table. "Where did this come from? I mean, how did he know how to reach me?" He was visibly shaken up.

"Elise. She found him and reached out to him. I know you have mixed emotions about this, and you will have to get your questions answered and resolve whatever issues at some point in the future. But for now, take this as an omen from Allah. It's no coincidence that your biological father is a Muslim. I believe this is a confirmation that Allah's hand is on your life and has been over your life. And it's time for you to make a clear choice. This is a pivotal moment for you: Are you going to choose light, or are you going to choose the darkness that is most certainly going to lead to your destruction? There is no more time to wait. Forget everything that has happened up to this point. Forget the evil your hand has put forth. Allah forgives you, but you must choose rightly, right now. It's time to leave here; evil is on the horizon."

Elijah wrestled with his thoughts. "I'll have to get my things—"

"No. Don't worry about any of that. Your uncle will take care of all that. You don't need to do nothing but get up and bring your body with us out of this place. Your keys, your phone, and whatever else will follow you. Just come now. For the life and love of your family, come." She stood up and reached out her hand to him.

Elijah slowly reached up and took her hand, rising to his feet. He grabbed the photo and letter with his other hand. She wrapped her arm around his waist, and he draped his arm over her shoulder as she led him out the front door into daylight that seemed to be shining even brighter.

As they walked down the steps, Elise and Lauren got out of the car and ran to embrace him with tears in their eyes. Sistah Raheema released him to their embrace.

"We missed you so much!" Lauren cried.

"I'm so sorry, baby." Elise gripped him tightly around his waist.

"I missed y'all too."

He turned to Elise. "I'm sorry too." He kissed her lips. "Let's get outta here." He held them as they made their way to the truck. Sistah Raheema had already gotten in the front passenger seat.

Elijah and Elise got in the backseat. Lauren closed the door behind them, then walked to the driver's side. She stopped and looked back at Big 9-Lives who was watching them from the porch. Lauren raised her hand to her forehead and gave him a hard, disciplined salute.

Big 9-Lives smirked and saluted back.

*   *   *   *

Big Teflon sat on his back porch smoking a blunt, watching Lil Akili play basketball on his plastic basketball hoop with breakaway rim, his mind preoccupied with a thousand thoughts. The weed was not working its intended purpose of calming his nerves, but instead was making him overthink things even more. He had not slept a wink since the phone call with Elijah the night before. He felt it in his heart that his brother's words were true. If he went to the meeting scheduled for tonight, he would never return home. He heard it in Elijah's voice—that distant, melancholy zone he'd get in when he was making a hard decision pertaining to others. He knew his childhood friend all too well. After all, he was there on many occasions when Elijah made those same decisions pertaining to others. And now he was one of those others.

But if he did not show up to the meeting, his Hood pass would be in question and he would have to look over his shoulder for the rest of his days, or until Elijah and his circle were no longer around. He knew he could not kill them all and really had no desire to even try. Why would he risk everything that he was doing with his life to fight a war that had no benefits at the end of the day?

There was a way he could ensure he and his brother would be safe without having to fire a single shot. But it was not an easy decision. He took out his phone; he paused one last time, questioning if he was sure. He dialed the number and put it to his ear, listening in anticipation as it rang.

"Hello?" a voice on the other end answered.

"Hey, it's me."

"Silver Fox?"

"Yeah. You got time to talk for a few?" He stared at his son, still running around playing.

"For you, of course. Shoot."

"I need you to turn it up now. There's no more time to waste. Time-Bomb's dead; Lil Bar-Dog hasn't been seen, so the safe bet is, he's dead. Now they callin' me to come to a meeting where I'm certain they plan to smoke me too. So you need to shake shit up like right now."

"Well, you know what the problem is with that, me just stomping into full action. The information you've been providing over this time is helpful but—"

"I know, I know." Big Teflon cut him off. "But you need me to be willing to testify if my information not strong enough to stand alone, blah, blah, blah." He stood up and paced with the phone to his ear. "Look, I'll do it. I was hesitant before about the testifying part. Giving information from the shadows is something all the way different from revealing what I'm doing where my name will be on paperwork. But now I don't give a fuck. I'll give you all them niggas. I'll tell you everything I know. The murders, the drugs, everything. And I'll testify to it all. But you have to move now."

There was silence on the other end.

"You there?"

"I'm here. Just trying to process. You must know if I jump the gun on what I'm doing based on your word, there is no turning back for you. If you fuck me, I'll make sure your confidential informant status is exposed."

"I got you, man. Just keep up your end," Big Teflon assured him.

"Let's get to work then, my man. Our usual location?"

"Yeah, in two hours."

"Sounds good."

The line went dead. Big Teflon put the phone in his pocket. "Come on, Akili, let's go get some snacks." Lil Akili dropped his ball and ran up on the porch to him. They playfully raced into the house.

It didn't matter anymore whether Big Teflon did the right thing. It was too late now. In a few hours, he would meet with Agent Berrigan and answer all of his questions, and everything would change. Big Teflon would never be able to show his face in the Hood again.

CHAPTER 40

Lil Wizard stepped out of the store on Ninety-Second and Western dressed in a fake leather Member's Only jacket, Wrangler jeans, and a pair of brown Wallabees, eating from a box of Lemonheads. He enjoyed walking through the Hood on foot, especially lately. The stares he got, the homies who got out of Dodge when he showed up, the visible fear he instilled, let him know that things were as they should be. They were the figures in the Set, and he would continue to apply pressure to make sure the opposition did not forget it.

He walked to Ninety-Fourth Street and turned toward the alley. As soon as he made it to the mouth of the alley and went to make the left inside, a black Crown Victoria with limo-tint sped to a screeching halt in front of him and two white men with pistols drawn jumped out.

"Little Wizard don't move! Get on the ground!" they screamed. "Freeze, motherfucker!"

Lil Wizard removed his hand from the butt of his gun and took off running. He hit the nearby brick wall, ran through a backyard, and came out on Manhattan Place.

One of the officers on foot was in hot pursuit behind him, screaming in vain for him to stop.

By the time Lil Wizard ran across the street and turned up

Ninety-Fourth Place, the ghetto bird was nearly on top of him, hovering. Unmarked cars came from everywhere. The three cars coming from Ruthelen Street pulled on the curb in front of him, blocking the path. The officers hopped out with their guns leveled at his head. "On the ground, now!" they screamed in intervals.

Lil Wizard knew it was over. He stopped and raised his hands in surrender.

Agent Berrigan, who had been the one on foot pursuit, ran up behind him. He roughly grabbed his wrist, placing him in handcuffs. He snatched the gun from Lil Wizard's waistband. "You won't be needing this anymore," he whispered in his ear, roughhousing him toward the nearby squad car. "I've been waiting on this day for forever. How does it feel to know this is your last day of freedom?"

Lil Wizard looked at him and cocked his head. "How does it feel when you get dick up your ass, you white cracka motherfucka!"

Agent Berrigan laughed. "I would expect nothing less from you. Gangster to the end." He shook his head, shoving Lil Wizard into the back of the squad car by the crown of his head and slamming the door shut.

Lil Wizard sat in the backseat watching as all the officers and agents high-fived and joked with each other. He was still in the Hood, but already feeling like he was a million miles away.

* * * *

The front door of the Hassahn family home crashed in and a team of agents dressed in paramilitary gear poured in, tactically making their way to every room. They canvassed every area before giving the call that all was clear. They tore up the house from top to bottom in search of guns and drugs.

Agent Berrigan stood in the middle of the room taking it all in. He had dreams about this day, of being able to kick in the front door of the Hassahn house and haul Big 9-Lives and Little 9-Lives off in handcuffs. Now there he stood, search warrant in hand, and even though the house was empty of anything illegal and both men were nowhere in sight, he knew it was just a matter of time before he had them in custody. He was as giddy as a kid on Christmas Day when the indictment was unsealed. A Continuing Criminal Enterprise case against Big 9-Lives and Lil 9-Lives, Big and Little Wizard, Hitter, and Elise. The US Attorney's office used Elise's recent cocaine dealings as the anchor to tie in a slew of charges against the others, although they had been out of the game for years. The case was presented to the grand jury as a long-running organized crime operation that everyone played a part in. Big Teflon had given them everyone and everything he knew. Now it was just a matter of finding everyone and bringing them in.

A picture lying on the floor caught his attention. He walked over and picked it up, flipping it over to see the faces. It was the childhood picture of Elijah, Ju-Ju, and the Teflon brothers. He shook the picture in his hand as he gave the living room one last look. He pocketed the photo and walked out briskly without looking back. Time was of the essence.

*   *   *   *

Lauren sat behind the desk preparing a legal brief in her plush office on the twenty-sixth floor of a high-rise building in downtown LA. Her intercom speaker buzzed. She pushed the button. "Hey, Cheryl."

"Ms. Kross, there's someone here to—"

Lauren's office door swung open before her assistant could finish the sentence. Two white men in suits barged in.

"Ms. Kross." They flashed their badge cards. "We have a search warrant here to seize all of your files and computers." The lead agent pulled the warrant from his inside pocket and handed it to her.

Lauren nervously scanned the search warrant. "What is this about?"

The agent smiled. "You lay with criminals; you get treated as one." He walked around the desk. "I'm going to have to ask you to go with my partner here for some questioning while we do what we have to do here."

A team of a dozen agents poured into the room with boxes and ledgers, already seizing items with total disregard to her presence in the room.

"Am I under arrest?"

"Not yet. But I think you'd rather go on your own free will, with a little dignity, rather than me arresting and holding you for seventy-two hours. You're a lawyer, you know I can do that, right? I can legally hold you for seventy-two hours without any charges with a flick of the pen. So, it's your choice." He stood over her with a smug look.

Lauren knew he was right. She hid the nervous ball growing in her stomach and stood up. She reached over to grab her purse. The agent stopped her.

"We need to take a look in there." He picked up the purse and rummaged through it.

"You find anything?" she asked sarcastically.

He smirked and handed her the purse. "Keep that smart attitude; you're gonna need it."

She snatched it from his hand and put her best courtroom face on. "Let's get this over with, I got shit to do." She brushed past them and walked out the door confidently, shadowed closely by the second agent.

* * * *

A series of raids and arrests ensued throughout the Nineties from LA to the furthest corners of the south. Even the Tiny Toons spots were hit and a few of them were thrown in juvenile hall and the LA County jail for murders and attempts on the Hoovers and Eight Tray Gangsters. The homies who were able to miss the first wave of the heat were now scrambling for cover, getting as far off the radar as possible. An unsealed indictment was now underway, and the long arms of the federal government were working at full strength.

* * * *

Elijah stared out the window as the city below grew smaller, fading away swiftly. The usual gray smog hung over the city as the airplane made its smooth ascent toward blue skies. Memories of the homies, his childhood, and all those who had passed away fluttered through his mind as the canvas below him gave way to patches of brown earth. He felt a sense of sadness and loss. Yet, there was a touch of hope for what new opportunities lay ahead in Jamaica.

I'll just give it some time, he thought. Or maybe I won't. Maybe I'll stay in Jamaica permanently. I can always travel elsewhere if I want to. My fake identity and paperwork let me go wherever the fuck I want, when I want, without no one really knowing who I am. I can be a ghost . . . ain't that some shit? He smiled. I get to meet Pops for the first time when I land. Maybe I can even go over to Egypt to see how he livin' at some point. He looked over at a sleeping Elise, with Amaru resting against her from the middle seat, asleep as well.

My family is all I need. His mind continued to race. *Lauren and Toussaint gon' be on they way soon as she tie up all our loose ends. When that happens, we gon' be complete, no matter where we at in the world . . . as long as we together, we straight.*

He peered back out the window, gazing at the bed of clouds. *Thank you, Almighty, for blessing me beyond measure.* His eyelids grew heavy. He reclined the seat and leaned against the headrest; soon, sleep overtook him.

*   *   *   *

Soft snowflakes drifted lazily to the ground around Big 9-Lives as he stood on Lewis Street on the South Side of Philadelphia, waiting for Big Wizard and Hitter to arrive. He blew into his hands and drew his goose down jacket tighter, anxiously looking up and down the block. He was relieved when he saw the black Suburban turn on the block. The SUV pulled over to the curb and he jumped in the backseat. He welcomed the warmth of the heat blowing at full blast through the vehicle.

"What's the word?" Big Wizard asked from the passenger seat.

"It's all bad." Big 9-Lives rubbed his hands together, still trying to warm up and shake the chill. The flurries outside started to intensify.

"Imma bend the block so we not just sittin' here." Hitter drove off.

"Good idea." Big 9-Lives settled back. "They said all of us is on the indictment. Neph and Elise is listed as the principals."

"How the fuck they indict us on some dope shit and we ain't really even gettin' down like that no more?" Big Wizard stated, frustrated.

"I don't know. The way the shit read is like they went back years ago to tie us in. The feds ain't gon' give up too much info until we in custody."

"This all fucked up, big bro," Hitter added, navigating traffic. "They kicked in my baby mom's door askin' for me."

Big 9-Lives shook his head. "They kickin' in everything, everywhere connected to us. We good up here for the moment though. Don't nobody know we got ties in Philly."

"How long do that last once they put us on *America's Most Wanted?*" The stress was evident in Big Wizard's voice.

"Shit, we cross that bridge when we get there." Big 9-Lives stared out the window.

"Well, I'm not gonna run from these motherfuckas. Y'all can stay tucked up here. I'm gonna head back, lawyer up, and go see what the fuck they talkin' 'bout." Hitter pulled into a McDonald's parking lot.

"Fuck you mean, you 'bout to go see what they talkin' 'bout. When we start turnin' ourselves in?" Big Wizard looked at Hitter in disbelief.

"We never have." Hitter parked. "But I'm not gonna live under all this stress. We haven't been heavy in the dope game for a while. I feel it's a scare tactic; they just shakin' the tree."

"Shakin' the tree or not, I wouldn't advise that, lil bro." Big 9-Lives lit a blunt and inhaled deeply. "Somebody tellin', and who knows where that go once we in that courtroom."

"Well, it's a risk that gotta be taken instead of runnin' from ghosts in the dark."

"Hell nah." Big Wizard shook his head. "Ain't no goin' go give ourselves up to those people and put ourselves at their mercy."

"I didn't say us; I said *I* was gonna turn myself in. Y'all stay put. If they keep me, at least I can let y'all know what we up against. And if it's niggas snitchin' on us, y'all can know who it is and handle it."

"Again, I don't advise it. Let's get ourselves situated here, give it some time, then make decisions. We all too stressed right now to make critical moves." Big 9-Lives passed the blunt to Hitter.

"That's a good idea," Big Wizard agreed. "The realtor supposed to have a couple spots ready for us Monday. We'll hunker down and breathe for a while."

An uneasy silence filled the vehicle. Finally, Hitter half-heartedly agreed. "Alright, I'll give it a few weeks to think on it."

"Cool." Big 9-Lives wrapped his scarf tighter around his neck. "We'll meet back up in a few weeks and go from there."

"That's what's up." Big Wizard and Hitter intoned.

Big 9-Lives reached forward and squeezed both of them on the shoulders. "I love y'all...We gon' come outta this on top like we always do."

"Inshallah," Hitter responded with uncertainty.

"I'll walk from here." Big 9-Lives pulled his beanie down on his head and exited the truck. He shut the door, tapped on the window, then turned and walked away. He heard the truck drive off; he did not bother to look back. The falling snow gradually surrounded him as he disappeared into a white blur of obscurity.

*   *   *   *

Lil Teflon was placing items in his open overnight bag when his phone rang. "Hello." He answered.

"Bro where you at?" Big Teflon's voice echoed from the other end.

"In the Hood. But 'bout to run up to Vegas, need to grab some shit from up that way. What's up?"

"Why you in the Hood? You know what's goin' on right now." Big Teflon sounded furious and frustrated.

"I'm in a tuck spot on the Orchard side, I'm good. Ain't nobody even be over here no more. And the shit with the pigs, shiddd, they ain't looking for me. All this heat actually help me. Don't have to worry 'bout them niggas because they all runnin' for they life."

"I know they runnin' for they life, that's why I did it. But you still need to be out the way till everybody for sure scooped up."

Lil Teflon paused and frowned. "Wait . . . what you mean . . . that's why you did it? I'm lost, did what?"

"Man, you know."

"Nah, I don't know. What you mean?"

Big Teflon smacked his lips, hesitant on what to say next. "Man . . . I mean, I did what I had to do. You know that Agent fool Berrigan been at me ever since you got shot."

"He was at me too. That don't mean I been talkin' to the motherfucka since then. I told him to suck my dick and get the fuck away from me. You mean to tell me . . ." He could not bring himself to say the words.

"Yeah," Big Teflon answered for him. "I been in touch with

him since then. Just givin' a little information here and there when the shit was goin' on after you got shot. I was hopin' they would gather enough to get Lil Wiz, Hitter, and Big Wiz, and that problem would be over. But it didn't work out that way. Once we was able to get shit squashed though, I figured we was good; I wouldn't need to talk with him no more. But now this shit flared up again. I felt this was the only way. Let the police get rid of these niggas for us. Fuck them niggas; they looking to kill us, so it is what it is."

There was a long pause from Lil Teflon's end, then he finally spoke. "I can't believe you just told me some shit like that." He shook his head. "What type of lame shit is that? You mean to tell me you the one who got the Hood gettin' raided and niggas goin' to jail? Since when we get down like that? We wasn't raised that way. We handle our business; we don't tell the police shit."

"I did this to protect us. I gotta think 'bout my son and everything I worked hard for. I couldn't just sit by and let them niggas do us in!" Big Teflon protested.

"Don't try and make it like this some art-of-war-strategy bull, this some coward shit, period—point blank. You better pull this back and make it right before you throw dirt on our names, nigga."

"I can't. What's done is done; it's already too late."

"You know what? You can lose my number after this. I don't know what happened to you, but you done turned into a real sucka. I can't change the fact that you my brother, but startin' now, I don't fuck with you, nigga. You shamed our name in the streets and all that we supposed to stand for. I'm a hoodsta nigga, and no matter how scandalous and cutthroat I might be, I'll never be a fuckin' rat . . . I'll die first. Don't call me no more, nigga,

I'm off you all the way."

"Nigga, how the fuck—" Big Teflon paused, realizing that his brother had already hung up.

*   *   *   *

Lil Teflon looked around the room in disgust. "Bitch-ass nigga," he mumbled, putting the last of what he wanted to take with him into the overnight bag.

A car outside honked three times. "Ha-ha, my new bitch here." He flung the bag over his shoulder, grabbed his keys and pistol from the table, and headed out. He kept the pistol in his hand as he locked the door behind him.

He glanced around anxiously, then quickly took the steps and headed to the car sitting at the curb with a woman behind the wheel. He got in the passenger seat and tossed his bag on the backseat. "You ready to hit the road?" He smiled at her.

"I'm always ready for whatever need to be done." A big, devilish, red-lipstick smile spread across Diabla's face.

EPILOGUE

Eras end, time goes on as the real warriors of yesterday pass away like particles of debris in the wind. Along with them goes the concrete constitution that we once stood on. We once treaded among the lions, wolves, snakes, and gorillas of the urban jungle. It was survival of the fittest, where no one else got the bully off you, you had to grow strong and brave enough to get him off yourself.

In our jungle, circumstances were far from perfect. Yet for the bulk of us, we stood on the code of honor that was given to us by the real OGs. Is it evolution that our ways in this thing of ours became outdated? The same code of honor that established the real ones also delivered us over to death and the prison house. While the fakes and nobodies who were among us bided their time until the real ones were all gone, then usurped what had been laid down by us under the guise that they were part of that pitiless tribe. It worked on the next generation of up-and-comers because they were too young to know any better.

I sit here looking out my window of what the Set has become. Active snitches, busters, and rats now run the Hood. They go from the witness stand to the head of the gang meeting. Money is now the determining factor of who is reputable when before, money would only make you prey if you were not warrior enough to defend it. The tough guys in the neighborhood now wear bright-pink clothes, tighter than what my woman wears. What happened? How did the style, grit, and masculinity of Raymond Washington and the old guard get watered down to this? I'm an old relic, they say, out of touch with the new wave. But I'm content with that. If being part of the new wave means I have to break bread with rats and relinquish what the real originals did, I'll pass. Y'all can have this shit. I'll take my tribe of elites and move to the realm where real mobsters play. The game has changed, so the real ones must change how we play it. Who's up next?

To Be Continued . . .

ACKNOWLEDGEMENT

We honor and salute all the Black kings and queens who have set a standard and paved the way for us to be today's revolutionaries. We stand in solidarity with our brothers and sisters who are still in bondage, victims of systematic oppression. Continue to shine even in the midst of the darkness.

We salute all those who are on the frontline fighting for the end of mass incarceration and genocide against our people. United we stand divided we fall.

Thank you to all those who were instrumental on this journey. A special thanks to three energies that inspire me daily to give my all even when I don't feel it: Big Moosie, Lil Moosie, and Gawk, my motivation.

AUTHOR'S BIO

Toni-T-Shakir, author and co-CEO of Shakir Publishing, is a Jamaican native who grew up in the Bay Area of Northern California, subsequently migrating to Los Angeles. She is an avid reader who acquired the love for writing at a young age.

Shakir Publishing is the culmination of Toni's dream of bringing awareness to critical stories throughout the world and being a voice for those who are often unheard. She has recently ventured into the film industry as a producer on the film adaptation of *Land Of No Pity*, written and directed by her stepson, Asim Jamal Shakir Jr. The film is slated to become a tv series in 2021.

Toni's debut novel, *Land Of No Pity*, introduced the world to her ground-breaking style of storytelling, that entrenched the mainstream into the gritty gang culture of South Central Los Angeles in a qualitative and poignant way. Her follow-up sequel, *Land Of No Pity II: The Lost Generation*, is the long awaited continuation of the saga readers have been highly anticipating.